the HANDSOME GIRL & her BEAUTIFUL BOY

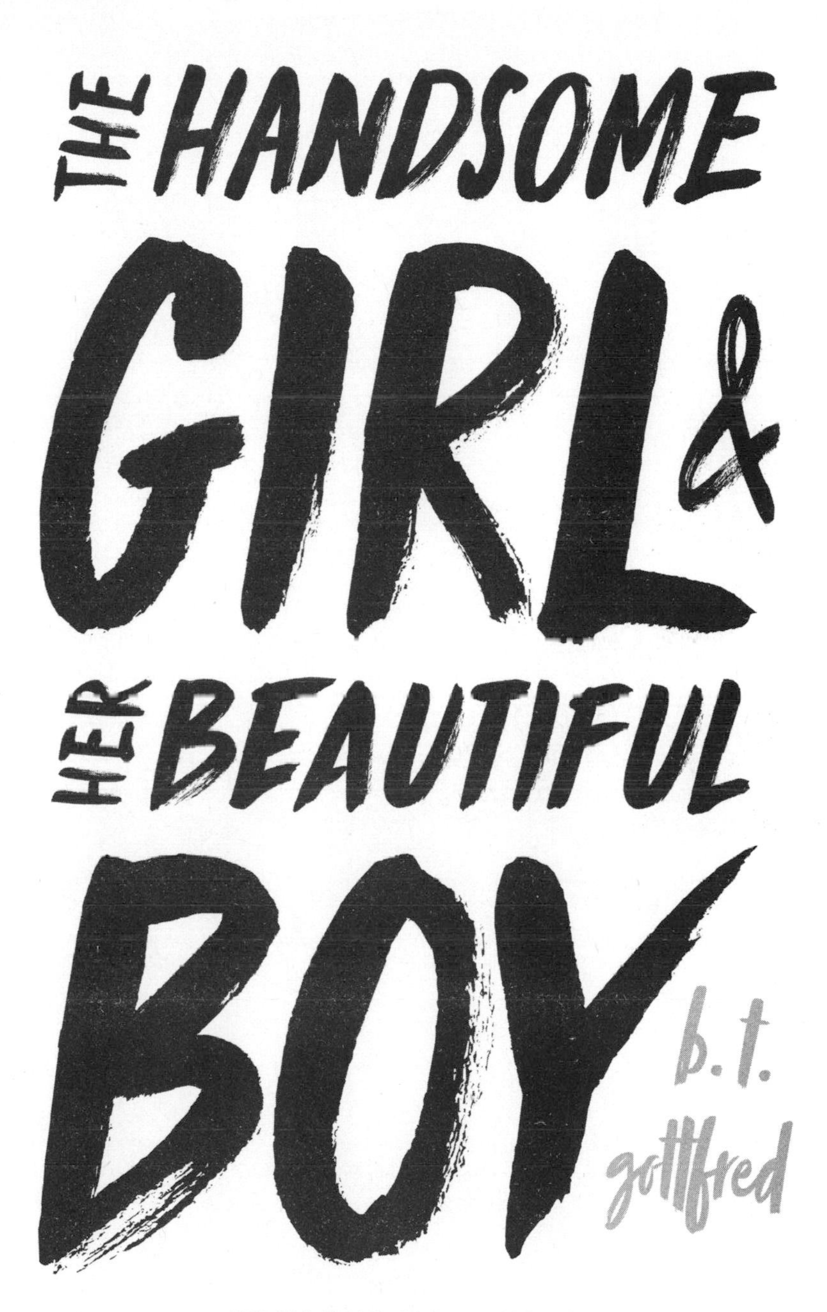

HENRY HOLT AND COMPANY
NEW YORK

Henry Holt and Company, *Publishers since 1866*
Henry Holt® is a registered trademark of Macmillan Publishing Group, LLC.
175 Fifth Avenue, New York, NY 10010
fiercereads.com

Image source: p. 415: Created by Carol Ly, based on Wikimedia/*Sexual Behavior in the Human Female (1953)*

Library of Congress Control Number: 2017945041

ISBN 978-1-62779-852-5

First edition, 2018 / Designed by Carol Ly

Printed in the United States of America

10 9 8 7 6 5 4 3 2 1

dedicated to everyone
who has embraced their own
unique, magical mix
of feminine & masculine
(and olux and xulo)
and then
embraced everyone else's
in return

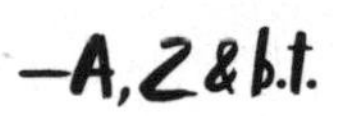

author's note

(Actually this is the Author's Note ABOUT the Author's Note. For reasons I can't explain at this exact place in your reading experience, I decided to put the Author's Note at the end of the book. If curiosity demands you read it first, it's on page 397. I promise neither I, Zee, or Art will judge. We like you exactly the way you are.)

Part One

MYTHICAL CREATURES MEET AT A PIZZERIA

ZEE

Listen, let's start with a list.

1. Everyone at school thinks I'm a lesbian. I'm not. Wish I was (sometimes, maybe) but I'm not.
2. Everyone feels sorry for me because my mom's dying. Don't.
3. My real name is Rebecca. But no one calls me that. Ever. Everyone calls me Zee. Don't ask.
4. Honestly, I don't even remember what four was going to be.
5. My mom taught me to love everyone. So I do. But I really don't like any-one.

Okay, I like one person.

Cam.

Isn't the word "like" lame? Yeah, it is.

But I can't think of a better one, so fuck it.

Disaster!

I don't even know why I thought that. Perhaps the universe is communicating in mysterious ways.

Or I'm bored.

I should *probably* do my physics homework, but instead I'm going to read your mind (just trust me on this). I can sense you're probably wondering, "Art, how can someone so witty and interesting like you be so lonely?"

The answer is, I plan to change this very soon.

How do I know this?

Because I know magic!

I'm kidding. I don't know magic.

I *am* magic. You'll see. Ha.

People Who Have No Idea That Magic Could Be Inside Them

People Who Will Never Believe Magic Is Inside Them

People Who Believe Magic Is Inside Them

People Who KNOW So Much Magic Is Inside Them That They May Explode

Me (And Maybe Only Me)

People Who Hope but Don't Believe Magic Is Inside Them

ZEE

So, yeah, I like Cam.

He's my best friend.

He's been my best friend since we played travel baseball together back in grade school.

We text all the time. I'll text him right now:

ME

Yo dude—usual time for our monday pizza?

So when I say I like him, what I probably mean is I might be in love with him.

Wish I wasn't.

CAM

you got it dude

Cam has no idea about my feelings. ("Feelings" is as lame a word as "like.") I should tell him. I don't want to, but I should. Because, listen, he's got a girlfriend. *Abigail.* She's nice to me. I secretly hate her.

art

"ART!" my sister Abigail yells from downstairs because everyone in my family loves yelling. My dad yells, my mom yells, my brother, Alex, yells, and my two other sisters, Amy and Alice, do too. All our names begin with "A." Oh, and our last name is Adams.

Isn't that cute? Um, NO, IT'S NOT! It's the most boring and annoying disaster in the history of boring and annoying disasters!

"WHAT?!" I yell back, because I've been brainwashed. I'm the youngest, the baby, the one nobody really notices. I'm feeling needy, which is boring, so I'm over it.

"DINNER!" Abigail yells again. She's a junior and I'm only a year behind her, but she acts like she's *so* mature. Everyone at Riverbend loves her but only because they don't have to share a bathroom with her. I'm hilarious. But, seriously, go to college already, Abigail. Her boyfriend, Cam, told her that I'm gay because I don't play any sports. Isn't it more gay to get sweaty with a bunch of guys and then take showers together? I'm kidding. I like to make jokes that I only tell to myself.

ZEE

Maybe I shouldn't tell Cam. Telling him would be even more stupid than not telling him. Instead, I should just say something like—

A voice behind me: "Cam, I love you soooooo much. Please dump Abigail because I'm soooooo much smarter and more interesting and more beautiful."

I slap my phone to my chest, spin from back to butt on my bed, and face her. She loves to sneak into my room when I do my "stare at the ceiling" thing, as she calls it. "Hi, Mom," I say, but I say it like I mean, *You suck*.

"Don't be mad at me. Stand up and give me a hug. I could be dead by tomorrow." My mom's been saying crap like this since I was ten. It's funny. Sometimes.

I do as she says. My mom is this tiny thing, like a fairy if she had wings, and I'm this tall thing, but our bodies fit just right when we hug. My chin on her head, her head against my neck. Connected so there's no separation. And she's super pale and my skin's super dark, so we're almost that yin-and-yang symbol. That's weird to say. I guess I'm saying we're more than just mom and daughter. We are two halves to a whole that occasionally spend time apart. After our hug, I say, "I've decided I'm not going to tell Cam."

"That's a good idea. Much better to spend your life regretting not telling him."

"Yeah, yeah." I plop back to the edge of the bed. "If I tell him . . . and he doesn't like me back, then it will be awkward and I'll lose my best friend."

Mom sits next to me. "Darling . . . I'm sure after I'm dead, you'll be like, 'My mom died! Telling boys I love them is so easy compared to that!' "

"I'm sure."

"See? I'll be the best mom even in the afterlife."

"You will be." I almost—*almost*—get sad. But then I let it go. Because, listen, my mom's had cancer on and off since I was three. Being sad she has cancer would be like being sad she's got brown hair. It is what is. Yeah, it's stage four now. But it's been stage four for two years and she keeps looking healthier. She'll probably outlive me.

"I'm going to lie down. Have fun not telling your feelings to Cam over pizza." Yeah, yeah. We slap five and she leaves.

I lie on my bed and go back to obsessing over Cam. Screw that. Stupid girls obsess over boys. I contemplate. Yeah. Contemplate.

And contemplating boys sucks, so I'm going to watch TV.

art

"OH MY GOD, ART!" Abigail says as she throws open my bedroom door. "DINNER!"

I leap to my feet and tap-dance on the carpet because I'm a crazy person, then spin and slide on one knee in front of her with my arms out wide. Maybe I should be a choreographer on Broadway.

"YOU'RE SO WEIRD!"

"Thank you," I say. "Do you want to see my latest Art Chart?"

"Not even a little bit. And don't annoy Mom or Dad over dinner because if you do, they won't let me go meet Cam and then I'll have to hate you forever."

ZEE

"Don't you have homework?" asks Michael when he finds me watching the Bulls game in the living room. Michael is my mom's boyfriend. (Michael Trust is his full name. If that last name sounds made up, it's because it is.) They grew up in Gladys Park together. He was the football captain, she was the head cheerleader . . . and she wanted nothing to do with him until stage four hit. She explained back then that "I always liked my men a little weird, and Michael, well, is very normal and maybe we need normal and boring right now."

I tell him, "Did it." Which is true. School has always been super easy for me. Everything has always been easy for me. Except getting Cam to think of me in a non-friend way. ("Non-friend" might be lamest of all.)

"Your mom's resting?" he asks. I nod. "Are you hungry? I'll make some pasta."

"Going to dinner with Cam like I do every Monday."

"You shouldn't go out on a school night, Rebecca." Michael tries to pretend he's my dad but I spent my whole life without a dad, so why the hell does he think I need one now?

"I appreciate your advice, Michael, but I'm cool."

"Rebecca . . ." And fuck him for always calling me Rebecca when he knows I hate it. I raise the volume on the TV. He marches over and snaps the controller out of my hands.

"It frustrates me that you don't respect me."

"I respect you, Michael." Sort of. He let us move into his big house, and he pays the lease on my truck even though he said girls shouldn't drive trucks.

"Can we please come to an understanding while your mother is still with us?"

And, yeah . . .

I get up, pat him on the shoulder with a "you're an insensitive idiot" nod of my head, then leave the house. Michael likes to think he needs to prepare me for my mom being gone. Like I haven't been to a thousand doctors' appointments, or seen her go bald twice, or noticed both her boobs were chopped off. People's sympathy is annoying enough, but having to deal with his or anyone's condescending tone makes me want to punch them in the face.

art

Per Adams family law, the parental figures are already eating in front of the television. It wasn't so bad when everyone was still at home, because you can't keep five kids quiet no matter how much Dad screams, but now that only Abigail and I still live here, it is depressingly dull. Dad watches his sports, Mom plays Scrabble on her phone, Abigail texts her friends, and I wonder if the universe screwed up by having me born on planet Earth.

It's Monday, so it's Boston Market day. Chicken, bacon loaded mashed potatoes, and macaroni and cheese. I'm a vegetarian. "How can you not like meat and be a man?" Dad asked when I explained to them at twelve that I would no longer be eating the dead flesh of animals. I offered to be the family chef and cook out-of-this-world dishes like mushroom and asparagus risotto. "Oh, Art, why do you have to always make everything so difficult?" my mom said.

I heat up some leftover broccoli and mix it in with the mac and cheese, sit next to my dad, and ask him questions about the basketball game so that he can pretend we have anything in common. He is this large, large, super-large man, over six foot five with baseball mitts for hands and a gut full of carbs and fried meat and cheap beer, and I'm not even five nine and would have to eat milk shakes every hour for a month to add on two pounds. He's some kind of manager at Allstate, and if you asked me, *Hey, Art, do you believe in hell?* I'd say, *Yes, it's middle management at an insurance company!* But I hate being negative about my parents. They're just parents and they seem sure of themselves and their life choices, so *Go do your thing, Mom and Dad! Eat your fast food! Watch your sports! Count your money! You be you! Just let me be me!*

ZEE

When I get to Penelope's Pizzeria, I just walk in and sit in the back at our usual table. Cam and I have been coming here every week since he learned to drive. The hostess comes over and drops off menus even though she knows we never look at them. Her name is Pen. Her dad owns this place. Pen's a chick in my class who I always thought was a bitch until she started dating the biggest dork in school over Christmas break, which is so fucking bizarre it actually makes me want to become friends with her. Now I sound like a bitch. Can't think about this now. Cam. I need to concentrate on Cam. . . .

Maybe my mom was right? Maybe I'll regret not telling Cam more than I'll regret telling him. So why not just do it tonight, right? Yeah, what the hell. Junior year will be over in six weeks; high school will be over in a year. Be pretty stupid to wait any longer.

When Abigail is done eating, she says to my parents, "I need the car. I'm going to see Cam."

"Absolutely not," my dad says. But it's a ten-beer night, not a five-beer night, so it's more like a phlegmy, gurgley "absowooley not."

"Only if you take Art," my mom follows, then gives a look to my dad that says, *We can have sex if both kids are out of the house.* My parents are boring and don't talk about much with each other besides food and money, but if my mom's having a four-glasses-of-wine night, they are pretty much guaranteed to go at it. That's probably how they got stuck with five kids even though they're both incompetent parents.

"Yeah, okay," my dad says, "take Art and you can go."

"I'm not taking Art on my date with my boyfriend!"

"THEN YOU'RE NOT GOING, ABBY!" My dad is the king of the yelling Adamses. He always gets his way by screaming, so I don't know why he'd ever stop.

"Ugh, fine! We are leaving in two minutes, Art!" My sister stomps off. I wait for my parents to ask me if I actually want to go on my sister's date, but only because I like to wait for things that are never going to happen. "AAAAAART!" Abigail yells after noticing I hadn't moved.

"Were you talking to *meee*, sister?" I say, because I'm hilarious.

"You're so annoying! Mom!"

"Don't be annoying, Art." Mom always takes her side.

Robot voice? Yessssss: "I. Am. Sorry. Did. Not. Mean. To. Disobey. Orders. Standing. Walking. To. Car. Will. Wait. For. Further. Instructions."

"MOOOOOM!"

Like I said, hilarious. Too bad I'm the only one who thinks so.

ZEE

"You already ordered?" Cam asks as he walks toward our table.

"Of course," I say as he sits across from me and does our usual fist-bump greeting. Cam's got great hands. Big, strong hands. And shoulders. And legs. And everything. I sound like a chick. I am a chick. But I hate sounding like one. Listen, okay, Cam's hot. Not pretty-boy hot. But hot like a man should be hot. Like he could wrestle grizzly bears. Push cars up mountains. That sort of shit. I also dig that he doesn't care how he dresses. Who wants a guy who cares how they dress? And Cam really doesn't care. Wears the same zip-up jacket for a week, same jeans for a month, and the same Cubs hat since I gave it to him two Christmases ago.

In the three seconds it takes him to settle into the booth and look up at me, I think about just blurting out, *Dude, I'm kind of in love with you.*

I wouldn't have said that.

Never could say that.

But that would be the coolest way to do it, right? Like it's a casual thing, like I'm totally comfortable about being in love with him and don't need anything from him but for him to know. But, yeah, listen, that's never going to happen. He's been my best fucking friend since I was ten. You can't just say something like that without preparing the guy. Preparing myself. I don't know. But, see, even before I could say anything else, Cam says, "Abigail's going to join us. Hope that's cool."

Not cool at all. *At. All.* But it wouldn't be cool to not say it was cool, so I have to say, "Yeah, it's cool."

He says, "She gets jealous of our pizza dinners."

She does? That's good, right? If Abigail . . .

with her curves,

with her high heels to high school,

with her big lips and big eyes,

with her flirty 24-7 voice,

. . . could be jealous of my tall, flat-chested, tomboy ass, that's something, right? Maybe Cam talks about me a lot when they're alone. Yeah. Maybe he talks about all the things I am that Abigail could never be.

"BABY!" a shrieky, hyperfeminine voice launches across the restaurant. Abigail. Beautiful Abigail. Beautiful fucking Abigail.

"What's up, babe?" Cam says as he stands. She jumps into his arms, kissing him all over the neck like he has just returned from some war. Like they haven't seen each other in years instead of hours. I wouldn't even know how to do that. Jump in a man's arms. Let him twirl me and hold me like that. Maybe I have to learn.

"Art?" says Cam to the kid I am just now noticing standing behind Abigail. "What the hell are you doing here?"

Abigail, trying to pretend the kid doesn't exist, says, "My parents made me bring him. Sorry."

"It's cool. Art's cool," says Cam.

"He's in a mood. I apologize in advance."

"Zee, you ever meet Abigail's younger brother?"

art

Have you ever seen a mythical creature that everyone says doesn't exist but then you see it and you're like *They're real! They're real!* Of course you haven't. No one has because otherwise they wouldn't be mythical.

BUT!

I saw one. I'm seeing one right now. I mean, I have seen her in the halls a few times and in the stands at a couple of Cam's baseball games, but I have never seen her up close. I have never touched her. I have never felt her energy so purely. And now that I have, you just have to believe me, this girl named Zee is a mythical creature and she is even more beautiful and magical than that.

I'm sure everyone at school thinks she's boring or ugly or a lesbian, but she transcends beauty, with her big cheekbones and thin face and long neck and eyelashes that would be a mile long if she even acknowledged she had them. She is—what's the word?—oh, yes, she's androgynous but not in an unsexy way. In a way that every boy AND girl should find mesmerizing. I'm going to become a photographer so I can say I discovered her and get her out of that hoodie and those cargo pants and put her in loose dresses over her toned body, add a dash of makeup just to highlight what is already perfect, and then have the world scream, *She's magnificent!* And I will scream back, *I know! I know!*

ZEE

"No," I say as I stand to face Abigail's kid brother straight on. And he is a kid. I think a sophomore. But a *young* sophomore. His face is just so . . . pretty. Like he had never gotten a zit in his life, or a sunburn, or even a bad cold. You know what he looks like? Like he belongs in a boy band. My cousin Malinda used to have pictures of those bands all over her walls. She was twelve and I was probably six, but even then, I was like, "How can you be in love with them? They look and sound like girls." And Malinda said, "They're gorgeous like girls and that means they'll be sensitive and good listeners like a girl but also they're still boys and that makes them perfect."

As we shake hands, this kid, this pretty boy, this Art, he pulls me in closer to him with this funny little smile and says, "And now your life will never be the same."

"See?" Abigail says. "He's in a mood. PLEASE ACT NORMAL, Art!" I've never heard Abigail yell like that. She was always so sweet and cute and harmless. (Harmless besides standing in the way between me and Cam.) But her brother got to her. Which was awesome.

"Sorry, sister, I'll try to conform to standard human operating procedure for the rest of the evening."

And I fucking laugh. I can't even help it. I never laugh. (Well, except at my mom's stupid death jokes. But besides her, never. I just don't.)

"YOU'RE JUST GOING TO ENCOURAGE HIM, ZEE!"

"Yes, Zee," Art says, "you're only going to encourage me." And then he winks right at me. No one has ever winked at me before. Not like that. Such a bizarrely confident wink. If he wasn't so young, and if I wasn't one hundred percent sure he was gay, I'd almost think he was hitting on me. But that's impossible. He's a pretty boy who likes boys, and I'm a tomboy who might not even know I like chicks. But who the hell cares why he winked, right? He made me laugh. So I wink back.

art

She winked back. BACK!

My whole body is tingling all over and I'm thinking I've just met my future girlfriend and probably the other half of my soul and we're going to live in a castle in the sky of another dimension and be king and queen and rule over advanced beings who worship us even though we insist everyone is equal. Oh-my-god, my thoughts are fireflies on fast-forward in Crazy Town. Slow, slow, sloooooooooooow down.

BUT I JUST CAN'T!

"Zee, oh, my gosh, Zee, I have to ask you something," I blurt out even though she, Cam, and Abigail are talking about something else.

"Yes, Art," she says, and she smiles and I can tell she never smiles but she smiles at me, which I think means she loves me. I mean, she probably doesn't know it yet, not like I know I love her, but she'll know it eventually.

"Do you believe in love at first sight?" I ask, because, let's face it, that is happening right this second.

Zee laughs. I just love her laugh. Seriously, it is the best laugh ever. Not fake or tired or like it laughs at just anything, but a unique laugh, a special laugh. Yes, a special laugh that has to be earned by someone special like me.

"Art, dude," Cam says, "you're acting like you're on drugs."

"He's like this all the time at home. It's such a nightmare," Abigail says.

Do you know what my future girlfriend says? This is what: "I think Art's super cool." *Super cool.* She basically just told me she loves me as much as I love her, right? Yes, duh! I need her number. I need to be able to talk to her and text her and see her every second of every day. That's insane. Don't be insane, Art.

"Can I have your phone number?" Sorry. I had to. I can't be stopped.

She laughs AGAIN, and then she asks with this really knowing glint in her infinite brown eyes, "Why do you want my phone number, Art?"

And because she is acting so bold and mesmerizing, I decide to just say it: "So I can make you fall in love with me."

"Art! STOP MAKING EVERYTHING A JOKE!" Abigail yells because she doesn't really know how to handle me any other way. But Zee would, wouldn't she? She would. She doesn't laugh this time. Maybe because she knows I am serious.

"Art," Cam starts, "for real now, buddy, let's just settle down and be chill for the rest of dinner."

"But, Cam, *buddy*"—I love messing with him—"it's hard to contain myself when I've just met the greatest love of my life."

"All right, cool, but now we're going to talk like normal people." Cam is normal. Abigail is normal.

"But Zee and I aren't normal. We are special and cannot be bothered with your boring normal-people talk."

"SERIOUSLY, Art!" It's Cam that yells this time. He has never yelled at me. "Zee is my best friend, and you're making this weird for her."

"He isn't making this weird for me," Zee says. See? Special.

"Zee," Cam says, "I know you try to be accepting of everyone, but he's making fun of you."

"How's he making fun of me?"

"Yes," I say, "how am I making fun of her?"

Abigail butts in. She likes to butt in. Stupid buttface butter-inner. "Because you know you two are like polar opposites. So you're making a joke out of it."

"We are *not* polar opposites," I start, in almost a serious voice because I am starting to realize they really can't see how perfect Zee and I are for each other. "We are the opposite of opposites." Zee laughs again. She can't help finding me hilarious.

Cam says, "I don't even know how this started, Art, but Zee would never be into you and you know you'd never truly be into her or any other 'her.' "

Cam just said I was gay. Out loud. In front of my future girlfriend and my sister. Everyone's pretending he didn't say it, but he did.

And, I mean, let's be serious, I dress well, I don't really like sports, I like almost all creative endeavors, and my best friend Bryan *is* gay. And I think most gay people are so much more interesting than most straight people! So, okay, I get it. No denial of how the world perceives this soul.

And even though I love Cam for saving Abigail after biggest creep ever Will Safire left her in a thousand, tearful pieces, I honestly don't care that Cam thinks it. I don't care that anyone thinks it, really. I mean, aren't we all a little gay? Cam sweats and showers with guys, Abigail cuddles and confesses with girls, and I don't put labels on them. But the problem is, I don't want Zee to think that *I thought* I was gay.

But see . . . see, see, see . . . I thought that was the problem. I *thought* that was going to be my biggest obstacle now between my and Zee's great love affair. Afraid not. Because after I spent not even a full single second stressing over what she might think of me after Cam's statement, I notice this brokenhearted little girl inside Zee's eyes.

ZEE

Cam thinks I'm a lesbian, doesn't he?

He didn't exactly say it, but like I mentioned, I know a lot of people at The Bend think it. But they're all idiots, right? So what the hell do I care what they think? But if Cam thinks it . . . if the one person who knows me better than anyone besides my mom thinks I do like girls, or should like girls, or will like girls . . .

I mean, my brain just can't operate right now. Just one big block of fuck-me.

"Zee? Dude? What's wrong?" Cam says. "I didn't mean . . ."

"Nothing," I say. Nothing except the one dude I could ever really like thinks I like chicks.

art

Zee is in love with Cam.

She is. She is in love with her best friend and my sister's boyfriend. In love with a boy who used to bully Bryan and me in grade school. In love with a boy who truly is my polar opposite.

I guess that makes me wrong about everything. I know who I am and know who I like. If Zee could "like" someone like Cam, then she isn't the girl I dreamed her to be. She's not special like me. She's just not as good at being normal as people like Cam and Abigail.

So I turn my magic off. No reason to annoy normal people with it if it isn't going to amaze my mythical creature at the same time.

"Okay, I apologize," I say.

"Cool?" Cam says.

"Cool, dude," I say, mocking him a little because I can't help myself. But he doesn't notice.

"It's a trick," Abigail says.

"No trick," I say, "let's discuss the Riverbend Renegades baseball season with its star and captain, Cam Callahan. Or maybe we should preview the upcoming football season with its star and captain—what's his name?—Cam Callahan."

"Don't push it, punk," Cam says, ruffling my hair like I'm five years old. I was planning on pretending Zee barely existed for the rest of the dinner, only I can't help but notice her gazing down at her lap, either too ashamed about not defending me or too wrecked over her dream-man Cam not realizing she is in love with him.

But then—

—oh, goodness, but then—

She lifts her head and with it the phone from her lap. She slides it across the table toward me and winks—winks!—as she says, "My number."

ZEE

Listen, I don't know why I gave the kid my number. Maybe to piss Abigail off? Make Cam jealous? Why the hell that would make Cam jealous, I don't know. I probably did it because the kid was just out there—you know, different—and I'm sure enough people have ignored him or made fun of him and I didn't want to be another one of those people. Or maybe I hoped he'd make me laugh again. Who knows?

art

Okay, okay, okay. I see . . . don't you seeeeeeeeee? Zee's not bad at being normal. No, no, no. That's not it at all. No, see, Zee truly is a mythical creature, but *she doesn't know* she's a mythical creature.

That would be like the only unicorn on earth walking to every corner of the planet, seeing every other living being and not seeing any other unicorns, and *still* not understanding they were special.

So, yes, Zee and Art's love affair will happen and it will be fabulous. But it will have to wait for now. First, see, I was going to have to find my unicorn a mirror so she could see how magical she was.

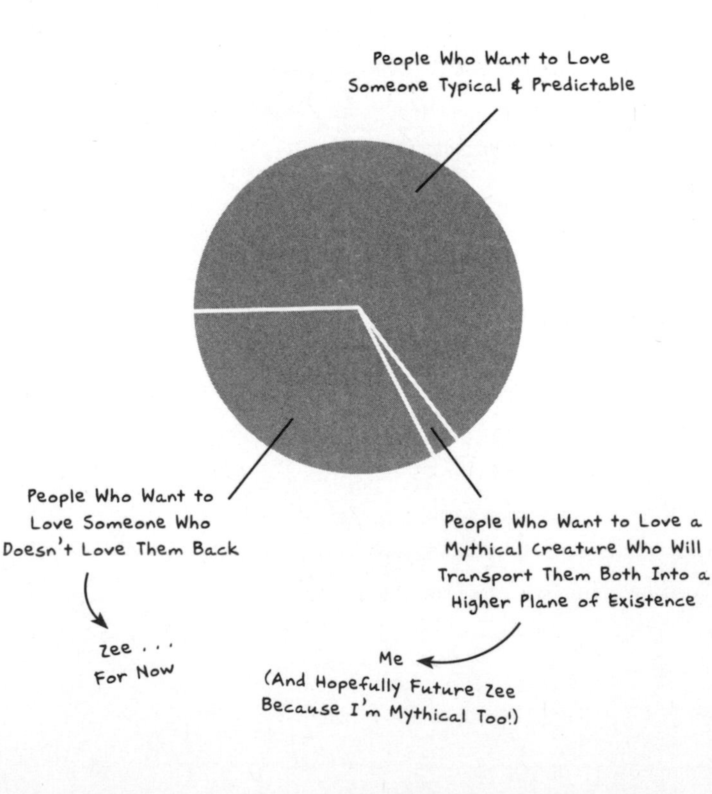

ZEE

The rest of dinner isn't nearly as eventful as the first bit. Art does calm down a little, though he keeps looking my way even if Abigail or Cam is speaking. It feels like he's studying me. Like he wants to draw me or some crap like that. I don't even . . .

After we eat, Cam says, "Zee, you mind sitting here with Art for a while so I can talk to Abigail in my car?"

He doesn't want to talk to her; he wants a blow job. From the first time Abigail did it, he couldn't stop talking about how great she was at it. (I swear their relationship is based on those fucking blow jobs.) After the fifth time hearing too many details, I told him I'd rather shove a pencil through my eye than hear about her "oral talents" again. And right now, the last thing I want to do is sit in a restaurant while the boy I love is getting it on with his girlfriend out in the parking lot. But I can't say no. So I say, "Yeah, cool." Fuck me.

After they leave, Art gets this little grin on his face as he says, "They're not going to talk."

"Yeah, I know."

"Does he know?"

"Does who know what?"

"Does Cam know you're in love with him?"

My first instinct is to say, *What the fuck are you talking about, kid?* But I have told no one except my mom and my mom's awesome but she's an idiot when it comes to guys so I think what the hell and say, "No, he doesn't, and if you tell your sister I'll end you."

"I want to be your best friend, so of course I'll tell no one."

"You like saying stuff like that, don't you?"

"Like I want to be your best friend and make you fall in love with me?"

"Yes," I say.

"It's just so boring to say boring things. I like to not be boring."

"You're definitely not boring, Art."

The kid inhales a deep breath, catches it, and then blurts out, "You're special."

"Thanks?"

"So why would you fall in love with someone so not special like Cam?"

"Don't be an asshole."

"I'm just saying . . ." Art starts.

"He's my best friend, so don't be an asshole and tell me he's not special, because he is."

I swear the kid almost cries. I feel bad even though he was the one who said the stupid thing.

"Listen, kid—I know you were trying . . ."

"Kid?" he says, and now, yeah, there is definitely water in the corners of his eyes. Crap. Before I can apologize, he says, "I have to use the bathroom." And he leaves. He's still in there when Abigail and Cam walk back inside with their faces flushed and her lips puffed out from, well, from whatever. I am exhausted from Art. From Cam. From my stupid "feelings." So I pay the bill, and as soon as they're back at the table, I stand up and say,

"Art's in the bathroom and I've got to go." They sort of say, "Cool," but I'm not really listening anymore.

art

Once composure is regained, tears dried, and my face again impossible not to love (ha), I exit the pizzeria bathroom to find Zee gone. Tears threaten to return before I remember: I have her phone number! Then all I want to do is text Zee every fifteen seconds until she realizes that our encounter is the most important meeting in the history of the universe.

Knowing that this is a brilliant idea but also, possibly, a horrible one, I distract myself by texting Bryan while Abigail and Cam bicker in the front seat on the drive home:

ME

I'm in love

BRYAN

You fall in love every week, Art!

ME

Those were schoolboy crushes.
This is my first grown-up love.

BRYAN

You fell in love with the girl in the
Old Navy commercial last Thursday

True. That Old Navy girl *was* perfection. Like fantasy perfection you don't touch, only admire from afar. Zee is perfection meant to be held. Zee is so real it makes me fly.

But Bryan isn't going to understand for a million reasons but mostly because he's in love with me. We've had the conversation so many times. He tells me he loves me. I tell him I love him too. He tells me he loves me *like that*. I tell him I like girls. He tells me I'm not being honest with myself. I tell him he's not being honest with himself that I simply don't like him *like that* back. He cries, runs off, doesn't talk to me for two days, and then texts me that he can't even remember why we're fighting. I pretend I don't either and we go back to being best friends.

Back at home, and still fighting the urge to stalk-text Zee, I instead text my sorta, kinda new BFF Carolina Fisher. She hunted me down at the end of our freshman year, basically begging to be my friend because her brother had just come out of the closet and she thought I was gay and, even though I told her I wasn't, I could tell she didn't believe me. But then she had a big, epic breakup with Trevor Santos and we were watching a movie and she's like, "Are you really not gay?" and I could tell she was lonely and she looked pretty and I needed practice kissing, so I kissed her. And it was . . . like making out with my twin sister without the scandalous excitement. Such a disaster. I didn't tell her that because that would be mean. We did go to homecoming together and it was fun but also a little awkward because I could tell she thought I was gay again but really we just had zero chemistry. (Which I couldn't say unless I was a jerk and I'm the nicest person ever!) So the reason she's only kinda, sorta my new best friend is because we don't really hang out in person anymore but we do text each other really intimate stuff like who we think about when we masturbate. So that's why all I had to text is:

ME

Zee Kendrick

And I know she'll know what that means.

CAROLINA

REALLY?

ME

Yes REALLY

CAROLINA

She's so . . . brooding

ME

I KNOW! It turns me on

CAROLINA

I liked when Trevor brooded

Oh, boy, she is having a "Trevor is my soul mate" pity party. Boring. So I tell Carolina she should just get back together with him already and then say I have to go even though I don't.

Because all I want to do, maybe ever again, is think about Zee. But the perfect text to win her heart for eternity has not yet formed! Maybe I should just go to sleep and send her one tomorrow after I've had more time to think about it.

Ha. Sleep. Not a chance.

ZEE

I fall asleep on the couch watching SportsCenter. Only wake up when I get this text:

UNKNOWN NUMBER

You're right, Cam's special and everyone in the world is special but you're so special it hurts my body

It's Art. The kid. I want to find what he wrote creepy. Or freaky. Or maybe just stupid. But no one's ever texted me stuff like that. I have really only dated two people ever. Two dudes from my CrossFit gym. Neither of them texted me anything besides *Want to come over and watch a movie?* Which meant come over and hook up.

I don't know if what the kid texted was romantic or poetic or dorky or maybe just super nice. Art is clearly confused and lonely. Not sure why he is latching on to me the way he is, but screw it, I like it. Who cares why I do?

So I text back:

ME

sorry for calling you kid

ART

I've decided you can call me kid as long as it becomes your pet name for me when we make love :)

So weird!

Fuck it, I feel like being weird back.

ME

deal—what will your pet name be for me?

He doesn't text back right away and I feel like an idiot for playing along. But then:

ART

Sorry it took so long. But I had to make sure

I thought of the perfect pet name: my queen.

ME

your queen?

ART

Tell me you love it or I'll die.

I want to tell him it's stupid. That I should go back to sleep. But like everything with this kid, what I want to want and what I actually want are never the same.

ME

i love it

Part Two

THE OPPOSITE OF
OPPOSITES

art

Mom drives Abigail and me to school every day, but she usually makes business calls while she drives (she's a part-time salesperson at the Mercedes dealership in Hoffman Estates), so mostly Abigail looks at her phone in the front seat and I look into my heart for profound revelations in the backseat. I'm so interesting. I know! (Ignore me, please, I'm in a mood.)

But today Abigail leans into the back and says, "Cam told me to tell you not to bug Zee or he'll be mad."

"Zee and I are in love."

"Art! This is serious! Cam and Zee already are way too close and if he hates me because you harass her, then I'll hate you forever."

"I promise not to bug Zee."

"Thank you," she says, but she doesn't like my answer the more she thinks about it, so then she screams, "WHEN I SAY DON'T BUG HER, THAT MEANS DON'T CONTACT HER AT ALL FOR ANY REASON!"

"I love you, Abigail." Which I say in a voice that makes me sound so mature and her crazy, which confuses her so much she doesn't say anything the rest of ride.

Bryan is waiting for me at my locker like he always is before first period. For the record, my best friend is a horrible dresser, so anyone who thinks all gay people are fashionistas needs to meet more gay people. He's a bit big (he says fat) and is super self-conscious about it, so he wears big baggy khakis and bigger, baggier blue sweaters (always blue!) to hide his body. I tell him he's not overweight, he's strong, but then he asks why I'm not attracted to him and, "Let's move on already, Bryan!"

"I'm sorry for not taking your new girlfriend seriously," he says first thing today, and that is like the opposite of what I expect him to say.

"She's not my girlfriend *yet*."

He goes on, "But she will be when she gets to know you. Anyone who truly gets to know you and doesn't love you is a moron." Which is nice but also a little manipulative, so I ignore it and say, "I can't wait for you to meet her."

"Me neither." And then Bryan punches me (hard!) in the shoulder because that's how he shows affection but also because that's how he shows me he wishes Zee was dead.

I texted Zee when I woke up but she hasn't texted back by the time first period ends so I text her again but she still hasn't texted me by lunch so then I text her six times in a row saying how sorry I am for texting so much only to realize this is like singing, *I'm sorry for singing!*

I tell myself to be patient, but then I tell myself patience is for people who didn't meet their soul mate last night, so I go and find Cam and Abigail before they leave for Midnight Dogs.

"Is Zee okay?" I ask.

"I hate you," Abigail says, but she says it under her breath because she has everyone in school convinced she's not constantly on the edge of hysteria, which she so is.

"Art, bud, she's fine. I know you think you two bonded last night, but you gotta remember she's a junior and you're a sophomore and she's into sports and you're not, so you two don't really have anything to talk about."

Boring. I say, "Just tell me she's alive and not trapped under a large vehicle somewhere, and I'll worry about what we talk about."

They both shake their heads and ignore me and walk away, which is fine because I am done talking to them anyway.

ME

ZEE! MY LOVE! TELL ME WHAT ALIENS KIDNAPPED YOU AND I'LL FIND THE CLOSEST SPACESHIP TO COME FIND YOU!

This is too much. Why do I always have to be too much?

ZEE

you're hilarious

She's so in love with me, she can't even take it.

ZEE

I go do CrossFit every day after school except Tuesday because on Tuesday my mom schedules her personal training clients so she always has the afternoon off. Michael has meetings (he does the church's finances), so from like three to eight, it's just me and her. Sometimes we do big things like go shopping downtown. (Mom tries to make me buy girly crap, but I always end up just getting another hoodie or workout thing.) Or we see a movie and get a large popcorn and dump peanut M&M's in it. But mostly it's low-key stuff. Her reading on the couch while I do homework on the floor. Or picking up Chinese food and then bingeing on Netflix. I like it all, the big or the small, because it's just me and her. My life has always been best when it's just me and her.

Today's going to be a special day. We're going to do a tour at Northwestern University. She wants me to go someplace exotic like California or Portland, but there's no way I'm going to school that far away from her. No way. Northwestern is a forty-minute drive. Plenty far for me.

She had been talking about this tour all weekend as if I was actually leaving for college today, so I expect her to have her purse in hand, psyching me up with some of her old cheerleader ra-ra, but when I walk in through the front door, the house is weirdly quiet.

I know she's home because her car is in the garage, so when I enter and it's silent, I freak out. My mom is *always* making noise, moving or talking or something, unless she's sleeping and she never slept during our Tuesdays.

And listen, I know it's coming, I know it is, I know my mom's going to die, but just because you know something's going to happen doesn't mean it can't freak you out.

"MOM!" I yell, and I almost never yell. When she doesn't respond, fuck, I yell so loud I expect the house to blow apart. "MOOOOOOOOOMMMMM!" I start running from room to room. Yelling. Yelling more. The last place I go is her room because I always figure the place she would die would be her room and if she is going to be dead I want to wait as long as possible to find out. Yeah, I'm running, so maybe I should have crawled to make it last even longer, but nothing makes sense when you think your mom is dead.

And there she is, on her bed, her eyes closed, hands crossed over her stomach. She looks pretty, but a peaceful pretty and my mom is usually a high-strung pretty. Her makeup is perfect because it's always perfect. She is dressed in a suit for our tour. She never wears suits because she likes to be as girly as possible in dresses or spandex. The opposite of me basically. So the suit is for me, to impress whoever needs to be impressed at Northwestern.

But my mom . . . right now . . . is still. So still.

Too still . . .

"You think I'm dead, don't you?" she says, with her eyes still closed.

"AAAAAH!" I scream, and then run and jump onto the bed next to her. She laughs. Thinking she's so fucking funny. I am so pissed. And so happy. "That's not funny, Mom!"

"When I'm dead, you're going to think back on this moment and say, 'My mom was *so* funny.' "

"Why are you lying down? Are you tired? Do you want to skip the tour?"

"No! I'm fine. I'm so, *so* excited for this tour. First one on their feet wins." And damn, my mom sits up, swivels, and stands before I can even turn over. But by the time I'm up next to her, her breath gets short and she needs to sit back down on the bed.

I sit back down next to her and rub her back. Her wheezing is rough, deep, like an overweight man instead of her frail self, and it sounds like her lungs are gurgling water, even drowning. "We're not going," I say.

"We're going," she says.

"You can barely breathe!"

"I'm fine, Zee." And she puts her head on my shoulder and closes her eyes for one second before leaping back to her feet and pretending she is invincible yet again. "You go change and I'll meet you in the car in one minute."

"I'm wearing this," I say, pointing at what I wear every day. Hoodie (black today) and cargo pants (dark khaki green every day).

"No, you're not. You're wearing a dress."

"HA!" I haven't worn a dress in, man, I don't even. Long fucking time.

"Then at least a blouse and nice jeans. And no gym shoes or boots."

"This is a tour, Mom, not an interview."

"This is a chance to make an impression, no matter how small. Go." She pushes me out and closes her bedroom door behind me.

Fine. I'll do it. For her. Listen, no way was I getting in a dress—did I even own one that fit anymore?—but if she'd put on a suit, I could do jeans and that white cashmere-y sweater from Banana Republic she got me. Fine.

I change fast. Feel stupid, like I'm pretending to be someone else, but whatever. I haven't heard my mom open her door, so I fling it open and say, "Look how much your daughter loves you."

She is still again. So still.

But this time crumpled on the floor.

art

After Zee tells me I am hilarious, I text her back that we should elope, and she sends me a wink back, which means she isn't taking me seriously. I mean, I *was* joking. Mostly anyway. But, oh, I can just feel in my heart that Zee is going to be my escape superjet out of this terribly boring and ill-fitting life I'm stuck in. I just know it! So I decide no more Zee texts until tomorrow. Or at least tonight. Or at least an hour from now.

Walking into the house after school, I find Abigail crying on the front stairs and I think, Yay, Cam broke up with her! But then I think if Cam had really broken up with her, she would be doing her overdramatic spectacle in front of everyone and not this small sob hidden away from my parents.

"What's wrong?" I ask, because maybe, just maybe, something really is wrong.

"Dad got fired," she says, and I'm not even sure my brain thought what she said was English. It was like she'd said, *Dad is a lizard and he just molted his human skin off.*

But then my head slowly deciphers the words, so I ask, "Where is he?"

"Watching TV." She sobs an epic sob, and I hug her to make sure her body doesn't come apart at the seams. Abigail hugs me back, and for a moment, we seem like siblings who actually like each other. When she seems to solidify, I tell her I'm going to check on Dad.

ZEE

I drop to my knees, turn my mom over on her back. I have gotten certified in CPR and I am ready.

But she doesn't need it.

Breathing . . . she is breathing . . . barely . . . but enough. It's that same gurgling from before, except this time it is fast, shallow, faint. Super-fucking faint. Stage four cancer basically means her breast cancer has spread to other parts of her body. For my mom, the tumors in her chest wall are causing malignant fluid to fill the cavity around her lungs. Awesome, right? Yeah, right. So breast cancer in her lungs. It doesn't even make sense. She told me a few months ago—in her "isn't this funny?" way—that eventually she'd suffocate but not really know she was suffocating because of the pain medication. That can't be now, right? She isn't even on any pain meds right now, so it can't be. It just can't.

My phone is dialing 911 while my free hand strokes her hair and tells her it's going to be okay. I always wanted to be that person who didn't tell people it was going to be okay when I knew it wasn't. . . .

But she's my mom and I want her to be okay so much, I'd be any person anyone wanted me to be if she'd just be okay for a little while longer.

It doesn't get worse as we wait for the ambulance, but she can't talk, so we just lie on the floor next to each other. I stare in her eyes, memorizing every flicker inside of them. Every tiny movement. I convince myself as long as I look at her, she'll stay alive. Like a watched pot never boils. She tries to stare back but keeps losing focus. As if her eyes can't decide to look at this life or the next. So any time I see her pupils drift, I whisper, "I love you, Mom," and she'll be able to concentrate on me for a moment or two. Then she smiles at me, just a bit, and squeezes my arm.

art

My dad is in his usual corner of the couch, feet propped on the coffee table, a beer in his hand and a bag of Doritos in his lap. His mouth and hands are pasted in that neon cheese. SportsCenter is on because SportsCenter is always on if no actual games are. Dad has this far-off gaze thing that makes me think his soul has left his body and all that's left is this empty shell.

"How are you doing?" I ask.

"Fine," he says, not turning away from the television.

"Can I make you a sandwich?" I ask. I don't even know why. I have never made my dad a sandwich or any food in my life.

"No."

"Do you want to talk about it?"

"Not much to talk about, Art."

"I'm sure you'll get a better job now."

"Yeah," he says, but his "yeah" is more of a *my life is over.*

"Maybe the four of us should go out to dinner to make you feel better."

"Can't spend more money when you have less."

"Yes, but . . ."

"Art, I just need to be left alone."

"Oh, okay, sorry, Dad. I'll be in my room if you need me." I wait for him to say something else, but he just goes back to being a soulless shell and so I leave.

ZEE

The paramedics arrive six minutes after I call. Which is great. But they break my eye contact with my mom—yeah, to save her, but what if it's my staying connected to her that's saving her?—and by the time I step up into the ambulance with her, she can't focus on me at all. Not even for a second or two. She only looks up and off, off to that other world. Or winces from the pain in this world. Like someone is hammering big stakes through her chest every other breath.

Should I tell her it's okay to go? She's fought this disease fourteen years now. All for me. I should. Listen, I'll be alone, but isn't that better than my mom always fighting? Always in pain?

"Mom . . ." I start. Not crying. But my voice isn't steady. "Mom . . . you . . . stay with me. Okay? I don't want you to go. I don't want you to go."

I know I should've said she could move on. *I know.* But I don't want her to move on. Isn't that okay that I don't want my mom to die? Ever. Someone please tell me it's okay. Please.

Even at three, I didn't smile a whole lot. Yeah, I know some kids see their parents are depressed and try to cheer them up. But I was the opposite. My mom had all this crap happening to her, all this horrible luck, and all she'd do was make jokes and say stuff like "No biggie, kiddo." That was her favorite thing to say to me every time I got upset about her cancer coming back or some jerk guy dumping her. So I thought it was my job to be serious for her. I'd tell the doctors, "If you don't make my mom better, I'll kill you." I didn't say it cute. Said it dead fucking straight. Really. And I'd give them the best evil eye any little kid has ever given. When she was cancer free for a few years, and dating, I'd do the same to her boyfriends. "If you hurt my mom, I'll kill you." And evil eye them until they laughed uncomfortably and Mom told me to be nice. *Screw being nice* is what I used to think. If the world isn't nice to you, you shouldn't be nice back.

When I was ten, my mom's cancer returned for the second time. I wanted to blow up the planet. The whole fucking thing. In fact, I stomped around the house screaming, "I'M GOING TO BLOW UP THE FUCKING PLANET!" The type of screaming that turns your face purple.

My mom waited for me to exhaust myself, then steered me over to our tiny kitchen table in our (pre-Michael) tiny one-bedroom apartment. She said, "Zee . . . cancer's not fun. A lot of things that happen aren't that fun. But you're getting old enough now that I think you can work on not being angry all the time."

"I like being angry all the time!"

"I know you do." She laughed. She liked to defuse my rage sometimes with her chirpy fairy laugh.

"Because things suck all the time!"

Mom then said, "How about if I told you that you working on your anger might help me fight cancer?"

I said nothing. Just sat there and stewed.

"You're right. A lot of sucky things happen. And you and I may have gotten more than our fair share."

"WAAAAAAAY more!" Purple face was back.

Mom continued with her big lecture, and even though that day I barely registered what she was saying while she was actually saying it, I really didn't forget any of it. Weird, I know. She said: "To deal with all these sucky things that happen in life, people try all sorts of things. Some work a lot or get a big hobby so they are too busy to think about the bad stuff. Church has helped me and a lot of others find peace when things become hard. And almost everyone uses things like TV or food or alcohol or drugs to distract themselves from the sucky things. Which is fine too as long as you don't distract yourself so much that you don't want to do anything else besides distract yourself. And you, Zee, you're addicted to distracting yourself using anger . . ."

"But, Mom . . ." I said, not yelling. More quiet. Like I knew she had a point but still had to argue with her anyway.

". . . but being angry about things being sucky is self-fulfilling because if you're so busy being angry, how are you going to look for things that might make you happy? And if you're so good at being angry, why are nice, fun people going to want to spend time with you? So of course things will keep staying sucky!" She tried to pretend this was funny. It wasn't. But then my mom hugged me and made us grilled cheese with tomatoes, which was my fave then, and that day became my fave forever.

You can't tell your parents lectures work or they'll do it all the time, but that lecture worked. Not like I became this fake, smiley person suddenly. But I stopped hating every person I met. I tried to talk to other kids like they might be my friends and not just ignorant idiots.

That summer is when I met Cam. And listen, my mom is right. When I let myself have a friend, someone I could have fun with, it was easier not to be angry all the time. I guess I'm thinking about this now because it's not like my mom is just this nice person who feeds me and clothes me and drives me places. She's got super-wise insights. And I want her around to give me more insights. About college and jobs and Cam. I want her here. Please.

Once at the hospital, a nurse directs me to the waiting room while they wheel my mom back into the emergency department. I try to argue, not really with words, but the nurse says, "We will bring you back there as soon as she's stabilized."

Can't sit, too much energy, so I hover near the admitting desk. Text Cam:

ME

At the hospital with my mom

He doesn't respond right away. Which sucks. Sucks. Sucks. Sucks. So I text Michael just to have something to do. Michael responds fast. Which is cool I guess. Says he is on his way. I keep looking at my phone, waiting for Cam to text back or call or maybe just show up. Wouldn't that be the best thing to ever happen? If Cam just strolled into the emergency room and then saw me from across the lobby. Without words, he'd be saying, *I'm here for you, Zee.*

If he showed up like that, I think I would run up and jump into his arms. Yeah, I totally would.

art

The one positive of my dad losing his job and our family possibly ceasing to exist is that I don't obsess over Zee every second.

Every other second?

Yes, duh, ha.

I finally text her again around seven. Which is basically a world record.

She doesn't text back.

But I'm a much more mature person than I was this morning, so I'm not going to text her again until after she texts me. Unless she doesn't text me back in the next ten minutes.

ZEE

Cam doesn't show up. No jumping into a boy's arms today.

Michael does show and does his grown-up thing and talks to the nurse. Doesn't do any good, but it's cool he did it.

Three hours. That's how long we have to wait. Michael makes business calls, but all I can do is just stand there. Yep. Nothing else. Don't really think anything either. Sometimes you want something to happen so much you can't do anything but wait for it to happen.

So three hours. The doctor first explains that they have opened her chest to release some of the fluid buildup in her lungs, which regulated her breathing. "So she's stable," the doctor explains, "but sleeping. The surgery and the pain medication will probably keep her resting through the night. But you can go see her."

A nurse then leads us back to the patient rooms. Michael and I both walk through the door to her room, and I expect her to look like she did when I walked into her bedroom after school. But now she's ghost white, drool down her chin, mascara smeared across her face, the hospital gown jagged across her left shoulder. Tubes and wires sprout from her body. My mom looks sicker than I've ever seen her, even the chemo days.

I grab a towel from the bathroom, get it wet, and wipe her face clean of the drool and makeup. After cleaning her up, tightening the gown, straightening out her blanket, I kiss her on the head. *Love you, Mom,* I say without saying it.

"I'll sleep on the chair here," I say.

"No, you are going home to get a good night's sleep," Michael says in his boss voice.

"One person can stay, but not two," the nurse says. "I'll let you two work it out." Then she leaves.

"I'm staying." I fire my evil eye. He gets the message.

"Okay, okay . . ." he stammers. "You call me if anything changes. I'll come back in the morning so you can go to school."

No chance I'll be going to school tomorrow but no reason to argue with Michael on that point now. He tries to hug me before he leaves, but I look in the other direction and he gets the hint, says good-bye, and leaves.

Cam has finally texted me back:

CAM

Zee, so sorry about your mom—Thinking of ya

I'm sure he had been lifting weights or maybe hanging out with Abigail. But three hours is a long time to wait for your best friend to respond when your mom is dying. And then to not say, *I'm on my way*, or even *Can I do anything?* or any *fucking* thing besides the most pointless thing in the universe. *Thinking of ya*. HOW DOES THAT HELP ME? WHAT AM I SUPPOSED TO DO WITH YOUR THOUGHTS, CAM! I want you here! I want you trying to hug me! I want you to love me like I love you!

Fuck me, I'm such a loser.

I go to type something back, something normal like *Thanks*, but my phone dies. FUUUUUUUUUUUUUUUUUUUUUUCCCCCKKKKK KKKKKK.

art

Four point two minutes later, suffering severe Zee withdrawal, sure I am about to die, I text Bryan to see if he can distract me from the pain:

ME

My dad lost his job. We're poor now.
I'm either going to work at TGI Fridays
or sell my body to lonely old women.

BRYAN

Sorry about your dad, Art. That's hard.

Bryan's parents are super-rich accountants—like big-deal accountants and I don't even know what that means, but if you have a house with a tennis court in the backyard, you must be a big deal, right? And Bryan is an only child, so he gets whatever he wants. New car. New clothes. (Even if he picks terrible ones.) New video games and computers and a credit card he can use to buy whatever food he wants whenever he wants. He's so lucky. His life would be perfect if I was his boyfriend and his parents stopped pretending he wasn't gay. So maybe it all equals out.

BRYAN

But if you're going to sell your body,
you should sell it to me.

Set myself up for that one.

BRYAN

I'm KIDDDING Art. Sorry about your gf

How does he know Zee isn't texting me back?

ME

What do you mean?

BRYAN

Her mom—you didn't hear?

ZEE

"Zee." The nurse steps back into the room.

"Yeah?"

"There's a young man in the waiting room here to see you. We can only let family back here after hours. Do you want me to tell him something?"

"No-I'll-go," I say almost as fast as I am walking back toward the waiting room.

Cam came.

Cam came.

Cam came.

Maybe he does love me. Maybe, right? I am definitely going to jump into his arms. That would be fucking insane, but I'm going to do it. No more waiting, no more planning stuff in my head. Just going to go for it.

I round the corner into the waiting area and there . . . he is.

The kid.

Art.

Holding two large potted plants.

I want to strangle him. Strangle him for not being Cam. For being annoying. For showing up at the hospital where my mom lies dying when I barely know him. But before I can yell at him or punch him, he sprints over, drops the plants to the floor, and bear-hugs me before I can tell him I don't do hugs. Lifts me off the ground even. Barely, because the kid is probably lighter than me. But my feet are definitely in the air.

I stop fighting his fucking weirdness and hug him back. I'll punch him or yell at him or never speak to him again later.

After I put Zee back down, I think about kissing her. Oh-my-god, a first kiss in a hospital! So epic! So dramatic! But I didn't. I'm crazy but I'm not that crazy. Tonight's not about all my mad fantasies of our love and life together; it is about her mom.

Sooooo, I say: "How's your mom? How are you? What can I do? Can I go get you something to eat? To drink? Is there someone I can call? Do you want me to talk to any doctors? Tell me, Zee, tell me. I'm here to do whatever you need."

Zee takes a step back. I am too much. DON'T BE TOO MUCH, ART! She says, "My mom's resting. She's fine. I'm okay. Thanks for coming."

Oh-my-god, she wants me to leave. No, no, no. "Let me do something. Anything. Tell me."

"I just need to be alone with my mom right now. Okay?"

My dad wants to be alone; now Zee wants to be alone. Humans are not meant to be alone! We are meant to love and connect and communicate and create *with* one another! But I can't say any of that. (Don't self-combust, Art!) Instead I fake composure: "Okay. Of course, I totally understand. Here, I figured you might need this." I pull an iPhone charger from inside my coat pocket and place it in her hand.

And, you wouldn't believe it, but it's a stupid phone charger that turns my stoic queen soft. Zee doesn't cry but her eyes get big, so big, and quiver, and then she wraps her arms around my neck and pulls me tight into her. Our bodies are both thin and I've always hated how skinny I am, but when we're pressed together like this, it's like we're one of those kids' shows where two people join together to create a singular superhero. Yes! Yes! I could see it all now. Apart, we are these mere mortals Art and Zee. But together, we will transform into the all-powerful, all-knowing, all-wonderful . . . Artzee!

(Or Zert. Yes, you're right, Zert's better.)

The all-powerful, all-knowing, all-wonderful . . . Zert!

Oooh, I'm going to write a comic book tonight and then I'll sell it and then it will be made into a movie and then the whole world will know our one-of-a-kind love story!

"Thanks again, Art," Zee says as she returns us to two mortals.

"Of course, my queen." And then, while ever so slowly backing away, I give her my best movie-star smile and wink that I practice in the mirror. Yes, I practice it every day! "Call me, text me, if you need anything at all." Then I twist away from her because I'm pretending to be cool and not super needy. I keep waiting to hear, *Wait, Art, wait, come back!* And then I'd turn, run back, and we'd have the first kiss to end all first kisses. But she doesn't. It's okay. . . .

IT'S NOT OKAY AT ALL! I want to kiss her and spend every minute with her until I know every inch of her heart, soul, and body!

But it's okay. Really. I'm maturing. Right? Yes, really, because the *old* Art would have run back, all pathetic, and asked/begged Zee for more time with her. Ruined my flawlessly executed good-bye. But not the *new* Art. No! This new Art keeps walking and walking—oh-my-god-this-is-so-hard!—and walking until the emergency room doors open and let me outside.

Of course, then I hide behind a cement column and watch Zee pick up the plants I brought, turn, and disappear back into the hospital.

And then, of course, I go back into the waiting room, sit, and stare at my phone. She'll text me, right? She will.

She doesn't!

I want to die from loneliness!

But then she does! Twenty minutes later! It feels like twenty years, but that's okay because I'd wait twenty thousand years for her. Her text:

ZEE

you're awesome

In my head, I interpret Zee's text to mean: *You're the best person to ever breathe and I can't wait to see you again*, and so I type out: *I'm here for you always and forever.* But that's too much. Or not? Yesssssss, Art, it's too much. New Art is not going to be too much! So I erase it and send a smiley face.

Which is so dumb and boring, but she's in a hospital room with her sick mom and needs me to be helpful, not needful, and true love knows when to be which.

ZEE

The fucking kid brought me a phone charger. Like he had read my thoughts. Not just read my thoughts, but read my thoughts *before* I had my thoughts and from miles away. Fucking kid. I don't even know what I'm going to do with him. He's so lost and needy and nuts . . . and yet . . . yeah, and yet . . .

After my phone turns back on, I text him. I shouldn't encourage him, or lead him on, but I can't just ignore Art's being awesome either. I look at Cam's text again. *Thinking of ya.* Oh, who cares? That's who Cam is. He's a man's man and man's men are aloof and almost never helpful with shit like this. I saw that with dozens of my mom's previous boyfriends. Michael is the first one who ever provided anything of substance. But he's also the first one who—and she admitted this to me—didn't "excite" her. Maybe that's how relationships are. The ones that excite you are only good for getting you excited (and I don't mean sexually although that's probably also true) and the ones that are helpful don't really excite you. Sucks that there aren't guys who can do both. Maybe there are. But my mom has never met one. And I certainly haven't.

art

An hour later, with no more word from Zee, I walk home from the hospital. Alone in the dark. It is miserable, of course, but also a very productive time and place to plot out the beginning adventures of *ZERT: THE SUPERHERO BORN OF SUPER LOVE*.

Yuck. That might be too dramatic even for me.

Ha, I'm hilarious. *Nothing's* too dramatic for me.

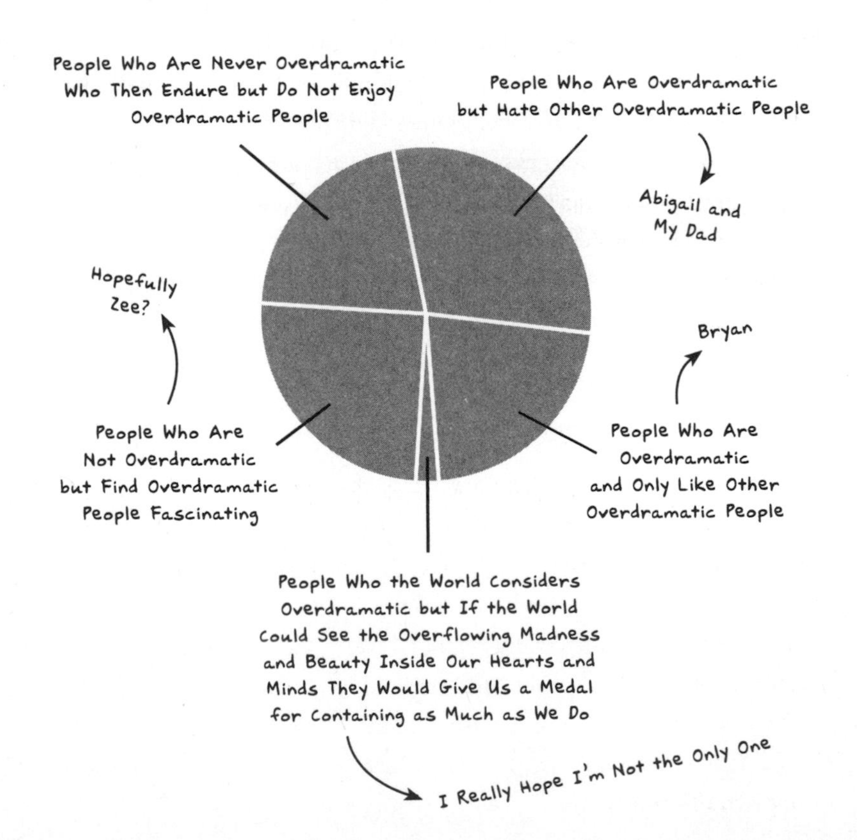

ZEE

I fall asleep without realizing I'm going to, and when I wake, my mom is staring at me.

"Mom! How long you been up? You should have woken me." I jump from the hospital room reclining chair, chucking the blanket, and crouch by her bed so our faces are level.

"I wanted to watch you sleep," she says, but her voice is a whisper. Not even a whisper. A wisp. A broken, scratchy wisp.

"You shouldn't talk. Should I call the doctor?"

"No, I need to tell you something."

What-the-hell-my-eyes-are-watering. Why the fuck are tears forming? There's no reason to cry now! She's fine! Doctor said she was stable! She just said she needs to tell you something. "You're okay, Mom."

"I know, I'm going to live forever." Making jokes. Always making jokes. She tries to smile. Tries. Too much pain. I stand but she grabs my hand. Her gaze wavers again, like last night. Vanishing into another time and place.

"Mom?"

She dials back to me and the now. "Zee . . . I wrote a letter. . . ."

"You'll be able to tell me. You'll be okay."

". . . It's under those dresses you never wear. Your bottom drawer. I should have explained some things. I was a good mom, right?"

No, no, no. "Mom," I say, and f me, f me, f me, I am crying and I don't want to cry because if I am crying my mom is probably dying and DO NOT LET MY MOM DIE!

"I was good. I was like the best mom ever." She grins even though it costs her a double shot of pain. "But I screwed up, darling."

"You didn't screw up. You're the best mom. THE BEST MOM AND I WANT YOU TO STAY WITH ME." I don't yell this. I just feel it so much my body cracks in half.

"Three things . . . the letter explains everything better . . . but three things . . . I'm being really dramatic, aren't I?"

"Yes, you are!" And I laugh. Laugh while crying! Who does that? That's like eating and puking at the same time!

"I like being dramatic. . . ."

"Yes, you do."

". . . First thing, you'll have some money. I opened an account under your name. . . . Michael knows all the details. . . ."

"Mom . . ."

". . . Let me finish, I could be dead any second. . . ."

"MOM!"

". . . I'm so funny. . . ."

"Mom!"

". . . Second thing . . . Michael said you could live with him as long as you want, but if that feels weird for any reason"—and it's weird that she's saying it might be weird—"then use the money to get your own place."

"Mom, you should rest."

". . . Third thing . . . oh-my-god, this is even more dramatic than I thought I could be. . . ."

Mom . . .

". . . Your dad . . ."

My dad? MY DAD?!

". . . I promised him you'd call."

"You talk to him?"

"See? I wasn't perfect."

"You're perfect, Mom." But what the hell? She told me my dad disappeared after I was born and now she's telling me she's been talking to him? I never even asked about him because I never wanted her to feel she wasn't enough. But she knows where he is? Knows what he's doing? WHAT THE HELL, MOM?

"I'm so sorry, Zeela," she says. *Zeela.* That was her nickname for me before I could speak—I have no idea why—and then when she tried to call me Rebecca, I hated it and so she started calling me Zee.

"It's okay, Mom," I say because everything will be okay once she's better. I'll eventually fucking yell at her about this dad craziness. It will all be okay.

"Hug me," she says, and I try. I can't get anywhere close to our seamless hug with her strapped to the bed. But our faces press together. We are united as one even if it's only our cheeks. Then, with her right hand, she turns my head back to face her. "I . . ."

"What, Mom?"

"I . . . actually thought I'd be dead by now."

"Stop it!"

"I'm feeling better. The pain meds must be earning their keep. So funny! My lungs don't feel like they are a million pounds. Oh-my-god, what if I wasted all that good drama and I live for another ten years?"

The doctor and nurse walk in, ask how she's feeling. They tell her about opening her chest. Draining the fluid. Tell her they thought the operation went well and her vitals are remarkably strong. My mom. She's invincible. She probably *will* live another ten years.

After the doctor leaves, the nurse says she'll be back with some breakfast. I go to the bathroom to pee and wash my face. I can't stop obsessing about my dad. Not obsessing. Pondering. Whatever. My dad . . . *dad* . . . so fucking weird . . .

I never missed having a dad before because I never thought about having a dad before. This is stupid. In a couple weeks, when we're back at the house and life is normal again, I'll grill Mom about everything, but until then it's pointless to think about him.

"Mom . . ." I say as I exit the bathroom. I don't even know what I was going to say. But I see her face, her gaze off to that other place. Her body still in a whole new way.

I see the machine, and that flat line, and then I hear footsteps.

I don't cry. No benefit to crying now. I just grab her hand as the nurses and then the doctor do their thing. They try to make me step away. They think they could save her. But my mom is my best friend and I know her better than anyone knows anyone. And I know she is gone.

Part Three

THE FIRST DATE (NOT-A-DATE) OF MAGICAL DESTINY

art

Zee, the queen of my heart and the mythical creature of my soul, doesn't come back for the last six weeks of school.

I send her a text every week, on Tuesday or Wednesday. (I switch it up so it doesn't seem like I'm waiting exactly one week between texts even though that's exactly what I'm doing.) I don't try to be funny or dramatic. Just super nice. I text things like *If you need anything, I'm here*. She responds with *Thanks* (four times) or *Thanks Art* (two times). The two times she responds with my name, I decide that's a signal that she wants me to text back right away. So I do. Except she doesn't respond to either of those texts. And I start to think I'll never see her again. That she'll move away to some aunt's house in France and forget about me and I'll spend the rest of my life searching for her except I'll never find her and, oh my gosh, I'm so self-centered for thinking about how her mom's death ruined my life. I know. Yuck. Double yuck.

In other news, my dad's great. He found a new job, he and Mom are more in love than ever, and he tells me thank you every day for joining the waiter ranks at TGI Fridays to help buy groceries.

Ha, I'm so lying.

Well, I did get a part-time job. But my dad's basically a corpse. He sits on the couch all day (drinking beer by the case), sleeps there most nights because he can't get up to do anything except to use the bathroom. That's even debatable considering how the den has officially created a new horrible smell that could be used to kill insects and small animals.

And . . . so . . . not so surprisingly . . . my mom moved out. She told us the Sunday before finals. Abigail literally melted down. I don't mean the word "literally" literally. Abigail did rotate between two volcanic states: enflamed rage or explosive tears. So either stomping floors and screaming "fuck!" in front of my dad (he didn't care) or wall-shaking sobs with an occasional wall-breaking "fuck!" for my dad's benefit. He still didn't care. My mom ended the conversation by saying, "If you need something, you can call me. But you two really need to stay here with your dad and take care of him." Thanks, Mom!

Abigail got an extension to take her second-semester finals later this summer. She told me I could do that too, but that just sounded like having homework in July. Not that I can predict the future, but after three days of my dad's post-job couch-planted existence, I could see the love literally die in my mom's eyes. (And I do mean "literally" literally this time! Love physically manifests in our eyes! It does! I know because I see my love for Zee every day in the mirror.) So, anyway, Mom moving out didn't shock me like it did Abigail and thus I got the stupid, boring finals out of the way and probably did my usual boring average because no test ever invented can capture my rare genius.

Our three older siblings—Alex, Amy, and Alice—did an impressive disappearing act. Bravo, sisters and brother! Alex lives in Ohio and he and my dad have hated each other since Alex went to work for Progressive insurance instead of Allstate but mostly they hate each other because they're the exact same person and you always hate yourself if you're not an evolved species like me. So there's no way we were going to see him no matter what. Amy will be a senior next fall at Drake University and decided to spend the summer there in Iowa once she heard about all the family drama. Alice came home from Northern Illinois University for approximately seventy-two hours until Abigail complained to Dad about the pot smell in the room they have to share. Dad decided he cared about that more than Abigail cursing at the top of her lungs, but really he just needed a good excuse to yell at someone and Mom wasn't around anymore. So Dad yelled and yelled *and* yelled until Alice ran off to crash at some unknown boyfriend's in Wrigleyville. I seriously doubt we will see her again until Christmas. Clearly I will have to be the one Adams child to reunite my parents and rescue this family.

What this all means is sophomore year's over, summer vacation has begun, and I should be doing cartwheels while holding firecrackers of joy.

But because my family is a bigger disaster than I thought we could ever be (and I already thought we were a pretty huge disaster!) and because the love of my life may be nothing more than a beautiful yet fleeting dream, I have spent the first weeks of my school-free life sitting in my room, sipping Diet Coke through a straw, charting dozens more Art Charts, and blogging about how I—writing under the pseudonym Zert—and only I can heal all the broken hearts and broken souls in the world.

I also check my phone every four point two minutes to see if Zee texted me.

In fact, I'll check right now.

And no. Nothing. WHY CAN'T SHE JUST TEXT ME?! PLEASE, ZEE, MY LOVE, PLEASE!

I'm fine. I'm being dramatic me. I'm totally fine.

But oh-my-god if she doesn't text me soon, I'm going to die.

ZEE

I couldn't sleep those first few nights.

I obsessed about that last day. Could I have done something different? Said something to my mom? To the doctors? I replayed every minute. Over and over and fucking over.

Then I did nothing but sleep for weeks. Whenever I'd wake up—middle of the night, morning, middle of the day, didn't matter—I'd have maybe five seconds where I forgot she was gone.

My brain and body had those five seconds to feel normal. Then

f-u-c-k-i-n-g

p-o-w

it would hit me hard like I was experiencing it fresh. My shoulders would snap-fold toward each other, my head would twist down, this black hole of a knot would engulf my core, and then my eyes would just pour. I didn't make noise. Never was a loud crier, even as a kid. But, fuck, my face just drenched itself.

Michael kept telling me I should get up, go to school, go to church, go somewhere. I'd tell him to fuck off in my mind and then pretend he didn't exist.

The little time I was awake, I'd flash back to random moments with my mom. Eating sushi on Thanksgiving. Both of us trying not to laugh after old Miss Anderson farted during a Sunday sermon. Watching *Law & Order* marathons on Netflix until three a.m. on a school night. So random, right? And tiny things, like looks on her face when she was worried about me or was excited to tell me something. And of course her stupid fucking jokes about dying. Damn, thinking about those hurt the most. Maybe helped the most too because I'd realize I was smiling way after I started smiling even though I thought I'd never smile again.

*

I found the letter.

It was where she said it would be. Under dresses I haven't worn since junior high and I'd never wear again.

I still haven't read it.

That's fucking weird, right?

My mom's dead (shit, it sucks to say the word "dead") and there's this one thing she left behind and I can't bring myself to read it. I can't even explain why. Maybe I . . . no, I don't know . . . truly, man, I don't even know why. I should just read it.

I should.

I crawl off the bed onto the floor because I can't be bothered to stand. Hand-and-knee it over to the dresser. Get it again from under those stupid dresses for the fiftieth time and the envelope isn't even sealed, just tucked in there, and . . .

No. Can't. Tears flow just thinking about opening it. Can you imagine me actually reading it? I'd probably fucking drown.

Put the letter away. Crawl back . . .

A text.

Art. This kid. Texts me every week but like he doesn't want me to know he's texting me every week.

Better than Cam. I really thought Cam would be there for me. He came to the funeral, sure, but so did a hundred other kids from The Bend I barely talk to. My CrossFit coach, Dish, and some of the crew came, and they've actually been the coolest. They sent flowers, and they check in even though I haven't gone back to class once.

But Cam? I got the hint pretty quick that he couldn't handle me. I didn't even cry in front of him. (Saved almost every tear for my bedroom.) So I don't know what he saw that scared him off so bad. He hasn't even called or texted to say *Thinking of ya* or some other shit thing that's shit but it's better shit than nothing at all. (I should note he's texted me three times about the Cubs pitching staff but I haven't responded to those and he sure as hell hasn't gotten the hint that I need more from him than baseball reports.)

Back in bed, I close my eyes but sleep isn't going to happen. Even thinking about reading the letter shot adrenaline through me. It's Wednesday? I think so. Yeah. It is. School ended a couple weeks ago. Principal Ruter e-mailed me personally saying that protocol stated the finals would have to be made up at some point, but my teachers agreed to assign me the same grade I had the first semester. I suppose that was cool of them. I suppose it's cool that I'm officially a senior now. But, truly, I don't care all that much about anything.

I go downstairs because my bedroom walls were closing in on me, but as soon as Michael sees me, he unleashes, "Have you given thought to what you're going to do with your summer?"

I. Can't.

"Zee, it's rude to ignore me the way you do."

"I'm sorry," I say. Guess I mean it.

"Until you leave for college in fifteen months, I'm your legal guardian and deserve some level of respect accorded to that position." Michael talks like he thinks he's a lawyer on TV.

And he is *not* my legal guardian. Mom asked me when I was fourteen if I wanted to be emancipated in case she died. I didn't know what it meant at the time, but I said I could take care of myself and she made sure I'd be able to do that no matter when she left.

"ZEE!" Michael yells. Probably because I'm just standing there, not saying anything.

"I'm going out."

"Where are you going?" he asks.

"I don't know. Out." I go back toward the stairs, but Michael follows.

"Hey, sorry about yelling." Michael's voice goes soft as he does his weird flip from bad cop to good cop. *Like, who are you really, Michael?* But I stop and let him talk because I'm not a total asshole. He goes on, "I'm still finalizing all of your mother's affairs. Just checking again if you remembered anything she talked about the morning she died—"

Hate. That. Fucking. Word. "Like what?" This is the third time he asked about that day. First two times, I told him I couldn't remember. Truth is, I don't want to remember.

"Anything that you might think I should know."

I pretend I'm thinking. Well, I *am* thinking. I'm thinking he's probably wondering if I know about my dad, right? But why's that his business? How can he possibly be threatened by some man who abandoned my mom and me seventeen years ago? And, anyway, unless Mom put my dad's contact information in the letter I can't bear to read, I have no way of contacting him. So I say, "I just don't know, Michael. I got to go."

I go upstairs, put on clean cargo pants—I spent at least three days in bed in the pair I had been wearing—clean T-shirt, clean hoodie, and my white Jordans. Okay. I spend too much on shoes. Or my mom used to. Jesus. What happens to my life now? How am I supposed to go from doing everything with her—EVERYTHING—and now I can do *nothing* with her.

And, yeah, tears. I don't even make it halfway to my truck. I should go back inside. Get back in bed. But I get into the truck just because. Look at my phone. And there's the kid's text. If I had even another minute to gather the pathetic mess that was my thoughts, I wouldn't have done it. But I don't take that minute. And find myself texting him:

ME

what ya doing?

art

At the sight of Zee's text, I attempt to quell the beams of rainbow light bursting from my entire being. But I quickly determine containing that amount of power might be fatal. Thus I text:

ME

Whatever you're doing, wherever you're doing it

This is too much. I know it before I even send it but I send it anyway. And then I have to wait. And then I know even if she responded in fifteen seconds, it will be too long.

Thus, I call. No one uses phones for actual phone calls. I'm sure if I haven't scared her with my text, seeing her phone ringing with my name on it surely would.

ZEE

He is calling me.

Calling. Me.

Jesus.

Who the hell calls someone? And, *fuck*, I answer it but only because I should tell him I can't hang out. Or do anything. Probably ever.

"Hey," I say, but before I can get another word in, Art says, "I know how weird it is to call. But I didn't want to give you too much time to think about why you *shouldn't* hang out with me or why you *shouldn't* have texted me instead of honoring your first instinct, which was *to* call me and *to* hang out with me."

This kid is . . . I don't even. He's just a lot. Overflowing with whatever he is. And, yeah, screw it. "I wasn't thinking that. . . ." I was. "Yeah, maybe I was . . . but yeah, okay. Wanna see a movie?"

"Yes. A thousand yeses."

A thousand yeses?

"Or just one yes if a thousand is too much. What time? Now is best. The Gladys Park Regal Twelve? I can be there in thirty minutes if I catch the five-twenty-five bus."

"No . . ." Everyone in Riverbend sees movies at the Regal Twelve. I don't want to see anyone. Or for anyone to see me. And sure as hell not see me with Art. I suck for thinking that, but I don't care that I suck for thinking that. So I say, "Abigail home?"

"She's out with Cam. Why?" Because I don't want Abigail seeing me and then telling Cam I went to a movie with the kid.

So I say, "I'll pick you up. I'm already in my truck. Can you be ready soon?"

"For you, my queen, of course."

I can't even respond.

"If you prefer I speak like a more typical teenage boy, I'll rephrase. Ask me the question again."

This kid! Jesus!

"I'll ask for you." Art, with a voice that's nothing like mine but maybe a little less like his, says, *"Can you be ready soon?"* And then he answers with this gruff, distant, disinterested tone, "Yeah, dude, whatever." To be honest, it sounds a bit like Cam. Then he goes back to *his* normal voice and says, "What do you prefer?" I don't even think he took a breath.

"Just text me your address, kid." I guess I'm smiling. Can't really be helped.

"Yes, my queen."

art

I've known what I would wear on my first date with Zee for seven weeks. If I admitted this to anyone—Bryan for instance—he would have said, *That's because you're gay, Art*. No, *Bryan*, it's because Zee is special, and I want her to feel special when she sees me, and *I want* to feel special when I see her. Bryan would probably then respond, *Anyone who says "I want to feel special" is definitely gay*. But who cares what Bryan thinks or anyone in the world thinks. I'm glad I picked out my outfit seven weeks ago because I have about seven minutes to be ready:

Black boxer briefs, gray no-wrinkle pants (affordable yet you'd never know it), a white button-down, no socks, and blue Bullboxer shoes (casual but beautiful and newly acquired from the second TGI Fridays paycheck). I debate, briefly, leaving my shirt untucked because Cam never tucks his shirt in and Zee probably thinks she's still in love with him. But the only way she's going to realize she's in love with me is if I'm me and not anyone else. I've studied every *GQ* magazine since I was eight, and the untucked look only works with shorts, some linen pants (and only if you're near water), and worn jeans (and only if the shirt isn't too long). These are just the facts.

I wasn't going to tell my dad I was going out, mostly because I knew he wouldn't care. But then I decide I want him to know I still care enough to tell him even if he doesn't care enough to care I care.

"I'm going out on a date," I say, loudly because some baseball game is on. As I say this, I realize I want him to hear I am going out on a date. His head moves just enough to acknowledge me. I add, "She's very beautiful, Dad. I'm sure you'll meet her soon." I guess I want him to know I am going out with a girl too. I know how ridiculous it is to have to point out that my date is a female, but I've just always had this feeling—even though he's never said a single thing about it—that my dad thinks I'm gay. If I *was* gay, I'd want him to know I was gay. Doesn't that make it okay that I want the only father I'll ever have in this lifetime to know that I'm straight? Yuck. I hate being all needy and it feels homophobic to point out you're straight. I leave without waiting for him to respond because he isn't going to respond anyway.

I wait by the front window for Zee to arrive. I'm not nervous at all. When I say I'm not nervous at all, what I really mean is that I think every nerve in my body has morphed into a flesh-eating virus and I will be consumed in entirety before she even arrives.

Maybe breathing might help?

Yes, breathing is always a good idea.

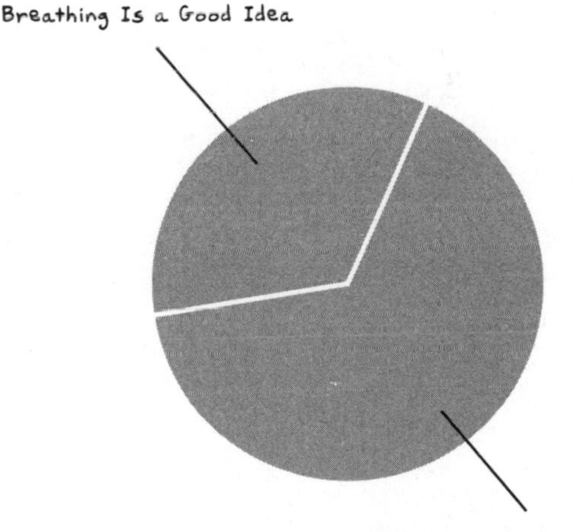

ZEE

As soon as he walks out the door, the hugeness of my mistake hits me. The kid thinks this is a date. He's dressed like we're going to see some Broadway play downtown and have dinner on Michigan Avenue. I don't even . . .

Art climbs into the passenger seat, sits, and faces me straight on. He's 24-7 intense.

"Hi," he says, and before I can say hi back, he continues, "First thing. Before we talk about why I'm dressed as if this is a date even though I know it's not a date or we talk about what movie we're going to see or anything else, I want you to know if you want to talk about your mom—or how you're feeling about *anything*—that that's the most important thing. If you don't want to talk about it, that's also the most important thing. Whatever you want, today and tomorrow and forever."

Kid left me speechless per usual.

Then he says, "Can we hug? Not because we're sad or we're in love but because we're human."

Art talked like he watched too many interviews with emo rock stars. But now I have to say, "Sure." And then Art leans over the center console and pulls me tight against him. Our heads even press against each other. I can smell him for the first time and—

Uh . . .

This is so fucking weird.

Or depressing.

Or I don't even know.

He smells like my mom. Not like when she wore perfume. But like the lotion she uses. *Used.* She'll never use it again because she's dead. But Art must use it. Or use one that smells the same. And that's so fucking bizarre! And this is the only hug I've really had since the funeral and, truly, the second most intimate hug I've ever had with anyone besides my mom. It's just too fucking much.

Fuck!

I start crying and yeah, I try to pull away because this is fucking embarrassing but he can sense I'm trying to pull away so he holds me even tighter and him holding me tighter—

—for who the hell knows why—

—makes me cry even more. My chest heaves. I never cry so much my chest starts heaving. Except now. With Art. And so I say, "Fuck, I'm sorry."

"Don't be sorry for crying! Crying is pure, it's real, it's vulnerable, and being vulnerable is beautiful and strong and I promise I'll only think how beautiful and brave you are when you cry in front of me and I'll think the same if you don't cry too."

I don't try to separate from his hug again until my body calms. I dry my face as best I can with my right sleeve. Then I pull back and this time he lets me. "Thanks," I say.

"Thank you," he says back.

"So . . . movie?" And as I say that, I start laughing. Who goes from bawling to asking about a movie so fast? Me. But Art doesn't care. He laughs with me and says, "So . . . movie." He looks at his phone. "Here are the movies starting at the Regal Twelve in the next hour—"

"I like the AMC at Northbrook Court better. Cool?" I say. He's gonna know I don't want other kids from The Bend seeing us, isn't he? But he doesn't even take a second to think about why I'd want to drive forty minutes to Northbrook instead of eight minutes to Gladys Park.

He just bursts out with a big smile and, "Of course! Wherever you like best, I like best."

"Great," I say, turning up the music loud enough that he gets the hint we don't need to talk on the drive.

art

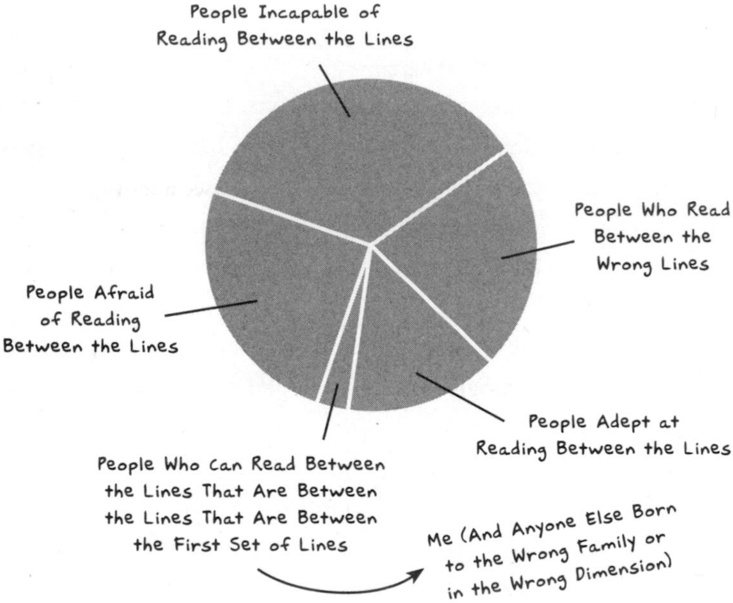

People Incapable of Reading Between the Lines

People Who Read Between the Wrong Lines

People Afraid of Reading Between the Lines

People Adept at Reading Between the Lines

People Who Can Read Between the Lines That Are Between the Lines That Are Between the First Set of Lines

Me (And Anyone Else Born to the Wrong Family or in the Wrong Dimension)

Zee doesn't want anyone from school to see us together. I'm perfectly at peace with this. And when I say I'm perfectly at peace with this what I mean is my inner child is bawling his eyes out on a leaky raft in the middle of the ocean. Of course I'll pretend not to know the true reason she wants to go to Northbrook—which is six million hours away!—instead of Gladys Park. I've pretended to not know a lot of things in my life. I had to. If my family and friends understood that I understood EVERYTHING, they would realize their souls were naked to my eyes and would flee at the sight of me. So pretend, Art! Pretend you're clueless so the girl you love doesn't have to be embarrassed to be seen with you in public! Pretend you're not the most insightful person she will ever know! Pretend!

"Zee . . ."

"Yeah?"

"I can't pretend."

"Huh?"

I turn down the music, begin again, "I wish I could but I can't pretend I don't know why you want to go to a movie in Northbrook instead of Gladys Park. I wish I could pretend. But I just can't."

Silence. I get it. She's the strong, silent type. I'm the strong, say-everything-that-goes-through-my-brain type.

"You're afraid kids from Riverbend might see us if we went to a movie at Gladys Park. That's why we're driving two hours to see a movie."

"It's forty minutes and . . ."

ZEE

Fuck.

Two choices.

Bullshit my way through this, see the movie, and never deal with this kid again?

Or:

Turn around, tell him it's too much for me the first time out after my mom's death . . .

Fuck. That was bullshit too. You want to know what my mom never did? Bullshit. She was so goddamn sincere and straightforward.

So.

I pull over, put the truck in park. "I'm sorry."

"No, *I'm* sorry. I should have pretended not to know. I'm being selfish. I don't care. *I care* but I don't care. I wanted you to know I can pretty much figure out what anyone means even when they don't want people to know. But I shouldn't have needed you to know that right this second. I'm so excited to see a movie with you, even if we have to drive to Antarctica."

And for some reason I make a joke. "They probably don't have a movie theater in Antarctica."

"They do, but they show films in penguin with English subtitles."

I laugh. "You're quick, kid. That was quick."

"We have good humor chemistry. This probably means we'll be good in bed together."

I try to smile through that one.

He says, "Dammit, I just killed our moment by making a sex joke."

Time to be clear? It's time. I say, "So no bullshit, Art, okay?"

"I never do."

"I meant me. I bullshit sometimes. Not all the time. But with other kids at Riverbend. I just don't relate to many people. . . . Anyway . . . yeah, I don't really want other kids from school seeing us hang out. I don't even know what I'm doing tonight. You're the first person I've seen from school since the funeral"—don't cry, you bitch—"but I needed to get out and now I'm out."

"And I'm being *so* high maintenance."

"No—"

"You said no bullshit, Zee." He nudges my leg.

"Okay, yeah. You're a lot to handle. I knew that. I don't even mind it. I might even need it so I can get out of my own fucking head. But what I don't need is Cam or Abigail or anyone thinking me and you going to a movie is something that it isn't and it's just easier to go somewhere far away from Riverbend to make sure nobody starts any stupid rumors. That make sense?"

"Yes. I believe you're saying our affair will be that much more exciting if we keep it a secret."

He isn't kidding. Not entirely. So I say, "Art . . . what you said about Cam the night we met, you're right. I am in love with Cam. I've been in love with him since sixth grade. And if he's my type—"

"And I'm nothing like him, then that means I'm not your type at all." He's wounded. Bad.

"Art . . ." I start, but before I can bullshit—

The kid shimmers his body, as if shedding a dramatic cloak for a coat of rainbows. Then, with this funny glint in his eye, Art says, "So . . . movie?"

art

Once at Northbrook Court, which is a gigantic mall that will surely be used as the last outpost of humanity in the coming zombie apocalypse, we park on the far side from the theaters, which means we have to cross through the mall and past every retail staple of American commerce. Do you know who didn't want to look into a single store? Like, not even window-shop while walking? Zee. How can you not even be an itsy-bitsy bit curious what Forever 21 or Lululemon has in their display windows this week?

Bryan would say my love of shopping and style is another checkmark in the "Art Is Gay!" column. (Oh, is that so, Bryan? Well, is your disdain for shopping and anything resembling style a check in the "Bryan Is Straight!" column?)

When I get out money to pay for the movie tickets, Zee says, "Let me buy. You did me a huge favor helping me get out of the house."

She's *trying* to reinforce that this isn't a date, so I say, "I started waiting tables at TGI Fridays, which means I'm basically a millionaire now."

"Can we at least split it?"

"You can pay for the tickets for the fifth movie we see."

"Art—"

"Zee." I nudge her hip with mine. It's a very understated flirtation. Not like me at all. But I can tell she likes understated flirtation, so I'll have to use it more often. I'LL STILL BE THE BIGGEST PERSONALITY ON THE PLANET. But a more subtle version sometimes.

I pay for the popcorn, Diet Coke for me, regular for her. Again, she tries to give me money, so I say, "You can pay for the popcorn every seventh movie we see."

"You're hilarious."

"I know." After we sit down in the theater, I realize I am seeing my first movie with a girl I actually like. Yes, I know, she likes someone else—that's not relevant information!—and so I turn to look at her and take a mental picture as a memento for this momentous occasion. Zee is watching the pre-movie commercials and aggressively eating the popcorn, and staring at her under the flickering light of the screen reminds me how breathtaking she is . . . and how I'm the only one who sees it. Cam certainly doesn't see it. He likes Abigail and her oversugared femininity. No other boy at The Bend sees it or they would have pursued her with the same passion as I have.

And thus, as the movie starts, I keep stealing glances of beautiful Zee (don't worry, she doesn't notice), and my bold new strategy in Operation "Make Zee Fall Madly in Love with Me" begins to crystallize: I'll have to show her she is a special kind of beautiful. The best kind of beautiful. The kind that is hard to see at first but once seen impossible to unsee.

I love this plan!

I know!

Wait . . . why do I love this plan?

Because if you show Zee she's a special kind of beautiful, maybe she'll realize it takes a special kind of boy to see it.

Ooooh.

I know.

Wait, who's the special kind of boy?

You're hilarious.

I know.

ZEE

The kid spends more time looking at me than the movie. At first his staring annoys me, but then I just let it go. The kid has a crush. Even if he really is gay and doesn't know it yet, Art looks at me with more interest than any straight boy has ever looked at me. More than both Bill and Glen from CrossFit and I got naked with both of them. Sure as hell more than Cam. Art's look feels like more than interest too. It's . . . I don't know . . . longing. Yeah, that's what it feels like. And I've never felt that from another guy. Ever. So I might even like it.

On the drive home, Art says, "We should stop for frozen yogurt to break up the cross-country road trip."

"Sure," I say, and even laugh. The kid *is* funny. If he can make me laugh, the least I can do is let him not so subtly have a crush on me.

He pays again. And again, just like back at the movie theater, I think how Cam has never offered to buy me a thing in his life. I pay for pizza because I work the desk at the gym a couple times a month. I buy him birthday and Christmas presents. I don't care Cam doesn't buy me stuff. I really fucking don't. I'm just saying Art paying was . . . nice.

As we near his house, Art says, "Drop me off at this corner. I'll walk the rest of the way."

I stop the truck even though I shouldn't. "It's six more blocks. . . ."

"But Abigail *and* Cam might be at my house. I don't want them to see you drop me off."

"I feel like such an asshole. I'm sorry. Let me drive you. I don't care if they see me and you hanging out—"

"I care . . ."

And I'm confused, but Art explains, in this almost wise voice, as if he has matured ten years in ten seconds, "I loved hanging out with you tonight, Zee. *Loved* it. And I want to hang out again—*soon*"—he taps my thigh, friendly, sort of flirtatious—"and my expert analysis says the best way to make you want to hang out with me *soon* is to make sure you feel safe. To make sure there's no stress. That when you think of me, you're not thinking, 'I hope Cam doesn't get the wrong idea if he sees me with the kid.' I want you to only be thinking, 'That Art is so fun, I want to hang out with him all the time.'"

"You *are* fun, Art."

"I know."

"You're also *hilarious*—"

"I know! But nobody else knows this besides you. Which is the real reason I want to hang out all the time. So you can laugh at all my jokes and tell me I'm a comic genius."

"Okay," I say.

"Okay, what?" His excitement boils over into confusion.

"Let's hang out all the time." What the fuck am I saying?

"Really? Like tomorrow?"

"I don't know. Maybe. But soon . . . because this was good for me. I know it already. So thank you."

He lights up. The joy inside him practically shoots fireballs out of his eyes. Jesus, the kid feels a lot, doesn't he? When he manages to contain himself just a bit, he reaches across the console and hugs me. Third hug tonight. This one is more for him than me, but it feels just as good. It feels comfortable this time. Then he kisses me on the cheek and whispers, "Good night, my queen," before jumping out of my truck, up and onto the sidewalk. He waves once, turns around, and walks on.

I watch him until the night makes it impossible. Then I say to myself, "Good night, kid."

A voice from the backseat:

"Oh-my-god, I think he's perfect for you! He's funny and smart and beautiful and has *amazing* taste in lotion."

I look in my rearview mirror.

She's so real.

She's *so there*.

My mom is sitting in the backseat of my truck. Hair in a bun, streetlamp light in her eyes, and wearing her black-and-white-striped dress she wore to my eighth-grade graduation. She's smiling. Carefree and glowing and so alive. And I try to smile back at her, try not to cry, but my shoulders fold, and my face caves, and the tears are stronger than me. And as the snot is falling and my body is shaking and my vision gets blurry from all the fucking tears, I say to her, "I miss you so much."

And she says, "I'm still here, my love. You think dying was going to keep *me* from watching my daughter grow up?" Always making jokes, and this time my body lets me laugh and she laughs with me. As our laugh fades, so does my crying, and so does she.

I use my hoodie to wipe my mess of a face, put the truck back in drive. Pause. Put it back in park, take out my phone, and text.

art

A text beeps on my phone as I walk inside my house:

ZEE

good night kid

After letting my heart soar out of my chest, into space, mate with the brightest star, and return to me, my instinct is to text her back *You fell in love with me after all, didn't you?* but I am trying to be understated. So I make myself wait. Which is easy. And when I say it's easy, I would have preferred a rubber band snapped into my eyeball five hundred times.

Cam's truck is parked in front of our house. Since my dad has taken up permanent residence in the den, their previous make-out headquarters, that means he and Abigail are probably getting naked upstairs in Abigail's room. And since I have no desire to listen to their sex noises, I have no choice but to watch SportsCenter with my dad. Yay!

After filling two glasses with water in the kitchen, I push through the swinging door into the den and am immediately gagged by the smell, which has, somehow, reached new heights of disgustingness in the four hours I was gone.

"Hi, Dad, how was your night?" I ask as I sit down on the chair. He doesn't move from his horizontal position on the couch, nor look away from the TV, but he does manage a:

"Hey."

"I brought you some water." I place the second glass on the coffee table so it will at least partially block his view of the television.

"Christ, Art, I didn't ask for water."

"I thought you might be thirsty." I also think one glass of water for every two dozen cans of beer might be a good idea. My placement works. He sits up, slowly, kicks the dirty dinner plates he had stacked on the ground to each side of his feet, and gulps down the water.

I debate telling him about my night with Zee, but I would just be talking to hear myself talk—which I've done my whole life, so it wouldn't be that difficult!—but before I can decide if I need to hear my own voice that badly, he farts. A big, long fart. The mystery of the smell escalation is solved. He says, "Frozen food's killing my stomach."

"Why don't you come into TGI Fridays tomorrow? I work the lunch shift."

"I don't think so."

"Come on, Dad. It will be fun to have you there. I get free food and you can sit at the bar and watch sports on the TVs there." I don't get free food. I get discounted food, which I'd happily pay for. It's the only way I can make sure he's going to get anything green and not fried-frozen-microwaved into his body.

"We'll see how I feel tomorrow."

"I'm sure you'll feel great." Then he farts some more, and I officially decide there would be no benefit to discussing my love (or lack of) life with him. But I do sit there with him, watching SportsCenter and texting with Bryan about Zee.

BRYAN

She's in love with you, isn't she?

ME

No. But I think we'll be great friends.

I cannot trust Bryan with too much information on the subject of Zee.

BRYAN

But not better friends than we are.

ME

Of course not.

Of course *yes*. Zee is the second half of my soul.

BRYAN

Hang tomorrow after your shift?

ME

Yes.

Unless Zee wants to hang. Duh.

When I hear Abigail and Cam descending the stairs, my SportsCenter torture watch is over. Before I leave, I do say, "Dad, why don't you sleep in your bed tonight?"

"No."

"I'm sure you'll sleep better. Then I can vacuum in here tomorrow morning before you get up."

"I don't like sleeping in there without your mom."

Oh. Because my parents are not terribly great parents, I forget sometimes that they're still human with actual emotions. I decide to start Operation "Reunite the Crazy Adams Clan" by texting my mom:

ME

Dad needs you.

MOM

I need to be alone right now.

Ugh. I give my dad a hug because someone should. "Yeah, okay," he says to get me to let go. Carrying what plates and trash I can, I leave my dad to his fart-filled den.

Abigail is begging Cam to spend the night by the front door when I try to sneak past them upstairs. "Please stay, please? Please don't leave me, baby. Please?" In the weeks since my mom moved out, Abigail's neediness has ballooned to ten times its already massive size. The look on Cam's face suggests he loves being around this new hyper-attention-seeking Abigail. When I say he loves it, I mean he might prefer being trapped in a tiny submarine with my dad's frozen food gases than endure another minute of her pleading. "Why are you going to leave me? You just wanted me to kiss your penis and then you leave me? Is that all you love me for? Is it, Cam? If you loved me for me, you would stay."

"Your brother is still on the stairs, Abigail. Come on."

"I don't care! He should know that some men just pretend to love you so they can get sex!" And that's the last I hear before I close my bedroom door behind me, find my earphones, and let Lana Del Rey transport me to another time and place.

After I wash my face, brush my teeth, and get into bed, I decide I have waited long enough to text Zee back. It has to be a great text. One that isn't dramatic or high maintenance—oh-my-god, I'm never being needy again after listening to Abigail!—but a text that is still sincere. That still communicates how much Zee means to me. How much this night with her means to me. I think about just texting, *So . . . movie?* because that's our inside joke now. But I think my brilliant sense of humor is already well established. So instead I keep it simple and sincere:

ME

You're a beautiful person

And then I turn off my phone because I don't want to stay up the next three hours waiting for her to respond when I know she never will. Maybe she'll respond tomorrow. Maybe the next day. Maybe a week later. But whenever it is, I can handle waiting because I knew Zee is worth waiting for.

And then, oh, approximately four point two minutes later, I have to turn my phone back on BECAUSE I CANNOT HANDLE THE TENSION.

Guess what?

Are you sitting down?

Zee has texted me back.

Already.

And guess what she texted?

If you were sitting down, you should probably stand because YOU ARE GOING TO WANT TO JUMP UP AND DOWN LIKE I AM DOING RIGHT THIS MOMENT!

She texted:

ZEE

So tomorrow . . . movie?

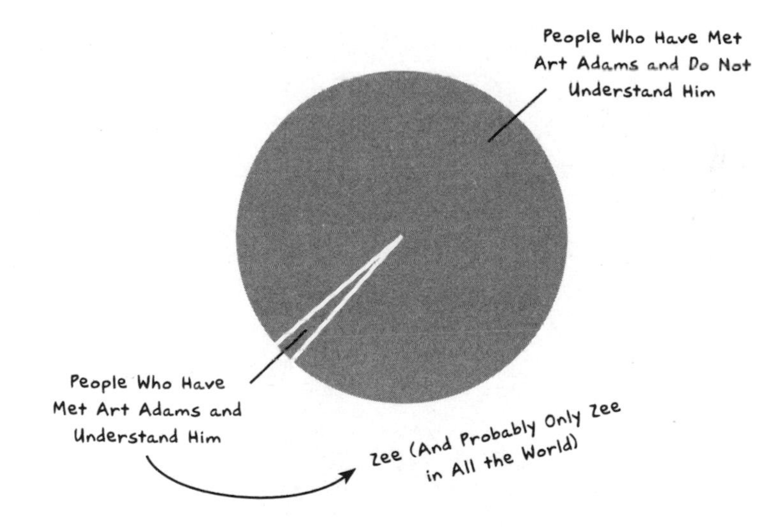

Part Four
SO...
COMPLICATED

ZEE

So, yeah,

I end up hanging out with Art the next day.

Then the next.

Then for two weeks straight. We even watch fireworks together in the back of my truck on the Fourth of July.

art

On the Fourth, I think about maybe, possibly asking if I could kiss her. We're sharing french fries and milk shakes, lying next to each other on a blanket in the bed of her truck (a bed!), staring up at the night sky as it explodes every few seconds in spectacular light. It's *so* romantic. . . .

It's not romantic at all. I never think about kissing him once.

I can tell Zee thinks about kissing me all the time.

Okay, maybe not *all* the time. But definitely a lot. Or at least once—

ZEE

Okay, maybe I think about kissing him once. We're watching a movie in my room and Michael has been an asshole to both of us after we walked in on his poker game with his former frat brothers.

Yeah, and so, look, I don't know . . . I was feeling alone . . . because Cam's a bigger asshole than Michael! And I'm thinking maybe we can just make out to pass the time. It isn't a big deal. It wouldn't have to mean anything. Just something to do. Like playing video games or watching Netflix or something.

So I give him that look, you know *that* look—

art

She gives me that "I'm in love with you but I don't know it yet" look, but I had promised myself I would be patient, that I wouldn't kiss her until I knew she knew she loved me and not Cam. So I give her the look that says "I love you so much that I won't even use my magical lips to make you fall in love with me."

(Because clearly my lips are *that* magical.)

But he gives me a look that says he has no idea what my look is. Probably because he really is gay or maybe asexual or who knows. The point is he doesn't kiss me the *one* time I think about kissing him. Which is good. We would have sexualized something that didn't make any sense to sexualize. I probably would have hated both of us if we'd kissed.

Listen, Art's great—funny, smart, buys me dinner, sees the movies I want to see—but maybe we are spending too much time together for a friendship that probably will end once school starts. I mean, Jesus, we must have seen each other almost every fucking day in July. That just can't be healthy.

art

When you see someone every day for a month, even if you don't kiss them, this means you're falling in love with them. Of course it does! So I start planning where Zee and I will get married, where we'll live, what the names of our children will be—

ZEE

So, yeah,

this is not going to end well.

art

Suddenly it's August and school is going to start soon and I'm beginning to have mental meltdowns that we won't be able to see each other as much because we won't have any classes together. So I pretend to be my mom (I can fake her voice better than my dad's) and call the school and switch around my schedule so that Zee and I have the same lunch period.

We'll probably go out to lunch every day and we'll probably be boyfriend and girlfriend by then and be able to hold hands and kiss in her truck and it will be the best thing since sliced bread except better than that because who cares about sliced bread compared to Zee and me being in love?

ZEE

Thinking about Cam seeing me going out to lunch with Art even once, let alone all the time, made me think it was time to cool off this weird thing the kid and I had. It would crush him, but it had to happen at some point and better now than after school started.

So as I'm dropping him off after our twentieth movie of the summer (not exaggerating), I tell him we can't see each other for a couple days. He's devastated but pretends he's not.

art

When Zee tells me she can't see me for a cruelly unspecified amount of time—AFTER WE WERE PRACTICALLY MARRIED—I act like it's no big deal. I doubt she has any idea that her words ripped open my chest and strangled my heart until all hope of love for anyone ever was murdered. Yes, everyone ever!

I'm not being overdramatic. If anything, I might be understating the seriousness of the situation.

ZEE

So the next morning, I try to make myself read my mom's letter but I am a fucking coward and can't even get it out of the envelope without feeling like I'm going to pass out. By noon I'm practically twitching from Art withdrawal. The kid is like a drug that (almost) makes me forget how much my life sucks.

But I'm still determined not to see him for a while.

At least not today.

Maybe tomorrow.

Not today, though.

Probably.

Then I get this:

UNKNOWN NUMBER

Zee: I'm texting because your mom said I should start with a text. This is Arshad. Your father. That must be as strange for you to read as it is for me to type. I would love to see you or talk or whatever you feel comfortable doing. But I also respect your choice not to. You have my number now (just in case you didn't) and I hope to hear from you.

So I send this:

ZEE

if you don't hate me—dinner tonight?

I was never worried. Ha.

ME

Yes times infinity.

(p.s. to hate you would be to hate

all that is beautiful in the world)

Too much? Always.

ZEE

I tell Art to meet me at Penelope's Pizzeria even though it's Cam's and my place. Maybe *because* it's our place. I haven't heard from Cam besides more fucking baseball updates and him not being around has made me hate him *and* want him more. Which is such a typical chick thing to do and I hate being anything a typical chick would be.

While I'm waiting for the kid to arrive, the hostess Pen comes over, lays down the menus, and says, "Sorry to hear about your mom."

"Thanks," I say.

"My friend Iris lost her mom, too. If you want to talk to her . . . Or the three of us could hang out. Just let me know."

"Okay, yeah, thanks." This is the longest conversation we've ever had and I've been coming to her dad's pizzeria forever. Dating that Benedict dude has made her a different person. Which is great, I guess. She's much nicer now. But I'd never let a dude change me. Then, two seconds later, her boyfriend shows up and she says bye and I nod and they sit at a table by the kitchen. Even though I could never date anyone so awkward like Benedict, the two of them look so fucking in love, it makes me jealous. And, crap, I hate thinking this, but if Cam said, *Change for me and I'll love you back*, maybe I would.

When Art arrives, I feel like I haven't seen him in a month instead of a day and that's fucking stupid. Then he does that too-pretty smile of his as he's sitting down and I don't like him, I don't, I like Cam, I do, but for some reason Art's looking handsome tonight too.

Can someone be handsome *and* pretty?

Why am I suddenly not stressed about my dad's text? I don't even want to talk about it anymore. I just want to bask in the high that only happens in the company of Art.

Then he says, "What you're feeling right now is called Art ecstasy. It's the best drug ever made, all natural, and I'm the only dealer." I laugh but, fuck, we're thinking the same thoughts. This can't be normal.

art

After I get home from pizza, I get a text from Bryan:

BRYAN

Let me know if I should find a new best friend.

Ugh. Because I still love him (as a friend) even when he's being passive-aggressive, I meet him for lunch the next day at Uncle Josh's Sandwich Shop. He asks me about Zee, but all he wants to hear is that I hate her or that she's moving to the moon. Then not even thirty minutes after we're there, my phone beeps.

I say, "Hold on—"

"IF YOU DITCH ME FOR THAT GIRL, I WILL DISEMBOWEL YOU!"

"I would never." And by never, I mean I would absolutely ditch him. I'm a horrible human being. My brother, Alex, once told me that all boys ditch their friends when they get their first girlfriend because "getting a hand job is a lot better than hanging out with a bunch of jerk-offs." I would have phrased it more eloquently, but I do think Alex had the right sentiment. He also said eventually you go back to your friends and they forgive you because they would have done the same thing. My only challenge is Bryan is my jerk-off friend who also wants to jerk me off. Ha.

ZEE

Do you want to go to crossfit with me at 4 pm?

I haven't been back since my mom died

and I don't want to go alone.

She's being so needy! I love it. But *then* I look at Bryan and, ugh, I guess I'm not *that* horrible of a person because I ask him,

"Do you know what CrossFit is? Do you want to go, and explain it to me on the way?"

ZEE

After Art tells me he (and Bryan) can meet me at the gym, I text Coach Dish:

ME

Can I come to class today with some new friends?

And I know she'll say yes, but maybe I need to hear it:

COACH DISH

Fuck Yeah! The dudes are getting weak
without the Vajayjay there to kick their ass

I'm the only girl that regularly went to the four p.m. class at GPCF (Gladys Park CrossFit, on the border with Riverbend), so Coach Dish started referring to me as the Vajayjay. If Dish wasn't a girl, it might be weird her calling me that, but I love my nickname. And I kind of do beat the guys most of the time, so my nickname makes me feel like even more of a badass.

When I walk into the gym—even though I get there early—all the regulars are already there (including my hookups matinee idol Bill and mucho macho Glen, and my super-buried obsession Taylor, who's this private school kid with the sickest abs in the gym) and they all circle around me and give me a big group hug and tell me they love me. They're still being meatheads and teasing me a bit, but it's sincere, and awesome, only I'm here to sweat not cry so I say, "All right, fuckers, thank you, but let's get to the part where I demolish you."

Art and Bryan show up two minutes later and immediately I realize I'm a fucking idiot for inviting them. Art's dressed in a neon-white Adidas tracksuit he bought five minutes ago. It's bad but not nearly as bad as Bryan, who's in cargo shorts, a blue sweater, and brown leather dress shoes. Who the hell wears dress shoes to work out? I'm about to say something to him, but Art beats me to it.

"I already told him we would pretend not to know him if he wore those shoes."

Bryan explains, "I didn't have time to buy lifting shoes, and I read that shoes with these heels are good for lifting." I turn to find Dish so she can explain he's an idiot, but she's already opening her mouth.

To say, "He's right. It's cool."

"THANK YOU!" Bryan yells, and hugs Dish. Then he fires a mean fucking glance my way. Dude wants to destroy me. And Bryan *is* such a dude. Gruff, angry-looking. Thick head, thick legs, thick chest. But he's gay, right? Yeah, he's out. So maybe Art and him are secret lovers but Art doesn't want anyone to know so he pretends he's in love with me? Because it makes no sense that surly Bryan is gay and peppy Art is straight and they're best friends.

art

The CrossFit trainer is five foot two, all muscle and freckles and spunk, and if Bryan was ten years older and straight, she'd probably be the love of his life. She makes us sign these waivers so that if we die while working out, our families can't sue them.

The trainer, whose real name is Meredith but everyone calls Dish for reasons no one has clarified, starts explaining what the workout is going to be, says we have to practice our "handstand push-ups." So I say, "I have no idea how those two things could be related." The class laughs because my comic timing is impeccable. Then I watch Zee walk over to the wall, throw her hands down on the ground, her legs up in the air, and do these mythical handstand push-ups. She looks so fluid and strong and sexy, I start to wonder if maybe she should be with another athlete like herself. I immediately forget this ridiculous notion and think about our wedding on top of a mountain overlooking an ocean.

Everyone is impressed that Bryan can do these silly handstand push-ups as well as anyone in class—except me, because I already knew Bryan was this weird superhuman—but then Dish asks me to try them.

I say, "If I tried to stand on my hands, my arms would break, then my face would break, then I would no longer be flawlessly handsome." I wink at Bryan and Zee. "And *then* I wouldn't be able to sue you, so I don't see the point."

She gives me a disapproving look and I feel like she's the mother I don't have or want anymore and, ugh, this was a terrible idea to come here and I wish I *was* gay because no gay person would ever be expected to be good at this sort of thing. Except Bryan. He's not really gay. Of course he is, but he's more Bryan than he is gay, so he doesn't count.

ZEE

The workout is "Diane" (all famous CrossFit workouts have names), which is twenty-one deadlifts, then twenty-one handstand push-ups, then fifteen of each, then nine of each. I've got the gym record, so it's one of my faves.

Art's a mess but he's making jokes about it, so hopefully he doesn't stress the f out and have a heart attack. Dish is making him do a super-modified version of just deadlifting an empty bar and then doing five-pound dumbbell presses instead of the handstand push-ups he refused to even attempt.

Bryan (who knew?) is doing the Rx weight, which is 225 for boys and no joke. And he's been giving me this look while we are loading our bars. He thinks he can beat me, doesn't he? Then, right before we start, he says, "Winner gets Art?"

No, but whatever, so I say, "Sure." I mean, there's no way Bryan's going to beat me . . .

. . . but then it's a go and he's done with his twenty-one deadlifts faster than me and no one's ever faster than me. I'm better than him at handstand push-ups, so I catch and pass him heading into the middle round. He flies through the deadlifts again and, fuck, even though I don't want Art, I don't want to lose him to Bryan.

We're even again as we start into the last round. He's breathing like a speared bull. It's a bit intimidating. And inspiring. Art's not even doing the workout anymore, just cheering us on as Bryan and I hit the wall for the handstand push-ups. My arms are noodles but, fuck it, I find a gear I didn't know I had. Emit grunts I didn't know I had either. Beat Bryan by three seconds. Not my best time ever but close.

We're on our backs next to each other, lungs bursting. Dish comes over, slaps fives with us. "That was an outstanding display of athleticism!" Which she says every class and I love it every time.

Bryan manages to get out between gasps, "I usually want to murder anyone who beats me at anything, but I don't want to murder you. I don't know what that means."

I try to laugh but my lungs feel charcoaled, so I say, "I bet you'd beat me if we did it again."

"Yes, I would." He shoves me. Friendly, but not softly. "Not bad for a chubby gay kid, huh?"

"Not bad for a fucking Olympian, Bryan."

He laughs.

"You really should play football or wrestle or something. You're a stud."

"I don't know, it's too late now. I'm going to be a junior. Everyone's already all friends and teammates and all that."

"I could . . ." I start. Was going to say, *I could talk to Cam about walking on for the football team this fall*, but Cam and I aren't friends anymore. Wow, that sucks to finally admit. Before I can get too depressed, Art leaps onto the ground between Bryan and me, and yells out:

"You two were incredible! You're like superheroes!"

Bryan says, "Since Zee won, you're her responsibility now."

"WAIT!" Art yells even louder. "You were competing for me? For meeeee?" He's giddy.

"No," I say, because I wasn't. I don't think.

"Yes," Bryan says.

Art looks at me and knows the truth because he always does. Then he does his Art nuttiness and says, "So does this mean you'll never tell me we need to spend a few days apart ever again?"

"Sure," I say, because I don't think I can handle my mom being dead *and* my dad being alive *and* Art withdrawal all at the same time.

I am gifted by the gods of love about five seconds to bask in the return of Zee's affections before one of the other CrossFit people—Taylor, with his black hair and smoldering Eurasian eyes—walks past us and says, "Welcome back, Zee, and welcome to class, boys. Bryan, you were incredible." Then he walks out and both Zee *and* Bryan gaze after him like he's some kind of Greek god. Ugh.

She whispers to us, "If he asked me out, I wouldn't say no."

Sorry. Let me pause time and cry for a year. Thank you.

"Yeah, he's hot," Bryan says, but in this uncomfortable way.

"He's fine," I say to Zee, "but he's not your type."

She says, "Taylor's like a more ripped Cam. With a dash of Spanish and Filipino."

"Cam's not your type either."

"I'm gonna go."

"I was kidding!"

"I know, kid. I'll text ya later." Then she just walks away as if each goodbye isn't a steak knife through my ribs.

Once Bryan and I are in his car, he says, "You still have the worst gaydar."

"Zee is *not* a lesbian."

"Well, that's debatable. She *does* have the lesbian Bieber haircut."

"I have no idea what you're referring to, and I know everything."

"Never mind Zee, Art! I'm talking about Taylor."

"He's gay? Really?"

"Absolutely."

"How do you know?"

"I know."

"Well, I hope you're right because all I can imagine right now is Zee and him sweaty together."

Then he asks, "We're going back tomorrow, right?"

"I'd rather be eaten alive by rats."

"I'm going back."

"You better not be falling in love with Zee too. I saw her first."

"You're a moron. Half that class is gay guys, and I'm going to lose my virginity to one of them."

"Half that class is not gay! They were all muscly jocks!"

"Art, for being so smart, you are *so* dumb. Your ability to recognize obvious gay people is astronomically bad."

"It is not," I say, because I never admit to flaws. But, actually, Bryan's right. My gaydar is terrible. Which is so not fair! I should have the best gaydar on the planet! But maybe it's because I think people's hearts shouldn't be pigeonholed. Yes. I like this excuse and am embracing it.

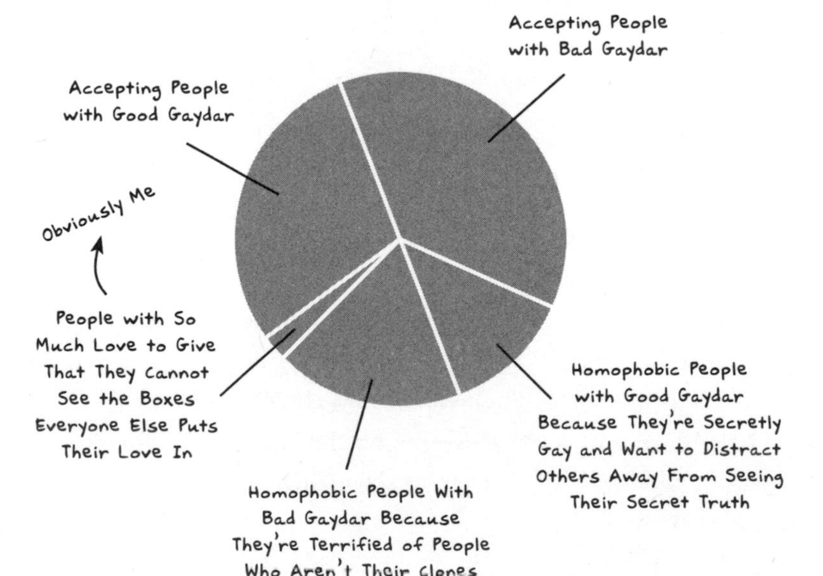

ZEE

On the drive home from CrossFit, I'm trying to figure out why I was so determined to win Art from Bryan. And then, five minutes later, throw my attraction to Taylor into Art's face. This is probably why girls have chick friends. Maybe I should have given Pen my number. But she mentioned Iris, didn't she? And didn't Iris sort of secretly date Stacy Ashton? Yeah, so really Pen thinks I'm a lesbian and is trying to set me up with Iris. Why does everyone think I'm secretly gay except Art, who is probably secretly gay himself?!

Once I'm back at the house, I go up to my room and find Michael in there.

In my room.

While I'm not home.

What the fuck. Which I don't need to say because my face is screaming, "WHAT THE FUCK, MICHAEL!"

So he looks up, down, everywhere but me. Then he says, "I was thinking of having the house painted. What color would you like your room?"

I don't respond because this is more than a little creepy. It's a lot creepy.

He says, "Think about it and let me know," to my silence, then leaves. I lock the door and know I need to get the hell out of this house. I'm about to call Art, when I see my bottom drawer slightly ajar. The dress drawer. The letter drawer.

I'm on the floor, yanking it open, and I know before I know. It's gone. The letter's gone. Michael took it. He fucking stole it. Before I ever read it.

art

On my bus ride to Fridays I get a Facebook invite from Penelope (the hostess at the pizzeria) for a back-to-school party at her boyfriend's house. Oh-my-god, was I getting invited to a popular upperclassman's party?

Art Adams's time has come!

Except Pen isn't really popular anymore now that she's dating Benedict the Nerd and I guess I'm a junior now, so that means I'm an upperclassman too, and there are a lot of juniors invited besides me, like Carolina, who I should probably text since I've been a bad text friend to her most of the summer, but STILL, history should note today just because.

Anyway:

ME

How's my favorite person named Carolina
at least until I meet a second Carolina
and then she'll still be at least in my top two?

CAROLINA

:)
Trevor texted me he missed me but then Kendra
saw him at Midnight Dogs with some new girl :(

That was like five new girlfriends for Trevor since Carolina and him broke up. I'd applaud him if it wasn't my duty to hate him for Carolina.

ME

He's just desperate to distract himself
from accepting he's destined to be with you

CAROLINA

I love you;) How's Zee Kendrick?

ME

Desperate to distract herself from accepting she's destined to be with me. Ha.

I thought I had done my duty as Carolina's text BFF, but then my phone rings and, oh-my-god, who actually makes phone calls. (Besides me to Zee, but that's different, ha.)

But I answer because I love vintage things like telephone conversations.

Carolina jumps right in. "So there's a girl on my travel soccer team who just moved to Winnetka from New York . . ."

As she starts, I'm thinking, *Is Carolina trying to set me up on a date with her friend because she's sure Zee will end up with Cam*?

But then she continues, ". . . and they go to New Trier, which is even more uppity than Riverbend, and her brother Jayden is having a hard time making friends. I met him, and he's super interesting and reminded me of you and I thought maybe you could meet him for coffee and just tell him suburban Chicago isn't the worst place ever?"

"Of course," I say, because I'm awesome, but I also have to ask, "Carolina, is Jayden gay?"

"Um, uh . . ." Caught her! "Maybe. Probably. Definitely. But I'm not trying to set you up, I promise, I know you like girls . . ." She doesn't believe that at all. ". . . I just think you two would get along. He's super interesting and amazing like you." "Amazing" is Carolina's favorite word, and I blame her for my overuse of it.

"But not *as* super interesting and amazing as me, right?"

"That would be impossible, Art." Get my sense of humor=I love you.

"Okay, Carolina, you can give him my number." And, anyway, the way these things work, I seriously doubt I'll ever hear from this Jayden boy.

ZEE

I stomp down the stairs toward the kitchen because I want Michael to hear me coming. He's standing two feet in front of his projection television, flipping through channels as if he didn't just hear me approach like King Fucking Kong. I seethe, "Where's the letter?"

He says, "What letter?" without even looking up from the remote. And, fuck it, let's do this:

"Give. Me. The. Letter."

"Your mom—"

"Do not bring my mom into this. I want the letter."

He finally turns away from the TV, tries to pretend he's a real man. "If you're going to live in my house, you have to allow me to protect you as I feel is best."

I want to laugh because he's so fucking creepy and pathetic, but I'm too fucking angry, so I say, "How do I get my money?"

He wasn't ready for me knowing about that.

I make it fucking clear: "The money my mom left me. She said you knew the details. How do I get it?"

He hasn't witnessed this side of me before. The anger monster my mom pacified long ago is back and she's fucking ready to blow. Michael's whole body does this tiny, nervous shake. He's terrified of me. He should be. "Rebecca, you're being incredibly disrespectful and rude right now. I refuse to speak to you until you have apologized."

"I want the letter and my money fucking now." Just a matter of time until blastoff—

"I wanted to get that letter so that we could talk about your dad, but it's obvious you're already talking to him. Did he tell you to get the money so he could steal it? There's things I know about your dad—"

And bringing up "Dad" does it. Boom: "WHERE'S THE FUCKING MONEY, MICHAEL?!"

"Your mom instructed me to keep that money in a secure account so that you weren't irresponsible with it."

"BULLSHIT! Mom would NEVER have said that! You're a FUCKING LIAR, Michael!"

"YOU'RE A SPOILED LITTLE BRAT!"

And I'm gone. Upstairs, locked in my bedroom. I want to throw my bed through the window and blow up this fucking house, but instead I'm about to text Art—what, I don't know—when I see *his* text.

Arshad.

What kind of name is Arshad anyway?

It's the kind of name my father has.

A sensation pulses in my gut, then builds, rises fast up through me. I'm up on my feet and I'm typing a text:

ME

This is Zee.

art

When I get home after work, Abigail's bedroom door is open and her light is on, which usually means she's feeling sorry for herself, and I try to do charity work at least once a week.

"Hi," I say, walking into her room and sitting down on her desk chair. She's lying on her stomach on her bed, feet in the air, flipping through a magazine. Abigail doesn't even look up.

"Cam hates me," she says.

I'm already bored, but that's why they call it charity work, so I ask, "What happened?"

"He saw you and Zee at the pizzeria last night."

Uh-oh.

"Art, oh-my-god, if you are stalking Zee, I will castrate you."

"I'm not. At all . . . stalking her." See what I did there? I'm terrible. Terribly awesome.

Abigail's nonchalant cool changes to the psycho channel as she spins to her butt, onto her feet, and then lunges with her finger in my face. "OH-MY-GOD, ART! YOU'RE GOING TO MAKE CAM HATE ME!"

"How is my hanging out with Zee going to make Cam hate you?" This is a legitimate question but only to a non-crazy person. Abigail is not a non-crazy person.

Abigail paces in tiny circles and cries out to the corners of her ceiling as she rants, "Because he already feels like he screwed up his friendship with her by not being there after her mom died and he'll think you're taking his place and then he'll blame me for you taking his place and then he'll break up with me and I'll get fat." All of Abigail's tragic nightmares end with her getting fat.

But, ugh, her stress is real. Time to be a good brother and not just a smart-ass. So I hold open my arms and let her fall fast into my hug.

She says, sniffling, "Cam is the only thing I have, Art. . . . You have all your creativity and stuff, but he's all I have."

"That's not true, you have . . ." I need to come up with something that at least sounds true in like two seconds so, ". . . you have passion, Abigail."

"You mean I'm crazy." Which is mostly true, but I say,

"You're not crazy. . . . Your passion just hasn't found the right way to express itself." This is even more true.

"Thanks, Art," she says as she nestles her head tighter against my shoulder. "This feels weird, but I don't hate you that much right now."

"I promise to forget you ever said that." Abigail laughs at my joke, which she never does, and then starts in on a whole new round of sobs and sniffles.

When I'm back in my room, I text Zee, *So tomorrow . . . movie?* because you know why.

But Zee doesn't text back and I try to fall asleep imagining myself scaling a castle tower to rescue her except she's probably the only one of us that could climb anything so then I imagine her rescuing me from the tower but no fairy tales ever end with the girl rescuing the guy because of how witty and fashionable he is.

ZEE

The nanosecond after I send that text to my dad, I throw the phone on the bed as if it's on fire.

Can texts be unsent? That must be possible, right?

And

then

my

phone

starts

ringing.

It's him.

Screw that. Fuck that.

Gonna let it go to voice mail.

Zee?

Yes, Mom?

If you're so busy being angry, how are you going to look for things that might make you happy?

Phone. Hand. Answer. Ear.

"Hello . . ." I say. I think.

"Zee, it's Arshad. . . ." His voice is soft, weathered, distant. Like from another planet. He speaks again to my silence, "Thank you for getting back to me."

"Yeah . . ." What does he want me to say? Who the hell is this person? I should hang up. THIS IS SO UNFAIR, MOM!

"I . . ." he starts, yeah, and you better say something great or I'm gone, ". . . am sorry to hear about your mom. She was a special person."

Nope. Not doing this. "This is weird. I have to go." And I hang up.

*

And then I can breathe again, which is better than not breathing, but I feel like hell. I'm a bitch to everyone. To Art. To Michael (even if he deserved it). To this stranger who knocked up my mom seventeen years ago.

A beep. A text.

FATHER PERSON

Zee . . . I shouldn't have called without asking if this was a good time. I apologize.

Yeah. And I'm a bitch. We're even. Except we're not. Because you abandoned us. But whatever.

FATHER PERSON

Let me know when a better time might be.

Or we can meet.

Whatever is best for you.

Take your time.

Forever. That's how long I'm going to take. *Forever.*

But instead I text:

ME

Okay.

I don't know what I mean by that. Hopefully he can figure out what I mean by that.

FATHER PERSON

Meeting is better?

No. I don't know. But I respond:

ME

Yeah.

FATHER PERSON

What works for you?

Are you free tomorrow?

No. Yes.
Why'd you make me do this alone, Mom?

ME

Yeah.

Part Five
A (LONG)
COLD
(RAINY)
DAY IN AUGUST

art

I wake up in the morning to a room so cold I wonder if I slept until December. It's past nine a.m., but outside it's as dark as dusk and the clouds are black and that means, in Chicago in August, that it's going to rain any moment. Not just rain. It's going to pour.

I close the window, get back under my covers, and check my phone because Zee *must* have texted me by now.

Except she hasn't.

So I decide I'm not leaving the house until Zee texts me or the thunderstorm ends.

Except there is no rain or texts by ten a.m.

Nor by eleven a.m.

Nor by noon.

Nor by four point two minutes after noon.

ZEE

My dad . . .

I don't think I can call him that.

Arshad . . . yeah, okay . . . Arshad suggested we meet at a coffee shop called The Forest, which is next to Lanrete Laedi College on the far north side of Gladys Park. No one from Riverbend that I knew ever went to that part of town, as it was a bit sketchy. And strange. But I preferred sketchy and strange to being seen by anyone, so I told him yeah.

Laedi College is this small private school for experimental artists, so it draws an eclectic collection of kids from around the country, even the world. Gladys Park itself is already strange enough. It was the manufacturing headquarters for Triple S Motors a hundred years ago and then when Triple S went under during the Great Depression the city became a ghost town until Laedi College opened in the 1970s. They finally opened a train station connecting Gladys Park to Chicago a decade ago, which started the ongoing transition from dead industrial city to up-and-coming suburb. All this means that Gladys Park—with its mix of artsy college kids, new suburbanites, and ancestors of a ghost town—makes for a dark, mysterious sister town to the Disney-ish sheen of Riverbend.

I know a ton about Gladys Park because my mom grew up there (her grandfather worked at the Triple S factory during the depression) and we lived there on and off during my childhood depending on my mom's job—or lack of job—situation. But Riverbend's school system is better, so she always made sure we had a Riverbend address when registration time came around.

Even though I knew a bunch about Gladys Park's history, my mom and I had never explored much of the north end. Like I said, sketchy. And so, even though The Forest is sort of famous as far as coffee shops go, I had never been there. Or seen it. So it isn't until I park out front that I realize it's located in a century-old gray brick factory building. A *gigantic* gray brick factory building surrounded by other gigantic factory buildings except the other ones are missing walls and roofs. These surrounding ruins blot out the view of the college campus to the east and Gladys Park downtown back to the south and make me feel like I've walked into black-and-white archival footage of post–World World II Berlin.

And then after I pass through a stone revolving door—yeah, *stone*—the inside of the café is even more trippy than the outside.

Trees.

Yes, trees.

A *lot* of trees. Guess that's why they call it The Forest.

And so much green on top of the trees, grass and plants and birds and, listen, this is a just a huge green house, like you would find on a space station in an old science-fiction film. Even though it's this super-bizarre dark, cold, cloudy summer day outside, inside it's super bright and warm. There are tables on cobblestone paths and students reading books on small hills as if everyone forgot that this isn't a neighborhood in Paris or New York but the inside of a football-field-sized coffee shop in Midwest suburbia.

I drift down one of the paths toward the center of the cafe where there is a tree-free clearing and a large circular bar with a half dozen baristas working cash registers and espresso machines. A bunch of red leather booths, most of them filled, line the ridge of the clearing. Tiny tables and wiry chairs fill the space between the booths and the bar. I sit down in one and, yeah, I guess I just have to wait . . . but . . .

All the surreal visual stimulation combines with the terror of meeting my dad to make me nauseous. I could have used the predictable environment of a Starbucks, Arshad! Christ. I almost text him I couldn't make it—how am I going to spot him anyway? I still have no idea what he looks like. I mean, I guess he could look like me, but I can't help thinking he'll be this male version of my mom. Small, pale, soft. But two of that type wouldn't make one of me. I should have asked to be texted a picture. Or, *Mom*, you could have shown me one!

God, I want her here.

*

I should leave. But I can't. Don't know why.

As I sit in this stiff chair that has one uneven leg, in the middle of this crazy coffee shop with its trees and factory stone walls, waiting to meet a man who is fifty percent of the reason I exist, I notice this boy staring at me.

A boy. A guy. My age probably. Sitting by himself at a booth, legs up on the seat, paperback book open in his lap.

Boys don't usually stare at me (besides Art), so it adds another degree of anxiety to my already off-the-charts level. The boy is dressed in black jeans, black Nikes, and a bright white button-down, sleeves rolled. His skin is darker than mine, and he has this mini-Afro that I'm weirdly jealous of. And I'm trying to look away, but I'm starting to freak out inside and I never freak out and then I notice his eyes—and it's pretty odd I can notice his eyes from twenty feet away—and they're green. Puncturing-my-brain green. So green eyes and probably—no definitely—the most aesthetically perfect face I've ever seen. Who is this must-be-a-supermodel-from-another-dimension and why is he staring at me while I'm waiting to meet a man who abandoned me before I was born?

"Zee?" A voice. Behind me.

I jump. Literally fucking jump. Not high. My heart feels like it jumps right through the skylights a hundred feet above me, but my actual body just lifts a couple inches off the chair. I mumble yeah, I think, or sort of, and I turn and there's this man. . . .

I should have left. . . .

I want to run or scream help . . . but I can't do that, can I? No, because this man . . . this man is . . . damn, I wish it wasn't . . . but it is . . . this man standing next to my table, waiting for me to respond to him . . . this man is my dad.

art

"She's not going to text you if you keep looking at your phone," Bryan says.

"Yes, she will because I'm sending telepathic text messages," I say, and then I shoot his Call of Duty character in the head even though we're supposed to be working as a team.

"Bitch." He's called me this seven times since I showed up at his house out of a desperate need to not be alone.

"Should we start calling hospitals?" Because amnesia is the most logical scenario I've conjured up so far as to why Zee hasn't texted me in twelve hours.

"Oh-my-god, Art, next time you want to talk about Zee, please remove my fingernails instead. I'd enjoy it more."

"Friends are supposed to listen sympathetically when the girl their friend loves has vanished!"

In response, he shoots my character in the head. His mother descends the stairs holding a snack tray filled with cute tuna sandwiches—crust cut off because Bryan gets whatever he wants except me—and Arnold Palmers over ice. In her sweet but secretly evil way, she says, "Did I just hear you have a girlfriend, Art? That's wonderful. Does she have a friend you can set Bryan up with? I just know he'd make the right girl so, so happy."

Bryan sinks into his recliner, probably wishing it would swallow him up and take him to a new house with new parents who want their kid to be happy more than they want their kid to be straight.

I say to her, "Bryan *would* make the best boyfriend ever to whatever person was lucky enough to get him." See how I went gender neutral? I'm awesome.

"He *would*. He's so lucky to have a friend like you, Art," she says, this chirpy innocence in her voice. Bryan's mom really is nice. If it's later discovered she skins cats alive and then eats their boiled flesh I won't be surprised in the slightest, but besides that possibility—and, of course, her medieval homophobia—I just adore her.

After his mom goes back upstairs, I shoot Bryan's character in the head just because and ask, "When are you telling them?"

"Never. Don't be a bitch."

"Quit using that word. You sound like a stereotype brainwashed by the Bravo channel."

He shoots me in the head. It's that kind of day.

"I'm serious, Bryan, just tell your parents. They'll get over it faster than you think."

"When are you telling *your* parents?"

Ugh.

"I'M KIDDING, ART!" He's so dramatic. I love it.

I say, "Unlike my parents, who barely register I exist, your parents worship you. They will throw themselves a two-day pity party and then start pointing out boys you should ask out."

"I hate you."

"You hate that you love me."

"BITCH!"

"Ugh, stop saying that! You're my best friend because you're original!"

Bryan is pouting because he's always looking for a reason to pout.

"Art, do *you* even know why people have kids?"

"Of course I do: because they hope they hit the lottery and have me as a son." I'm the best.

"They have kids," Bryan begins, after calling me a bitch with just his eyes, "because they want to have little versions of themselves so that those little versions will have more little versions of themselves. Basically, people have kids so they can delude themselves into believing they have cheated death and are now immortal. So do you know what happens when two people have *one* child and that *one* child is gay?"

I don't say anything.

"The delusion of immortality dies. IT IS MURDERED BY GAY CHILDREN! And when the delusion of immortality dies, a part of them feels like they're already dead. *That's* why my parents and other parents are terrified their kids are gay. All the church, religious, moral stuff is just a bunch of baloney. It just allows parents not to have to admit the truth. Saves them from having to sit down, look their kid in the eyes, and say, 'But, *Bryan*, we only had a child so you would have a child so that our DNA can live forever and now that you have killed our family tree we wish you were never born so we could travel more.' "

Um, wow. Honestly, this is the most intelligent thing Bryan has ever said besides "Art, you're the best person ever." Ha, ha. I'm sorry for making jokes! It's uncomfortable to discover your best friend might have all these profound thoughts in his head he has never shared with you!

My lack of response leads to him shouting, "Why aren't you saying anything?!"

"Because . . ." Oh, just one more joke. ". . . I'm finding you attractive for the first time ever."

And Bryan is out of his recliner, hoisting me out of mine, and body-slamming me into the couch so fast that if that were a sport, he would be the world champion. "You're so annoying!" he says as he's shaking me up and down against the cushions.

I have to say, "Okay, I submit. You can kiss me."

Except my joke doesn't inspire more unrequited love physical frustration. Nor does he laugh. He lets me go and falls back to the floor, pounds all four of his limbs against the carpet in a three-second temper tantrum, and then goes still.

Ugh, I'm such a jerk. I crawl on the floor next to him and try to hug him. "I'm sorry," I say, and I really am! But he pushes me off of him. Doesn't even look at me. Just keeps staring at the ceiling. So I start my apology again. "That was . . ." Time to be sincere. ". . . beautiful. Everything you said. Seriously, I'm sorry I made those jokes. I just do it because . . ."

"Because you're a bitch."

And he smiles, so I smile, and continue, ". . . because it's how I deal with tension and heavy stuff like your so-brilliant-we-should-put-it-on-YouTube-and-get-a-billion-views explanation of your parents' weird gay fears. I mean, really, you might be almost as smart as me after all. . . ."

He kicks me. A best friend kick.

"Bryan, I *do* love you . . ."

"Just not in 'that' way . . ."

"I wasn't going to say that!"

"I WAS MAKING A JOKE, ART! You don't have a monopoly on funny!"

I mean, I *almost* do. Ha.

From lying down, he jumps to his feet without using his arms. Jeesh, he's like the best athlete in school and nobody knows. He says, "Come on, let's go run a mile or eat Ben and Jerry's until we feel sick."

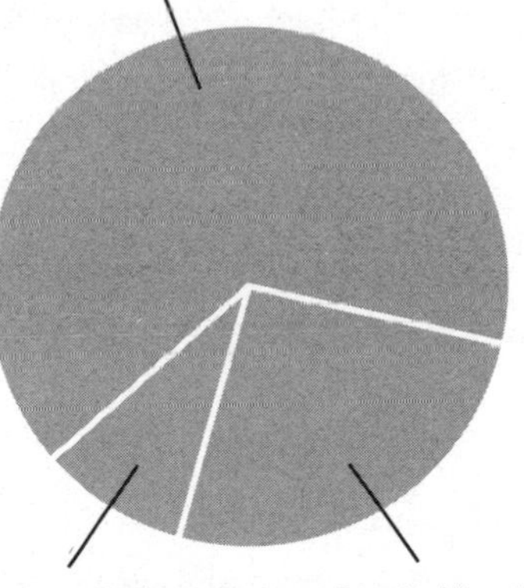

ZEE

My dad's Arab. Or Middle Eastern. Or something this sheltered and shallow suburban white girl never thought he'd be. But my cracking identity points out this means I'm not even really white anymore.

He's tall. Thin like me. His hair is thick, curly, in a ponytail that falls to the top of his back. His beard needs to be trimmed, especially the gray splotches. He's dressed annoyingly similar to me: cargos (gray), hoodie (gray), and work boots (brown). Did he see a picture of me and think this would be a way to fucking bond?

I hate the way he looks. I hate myself for feeling it and I hate myself for agreeing to meet him and I hate myself for being related to him.

"Zee?" he says a second time. But I don't jump again, don't say anything. I just go rigid. Like if I'm still enough, he won't be able to see I'm there. I'm psycho right now. Totally psycho. "Do you mind if I sit down?"

I guess I nod my head, because Arshad—*definitely* not calling him Dad—sits in the chair across the tiny table from me. (I should have gotten a booth so there'd be more distance between us. Fuck.)

"I'm, uh . . ." he starts because I sure as hell am not saying anything anytime soon, ". . . this is hard, isn't it?"

Not answering.

He looks up. Looks around. He looks nothing like me. Or maybe he does. I have no idea because his existence has made it impossible for me to form a mental picture of myself right now. I feel so far away from my mom right now. Like she never existed. Like I should have never existed. Fuck you, Arshad, for making me feel this way. He starts again, "This place . . . have you been here before?"

"No." I speak. I can speak. For now.

". . . I thought your mom . . . We, uh . . ." He's a fucking mess. Be a man,

Arshad! This is awkward because of YOU. "... we met here ... I thought maybe ..."

"I didn't know you were alive until the day she died." Don't cry. Not in front of him. Don't you fucking dare.

"I wondered ... that's good to know. So did Katie tell you anything about me?"

I have so much and so little to say all at once. All I say is, "No."

"Okay ... well, is there anything you'd like to know? I'm sorry. That's a strange question. But ..."

He stops, hopes I'll save him. No way.

"... I'd much rather hear about you. Your mom told me a lot over the past two years. But I'd love to hear about ... school. Or CrossFit? Or Cam?"

Fuck you. No. He waits again. He's about to bumble on again, but I can't take this any longer. So, fuck it, I ask, "Why'd you abandon us?"

My question isn't a slap to his face; it's a shotgun blast. His eyes close. As if deciding if the blast killed him or not. When he opens them, something's different. I don't know what exactly. "You deserve every truth I have to give," he says, his nervous stammering replaced by some kind of wannabe-poet bullshit.

"Yeah," I say, because I do, and because he deserves nothing else.

"I told your mom ..." Again, he closes his eyes. OWN IT, ARSHAD! "... after she told me she was pregnant ... I told her ... that if she didn't get an abortion, that she would never see me again. ..."

I laugh.

Truly. I laugh.

The man who put his dick in my mom to create me just told me he wanted to murder me in her womb and abandoned us when she refused and *I fucking laugh*.

He tries to talk, to explain, to something, but I'm free—I'm so fucking free of pretending I care about connecting with this stranger—and so I smile at him, the biggest "fuck you" smile ever smiled, and say, "Bye," and I'm gone.

Up, walking, outside, in the truck. SCREEEEEEEEEEEEEEEEEEE EEEEEAAAAAAAAAAAAAAAAAAAAAAAAM.

And breathe.

Start it up, drive.

Mom! Mom, Mom, Mom, Mommy, Mom . . . Mom . . .

Tears. So tired of tears. *Mom* . . .

I grab my phone and—

art

At four point two minutes after two, it still hasn't started raining and Zee STILL HASN'T TEXTED ME, so I let Bryan drag me to Ben & Jerry's in downtown Riverbend. Only, I do something dumb and tell Abigail that's where I am going, not thinking—*not thinking at all!*—that she'd show up there with Cam.

"What is *he* doing here, Art?" Bryan asks the moment he sees Cam walk into the store with Abigail.

"Oh, boy" is all I can utter because Cam used to pick on Bryan (and sometimes me) in grade school, called him "faggot" and other Neanderthal insults. He only stopped picking on him when Bryan got Cam in a headlock in the sixth-grade boys' bathroom and told him if he didn't stop calling him names, then Bryan would beat him up in public next time and the whole school would know that "Cam the Jock got beat up by Bryan the Faggot." It was my favorite thing Bryan ever said until his True Origins of Homophobia theory in his basement an hour ago.

Since I haven't answered Bryan, and neither Abigail nor Cam has said anything, Bryan stands up as if ready to fight. "What are *you* doing here?"

Abigail ignores Bryan, stares me down. "I told Cam you were BFFs with Zee now and he wants you to fix their friendship and you better or I'll go back to hating you."

Cam mumbles under his breath to Abigail, "You didn't tell me Bryan would be here." And Cam can't even look our way. Never seen him this fidgety.

Abigail's so confused she starts wiggling her hips like she's stuck in cement. "Do you and Bryan have some thing I don't know about?"

And because I feel abandoned by Zee (and because I love drama!), I say, "Yes, back in grade school Cam was a bully who used to call Bryan the f-slur and then Bryan beat him up."

"He didn't beat me up!" Cam cries out like, seriously, a girl.

"OH, YOU KNOW I COULD HAVE, BITCH!" Bryan shouts, fists clenched, and I have to admit that the use of "bitch" in this instance is quite brilliant.

"I was eleven, Bryan!" Cam says, and it's so, so, so weird seeing six-foot-four Captain Sports look so, so, so small.

"And I was ten!" Bryan says, and his tough exterior is melding with his quivering interior. This is tense! Cam, the childhood bully, being confronted six years later by Bryan, the victim, except the victim beat him up, and to be honest, I'd *still* put my money on Bryan.

Abigail doesn't know what to do, and I know I have to be the mature one even though I find this whole scene fascinating. So I say, as I stand up from the table, and I'm serious because I always know when it's time to be serious, "Cam, I'll help you fix things with Zee, but first you have to fix things with Bryan." Maybe I should be president of Earth.

And, again, there's this silence. Bryan standing beside me, hands still clenched, and Cam hiding behind Abigail, not able to look our way. For a moment, I think Cam is going to leave. But instead he takes two steps toward us and looks toward Bryan, even if he can't quite look him in the eye, and then Cam says, "I'm sorry, okay?"

Bryan waits. Good for him.

Cam continues, "I was dumb and insecure and I picked on you 'cuz it made me feel better about myself, which is even dumber." Deep breath. He finally meets Bryan's eyes as he says a final "I'm sorry."

"Okay," Bryan says after the world starts spinning again and then he says, "I have to go," and he takes a wide path around all of us and out of Ben & Jerry's.

"I'll be right back," I say to both Abigail and Cam, and I run and catch Bryan by the arm out on the sidewalk.

"I'M FINE, ART! I'M FINE!" Bryan yells, tiny tears trapped in the corners of his eyes.

"You were amazing," I say, and hug him.

"I always am." He goes soft, lays his forehead on my shoulder for a moment, then pulls back. "Go tell Cam now that's he's apologized that when he comes out of the closet, I'll be waiting for him."

"You think . . . ?"

"No, not at all, but I like to torture myself by finding unavailable boys attractive." And he punches me in the shoulder—not that softly!—and walks on.

I watch him for a couple seconds and can't decide if our friendship has taken an evolutionary leap or I'm just feeling the effects of Zee withdrawal. Then I turn back toward the store and try to determine just how helpful I want to be in mending the Cam-Zee friendship.

I mean, she might love me for making things great between them again, right?

But, ugh, what if I make things *so* right—because I'm brilliant—that Cam dumps my sister and falls in love with Zee and I lose my One True Love to a boy who wears black socks with brown shoes? This would be a disaster. And when I say "disaster," I mean it would probably be the worst thing that happened in human history.

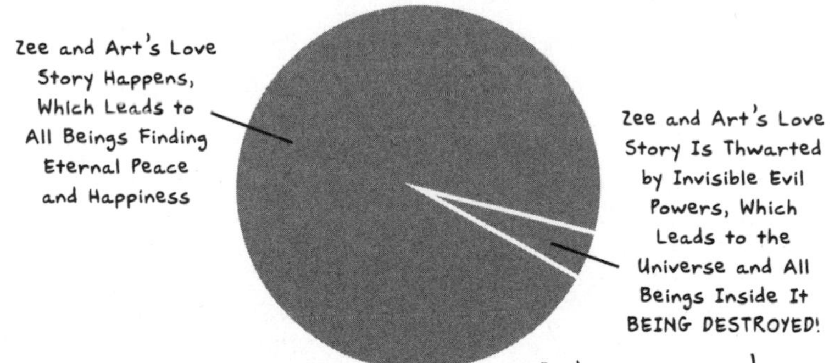

ZEE

—I call her.

Psycho me calls my dead mother's cell phone.

But it's a dead number. Dead like her. Michael cut it off. Asshole. Not as big of an asshole as my dad, but an asshole.

Need. I need. What do I need? "I NEED TO BLOW UP THE FUCKING PLANET!" I laugh. I'm so nuts.

I kill time listening to sports radio until CrossFit starts. Taylor goes back to forgetting I exist, Glen flirts with some new girl who will never come again, and Bill doesn't even show up to class. Know who does show up? Bryan. And he kicks my ass.

Fuck him,
fuck boys,
fuck Art,
fuck everyone.

art

After I babble on and on to Cam (and Abigail) about how Zee isn't ready to meet with him right now, which is a lie even if it might be true, Cam asks, "Can I see her today?" because he clearly hasn't listened to a word I've said.

I say, "Not today, Cam. But I'll ask her tonight when she might be ready to consider seeing you." This is a lie because Zee hasn't texted me in over fourteen hours and that's way, way, way, way, way, way, way too long.

Abigail does what she does best and butts in. "But you're going to make this happen soon, right? Cam is super depressed about it."

"I'm not super depressed . . ." he starts.

"Baby, you never want to see me, and when you do, you never want to do anything besides watch TV."

"Babe, we see each other like every day—"

"We didn't see each other yesterday!"

"But every day before that!"

Fight, drama, action! "I'm gonna go," I say, and leave them to do their dysfunctional relationship thing.

Once I'm out of Ben & Jerry's and walking to work—STILL NO RAIN!—I text Zee because I have no self-control:

ME

Ran into Cam and Abigail and Cam really misses you. I didn't tell him anything but let me know if you want me to.

And as soon as I hit send, I'm sort of sure Zee will hate me for talking to Cam about her, and I'm suddenly, absolutely, one billion percent sure that I have literally no idea what I'm doing.

YES, LITERALLY.

Actually, I literally don't even know if I know what "literally" means anymore.

ZEE

When I drive home from the gym, I see Michael's BMW, and I want to scream my fucking head off demanding he give me the letter back except Michael's right, isn't he? My dad's a bigger asshole than he is. Maybe the biggest asshole ever born. But it only makes me hate Michael more that he's right. No way I can go into his house, maybe ever again.

So I'm in my truck in workout clothes with a sweat that's cooling fast. I have no idea what to do or where to go. Then my phone beeps and it's—fucking of course—a text from Art.

He saw Cam.

Says Cam misses me.

Every feeling (and I hate that word!) that I've ever felt about Cam since sixth grade forces itself down my throat and into my gut. Only I want to be angry, not sad, so I start wondering why Cam would have told Art that he misses me *unless Cam knows I've been hanging out with Art* and suddenly I feel like Art's sabotaging my entire life. I'm about to rage-text the kid when I remember he's working and so—

art

After I close my last tab at just past ten p.m., I turn my phone back on—OH, PLEASE, TEXTING GODS, LET THERE BE SOMETHING FROM ZEE—but no . . . nothing . . . I contemplate moving to South America (probably Uruguay since that's the best name of a country ever) but the only reason to move would be to make Zee miss me and the only reason to make her miss me is so I could *see* how much she misses me but how can I see that if I'm in Uruguay?

There is a stupid text from Abigail and then a message from an unknown number:

UNKNOWN NUMBER

Art, this is Jayden. Carolina gave me your number and said you were the only interesting person in all of Chicago so i am writing to find out if this is true.

Oh, well, guess I'm not going to get away without having to meet Carolina's friend's brother. He did win points with his better-than-boring text message introduction but my brain can't engage in any non-Zee conversations right now, so I ignore it.

And guess what?

It finally starts raining!

Right as I have to leave the restaurant and walk to the bus stop!

I'm going to get soaked!

My life is a disaster!

But then—oh, yes, but *then*—when I walk out of Fridays, into the downpour, and toward the bus stop, I see her leaning against her truck.

*

If I *ever* claim that I was happier than I was when I saw Zee in the parking lot, call me a liar because I don't care what happens for the next billion years, I'll never be happier than seeing the love of my infinite lives at that moment.

She's here.

Here.

Here for me, to see me, standing in the rain, and she's wearing a white sports bra and black shorts and she's even more rippling with muscles than yesterday and the sight of her is making my body tingle everywhere. And the way she's leaning against the truck in the rain! It's so intense, and so confident, and so . . . oh, my, I'm soooooooo in love.

So I, of course, smile and start moving fast toward Zee—I almost run because I'm *that* excited, but then I decide I should pretend to be as cool as her, so I walk but walk super fast (and also in slow motion! I know that's impossible but it happens)—*and then* she steps toward me and I see the fire in her eyes.

Oh no.

Not a good fire. Not an "I yearn for Art as much as Art yearns for me!" fire. No, not even close. This was more like an "If I had X-ray vision, your face would have a big, burning hole through the center and you'd be dead!" fire.

She tries not to yell, but her whole body is screaming, so I feel her words pound into me. "How does Cam know we are hanging out, Art? Did you tell him? After all that bullshit that you said about not causing me drama? Was it all an act? WERE YOU LYING TO ME THE WHOLE TIME?"

I'm a small child, and my dad's yelling at me for pouring the dishwasher detergent on the kitchen floor in my attempt to emulate Olympic ice skaters on the tile.

But also . . .

I'm turned on. My penis . . . is excited. Zee is yelling, and yelling, my great love hates me greatly, and I'm sexually aroused. . . . Why would her yelling at me make me *more* physically attracted to her?! That's so confusing! I feel so pathetic, so gross, and my body is even more confused than I am and she keeps yelling—

"WHY ARE YOU JUST STANDING THERE, ART? JUST TELL ME HOW CAM KNOWS WE HAVE BEEN HANGING OUT!"

Remember when I said seeing Zee leaning against her truck outside of TGI Fridays was the happiest moment of my life? Well, this is now the *worst* moment of my life.

ZEE

And the kid's crying. Crying! I want to scream, *I'm glad you're crying!* but, fuck me, I can't even stay mad at him for a second longer so I say, "Fuck you," and pull him against me for a hug and then I smell the lotion, and now the memory of my mom is in my nose, and all that crap today with Arshad and Michael is in my brain. "I'm sorry," I whisper.

"*I'm* sorry," he manages through tiny sobs, "I thought I could help you and Cam be friends, maybe . . . I don't know . . . I'm *so* sorry, Zee. . . ."

He babbles on, burying his face into my shoulder, so I just hold him tighter.

It feels good to hold him against me. To let him cry. The chill from the rain and my cold sweat fades from the warmth of his body, and that warmth from Art is making me . . . I don't know. Listen. I'm feeling . . .

For some reason, the image of Cam picking up Abigail and twirling her at the pizzeria flashes through me. *That's* what I should want. Right? I want to be twirled. Right? I'm a girl—girls want to be twirled. Girls want to be held, not do the holding. Not be consoling some crying, pretty kid in the rain in a TGI Fridays parking lot.

But my body is vibrating, with adrenaline and . . . lust? I don't even . . . Maybe I'm just alone. Yeah. I'm so alone and I'm so tired of being alone and . . .

. . . and *then* I feel him. His penis. It's hard. Against me. *He's* turned on too. What a fucking pair we are.

"Let's get out of here," I whisper when he's stopped talking. He nods. I take him by the hand, walk him to the passenger door, and help him into the cab.

art

I start saying "Sorry" again as Zee drives out of the parking lot, but as soon as I begin, she says, "Let's not talk about it. Not now. We're drenched, we're freezing. We need to get dry and warm."

"Okay," I say, because she's in charge and I like her being in charge. Zee's eyes have transformed from rage to . . . oh-my-god, I can't even say it . . .

"We can't go to my house. Michael and I are fighting and I don't know if I can ever go back there . . . and we can't go to your house. I can't deal with Abigail and Cam tonight."

"Cam and Abigail went to the Cubs game—"

"How do you know?" She hates hearing this. "Never mind."

"And Abigail texted me they were going to stay downtown at my sister Alice's place, so we *could* go to my house."

She thinks. But my Zee doesn't just think, she broods, and when my Zee broods, she's radiant. Her short wet hair is slicked back, and raindrops dot her exposed skin, and the tiny shiver in her body makes every inch of her taut and vibrant.

I should kiss her!

No, absolutely not!

Yes, absolutely yes!

Your lips will not magically make her love you instead of Cam!

Of course they will!

I'm so confused!

I know!

"Okay," she says.

We don't say anything on the drive to my house. Me not talking is totally normal. *So* normal. And when I say that, I mean that I have no idea what alien has taken control of my body and insisted on bathing in all this silent tension in the truck. Oh, my gosh, it's unbearable. I'm going to explode. But maybe in a good way.

I tell Zee to park down the block *just in case* Abigail and Cam get in a big fight (or something) and come home. After I make sure my dad is passed out in front of the television, we sneak up the stairs on our toes even though we could play trumpets and my dad wouldn't budge.

I lead her into my room and I close the door and—

ZEE

His room has two single beds. On the walls above the bed with the navy-blue blanket are posters of Michael Jordan and Derrick Rose. Then pinned brochures of Lamborghinis and Porsches. And a five-year-old swimsuit model calendar. It screams Typical American Teenage Boy, and I have half that crap up on *my* walls.

The other half of the room looks like a showroom for Restoration Hardware, pristine whites, grays, and ivory. Framed magazine covers of *GQ* and *Vanity Fair* on the wall in two columns next to the closet. Above the headboard is a poster of a kitten in a pink tie and black sunglasses, a quote underneath reads, *I'm Everything I Pretend to Be*. This side of the room doesn't just scream Art; it broadcasts it.

If the chill from the three-hour-old sweat and recent rain wasn't shaking my bones, I might have been able to ask myself, *Why the fuck aren't you with the boy with sports posters and swimsuit models on his walls?*

And then, as Art lights a scented candle on his nightstand, he says, "You're probably wishing I liked sports like my older brother. . . ." Further confirmation the kid can read my brain.

"I don't care." I don't? I do. Maybe. I don't even know. What I know is I need—

"Oh-my-god, you're shaking. Let's get you in the shower. Here—" He grabs a clean towel from his closet, hugs me, rubbing his hands against my back to warm me a bit, and then leads us to the bathroom. It's tiny. And making it feel even smaller is all the crap crammed in here. Lotion crap. Makeup crap. Feminine crap. On the sink counter, top of the toilet, windowsill. "I just want you to know, only the stuff in here is mine." He opens the cupboard under the sink, where two rows of products are neatly lined up. "The rest of this madness is Abigail's."

"I wouldn't know what to do with half this shit."

"You don't need it because you're naturally gorgeous." And he holds his eyes on mine. We're a foot apart because it's impossible to be farther apart in this bathroom.

I have a weird fucking thought.

I want to take a shower with him.

Not in a sexual way.

I don't think.

More like girlfriends might take a shower together. Just to be together. *I've* never done that because I've never had a girlfriend close enough that I would even think about doing it with. But I've seen it on television.

But it's just a stupid thought. Weird and stupid and—

art

"What?" I ask because Zee has the *weirdest* look in her eyes.

"Nothing."

"Are you sure?"

"Yeah." She's lying. Ugh.

So I pretend I don't know she's lying and say, "Water takes forever to warm up. But it gets hot, I promise, and then after you're done, I'll have some clothes picked out that you can wear." I turn around to start the shower, maybe just to escape her gaze—it might swallow me, I swear!—but when I spin back to face her, those eyes of hers are still pulsating with so much intensity that my lungs cease to function properly. "Oh-my-god, tell me what you're thinking or I'll die," I say, and I didn't mean to say that out loud even though I always mean to say things out loud.

"You . . ." she starts. She's nervous. If she only knew that I worship every word that comes out of her mouth, she'd never be nervous around me again. ". . . should probably shower too."

"Yes, but you first. You're shivering and—"

"We could shower together," Zee says. She said that. She totally did, didn't she? Am I nodding? I think I am. I totally am. I can't speak.

I can't speak.

I'm not ready.

Not ready for what?

I don't even know!

I say or whisper or maybe just mouth, "With our underwear on?"

"Yeah . . . yeah, then it's not weird. . . ."

"Why would it be weird to take a shower together with our underwear *off*?"

She laughs because I'm hilarious, but I don't laugh because I'm fending off a nervous breakdown.

We stand there for a moment, not moving, not talking, and is this going to really happen or am I going to wake up?

But Zee takes off her shoes, then her socks, and then her shorts and I guess she can't take her sports bra off because that's why they call it a sports *bra* (I'm so immature!) . . . and I'm seeing a girl in her underwear (they're black boxer briefs, but that's still underwear!) for the first time ever and I'm just studying her, every inch of her, like she might disappear at any moment and I'm going to be tested on how many freckles she has on her left hip when I'm eighty-six years old.

"Are you going to take off your stuff? Do you not want to do this?"

"No, I do . . ." I say. "I'm . . ."

She knows I'm a disaster. So she says, "I'll get in and then you take your time. If you change your mind, it's cool." Zee's eyes offer a final burst of their burning light before she turns and steps through the shower curtain and out of view.

So . . .

Yes?

No.

Yes!

. . . shoes off and then socks and then pants and then shirt and my penis is calmer than me, so that's good and so I say, "Coming in!" like she needed to be warned, and I pull back the curtain and—

ZEE

My head's under the water, the heat bringing my senses back to life. Including my common sense. *This is the dumbest thing I've ever done.* But it's too late because Art yells, "Coming in!" so now all I can do is wait for him to step inside this insanity with me.

Then he's there at the far end of the shower. Standing. Shivering. Skinny. His bare chest is hairless, pale, pristine. His eyes are so wide and white and innocent that I feel he can lighten everything dark inside me. The steam reveals this faint glow pulsating from him. Flawless bright face, lips bursting with roses, and glowing skin. Art's a fucking angel, isn't he? Right. If he's the bright angel, am I the dark devil? I don't know. But I do know he's . . . fucking beautiful. Did I just call him beautiful? I'm in a shower with a boy I think is beautiful. But that's what he is. He's a beautiful boy.

"Come here," I say, pulling him under the showerhead with me. Our bodies are touching everywhere. And everywhere he touches . . . this isn't like taking a shower with a girl.

"Is it okay if I hug you?" he asks.

"You can always hug me. . . ."

"I know, it's just this is different—"

"Yes," I say, so neither of us overthinks this. He wraps his arms around me and lays his head in the crook of my neck and collarbone. I hook my right arm around his head, use my left hand against the small of his bare back to seal us together. We're one. Singular.

"This feels so good," he whispers. He's so gentle now, so . . . feminine. No. That can't be. I'm the girl. Maybe there's another word. But I can't think of it. All I can think is he's feminine, and I like it, and that makes me masculine, and maybe I really am a lesbian? Except I can feel him getting aroused and that's getting *me* aroused. Maybe I like boys that are half girls because I'm a girl that's half boy and maybe we make sense even if common sense says we shouldn't.

art

This is the most romantic embrace that has ever occurred under a shower, so please, please, please, please don't do this. No, no, no, no, no, no, please, penis, no . . . *please*?

"I'm sorry . . ." I say, mortified. I always thought I'd be able to control when this happened!

"It's okay . . ." Zee says.

"Do you want me to get out?"

She laughs. Laughs! She must think I'm so inexperienced, so immature. I should have practiced with other girls more!

"I'll go . . ." I try to break from the best hug in history, but Zee doesn't let me. She pulls me tight.

"I didn't mean to laugh . . . I'm sorry . . . I'm nervous too . . ." And you're not going to believe this, but she presses her pelvis *tighter* against my penis.

This . . .

. . . she's . . .

. . . I don't know . . .

. . . I lift my head from her neck and our eyes are *so* close, but the water is also still pouring between us, so nothing is clear. . . .

Ask her if it's okay to kiss her.

Okay.

You were supposed to argue with me on this!

My lips are magical! They'll make her forget about Cam!

No they won't!

Too late.

"Zee?" I say. Ask. Oh-my-god, my heart is beating so fast it probably could power all the lights in the world.

"Art . . ."

"You're my best friend. . . ."

"You're my only friend," she says.

"But even though you're my best friend and I told myself to wait until you knew for sure that you wanted to be more than my best friend . . . would it be okay if I kissed you?"

And then she makes me wait six thousand years for an answer.

It probably wasn't that long.

But it was close.

And she says, "Yes, it would be okay."

I take a deep breath because I know before it even happens that this will be the greatest kiss ever kissed—

ZEE

—something changes between the moment I tell him it would be okay to kiss me and the moment he leans in. I don't know what. Something. But I feel like I grow small, and he grows tall, and his lips are as confident as his words have always been. I expected . . . I'm not sure what I expected. Yes, I am. I was sure his lips would be limp against mine, but instead they are full and alive. He's alive. He's so alive, and now his arms wrap around me and I'm the girl. . . .

I was always the girl. . . .

I mean . . . now, I'm feminine . . . or whatever he was before . . . and he's whatever I was . . . and this kiss, Art's kiss, is beautiful like him, but strong like me . . . or strong like him? And beautiful like me?

This is the best kiss of my life. I haven't kissed many, maybe ten boys, but all those kisses felt like they happened to another person. This kiss is the first kiss I felt like I was present for. The first kiss that happened to the real me.

And he doesn't let up, his lips explore my lips, not aggressively, but with a tender longing to take me in. He's so in control, which I love, I do, but now something's building inside me, and I need more, I need to taste him like he's tasting me, I need to consume and not just be consumed. . . .

art

I almost stop our kiss after a few minutes to say, *This is the best kiss ever, isn't it?* because sometimes I just need to say things to make sure those things are really happening, but I stop myself from saying anything because this kiss—*our* kiss—is so good that it leaves even me speechless.

Our rhythm is slow, sensual, almost musical. It's a love song. Our kiss is a love song. And I could do this forever, literally—yes, literally!—but Zee starts nibbling at my lower lip. One nibble. Another nibble. Then a bite—

I want to say I don't like it, but I do like it, or I don't know if I like it. She grabs the back of my head with her hands and her lips overwhelm mine and I fall back under her power and let her devour me and it feels like she's lifted me off the shower floor even if that's impossible. Her nails dig into my neck and it hurts and I don't like it—but I want her to do it harder too—and I'm yours, Zee, I'm yours . . .

. . . and her hands, her arms, they grab at my back now, lowering, touching all of me, and then they take hold of my butt and it feels good but I'm not sure how good I want this to feel, and then her hands slide quickly around to the front and grab at me, at my penis, and—

No.

I can't.

It's too much.

It shouldn't be too much! I love her, she's the only person I ever want to love, there should be nothing that's too much. . . .

But it's too much anyway and I say—

"I'm not . . ." And my lips stop kissing and so she stops kissing me and her hand retracts from my—

"Doesn't it feel good?" she asks.

"Yes . . ." I think. Yes! But also no.

ZEE

I say, "Art, if it feels good, then that's all that matters." As soon as I replay those words in my head, I hate myself. Didn't Glen say that the first time we slept together?

"You're right," he says, but doesn't believe it. He leans to restart our kiss.

"No, I'm sorry, Art. . . . I'm sorry. . . ."

"Don't be sorry. I'm just inexperienced. . . ."

"Inexperienced? You're like the best fucking kisser ever." I get serious. Why'd I get serious?

"What's wrong?" he asks.

"Nothing . . ."

"Zee?"

"Nothing . . ."

"Zee . . ." He leans and kisses me just once, but it's so patient and tender that it's like a truth serum.

"I just never would have thought me and you would work."

"I knew the second I saw you."

"But you're nuts." I laugh.

"I'm a genius."

"Maybe you are."

"I fell in love with you the second I saw you."

He just told me he loves me. I knew he did. Or I knew he thought it. But now, after our kiss, I believe him. So I should tell him I love him too. I do, right? I do. I think. I don't know.

"Zee . . . this is where you tell me, 'I love you too.' Or, and this would be even more romantic and amazing, you could say, 'I fell in love with you just now.' That line should be in the movie made about our lives, so you should use it."

And he's waiting for me to say it back to him. Anything. He just needs to hear something. But is what I'm feeling love? I don't know. I've never loved anyone but my mom.

And Cam.

Cam.

Cam.

"Zee?" he says. Every second I don't say anything crushes him.

So I say what he wants to hear even if I'm not sure it's what I want to say. "I fell in love with you just now."

"I know," he says, and nudges me with his elbow. "But the actress we hire to play you in the movie will say it with more flair."

"You're funny," I say even though I'm not smiling.

"What's wrong?" he asks.

"The water's getting cold."

art

Zee doesn't love me.

I don't cry. Okay, maybe I tear up a tiny, tiny bit. Wouldn't you cry if you just shared the kiss-to-end-all-kisses, which made you fall *deeper* in love with the girl you already loved more than you thought possible, and then she didn't fall in love with you even a little bit? Oh-my-god, I'm numb. My body is numb from the pain of a broken heart and—

"Art?"

"Yes?"

"The water is really getting cold. Come on." She turns the shower off.

Now it's quiet and now the water isn't going to hide my tiny tears, so I say, fast and casual like my insides aren't withering, "Let me go first, you take your time drying off. The steam will keep the bathroom warm for hours. I'll bring you back some clothes in two minutes."

"Okay. Great," Zee says, and doesn't suspect a thing. Maybe I should move to Hollywood and be the best actor ever.

I grab a towel, run across the hall to my room, and I'm even colder now than I was before the shower. I put on my brother's old cargo pants. . . . Ha, I would *never* wear cargo pants in front of another breathing person. Seriously, I put on my nice pair of jeans but they're jeans so they don't look like I'm trying to look nice and then I put on a white thermal henley because even I look like I have muscles in it. I know Zee would be fine wearing some of my clothes—probably more than fine—but I'm feeling like making her uncomfortable because she's made me uncomfortable in my unloved soul so I steal a black jean skirt and an orange halter top from Abigail's room, knock on the bathroom door, and say, "This is all I could find in Abigail's," and close the door before she can respond.

I go back to my room and wish I never kissed Zee at the same time I wish I never stopped kissing her and that's when I hear the familiar sound of a Nissan Rogue pull into the driveway.

It's Abigail . . . and Cam.

ZEE

Art knows I was lying about loving him too. Of course he fucking knows.

He fakes like he believes me but the kid is a worse actor than me and then he races out of the shower the first second he can. CRAP. I take the towel he gave me and pull it over my head and—

What. The. Hell. Was. I. Doing. Kissing. Him?

Jesus.

I fucked up bad and I hate myself and I kind of hate him, just like I knew I would. Even if it was the best kiss of my life it was also the *dumbest* kiss of my life. I've fucked things up with the only friend I have by sexualizing something that wasn't meant to be sexualized. SO FUCKING STUPID, ZEE.

Then he knocks, and I stop suffocating myself with the towel, wrap it like a normal person, and open the door. He's there and he's crushed—but he looks gorgeous and why can't I love gorgeous boys instead of grizzly ones?—and he hands me clothes, closes the door, and runs off. No idea how I can fix this. Maybe I can't. Maybe I shouldn't. Then I look at the clothes and the asshole gave me a skirt. *Asshole.* I laugh, sort of. No chance I'm putting this on. But he knows that. So when he knocks, I'm assuming he has clothes I could actually wear, except—

He's panicked, saying, "They're here."

"Who?" I say, but already know and let him grab my hand and lead me fast across the hall back to his room. I'm still in the towel, I got the skirt but not my clothes. Art's a step ahead of me:

"Your clothes—I'll be right back—"

art

OH-MY-GOD, Abigail and Cam are already walking up the stairs by the time I'm back in the bathroom. They're arguing. These days this is like saying they're breathing.

"You wanted to have sex with my sister's friend, baby, just admit it and I'll forgive you. JUST ADMIT IT!"

"You're acting crazy, Abigail. I should go home."

"Yes, go home. Or go back to my sister's place and have sex with that girl. *Kelly.* She's so sexy. Her tits are fake, but whatever, you'll probably like them."

As they reach the second floor, I pile all of Zee's stuff—even her sweaty underwear, which I don't even mind touching—into another towel, fold the towel over it so it looks like it's *just* a towel and not like I was just almost naked with Zee in a shower—oh-my-god, that really happened—and I turn and they're right there. Stopped. Even their argument.

"What are you doing?" Abigail asks.

"I took a shower."

"You never take a shower at night." My sister is clueless about just about everything except she's like a genius detective when anything is off even by four point two mini-millimeters.

Cam saves me, says, "Let Art shower whenever he wants. You're always trying to control people, Abigail."

"I'M NOT TRYING TO CONTROL YOU, CAM! I'M JUST TRYING TO LET YOU KNOW IT'S OKAY THAT YOU WANTED TO SLEEP WITH FAKE TITS AS LONG AS YOU ADMIT YOU WANTED TO SLEEP WITH HER!" Oh, Abigail, no, not tonight. You can be the least appealing girlfriend every other moment of your life, just not tonight.

I duck around them, open my door a sliver so I can slip inside, and I regret it because if Abigail saw me walk inside like that she would *know* something was wrong.

And then—

Oh no, and then . . .

—I see Zee and she's put herself in Abigail's skirt and halter top, except she's four inches taller than Abigail, so everything is tighter and shorter than it should be. She's mortified and terrified and doesn't know how to stand like a normal person in those clothes, but, god, she also looks *so* sexy. Not sexy, sexual. Is there a difference? I don't know. I hate it. I think. But Cam is standing on the other side of my bedroom door, and if *he* were to see her look like this—like a taller, smarter, *saner* version of my sister—he'd fall in love with her instantly. Or lust with her. But he doesn't know the difference and neither would Zee.

I know I said the universe would end if Cam and Zee got together, but now, after kissing her, I'm sure it would be even worse than that.

So I whisper, mouth even, "I'll get you real clothes."

And she mouths, *Thank you*, and is so relieved she starts breathing again except Abigail is a witch with evil powers and she screams from the hall,

"WHY ARE YOU ACTING SO WEIRD, ART?"

And I didn't lock the door—why didn't I lock the door?—and I lunge toward it, but she swings it open with such violence it slams against the wall and knocks down my kitten poster, where the glass frame shatters on the floor.

ZEE

Abigail's fury freezes on her face at the sight of me. She tries to find words, but her mouth just opens and closes like a fish out of water. Cam emerges from the hall shadows into the light of Art's room. This is the first time I've seen him since the funeral. Over three months. The longest I've gone without seeing him since we met in sixth grade.

He looks . . . the same. Wide shoulders on a big frame, a tiny stubble, my Cubs hat on backward. He's a man. Not a boy. He's handsome. Not beautiful. I would never wonder who was masculine or feminine with him. I'd know my role. That's what I want. *He's* what I've wanted since before I even knew boys were something I should want.

"Zee?" he manages to say. The look on his face. *The look on his face.* He knows. Knows I just made out with Art in the shower. Knows I hooked up with his girlfriend's kid brother. That marks me forever as someone he could never consider seriously. And I want him more than ever right now. Probably because my gut is finally admitting I'll never get him.

Wait.

Wait.

Fuck.

Wait.

No.

That's not . . . is he?

He is . . .

His eyes . . .

They're drifting. Down me. Down my body. My bare shoulders. My exposed stomach. My naked legs.

That look . . . He doesn't know about Art, does he? No.

That look . . . He's having thoughts about me he's never had. That's why I misread it. I've never seen it before. Barely seen it on anyone.

It's this fucking skirt and halter top. I feel like a fraud. But Cam likes it. Cam likes it *a lot*. I could dress like this. For him. I could? Yeah, I could. For him.

"I'm sorry . . ." Cam says after an eternity of all four of us just standing there in silence.

"It's okay." It is? It is. Fuck it.

"I'm glad Art's been such a good friend to you when I've been such a shitty friend." That definitely confirms Cam has no idea that I just spent an hour in the shower half-naked with my "good friend" Art. Good. Cam can never know that. I want him to look at me the way he's looking right now and that would be fucking impossible if he knew about my kiss with Art.

I look toward Art, hoping he can read my brain like usual and knows never to mention any of what happened. But when I see him, it's even worse than I feared. He's wobbling, like I just shot an arrow through his chest, and there are tears threatening in his eyes and, listen, someone's going to see those tears when they fall. Cam will see those tears and know. But Cam can't take his eyes off me—really, Cam, all it took was a fucking skirt?—but I can't judge it now, I want it too much to judge it. And it's Abigail who's the problem because her fury is unfreezing itself:

"WHY THE FUCK ARE YOU DRESSED IN MY CLOTHES, ZEE?"

I search for some bullshit answer but I can't find anything and it's all going to blow up in my face but then Art says, "Her mom's boyfriend kicked her out and she got stuck outside in the rain and needed a place to shower. She didn't have any clothes, so I borrowed the first thing I saw." Almost scary how fast he came up with that half-a-lie.

"I TOLD YOU NEVER TO GO THROUGH MY THINGS, ART!"

Cam breaks from staring at me, turns to Abigail. "Abigail, babe, calm down. Art was just helping her out."

"Don't tell me to calm down, baby! You're being the worst boyfriend ever today, and I hate you! So leave! Go! I hate you!"

"Just calm—"

And then Abigail unhinges and unleashes: "AAAAAAAAAAAA AAAAAAAAAAAH!"

Cam counters, "FINE, I'M LEAVING!" and it's manly to yell like that. Right? Caveman shit. It's hot. It is. I think. And then Cam calms, turns to me, "Hey, Zee . . ."

My whole existence holds its breath.

". . . it's Monday on Monday . . . I mean, do you think Monday we can . . . do our pizza night?"

The girly girl who's somewhere deep inside me twirls and giggles and crap but the me on the outside is motionless. Motionless except for a tiny nod. Cam nods, smirks the sexiest smirk I've ever seen, then leaves.

Once he's gone, Abigail throws her batshit-crazy venom back on me: "Take off my clothes and get out of my house."

I'm twice her size, but I'm pretty sure she could kill me right now if she tried. Before I have a chance to even blink, Art says, with his larger-than-life charm, "Abigail, I love you like a sister, ha, but you clearly didn't take your Don't Be Crazy medicine today, so why don't you double the dose and get some sleep."

She's ready to fight him, but Art's an expert at handling her, grabbing both her hands at the wrist as she tries to swing at him and then guiding her out his door, locking it fast behind her. She kicks it hard twice, yells again, but then goes silent.

"Thank you," I start before Art turns back to me. Maybe I can explain? Maybe he'll understand? But the tears he hid from Cam and Abigail are bursting free all at once. He tries to hold himself together, but that seems to only tear him apart all the more:

"Oh, Zee, my love, I love you, I love you so much, I love you so much I don't know how to breathe normally around you . . . but you don't love me, even after our kiss, you don't love me . . . you still love him . . ."

"I . . . I'll go."

"No, you know you have nowhere to go. Let me be the friend I promised to be to you. Stay here. By morning, I'll let the dream of Zee and Art be just a dream."

He turns to leave, pauses, turns back. "But you should lock the door behind me because Abigail really is crazier than I've ever seen her. Ha. Bye, my love."

And then he leaves for good.

Part Six

NATURE & NURTURE & TWELVE HUNDRED DOLLARS CASH

art

I'm shaking and can barely breathe and my heart is in six million pieces at the bottom of my empty soul, but at least I stayed my brilliant self while experiencing this cosmic pain, right?

After writing down what I could remember of my wrenching good-bye speech on the notepad my mother keeps by her nightstand, I realize I could just sleep in here. Sort of gross to sleep in my parents' bed but they haven't used it in months. Maybe they'll never use it again. Thinking about that makes my parents splitting feel real.

If I couldn't make Zee fall in love with me with a kiss, maybe I won't be able to get my parents back together either. And if everything I dream doesn't come true, why should I dream at all?

Ha, I'm hilarious. *Of course* everything I dream will come true.

But maybe the problem is my dreams should be smaller?

That's even *more* hilarious.

The problem, clearly, is my dreams aren't big enough.

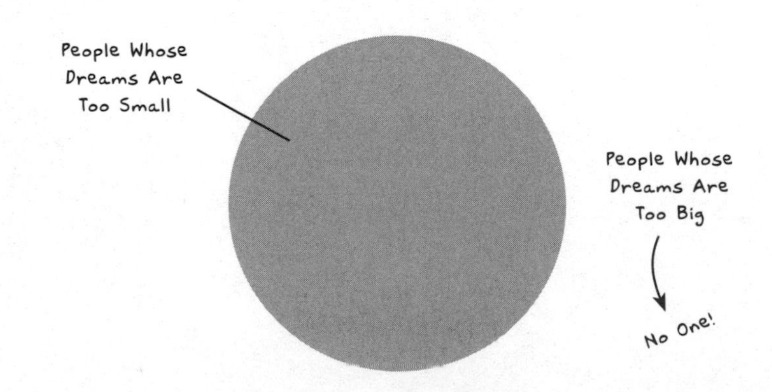

ZEE

I almost chase down Art after he leaves. But I don't know what I could say. Nothing. I could say nothing to make things right. Then I think I should leave. Sleep in my car, maybe? Or get a hotel. But I have almost no money, and if this fight with Michael is going to drag out, I need to preserve whatever cash I can.

So I stay in Art's room. Get out of that skirt and halter top, into sweatpants and a T-shirt. I go to bed in his brother's bed first because I think I'll be more comfortable but it smells like unshowered dude. So I move to Art's bed, which I know will smell like that lotion. I sleep and sleep well despite everything.

Sleep *so* well I don't wake up until Art is nudging me in the morning, which is better than Abigail strangling me after I forgot to lock the door. He's already dressed and dressed way too nicely for seven thirty or whatever hell time it is. He is also fucking smiling and has those beams of joy flying off of him as if he didn't give me the most dramatic, heartbroken speech last night.

"Hey, Zee," he whispers, "we should try to get out of here before Crazy Abigail wakes from her slumber and starts asking questions we don't want to answer."

I nod. I mean, he's right, but why is he doing me favors?

"Here," he says, handing me a folded stack of clothes. "These are a couple pairs of jeans and sweatshirts of mine I never wear anymore and you'd look amazing in them and would probably prefer them over anything Abigail has."

"Yeah . . ."

"And I washed your workout stuff too." He lays those next to me.

"Didn't you sleep?"

"No, I've decided I've wasted too much of my life sleeping already, so I'm not going to do it again until I'm twenty-four and a half."

I get dressed in his stuff and it's fucking weird how well it fits me. Far, *far* better than Abigail's stuff. And much more my style. But girls and boys shouldn't be able to wear each other's stuff and it's another reason I should want Cam and not him, right?

Once I'm ready, Art leads me downstairs to the kitchen, starts the coffee, and lays out a bagel for his dad (who's still passed out on the couch), and then we head outside to my truck. I'm thinking this is his brave good-bye after his messy one last night. Since this might be the last time the kid ever talks to me, I say, "Thanks, Art, you really are fucking awesome. And I'm sorry . . ."

"Zee, no sorries and no good-byes. I told you I'd be no drama, did I not? I did and then last night I kissed you when I promised myself I wouldn't. But today is a new day, and I'm going to be an even better friend for you than ever. And we'll start by me taking you to breakfast."

I don't quite believe him, but I want to believe him. And I'm fucking hungry.

We go to Roth's Diner and share the lumberjack special of blueberry pancakes and eggs. After we've settled in, most of the food eaten, Art starts:

"First, you should know I'll never tell anyone we kissed in the shower. And I can assure you Cam doesn't suspect a thing."

"How do you know?"

"Because he thinks I'm gay and if you do like boys you would never like a boy like me anyway." His stoic exterior shakes for a moment, but he regains it fast and continues, "But Abigail, despite being insane, has got a sixth sense for secret drama, so I'll have to throw her off the scent."

"Why are you being so good to me after everything that happened?"

"We can talk about that later. More pressing is what happens next. If I know anything about human nature—and, Zee, you at this point should know I know *everything* about human nature, ha—Cam is going to get back into your life in a big way, which is going to make Abigail more needy and unbearable, and then he'll break up with her and you'll be there to pick up the pieces."

I want this to be true and hate that I do, so I say nothing.

"But you'll need to begin some subtle preparations for this moment."

"Like what?"

"You saw how he looked at you in the skirt and top last night?"

Yep.

"Of course you did. Boys like Cam need a little boost to their imagination and showing off a little skin can go a long way. Showing what you showed last night can hypnotize a boy like Cam until you're both dead."

"I fucking hated wearing that—"

"I know, Zee, and you won't have to wear something that blunt. That's for girls like Abigail who have to overdo it on the 'Get Sex Right Here!' neon lights."

Art is telling me everything I always wanted to hear.

"But you will need to leave the baggy cargo pants and hoodies behind, at least for the first few times you see Cam. Like for your pizza with him tomorrow night."

I know he's right, but I have no fucking idea how I'm going to pull that off. But, like always, Art already knows what I'm thinking:

"Don't worry, I'll help. I know exactly how to add a pinch of feminine that will still be you but you in a way that will make it easier for Cam to appreciate." He starts rattling off some examples, but my brain drifts the moment anyone talks clothes and shit. What I start thinking is this doesn't seem right. I kissed this kid last night. Kissed him and it was a great kiss and he loves me. Yeah, in his Art way but it's love and how can I just let him help me get together with Cam all the while this must be some weird torture for him? "Zee . . ."

"Yeah?" I snap back to the present.

"Don't worry about it."

"Worry about what?" I ask.

"Me."

"Art . . ."

"Shhh . . ." He takes a sip of his tea. "On to less important things, like where you're going to live."

art

Personally, I thought my performance at breakfast was brilliant. Of course it was. Yes, every time I'd look at Zee, I'd see her lips and want to kiss her and then my heart would break yet again, and then I'd die because you can't live with a shattered heart but then I would come back to life because I'm magical.

My big strategy for finding Zee a place to live was to basically guilt my mother into letting Zee and me move in with her. And after last night, I was more sure than ever that Cam was going to dump Abigail for Zee. It might not be safe under the same roof with my sister.

With the exception of a few texts, and a few digital cash transfers from her, I had not spoken to my mom since she moved out. I didn't miss her, but I was annoyed she didn't at least pretend to miss me. Since I had no idea where her new apartment was, I knew I'd have to spring this move-in plan on her at work. Zee didn't have much choice but to join me since (1) she had nowhere else to go and (2) she was my only ride to the dealership in Hoffman Estates.

I drag her inside with me too, since I want to show her off to my mom even if I am showing off a girl who doesn't (yet!) love me. We snake past the cars in the showroom and then through the labyrinth of offices. Hers is at the very back, and I love my strategy of surprising her at work right up until I see her sitting at her desk . . .

. . . getting a neck massage from her sales manager. Stephen something. He is at least ten years younger than her. I'm going to throw up.

Zee whispers, "Art, we should go." Not a chance.

"Mother," I start as I step into her office. Stephen looks up, eyes wide in panic, then mumbles something about paperwork as he races out. Once he's gone, dear ol' Mom sits up tall in her chair as if she has nothing to be mortified about.

"Art . . . you should have . . ."

"Called? And missed this? Not for the world. Don't worry, I won't tell your suicidal husband how horrible you are. But my friend Zee and I need to stay at your apartment and thank you in advance for giving me the keys and the address." I'm so good at being vengeful.

But my mother doesn't respond, just looks at me like she knows she's an even worse person than I thought she was one minute ago because, oh-my-god, she doesn't have an apartment, does she?

"You moved in with . . . Ugh. OH-MY-GOD, MOM, YOU'RE THE WORST PERSON EVER BORN!" And she doesn't say anything *still*, which is fine because I've got so much anger I could yell all day (maybe Abigail and I are related after all), but Zee pulls me back and I don't fight her (much) as she drags me outside to her truck. She drives us out of there right away, but once we are far enough that I can't run back and make a bigger scene, she parks and we just sit there in the silence until my head has stopped spewing boiling-hot oil.

"So . . ." I start, ". . . movie?"

She tries to smile.

"Come on, that was funny."

"Art, let's talk about it. That must have been hard to see."

"Oh, please. I knew she was a terrible mother and now I know she's a terrible person too. Her not having an actual apartment does make it harder to move into." I laugh because I always laugh when my life somehow gets even worse than I already thought it was.

"Can we please talk about it?"

"Sure."

"Thank you. How are you feeling?"

"I'm feeling I'm over talking about it."

Zee can't help but laugh now.

"I'm fucking hilarious."

"You never swear."

"It's that kind of day, darling. It's that kind of day."

We go find a Starbucks and I slurp down sugared coffee until I feel like I could throw my mother over the Sears Tower. Oh, wait, it's the Willis Tower now because this world is stupid and inconsistent and annoying! Ugh, I'm so gross right now.

Zee doesn't say much because she could go weeks without talking, and I'm not talking much because I want to blame Zee for my mother sleeping with another man and blame her for being unloved and alone when we should be planning our takeover of the world as Zert! I even hate that stupid name Zert now, and because I want Zee to suffer even four point two percent as much as me, I say:

"You should just call Cam and tell him you'll wear skirts and halter tops all the time if you can move in with him."

She can't look at me because she knows I'm a big jerk but she's trying to be the better person and I hate her thinking she can be the better person so I get up and go outside and I just SCREAM until I throw up every ounce of my grande butterscotch frappuccino all over the sidewalk. I'm about to collapse to the ground when Zee hooks her arm under mine and pulls me back to her truck.

She opens the flatbed, hoists me up, hops up beside me, and wipes my mouth with her sleeve. Technically, she's cleaning the puke off my mouth with my sweatshirt, but it's the thought that counts. "I'm sorry," I say.

"It's okay."

"I have like six hundred dollars in my bank account from work, plus another two hundred in cash from tips. I could get you a hotel room for a week. Maybe you can get your money from Michael by then?"

"I'm not taking your money."

"After what I just said, you can extort me for years and I won't mind."

She ignores me and says, like it's not the biggest deal ever, "I saw my dad yesterday. . . ."

And I didn't think it was possible, but I feel even more selfish and gross. "Could you move in with him?"

"I asked him why he abandoned my mom and me and he said that he wanted me aborted."

Oh-my-god, I laugh. HOW COULD I LAUGH? "I didn't mean to laugh, I just . . . we . . . the two of us have had just a really, really dramatic two days and I couldn't help it."

"I laughed too when he told me. Not for that reason, but . . . I don't know. I laughed in his face and left."

"And has he called?"

"No. I don't expect him to."

"Would you want him to?"

"I didn't . . . now, I don't know."

"When you say 'I don't know,' it usually means yes."

She thinks, then, "You're probably right. It's fucking annoying how well you know me."

"Text him."

"No."

"I'll text him."

"No."

"Give me your phone."

She says, "No," but lets me slip it out of her hand when I reach. The conversation with the unnamed number has to be him. "What are you going to say?"

"Something brilliant." Then:

ME (WRITING AS ZEE)

I want to meet again. I'm bringing my best friend Art this time because we protect each other from our parents' horrible life choices.

"Jesus, don't," Zee starts, but,

"Too late." I send it.

"He won't respond. After how I acted, he's probably like, 'That's why I wanted to abort her.'"

I laugh. "You're funny."

"I know." Then:

ZEE'S DAD

Thank you for giving me another chance. whatever is best and most convenient for you. And I'd love to meet your friend.

"Ooh, good answer by him, right?" I say.

"Whatever."

"What do you want me to say?"

Zee doesn't respond, which I know means she wants me to handle it. So I text:

ME (WRITING AS ZEE)

Lunch at the P.F. Chang's at Northbrook Court in two hours.

"Art, no!"

"Oh, please, you love when I take control."

Zee goes silent.

"I was referring to our shower kiss in case you couldn't tell."

"Yeah, I know."

"I'm making jokes about the awkward tension between us, which means I'm feeling much better."

"I'm glad my crap with my dad is helping you get over your crap with your mom."

"It is, isn't it? Maybe that's the reason we're friends. To show each other things could always be worse."

ZEE

On the drive to Northbrook, I tell Art how I think my dad is probably a terrorist and that I'm definitely a racist a-hole for thinking he's a terrorist.

"He's not a terrorist, Zee."

"Wait till you see him."

"I don't need to see him. I can tell through his texts."

"You'd be a terrible FBI agent."

"I'd actually be the best FBI agent ever, but I can't be one because I have more important things to do like take you shopping so Cam can fall in lust with you and then both of you can pretend it's love."

Jesus.

He drags me to Macy's and then ropes an energetic saleslady named Luanne into helping us pick out clothes I will never wear. I tell him, "I've changed my mind. If Cam doesn't like me in cargos and hoodies, fuck him."

"You don't mean that. And I refuse to let you even pretend you mean that because then you'll harbor buried feelings for him instead of discovering much more amazing feelings for me."

"Art." Stop.

"You're right. I'll stop." Luanne brings over colorful skirts and dresses and the sight of them makes my insides clench into a knot but Art saves me and says, "Only pants, beautiful Luanne. But ones that fit." He hip-nudges me. Art does try to make me try on two-hundred-dollar Makkabi designer jeans that have holes and don't even reach my ankles.

"I could buy ten pairs of cargo pants at Target for this one pair of fatally fucking flawed blue jeans."

"But we know Cam doesn't think of you as a girl in cargo pants. We want Cam to think of you as a girl, and for him to think that, his creatively limited brain needs to see hips and ass."

"Don't say that about Cam."

"Even if it's true?"

"Even if it's true."

"If you try on the jeans, I won't talk about Cam's lack of imagination ever again."

"Asshole." I grab the jeans from him, head back into the private dressing room Luanne got us. He throws a white tank top with strings for straps over the door and yells,

"And that too."

Asshole. Takes me five minutes to slide the jeans over my legs. Who the fuck would spend five minutes putting on a pair of jeans? For two hundred dollars, they should materialize on your body!

"No bra!"

I do it because I already feel like an idiot and what's one more fucking thing at this point. I'm trying to avoid looking in the mirror, but I'm catching glimpses and I look like a kid playing dress-up. Fuck this. About to yank off the tank top when Art throws open the dressing room door. "Get out," I say.

"You were going to take it off without showing it to me!"

"Because I look like a girl pretending to be a girl!"

"Ooh, good line. But come, let's look." He stands next to me and turns my shoulders to force me to face the mirror straight on. It sucks. I look naked and yet I can barely breathe or move in the jeans. I suppose it's better than a skirt. And even with my short cropped hair and small tits, you can certainly tell I'm a chick. Cam would like it. But Art's not saying anything.

"WELL?" I finally yell.

"Cam would love it."

"Do you like it?"

He hesitates. Which means he hates it.

"Why did you make me try this on if you don't even like it?"

"Because we're shopping for what Cam would like."

"You want me to wear some super-frilly skirt, don't you? You'd love if I was into this clothes crap as much as you are."

"Zee . . ." But he stops.

"What?!"

"No, we have to go soon and we need to focus on you."

"Screw you. Tell me what you're thinking."

"I thought I would like you in it . . . I did . . . and I truly think it will make Cam drool . . . but you don't look like my girlfriend in it, you look like a girl that's just my friend."

"That's because I'm not your girlfriend." I didn't need to say that. Everything feels awkward again. "I'm never going to spend this much money on clothes anyway."

"I'm buying it for you," he says.

"No way."

"Too late." He winks at me and walks away.

"Get back here, Art, so I can yell at you more."

"We don't have time. We're supposed to meet your dad in five minutes."

Yeah.

art

Zee changes back into my old baggy jeans and sweatshirt and then refuses to carry the clothes I bought her. I know she'll eventually wear them for Cam and it makes me want to puke how much he'll love her in tight jeans and he'll want to touch her and I'm never thinking about that again even though the image is now etched into my brain.

On the walk to P.F. Chang's, my phone buzzes with a text. The only person I really care about texting me is Zee and she's walking next to me, so I decide I won't look. But then I look anyway because that's just what I do:

JAYDEN

I found you on instagram and I shouldn't tell you this but I can't NOT tell you this: you're the most handsome boy I've ever seen in my life.

Don't worry, when we meet (if you still will meet me after I admitted I'm crushing) I'll act aloof and disinterested.

You should text back at some point to let me know I'm not sending these texts to some old christian lady in texas -J

It's not that I don't want another gay friend, I just don't know if I can handle another gay friend who wants me to be his boyfriend. But I'm the nicest person on earth and Jayden's texts are clever and he clearly has great taste if he thinks I'm the most handsome boy ever, ha, so I text back:

ME

This is Art

and

an old Christian Lady from Texas-

I'm THAT interesting ;)

Let's find a time to meet when things

clear up in a couple weeks

I feel this was a worthy response to him while also sending the message of *I'm flattered you find me handsome, but I prefer the ladies.*

"Who are you texting?" Zee asks, and I resent Jayden for distracting me from my lady love.

"Some person I promised to meet."

"A girl?" she says, and, oh-my-god, I think she's jealous. Which I love, but I can't lie, so I say:

"You're the only girl for me, my queen." But she doesn't respond to my flirtation because she has stopped walking, eyes fixed ahead. I follow her gaze to see her dad waiting outside P.F. Chang's.

"He's fucking smoking," Zee says, starting to take small steps backward. "That might be even worse than wanting me to never be born."

I block her from retreating further. "Zee. You're malfunctioning. That's okay. And yes, smoking's gross, but we need, right now, to start opening our minds and hearts to this man. Me and you, more than anyone, should know we don't want to be judged prematurely."

She nods and her eyes grow large with tears and she shrinks into a tiny, terrified little girl. I take her hand in mine.

"I'm here for you just like you were there for me this morning with my mom."

She nods a second time and lets me guide her to meet her dad again for the first time.

Once he sees us approaching, he drops the cigarette, steps on it, and throws it away in the garbage. "Sorry about that. The last vestige of another life. You must be Art? I'm Arshad. Thank you so much for inviting me to lunch."

Zee's stiff beside me, her hand squeezing mine with increasing pressure. "Arshad . . ." I start, and I decide as our eyes meet that he can handle All That I Can Be and that Zee wouldn't want me to pretend to be anything less anyway. So I let it fly: "This is going to be a very fascinating and dramatic lunch and I love fascinating and dramatic things so should we get a table and some chicken lettuce wraps and dive into the many great mysteries of Zee's dad?"

He laughs. He laughs like Zee.

"Zee thinks I'm hilarious too," I say, and, OUCH, she crunches my hand and I take it because that's what you do for the girl you love.

"Having a friend who makes us laugh is a great gift."

"Wise words, Arshad. Wise words." I *almost* say *having a boyfriend who makes you laugh is an even greater gift* but I've banned myself from making this lunch about me—WHICH IS ALMOST IMPOSSIBLE—but I can do it. For Zee.

As Arshad speaks to the hostess, I notice that he dresses like Zee. So, of course, when we follow him to the table, I have to say, "Did you and Zee always dress alike or just since yesterday?" (He also looks *exactly* like her, but I bet she doesn't want to hear that right now. Same beautiful dark skin, same intense dark eyes, same beards. Ha, I'm hilarious.)

Zee gives me a murderous scowl as he answers my question while looking at her, "Katie told me we dressed alike. I almost wore something more formal to our coffee yesterday since I didn't want it to look like I was dressing like you on purpose, but I would have felt like I was faking something and I was already so nervous. . . ." He trails off. Probably because Zee is now giving him the murderous scowl.

"Zee turns silent when she's nervous—"

"I'm *not* nervous," she says. "I'm observing."

Before I can inject a clever aside, Arshad says, "That makes perfect sense. I respect that greatly."

She shoots back, "I don't need you to respect it."

"You're right, I didn't mean . . ."

Oh, boy. I say, "Arshad, let's let Zee observe a bit longer." The waitress delivers the menus just in time. "While we casually look over our lunch options, why don't you tell us about yourself? Where you're from, how you met Zee's mom, what you've been doing for the first seventeen years of her life."

And I push too hard. Zee's tolerance for the tension snaps, and then she leaps to her feet and says, "I gotta go." And is off.

"Order her a Coke, me a Diet, and I'll go get her. Don't worry, you're doing great." Sometimes it's okay to lie.

ZEE

Art catches me before I get out the door, pulls me down to the bench by the hostess table. I don't fight him. I want to kill him. But I don't fight him.

First thing he says, "Do you want me to go and leave you two alone?"

"Fuck no. I want to go."

"No, you don't."

"Yes, I do."

"No, you don't."

"YOU'RE SO ANNOYING, ART!"

"I know." He smiles.

"Just stop trying to make this funny and light. It's not. He ditched my mom and me and we were broke and she had cancer and it sucked and I thought he was dead. So this isn't funny!" I'd cry about this if I didn't want to punch my fist through the wall.

Art doesn't respond. Not for a long time. (Well, long for him.) Then, finally, he says, "No."

"No what?"

"If I'm going to be here and endure the tension between you two—and oh-my-god, it's so tense I can feel the blood inside me race around looking for an escape hatch—then I'm going to try to keep it as light and funny as I can. Because that's what he needs and that's what I think you need too."

"Well, you're wrong."

"Then I'll go." He's being so fucking stubborn. And confident. It's kind of a turn-on. And getting turned on makes me think about our kiss. And I need not to think about that ever again.

So I say, "Fuck. Fine. Do what you want."

"I always do." And he winks again! After his big teary good-bye last night, I thought I'd never see this side of him again. But he's more . . . just more . . . than ever.

*

I follow him back to the table, where Arshad has drinks waiting for us.

Art says, "Zee's going to sit on the inside of the booth this time."

No. Asshole. Fine. I scoot in first, accidentally take a sip of his Diet Coke, which tastes like acid. Switch the drinks, try to look at Arshad. Can't. Now I have to look at the wall because I'm on the inside. I feel like an idiot, so I try to look at him again and *he's looking right at me.*

Arshad says, "Is this too much? Too soon? I only want what's best for you."

He's so patient and present. Fuck him. "Stop being so fucking nice. You can't be a nice person. Nice people don't abandon their kids when they don't get aborted." Art tries to take my hand in his. Fuck him too. "I don't want to hold your fucking hand, Art. I'm fucking fine. It's you two that are being a couple of frauds."

Arshad's face shoots straight down with shame. Good. Sort of. But now I feel like I'm the asshole. That's not fair!

"Zee . . ." Art starts, then leans into my ear and whispers, "Open mind, open heart."

"I hate you, Art," I say, loudly.

The kid tells Arshad, "That's Zee-speak for 'I really appreciate you.' Don't worry, you'll learn it over time."

But Arshad can't smile at Art's charms this time. Good. Neither can I. Arshad closes his eyes, like he did yesterday at the café. Probably wishing he'd given up on me after that fiasco. Fuck it. I'm gonna pretend I'm Art and just say what I want. "Why do you do that?"

He opens his eyes to say, "Why do I close my eyes?"

"Yeah. It's weird."

"I apologize if it's off-putting. I do it when I'm feeling overwhelmed. It helps slow me down so I don't say or do things I might regret," my dad says. Arshad. Whatever. It was a good answer. Whatever a second time.

"Oooh," Art starts, "I like that. I never regret anything, but I still like that. I'm kidding. Not about liking that. I do. But about not regretting anything. I already regret saying I don't regret anything."

"He broadcasts his internal monologue," I tell Arshad.

He says, "I think it's very refreshing."

So Art says, "Thank you, Arshad. Zee loves it too. That's why we're BFFs now."

"Zee, can I address your comment about my not being a nice person?"

"I didn't mean . . ." I start, but I did mean it so I stop.

"No, you were correct. I was not a nice person. I was many things, but nice was never one. It is something I'm still striving toward. I have a theory if you don't mind my sharing it."

I don't respond. Fucking Art does: "We'd love to hear it."

Arshad goes on, "Kindness, I believe now, is not something you give others. Kindness is something you give yourself and only after you have given it to yourself does it flow freely and effortlessly toward others. Your mother . . ." He pauses. A memory. Oh, fuck, Arshad, you better not cry over my mom now because it will make me cry. Crap. He's tearing up. Oh, here I go now. So sick of crying! I choke it back as best I can as he continues, ". . . your mother, she overflowed with it. When I was young, and we were dating, I thought it was my job to show your mother how cruel and unfair the world was. So I said and did cruel and unfair things. Only years later—years and years of therapy and self-analysis—did I realize that I was not drawn to your mother because I wanted to teach her how unkind the world was. I was—subconsciously—drawn to your mother because I was hoping she would teach me how to be kind to myself."

Uh . . .

Yeah.

If you're so busy being angry, how are you going to look for things that might make you happy?

Yeah.

Open mind, open heart.

Okay.

But first I've got to unleash these tears. It's suffocating trying to hold them in. So I let my body shake, put my face in my napkin, and just let it pour. "I'm sorry . . ." I gasp out.

"I didn't mean . . ." Arshad starts.

But Art interjects, while rubbing my back, "This is good. It's good,

Arshad. What you said was very, very good. And I keep telling Zee that tears are good too and someday she'll believe me."

The emotions calm. The napkin clears my tears. "Okay . . ." I say, "Okay . . ." Whatever crap he did to my mom back then, I'm not saying I forgive it. I'm just saying I know he understands her now. And not many people do. And that means something. "Arshad?"

"Yes?" he says.

"I'm ready for you to tell me everything."

art

Before Zee's dad tells us about his past, he says, "Let's order first and you two should order whatever you feel like," which is code for "I'm picking up the bill," which is code for "Art's going to get an appetizer and a salad *and* a main course." Ha.

And then he begins.

I'm going to have to Wikipedia a bunch of the political, religious, and geographical stuff later (okay, all of it) but here are the CliffsNotes: Arshad Ghorbani was born in Iran just before the revolution. Both his parents were progressive professors and became refugees soon after Ayatollah Khomeini took control of the country. They were moved through Belgium, Germany, and England before ending up in Chicago in 1981. His sister, Christine, was born here soon after. His parents raised them in Gladys Park.

"My parents couldn't get work in academia here, so my father was forced to drive a taxi while my mother worked part-time at a junior high cafeteria. The vague memories I have of them in Iran were of passionate, patient people. But here, ashamed of his job, my father became angry and violent. My mother's misery led her to medicate herself numb and fall silent."

"I'm sorry," I say. I guess parents *could* be worse than mine. Yay!

Zee, my blunt Zee, says, "That's not an excuse to abandon your kid."

"You're right. You're right. . . ." He closes his eyes. God, he looks so serene when he does this. After his moment, Arshad says, "There are many kids who are raised by parents who hit them and ignore them. Or worse. And they quickly rise above and beyond these challenges. But I turned to anger. Deep, deep anger. I never made friends in high school. I had a soccer scholarship to the University of Wisconsin, but I dropped out my sophomore year because I was sure every teammate of mine thought I was a terrorist. I returned here, took philosophy classes at Oakton Community College while working at The Forest Café. . . .”

“Oooh,” I say, “I hear that place is amazing. Zee, we should go.”

“I’ve been. Not going back,” she says. “It’s where he met my mom.”

“I was twenty-two and absolutely sure of two things. First, the world was meaningless. And second, I was the only one smart enough to tell everyone how meaningless it was.” It’s like me, except I’m the only one smart enough to tell everyone how meaning*ful* it all is.

“What did my mom see in you?” Zee asks.

He laughs. “Besides being a barely employed coffeehouse barista who wanted to make everyone as miserable as I was?”

“Yeah,” she says, and almost even smiles at him.

He goes on, “Well, it’s always complex and fluid as to why we are drawn romantically to someone. In my defense, I was quite eloquent, even charming in my meaninglessness. And, despite the aged, withered, bearded man before you, I was young, athletic, and, if you’re into dark and exotic—which your mother was—I might have been considered attractive.”

“I’m sure you were,” I say. Ugh, why’d I say that? That was odd, even for me.

“That’s very nice of you, Art.” He nods at me. Wish he was *my* dad. Even if he wanted to abort me before I was born, he’s still better than the zombie corpse on my couch. That’s horrible of me to think. True, but horrible. Arshad goes on, “I also think your mother thought she could save me from my darkness. I reminded her of her mother, who had died when she was a teenager.”

Zee adds, “Her mom committed suicide.”

“Yes. She did. I believe your mom thought if she could save me, she could, in a way, save her mother at the same time.”

“Oooh,” I say. “That’s so complicated. I love it.”

Zee stays on point. “So were you in love with my mom? Or was it just sex?”

“I was incapable of love at that time, but it remains the most important relationship of my life. When she got pregnant with you, I assumed she would get an abortion. She knew well that I thought it selfish and ignorant to bring a child into this meaningless existence. But she was equally sure being a parent was the most meaningful thing someone could do. She almost had me convinced. . . ." Arshad pauses. Zee and I lean in. "Then 9/11 happened. The racism I endured went from subtle to vicious. My anger went from hot to boiling. That's when I told her to get an abortion or I'd leave forever."

"And you were gone," she says.

"I was gone. Moved to Los Angeles . . ."

"To act?" I ask.

"No." He laughs. "Mostly to run away. But I might have thought I could write movies. I'm sure you can imagine the market for doomsday screenplays written by a dark-skinned Muslim after 9/11 was not robust. So I became a cliché and began a slow, then fast descent into addiction and then homelessness. My parents and I had long ago stopped speaking, but my sister, Christine, found me in a shelter and brought me back to Chicago. Without her, I can assure you with one hundred percent probability, I'd be dead."

Whoa. Right? So dramatic. I love it. (Not that he had to go through that! Just that he was so brave to tell us everything.)

"I had a couple minor relapses with the drugs, but it took me five years to truly recover from my biggest addiction, which was to be angry about everything. To being *fucking* pissed off all the *fucking* time. Excuse my language."

"We've never heard that word before," I say, because I'm hilarious.

"Is that when you tried to get back in my mom's life?"

"It took me a few more years of therapy to come to terms with the fact that there was a human being on this earth that, if I'd had my way, would not be on this earth . . ." Arshad stops. The corners of his eyes fill with tears, just like Zee's often do. He pushes on. ". . . but, yes, eventually I came to peace with my deep shame and reached out to Katie. She held me at arm's length, as she should have, and her health never gave her a break, so I waited."

"Until she died," Zee says.

"I think your mom had the kind of magic that would have made this much easier on both of us."

"So . . ." Zee starts, and I can feel her anxiousness in my bones, ". . . what now?"

"That's up to you, Zee. I deserve and expect nothing but wish for anything and everything."

This guy is amazing. Maybe *too* amazing? I have to ask, "Are you like a Buddhist or a wizard? You're so wise and interesting."

Arshad laughs. Zee adds, "What Art's trying to say is you're saying all the right things, which makes it hard to believe you."

Her dad pauses, thinks, eyes open. "Well, first, thank you, Art, for thinking I might be a wizard. I am, sadly, not one. And while many recovering addicts turn to spirituality to aid them, I never found religion helpful on my journey. I do meditate, which helps calm my sometimes overactive mind. As for saying all the right things . . . I doubt this is true and I assure you it will not remain true. I am an immensely imperfect person. I do try to be honest, with myself and others. But I have and will fail at this as well."

"Are you a professor?" I ask. "You sound like a professor."

"No, not a professor. I never finished school. Currently, I . . ." Arshad hesitates. ". . . work at a coffee shop."

This seems like as good a time as any to just come out and say, "So I guess this means you won't be able to lend Zee money? 'Cuz her evil not-a-stepdad kicked her out of the house."

"Art, shut up," I start, "and, Arshad, I don't want your money."

"What happened with Michael?" he asks. Something about the way he says Michael's name—

"You know him?"

"Your mom, Michael, and I met for dinner about a year ago."

What the fuck. Maybe someone could have invited me?

"Did something happen with Michael, Zee?" he asks again.

"You don't like him, do you?"

"I . . . That's not true. We didn't get along as well as I'd hoped."

"What did you talk about?"

"You."

"What *about* me?"

"What would happen to you when your mother died." Arshad says "when" not "if" and I fucking hate him again.

So I pop: "All you adults make stupid decision after stupid decision, yet you still fucking think you should be making decisions *for* us."

"Zee . . ." he starts, but he's making me uncomfortable in my skin again.

"No, that's enough for today. I need to go." I hop up on the booth seat, leap over Art, and am gone.

art

I don't chase after Zee this time because I know her tolerance for the situation has expired.

I do flag down the waitress and ask her to pack our food to go. Only afterward do I ask Arshad, "Is that okay? We're going to be starving, and I hate to see it go to waste."

"Of course . . ." He wants to say something.

"Arshad, you did great. It's a lot for her."

"Thank you . . . can you take this to Zhila?" He reaches into his wallet, removes a stack of cash, then hands it to me.

"Zhila?" I ask, and as I do Arshad winces.

"Zee, I apologize . . ."

I lean over, whisper, "Is that her real name? I thought her real name was Rebecca."

"No, I mean yes," he stumbles. "Her real name is Rebecca. My grandmother's name was Zhila. It was just a slip." But I am Arthur Adams, Master Reader of the Imperceptible Truth—

So I say, "Arshad, weren't you just telling me how you always try to be honest?"

He winces again, does his close-the-eyes-and-find-inner-peace thing. When he opens them, "Art . . . I ask you . . . to treat what I said as a slip. For a time."

Ugh, he asks too eloquently for me to refuse. "Yes, okay. But you should know you're asking me to withhold information from the girl I love."

"I assumed you two were friends," Arshad says, which is annoying.

"Why? Do you not think I'm good enough for your daughter? Not manly enough like Cam?"

"I did not mean it that way. You would make an amazing partner for anyone, including Zee."

"Yes, well, now you're just saying that because you know I can blackmail you. Ha, I'm kidding." The waitress arrives with the food in a bag. I take his out, stand up with ours. "Arshad, don't worry too much about Zee running off at the end. That's just what she does to everyone. You made great progress today by being really open and honest. I'll keep your secret because I said I would, but you'll blow it if you try to hide things from her."

Then I leave because you should always leave after saying something that mature and profound so you don't undermine your point by saying something else.

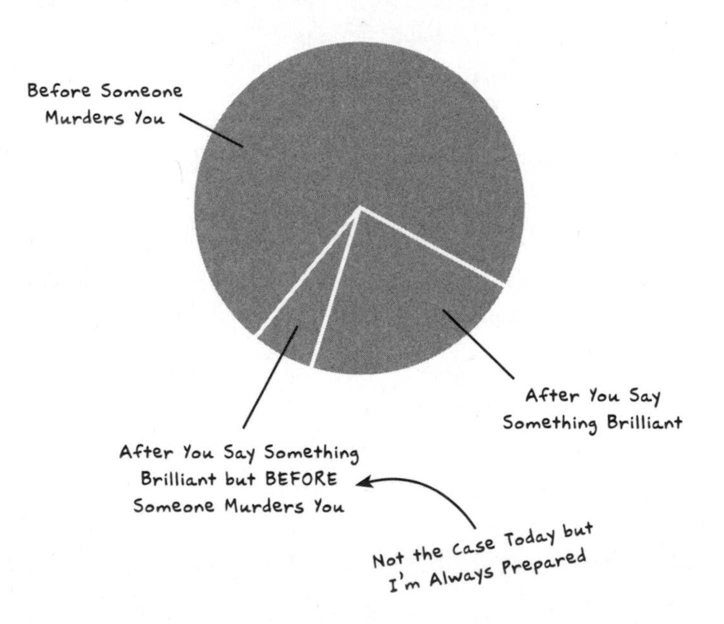

ZEE

It takes Art fucking forever to get back to my truck.

As he gets inside, I shoot at him, "I was about to leave."

"I was waiting for them to make the food to go." He places the bag of P.F. Chang's in my lap. I shove it back into his.

"Liar . . . what were you two talking about?"

"I told him how we had the greatest kiss ever last night and then today I bought you clothes so you could seduce another man." *Asshole.*

"ART, WHAT DID YOU TALK ABOUT?"

He reaches into his front pocket and places a wad of cash in my hands.

I say, "I told him I didn't want his money."

"Then go give it back to him."

"Fucker." I start fingering through the bills. "Shit."

"What?" Art asks as he picks through our lunch.

"Did you count this?"

"No, why? He just grabbed what he had in his wallet. I assumed it would be like fifty bucks."

"These are *hundreds*, Art. Twelve of them."

"That's . . ."

"Twelve hundred dollars." What the hell. "Didn't he say he worked in a coffee shop?"

"Yes . . ."

"What kind of forty-year-old Starbucks barista carries around this much cash?"

"He's not a terrorist, Zee!"

"Yeah, yeah, I never really believed that. But after what he told us—and this money—I bet he's a drug dealer."

"Drug addicts don't become drug dealers, Zee."

"He did."

"You just want him to be a terrible person," Art says.

"He *is* a fucking terrible person."

"He's one of the most well-spoken, deep-thinking adults I've ever met!"

"He abandoned my mom when she wouldn't abort me!"

"Doesn't that just make him pro-choice?" Art says, and regrets it the moment I unload my evilest of evil eyes.

"No, Art, that makes him part of a patriarchy that wants to make women a subservient reproductive class serving the whims of a man's timeline. Pro-choice means it's the woman's choice."

"When's the man's choice?"

"WHEN HE DECIDES TO HAVE SEX WITH THE WOMAN!"

"You're right. I'm wrong. Can we eat?"

"I'm too angry to eat."

"I'm too hungry not to. I will say if you feel uncomfortable taking his 'drug' money, I'll take it."

I almost do give it back. And then I remember I'm homeless and broke. Even my truck may be on borrowed time.

When we're back on the road, I ask Art, "What's the cheapest hotel in town?"

He says, "There's that motel by the Home Depot, The Last Riverbender, which is far too clever a name for such a crappy hotel."

art

Zee drives us to the decaying motel, parks, says, "Wait here," goes inside the office, and returns five minutes later with a key. "Come inside and check it out."

We go up these rusty stairs to the outdoor entrance of room 11. She opens the door, and I hold my breath as I walk inside because I think I'm leaving my real life and entering another one where I visit scary suburban motels only serial killers use.

The motel room itself isn't nearly as terrifying as the rotting exterior. It's clean, has a flat-screen TV, and despite the faint smell of cat pee, it feels welcoming. There are two beds, and before I can get myself in trouble by making a smart-ass comment, Zee says, "I got two beds in case you wanted to stay here with me."

Let us take a moment to be overwhelmed by ALL THE MIXED SIGNALS this girl sends me.

Okay, moment over.

"Yes . . . I mean, yes . . ."

"So do you mean yes?"

"Ha, you're hilarious."

"I know."

"But if you ask me to take a shower with you again, I'll refuse."

"*You're* hilarious."

"I know." God, our flirty banter is so good, it's annoying she can't skip past this Cam mistake. But, alas, not everyone can see the future like me.

"So," she starts after she throws her gym bag onto the floor, "here's what I'm thinking as far as a game plan for the rest of the day. Michael should still be at the church, so we go pick up some stuff at my house. Then we can get some of your stuff from your house. Then we get a bunch of junk food, come back here, and watch movies and stuff until we pass out."

This plan feels so romantic and perfect, I can't speak.

"Art?"

"Yes." I'll marry you.

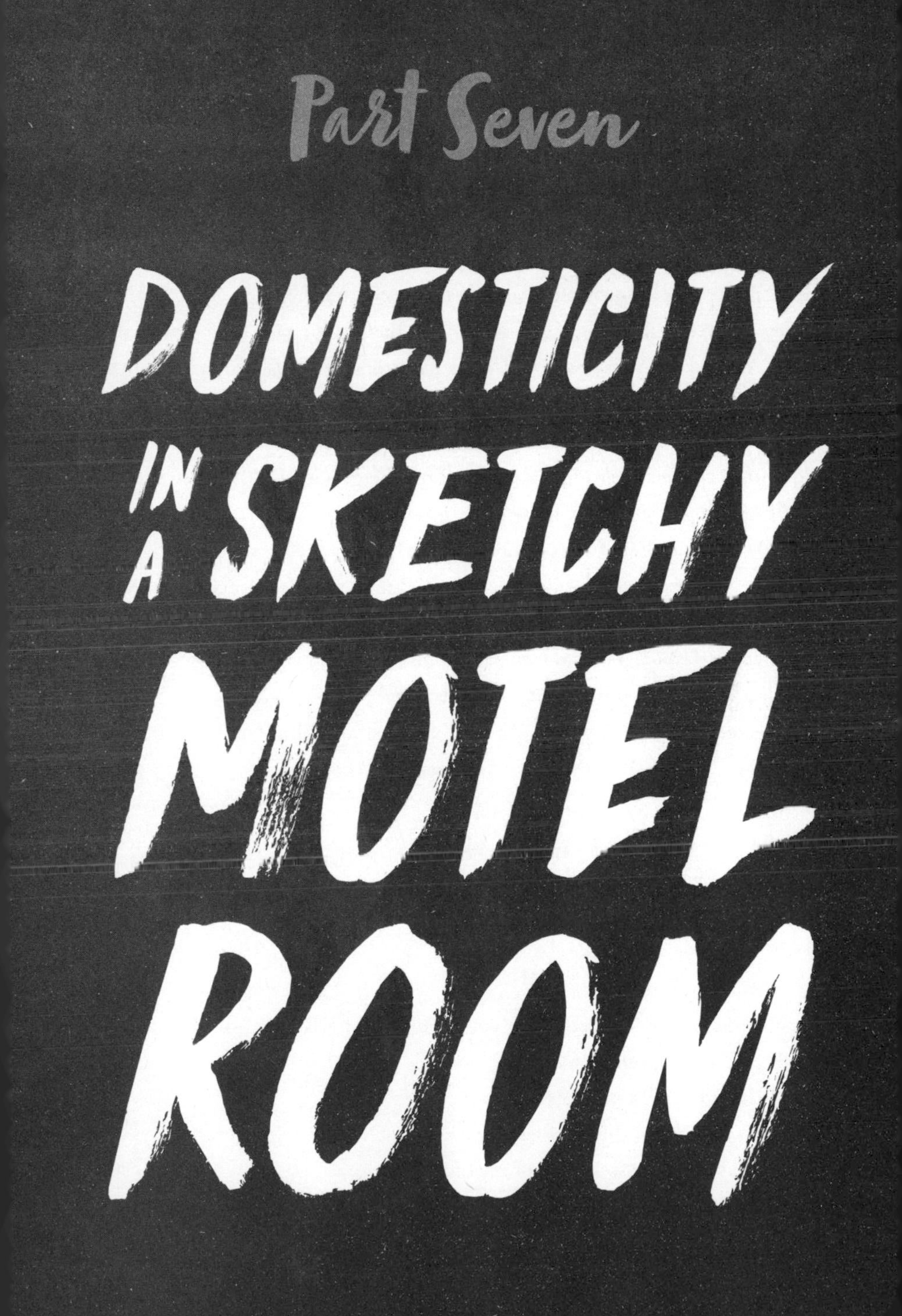

Part Seven

DOMESTICITY IN A SKETCHY MOTEL ROOM

ZEE

Art packs twice as much stuff from his house as I do even though he, unlike me, can go back at any time. We pick up pizza for the motel room. Yeah, I know we had it three days ago and I'll be having it again tomorrow with Cam. We also get pop, chips, and Nutter Butters for later.

We sit on the floor in front of the TV to eat and stay there way after we finish. Then I want to lie down, so I climb up onto my bed. Art stays on the floor until the next commercial break. Then he gets up and says,

"I'm going to get ready for bed."

"Okay," I say. What does he need to do to get ready? I just need to flip off my shoes and maybe my pants if I get hot. But he spends twenty minutes in the bathroom. Comes out with a scrubbed face, fancy boxer pajamas, and a clean white T-shirt. The kid is so pretty and pristine, sometimes it makes me feel like I'm anything but pretty and pristine.

He gets in his bed, which is good. Not that anything would have happened between us. But it's good he understands that.

But,

fuck,

DON'T BE PATHETIC, ZEE!

Whatever.

I say, "Hey, kid . . ."

"Yes, my queen?"

"No kissing or anything like that, but maybe . . ." Before I finish, he's out of his bed and slipping into mine.

"I thought you'd never ask."

"You were lying there for less than a minute!"

"It was the longest minute of my life."

"You're so fucking dramatic."

"You love it."

"Sure," I say. I don't know if I love him being dramatic. I do know I love him lying next to me. Just feels like he belongs there. I don't tell him that. No way. I also don't tell him I wish we could kiss again. A guy could get away with telling that to a girl. He could say, *Tomorrow I'm seeing the girl I love, but for just tonight can we find comfort in each other's arms?* A guy wouldn't say it cheesy like that, but he *could* say it. And then, even if the chick went ahead and made out with him (and did whatever else), the guy could tell himself (and the girl) that he never misled her. He could claim he was honest.

But I can't tell Art that. A girl can't tell a guy that. No matter how lonely she's feeling. No matter how much she wishes she could kiss him just one more time.

Actually, screw it.

"Art?" I whisper.

No answer.

"Art?" I whisper again. Then I peek down and see his eyes are closed. He's asleep. That sucks. But it does save me from fucking everything up a second time.

art

Of course I didn't fall asleep that fast! I just wanted to see if Zee would want to kiss me, which of course she did because our kisses should be captured and studied by future generations. But I had to protect both of us and pretend I was asleep so she didn't break my heart two days in a row.

When we wake up, we're in the exact same position. This probably means we could spend forever together. Zee paid for three nights at The Last Riverbender Motel, so we get to leave our stuff there. And *that* feels like we have our first apartment together and I really want to say something grand about this as we walk to her truck but she has a date with Cam tonight even if she doesn't realize it's a date and thinking about that breaks my heart even though I thought not kissing her last night would save me from that. Ugh.

We stop at Starbucks, then go to my house so I can help my dad with breakfast. Zee comes inside because we do everything together now but I bet she wishes she didn't because Abigail walks in while I'm putting cream cheese on Dad's bagel and she says, pretending Zee is invisible, "Where were *you* last night?"

"I could tell you . . . but I don't want to." I'm a brat sometimes.

"Will you tell your friend who steals my clothes that when she sees my boyfriend tonight that she should tell him he better call me today or I'm never giving him a blow job again? Thanks." Abigail fires a "die, bitch, die" glare at Zee and saunters back upstairs.

After she's gone, I say, trying not to smile, "Hey, Abigail wanted me to tell you—"

"Asshole," Zee says, which is code, in this instance, for "you're the funniest person ever born."

I put the bagel and coffee on a tray for my dad. This is more than I usually do, but maybe I'm feeling guilty about not telling him about Mom or that I spent the night at a motel with a girl even though he wouldn't have noticed if I spent the next month in Istanbul. "Hey, Dad," I say as I walk into the den, place his breakfast on the coffee table, and then open the shades so that he can be reminded that there's a place called "The World" outside this smelly, horrible room. "I'm working the lunch shift today, if you want to come in and eat."

"I don't think so," he says, still lying horizontal, eyes staring off into some netherworld.

"I have a great idea. You should walk! It's less than a mile and it's not too humid today, so you could get fresh air and sunshine and then I'll get you whatever you want from the menu this time, I promise."

With his gray, tired, numb, droopy, zombie face, my dad says, "Jesus, Art, who the hell taught you to shove your face in people's business so much?"

I don't say anything back because I'm trying not to cry—why would I cry? I haven't cried in years over any of the horrible things my parents have said to me!—but a *lot* has happened the past couple days, even for someone who loves lots of things to happen, and I can't hold myself together. "I'm going to go."

And then I'm into the kitchen and Zec hugs me even before I can tell her what he said.

Once we're back in her truck, I say, "Platonic wife, your platonic husband should get to work so he can pay for the motel room when our stolen drug money runs out."

"Platonic wife?" she says as she starts the car.

"Yes, tell me you love it or I'll die."

She laughs. "I love it."

ZEE

After dropping Art off at his job, I decide I'm going to go back to the motel and try on the tight jeans and frilly tank top he bought me at Macy's. I haven't told Art, but Cam has texted me five times since our big scene Saturday night. Not our old banter either. Stuff like *Excited to see you Monday, Z.* This might not seem like a big difference, but it's a *big* fucking difference. Then after Abigail's thing this morning, I just have this feeling . . .

. . . yeah, this feeling . . .

Actually, fuck it, I'm going to ignore that *feeling* until it's real or not real. Projecting how a boy might feel about you is fucking dumb. You know what else? No way am I wearing these jeans and tank. It took me even longer to put them on than it did at Macy's. And all I see in the motel mirror is a gangly imposter uncomfortable in her own body.

I text Michael, *I need the letter and my money or I'm calling a lawyer.* He responds a half hour later that *If this goes to court, you'll lose.* I ignore it and then a minute later he sends another text: *I'm sorry for getting defensive. Of course you can have your money if you want it. I'm only looking out for you, Zee.* His usual flip-flopping. Going to ignore that too.

I text Arshad:

ME

thanks for lunch and helping with money. sorry i ran out.

He responds right away. That's because he's a drug dealer who has his phone on him all the time.

ARSHAD

Anytime. You doing okay?

I tell him "yeah" and he asks if he "can do anything" and I say "I'm good" even though I'm living in a sketchy motel with only his fast-disappearing cash to my name.

I go to CrossFit, and when I get back home—the motel room, whatever—Art's taken over the bathroom counter with girly crap. Makeup, all that.

"Whatever you're thinking, stop thinking it," I tell him when I see it.

"I promise it will be subtle."

"I'm not wearing your clothes either."

"Zee! If you go on your date with Cam—"

"It's not a date!" It's probably a date.

"Ugh, you're being stubborn and dumb."

"I'm going like me, and if he doesn't like me, fuck him." Who the hell knows if I mean this, but now I'm pissed and, when I'm pissed, discussion is pointless.

I shower, put on my cargos and hoodie and Jordans. I guess I check myself twice in the mirror, which is once more than usual. But I look good.

For me.

I'm me.

Fuck.

I can't go looking like me, can I? I mean, *that* me. He needs to see the me he saw in Abigail's skirt. I turn to Art, say, "Fine. Dress me and makeup me and whatever." He leaps from our bed—*my* bed—and to my side.

"At your service, my queen."

"Just get it over with, asshole."

After I've shoved myself into the designer jeans, the fancy tank top (with no bra) and a pair of Art's shiny white girly shoes, he has me add a bit of mascara but I refuse to put on lipstick.

"What do you think?" Art asks our reflections.

"I hate it."

"But Cam will like it."

"He better. I'm going. I'll text you if I'm going to be late."

"Have fun, platonic wife."

I try to say it back, but I can't.

"Call me your platonic husband!"

"No. It's weird. Bye."

art

As soon as Zee leaves, I start to crumble and disappear into nothingness—but, boy, did I fake being supportive of this terrible date with Cam!—and I need to distract myself so I go through my text messages and text *everyone*: Bryan, Carolina, my brother, both my sisters not named Abigail, and, god, I need to find more friends.

ZEE

I get to the pizzeria early, and Pen, the hostess chick from my class, lays down the menus we never need and says, "I forgot to give you my number last time. And no pressure if you can't hang out with Iris and me for whatever reason."

"Yeah, no, we can . . . I will." And she really wants to hook me up with her friend, doesn't she? Or maybe she just wants us to be friends. Which is fucking just as weird, right? I give her my number anyway.

Then she asks, "Where's Art?" I didn't even know she knew Art's name. And why the hell would she think I'd be meeting Art? I've met Cam here a hundred times and Art *once*.

"I'm meeting Cam."

"Oh," she says. "Interesting development." Then she pauses, which is weird, then says, "Okay, until later," and walks away. Her mentioning Art does make me think I should text him some platonic husband joke. But I don't.

Then I get this anxious pulse in my stomach wondering when Cam might arrive and I realize I'm fucking nervous and holy shit that's so dumb. I've known him six years! Whatever. All this stuff is in my head anyway. This will be the same Monday pizza we've always had.

Right.

Yeah.

Nope.

Cam walks in and he's wearing a button-down and no Cubs hat. A *clean, pressed* button-down and gel in his hair. He says, "Hey, Zee," and instead of sitting, he leans over and hugs me. It's unbearably fucking awkward, but I try to pretend it's nice.

"Hey," I finally say as he sits down. He looks around, so I look around. Then he looks right at me, which is even worse than him looking around. But he doesn't say anything. Is he sweating?

"You . . ." he starts, and he gets this look. Oh, it's *that* look. Then he finishes, ". . . look great."

I smile. I try at least. "Thanks." I'd rather be comfortable, but whatever. Maybe if I fake this long enough, I'll like it.

"I shouldn't have said that. Sorry."

"It's all good. You look nice too." I'm the lamest person ever born.

"Zee . . ." he starts.

"Yeah?"

"I'm really sorry about not being there."

"It's okay."

Then he takes this deep breath. "Abigail and I broke up today."

It's getting real fast. "Yeah?"

"Yeah . . . we were always fighting. You saw us Saturday. So much drama. Even before I saw you, every time I was with her I'd wish I could just be chilling watching the Cubs game with you."

I like hearing that. I do. Wish he'd said it months ago. But it's good. "You're my best friend, Cam."

"Is that all you want to be?"

"What do you mean?" I'm gonna play the airhead. Maybe.

"It's just so great hanging with you."

"I love hanging out with you." I think I say this coyly or suggestively. Fuck, I don't know. Probably not. Whatever. It works.

He says, "I know, when I saw you last Saturday, I just knew . . ."

"Knew what?"

"We could . . . could be perfect together."

He just said what I've been fantasizing about him saying since I was eleven. I must be happy. I mean, I should be happy. *I mean*, I am happy. Really.

Then he says, " 'Cuz when you try just a little bit, like tonight, you're fucking hot, Zee. So hot."

Cam's not exactly artful, is he? Nor is he Art-ful. The kid would have liked that. No thinking about him! Don't sabotage this, idiot. *Fake it until you like it.* "I like looking like . . ." Don't gag. ". . . this for you."

He gets this childlike grin. "Can I sit on that side of the table with you?"

Oh. Uh. Not ready. But, "Yeah."

He flings himself out of his seat and is next to me in less than a second. "Hey," he says with this macho attitude thing.

I laugh because I think he's being funny. Nope.

"I'm sorry," he says.

"Jesus, no sorries, Cam. It's cool. I'm nervous." Am I still?

"Me too. I've been with Abigail so long and we've been friends so long. I'm not sure how to act around you."

"I know . . ." Wait. ". . . me too."

"Should we just kiss to break the tension?"

Oh, shit, I'm about to kiss Cam. I've thought about this since I was eleven years old and it's about to fucking happen.

"Zee?" he says to silence.

"Yeah. Okay," I say. He closes his eyes and opens his mouth and—

art

No one's texting me back! So I go through my phone trying to find someone, anyone (!), that will distract me from images of Zee and Cam kissing. (OH-MY-GOD, IT HURTS TO EVEN THINK!) And so I text a bunch of people I barely know, including that boy Jayden, even though my gut says he's got the potential to be a stalker and not the good kind.

ME

I know Carolina wanted me to tell you that
midwest suburbia was just as great as manhattan
but you should know up front I'm a terrible liar ;)

Of course, out of everyone, *he's* the one that texts back three seconds later:

JAYDEN

If you lied, I would have still found you gorgeous,
I just wouldn't have respected myself in the morning ;-)

Yep, definitely stalker potential. So I respond with just a smiley face to let him know I can't text anymore. But he ignores my obvious signal:

JAYDEN

I apologize for being so forward.
I'm a new yorker until death!
But I promise I'll temper my aggressive flirtations henceforth.

Maybe only because he used the word "henceforth"—and because no one else has texted me, not even Bryan, that bitch! Ha—I give Jayden another chance:

ME

You watch HGTV?

JAYDEN

yes, I also breathe.

That is funny. Kid is funny. So I ask if he's watching it now, he says yes, so then we start texting about whether they're going to "love it" or "list it" and I'm never wrong but Jayden says *he's* never wrong either *and* we disagree so we decide to make a bet. Jayden says the loser has to buy dinner when we meet. I tell him it will probably have to be a lunch because of my work schedule. (And dinner would send the wrong signal.)

Of course I win the bet because, unlike Jayden, I really am never wrong. Ha. Then he sends me a Facebook friend invite, and even though I know he's probably the stalker type, I click Confirm and click on his page to see what he looks like.

Ugh . . . I think he's a better dresser than me. Of course, he grew up in Manhattan and now lives in Winnetka, which means his parents are rich and he probably has his own high-limit credit card like Bryan except he clearly knows how and where to buy clothes.

He's also prettier than me, but this doesn't bother me as much as his superior wardrobe. And, if anyone ever calls me pretty again, all I'll have to do is pull up Jayden's profile, point to his picture, and say, *That boy is pretty, and if that boy is pretty, that clearly makes me flawlessly handsome.*

Time-out.

Why?

Do you think Zee is making out with Cam in the back of his Nissan Rogue right now?

Oh.

ZEE

His stubble.

Cam's kissing me, but all I feel is his stubble. Yeah, now I feel his tongue. A little weird to go for the tongue two seconds into our first kiss while we're in a restaurant, but whatever. I remind myself I love him, I do, I always have, and I need to stop being such a bitch. So I concentrate on what I like.

Mmmmh. *What do I like about his kiss . . . ?*

You know what I like?

That he did it. That it's happening. That even if it took me playing dress-up for him to see it, Cam finally saw we belong together. (*Belong together.* Lame thing to say. But you get it.)

Eventually the kiss ends, he pulls back, and fuck, I'm glad that's over. (Stop being a bitch!)

"That felt awesome," he says.

"Yeah." I smile. I do. I'm happy. For sure.

We spend the rest of the meal eating and watching the Cubs game, which I have never cared less about. I mention how Bryan has been coming to CrossFit and he's super athletic and he's got the build for football.

"Did Art tell you to talk to me about him?"

"No. Why?"

"Never mind. I don't know if Bryan would fit in."

"Because he's gay?"

"Christ, Zee, Art *did* tell you to talk to me about him!" He just yelled at me, didn't he? He's never yelled at me. Guess what? It's not hot at all.

So I say nothing and simmer.

"I'm sorry for yelling. It's not because he's gay. Fine, I'll talk to Coach Pollina even though that's a lot of drama for his first year as the head of varsity. But you have to kiss me first."

I do, and we go back to watching the game. Like we're friends again. Except we're *not* friends again. We've kissed. But this is why I always thought it would work. Because we're friends that can *also* kiss.

The bill comes. He reaches for it. That's awesome. But I'm awesome too, so I say, "Want to split it?"

And he says, "Yeah, oh, yeah, cool." Art would never have let me split it with him—STOP THINKING ABOUT ART! Cam fishes out some cash, lays it down on the bill, and slides it over. He put exactly half of the total, forgetting about the tip. But whatever. I don't care. I don't. I throw down my half plus the tip and we get out of there.

He walks me to my truck, which he has never done, and then kisses me again. This one's better. It is. But it's all mouth; his hands never reach for me. I'd reach for him if I thought he was ready to see my aggressive side, but I don't know if Cam will ever be ready for that.

I say, mostly because I need a break, "You're a great kisser." WHY AM I LYING FOR NO REASON! Maybe I think this is what girls do.

Then *he* says, "Am I the first guy you've kissed?" Motherf-er. He thinks *I'm* the bad kisser!

"No," I say, and crap, I think I laugh.

"You've been with other guys?" His lips are doing this macho pout. Like I've wronged him.

"Yeah."

"Who?" Dude wants me to name names.

"Why, you gonna beat them up?" I try to lighten things up. Doesn't work.

"Yeah, maybe!"

Then the raw me can't stop myself from saying, "Holy shit, Cam, ease back on your stupid jealous-dude thing. You've been with Abigail for almost two years. I'm not the type to sit in my room and pine for a guy." Even though I sort of did.

"I thought you were a lesbian!"

"Are you telling me that seeing me in that fucking skirt is the first time you thought, 'Hey, wait, maybe she's straight'?"

He says nothing because that's exactly the first time he thought it.

"News flash: Not all straight chicks like to wear skirts and not all lesbians wear cargo pants." Asshole.

And he knows it. He's fucking crushed. He slumps, eyes big and wet, mouth quivering. Jesus! Thought I'd be done with crushing boys when I was done with Art.

"I'm sorry," I say, even though he was the jerk.

"You've never talked like that to me before."

"I was upset."

"I thought I was done with the drama when I broke up with Abigail," he says. If he thinks he's laying his fake jealous righteousness on me, well.

"Fuck you."

We stand there, in the parking lot, in silence. I'm thinking this is it. Cam and I had one date, three kisses, and that's all.

Then he says, "Can I say something weird?"

"Sure." Whatever.

"I'm really turned on right now."

Holy fuck, drama turns him on. No wonder he and Abigail lasted so long. Guess what, Cam? *I'm as turned off as I get.* But saying that really would have ended it. So I try to fake being turned on and say, "Oh, yeah?" And I even glance toward his crotch. So lame.

But it works, I guess, because he lunges back into me and we're making out again. I go with it because I want to be with him, eventually, even if right this second I'd rather be doing just about anything else.

Then he stops and says, "Think Michael will care if I come to your place to watch TV?"

I'm not gonna touch the Michael subject with him, but I guess this means Cam wants to hook up. This is cooler than him not finding me attractive. But maybe it would be cool if he wanted to take things slow?

So I state it straight: "I'm actually pretty tired. Can we do a rain check?"

"Yeah, yeah, totally." Then he kisses me again and he's doing these little grunts, which is code for *Please don't leave me hanging*, but I'm definitely leaving him hanging, so I say, "Tonight was awesome," then kiss him on the cheek and get into my truck before he can try again.

As I'm driving away from Cam, I think of going home to Art and the thought releases every tension inside me. I suddenly can't wait to see him. I'm more excited to see him at our stupid motel room than I was to keep kissing Cam. So I text him:

ME

On my way home with leftover pizza, platonic husband.

But he doesn't text back.

And when I get back to the motel, the room is dark, his stuff is gone, and so is he.

art

Have I established I'm hilarious?

Good. Just wanted to make sure.

ZEE

I sit on the motel bed and look at my phone again. Still no response from Art. Would he really have just left without telling me? I text him again *Where are you?* but the kid who always texts back in three seconds doesn't text back at all.

Art . . . I should have . . .

Known?

Known what?

I don't know. As I'm sitting on the motel bed in the dark, trying to know what I don't know, I hear this dripping sound. Drip. Drip. Drip.

The bathroom. Creepy. But okay.

So I start moving toward the door, and the drip starts getting louder, which doesn't make sense.

Drip.

Drip.

DRIP.

And fuck, no more horror movies if I'm going to be on my own. I turn on all the lights, which helps a little. But I still hear the drip from behind the closed bathroom door—and it's getting faster, drip-drip-drip-drip—and now I *have* to turn off this faucet even though that's exactly what the dumb chick in a movie would do. So I open the door, flip on the bathroom lights and—

It's not the sink faucet.

It's the fucking shower faucet. DRIP-DRIP-DRIP-DRIP-DRIP and I'm thinking I should just get the hell out of there but *Don't Be a Pussy, Zee!* and I throw back the curtain and—

He yells, "AAAAAAAAAH!" with that pretty grin of his.

And I *fly* backward, screaming something, stumble out of the bathroom hard to the motel carpet, and he's already laughing.

"ASSHOLE!" I yell as Art leaps from the tub (where he and all his crap were) and onto the ground.

He's trying to hug me as a sort of apology but he also can't stop laughing. Which is annoying. But I guess I start laughing even though I think I had a heart attack.

"How long were you hiding in there?!" I'm yelling and laughing at the same time.

"Since you texted me I was your platonic husband."

"A *good* platonic husband wouldn't scare the living crap out of his platonic wife!"

"Maybe, but a *great* platonic husband would because he would never let their platonic marriage go stale."

Then I stop laughing and he does too, and I'm going to cry, aren't I? Yep.

"What happened?" Art asks.

art

Cam was a jerk to her! She hates him now! The grand love story of Zee and Art can finally take flight! Yay!

But then—

oh,

Zee says, "He kissed me. Abigail and him broke up and he kissed me." And then she sobs! So not only did the one girl I could ever love just tell me she kissed another boy, but *she's* crying, so I can't even be sad! Or mad! Or anything but the nicest, most understanding person ever.

Sooo, I pull her against me, let her cry her maybe-happy, maybe-crazy tears on my chest, and say, "That's what you always wanted, right? Why are you crying if that's what you always wanted?"

"I don't know!" Zee kind of yells and then kind of laughs.

"You're being very . . . interesting right now," I say.

"That's Art's way of saying I'm being insane."

"Maybe." I kiss her on the top of the head to let her know that it's okay that she's become an irrational disaster.

Then, after a bit of just letting me hold her, her sobs slow, quiet, and then she says, "Can you hold me tighter?"

My wiser, more mature self says I should lock myself in the bathroom until morning, but instead . . .

ZEE

Art slides his arm under my neck and pulls me onto his chest. My nose is pressed into his neck, which is so fucking soft because of that lotion. My body wants to be closer, so I wrap my leg around his leg, wrap my left arm around his waist, and pull him tight against me. Then the words—*these fucking words*—start rising from this deep, deep, deep place in me and they're building speed as they rise and I can't stop them even though I should. Even if they're true, I should stop these goddamn words, but I can't and so they just leave me and come alive and can never be unsaid again. "I love you, Art."

art

Oh-my-god, now *I* start crying, and have to say, have to know, "Really?"

"Yeah," she says.

Really really?

"Yeah," she says again.

"Like as a friend?"

She hesitates. "I don't know."

"As your platonic husband?"

She smiles.

"Or as the one person meant to travel with you through all time and space?"

"I don't know, Art . . ." And she just stares into me. ". . . but will you kiss me again even if I don't know?"

Yes! But, "What about Cam?"

"I don't know."

Oh. "I need you to know."

"I feel so confused, Art, I may never know."

"I'm not confused at all."

But this doesn't make her feel better. It might have made things worse. Oh-my-god, I can't believe I'm thinking what I'm thinking even as I'm asking, "So . . . you want to kiss me tonight?"

"Yes."

"But tomorrow you may kiss Cam again?"

She doesn't say yes. She doesn't say no.

"Okay." Okay?! This is the worst idea ever!

"You're sure?"

I lift her chin up and I look into her and I can see it. *The love.* It's literally in her eyes like it's literally in mine and, yes, I know she's going to break my heart! But I want her more than I want a whole heart. So I say, "Okay, I'm going to kiss you again, so you should probably prepare yourself."

"Okay," she says, smiling through her fading tears. I lean toward her, but she's nervous, which I like, so I say, "Close your eyes."

"Okay," she says again, and then I close mine and—

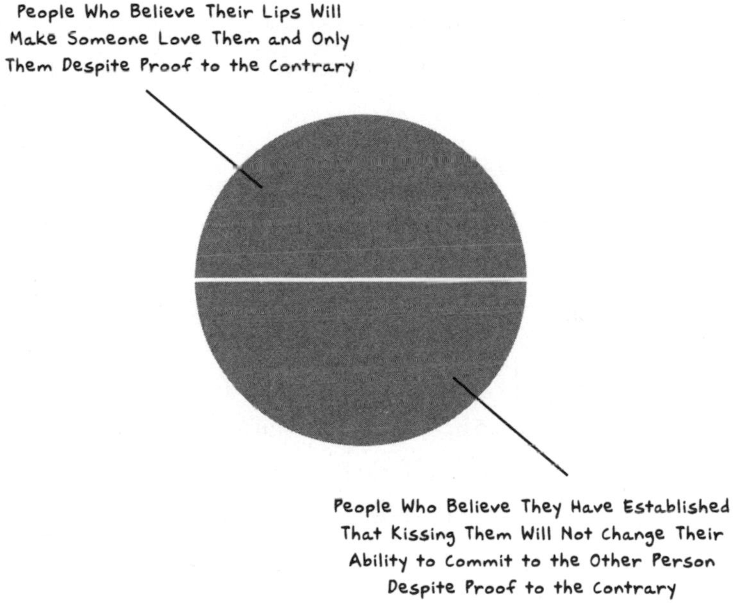

People Who Believe Their Lips Will Make Someone Love Them and Only Them Despite Proof to the Contrary

People Who Believe They Have Established That Kissing Them Will Not Change Their Ability to Commit to the Other Person Despite Proof to the Contrary

ZEE

Art's kiss, if I was a girly girl who fantasized about shit like that, would be the type of kiss I'd imagine my knight in shining armor would give me when he rescued me. I never fantasize about that stuff and, yet, him kissing me makes me *feel* like a princess. Which I like. Fuck you. But I do. I feel so safe with him. I've never cared about feeling safe because I never thought it would be something I should care about. But now, after my mom and Michael and Arshad and even Cam—Jesus, feeling safe feels like the most important thing in the world.

We make out for a *long* time on the motel room floor. We smile, we laugh a little, but mostly we just kiss. Him always in control. Me always safe. Him my gentle, soft, beautiful knight. Me the princess I never planned to be.

And

then

I decide it's time. So I say, "Want to get into bed?"

Art knows what I mean by this even if I didn't exactly know when I said it. So he says, "Yes, but is it okay if we only kiss tonight?"

"Oh, yeah." Aches ache. But I say, "Yeah, of course."

He goes and does his twenty-minute before-bed bathroom thing. I get into bed like yesterday, except this time I take off my pants. It was hot last night, I tell myself, but this is bullshit and I know it.

He takes longer than last night, so I get up and turn off the lights. Then I just stare at the door waiting for him to come out. Then he exits, and in this light, and on this night, and listen, I have to say it: "You're fucking beautiful." He blushes and slides under the covers with me. We kiss. Entangle our bodies. His bare leg is against mine and I think I have more hair on mine than he does on his because it's a pain in the ass to shave your legs all the fucking time. He doesn't say anything, so I guess he doesn't mind.

But then he says, "You took off your pants."

"It was hot last night," I lie.

"I like it."

"Sorry I didn't shave."

"I like how they feel."

He kisses me again and I say, "I love you," again. Maybe I'm ready not to feel safe. So I press myself into him.

art

Zee wants to have sex. Oh-my-god, she wants to have sex. I know this because I know everything but I also know this because her kissing is getting more aggressive by the second and I can, through her underwear, feel her, um . . . wetness? . . . oh-my-god, I said that, or thought it. She's pressing herself against my bare leg so it's impossible for me not to feel it. She wants me to feel it because she wants me to know she wants to have sex, doesn't she? But I told her I only wanted to kiss and having sex feels like trying to fly through space when I'm just learning how to walk and god, I love my metaphors, but mostly, I want her to read my mind and tell me it's okay that we just kiss tonight. But her lips start to nibble, which means her lips want to devour and . . .

"Zee . . ."

"Yeah?"

"You want to have sex, don't you?" I say everything, but I can't believe I just said that.

"No," she says, pulls away. She's five inches from me but it feels like a mile. "Maybe . . ." She thinks. "No, I don't . . . maybe I do, maybe I would, but no, it's not that. . . ."

"You can tell me anything."

She laughs. "I know, that's why you're my platonic husband. . . ."

"We're not being very platonic right now."

"I guess we're not." She gets serious, sure of herself, and it's mesmerizing when she gets still and intense and internal. "I love how you kiss me."

"That's because I'm the greatest kisser ever." Tension must be handled with humor!

"You probably are. . . . Listen . . . you're that good . . . but I want to see if you love how I kiss you."

"I do."

"No, you love how much I love how *you* kiss *me*."

"We're kissing each other—it's about how we kiss each other. . . ."

"I don't know," she says. "I don't think so. I think one person is always doing the kissing and the other person is the one being kissed. And it can switch back and forth every five seconds, but I think one person is always the lead."

"Um . . ." I start and, um again, and, "I'm sorry, I actually have to pause and think about what you just said because you might have just stated a revolutionary new theory and I thought I knew everything."

She laughs because I'm funny even when I'm sincere.

"Zee . . . yes . . . maybe . . . oh-my-god, yes . . . mmmh . . ." I have to think more, don't I? I do. I never have to think before I talk! But I do. I do and then I know what I have to say. "And you like to kiss aggressively."

"Maybe, I don't know. Maybe I didn't know how I liked to kiss someone until you, but now I want to try."

"And I kind of stop you every time you try to kiss me aggressively, don't I?"

"You don't 'kind of' stop me, you do stop me. Which is fine, Art. God, I don't want to be the creepy dude here trying to get in your pants. I just want you to know I love how you kiss me, but you have to tell me straight up if you don't love how I kiss you."

"I . . ." But I stop because I have to think *again* before I talk. Exploring new worlds tonight! Ha. Okay, yes, I know. ". . . I don't know."

"You don't know what?"

"I don't know if I like how you kiss me because I get super nervous every time you start taking control."

She doesn't know what to say.

So I try, "What if . . . what if . . . I let you take control, I let you be the lead kisser . . . but we have to keep our underwear on."

She laughs.

"I didn't want you to laugh this time! This is a great plan and tell me you love it or I'll die!"

"I'm sorry, you said the same thing in the shower, which I thought was cute . . . but, yes, that sounds awesome. I love your idea. I love your 'Keep Our Underwear On' rule."

"Okay, thank you," I say, and I kiss her and she kisses me and then I roll onto my back and she gets on top of me and I say the scariest thing I've ever said, "I'm yours." She laughs because that *was* a bit cheesy of me, but I can't laugh because I'm pretty sure she's about to eat me alive.

ZEE

Art shrinks under my lips, like he's making himself small enough for me to eat. That doesn't make sense. But whatever is happening, it feels good. It feels like I'm devouring him and devouring him only makes me hungrier, which makes me want to devour him more. He raises his chin, like a willing victim to a vampire. Does that make me the vampire? I hate feeling like a vampire. I kiss, lick, bite . . . lips, cheeks, ears, neck. Maybe I love feeling like a vampire.

I'm straddling him, our underwear on, but I've been staying high, on his stomach. I lift and lower myself down on him. He's excited. His penis is excited. Does this mean he likes how I'm kissing him? I wish he would tell me. And then I stop wishing and remember I'm in control and say, "Do you like this?"

He nods, gasping, vulnerable. Despite our underwear and because of the wetness, I can slide against him. I start slow. This isn't sex. But it isn't just kissing.

"This okay?"

He nods again, but manages the words "This is so intense."

"Too intense?"

"No . . ." Then a mesmerized smile. "Maybe, but I think I love it."

art

Her wetness has enveloped me. From her mouth to my face. From between her legs to everywhere else. I know we're not naked, but I feel like we're naked anyway. It feels like she has seeped into all my openings and is now touching me from the inside out. As if the only way she's going to get out from inside me is if I explode. And, oh-my-god, this metaphor is about me—

ZEE

He cries out in six, seven, eight high-pitched moans as he orgasms beneath me. I'll admit to myself what I'd never tell him or anyone else: He sounds like a girl when he comes. A girl crying out in extended, surprised, almost reluctant pleasure.

The other thing I'd never admit?

That's what did it for me.

His feminine moans.

That's what made me come.

My first orgasm with a boy happened when the boy cried out like a girl.

art

I'm mortified those sounds just came out of my mouth. Oh-my-god, I sounded like such a girl! Zee must be so disgusted by me, but when I open my eyes, she's smiling down at me, that love still in her eyes—

"How do you feel?" she asks.

"I don't know," I say, the embarrassment not subsiding despite her care.

"You didn't like it?"

I can barely look at her but I manage to say, "I liked it more than I was ready for."

"Art—"

"Yeah?"

"Kiss me."

"What do you mean?"

"*You* kiss *me*."

Oh. I twist so she falls to the bed beside me, then I prop myself on my elbow, and I lean in over her, pull her face in toward mine with my hand and kiss her, inhale her, sweetly, through my lips, and Zee says, "I'm yours," because she's my mythical creature and I'm hers.

ZEE

I fall asleep on Art's chest, and we wake up in the same position. That's two nights in a row we both haven't moved the entire night. I would think something was wrong if they didn't feel like the best nights of sleep in my life.

Same routine as yesterday. Starbucks (coffee for me, tea for him). Then his dad's house despite his dad being an asshole yesterday. I stay outside in my truck this time because Abigail might shoot me with something more than her eyes if I go inside. As I'm waiting, I think about last night.

About all that happened.

Me imagining I'm this girly princess safe in Art's knightly embrace.

Then, five minutes later, I'm mounting him like a guy and he's crying out like a girl.

Fuck, we're weird. Too weird? It's got to be wrong. Right? This isn't how people are supposed to act. Right?

Then I get a text:

CAM

Thinking of how hot it was to kiss you ;)

I wink back because I should text something but don't want to get into anything. But then:

CAM

Can I see you tonight?

I ignore it. I should say I wish I could fucking ignore it. I can't do this. Juggle both of them. I have to tell Art that last night was a mistake . . .

. . . but then I watch the kid glide out from his house toward my truck and all I want to do is swallow his pretty face. So we go back to the motel room and I throw him on the bed, take off everything but his underwear and then I take off everything of mine except my underwear. I even take my bra off.

"Those are your boobs, Zee," he says, trying not to smile.

"More like my mosquito bites," I say, because I fucking hate my body.

"They're your boobs and they're sexy and they're perfect," Art says, and I love how he loves me just the way I am even when I hate the way I am. And so I—

—she eats me alive again just like last night and rides me with our underwear soaked between us again and I cry out like a girl again and she grunts like a guy again and I'd nominate us for the most interesting couple ever if I wasn't sure there was something seriously wrong with us.

As we're cuddling on top of the motel bedspread, Zee says, not looking at me, "Is it okay if we don't tell anyone about this? At least for now?"

"Yes," I say right away, before I can say anything else. It doesn't bother me that Zee doesn't want anyone to know we are getting sweaty and dirty inside a sweaty and dirty motel room. And when I say it doesn't bother me, all my vital organs are disintegrating.

"Thanks," she says, breaks from our cuddle and stands to dress.

"When are you going to see Cam again?"

"Art . . ."

"I'm sorry."

She gets back on the bed with me, takes me into her arms. "I've wanted Cam for six years. . . ."

"I know. Never mind."

"I don't want to hurt you. But I don't want to lose my chance at being with Cam."

Don't cry, Arthur Adams. You agreed to this! You're a grown-up now! Even if you're not, you have to pretend to be.

I say, crying only on the inside, "I'll be fine, Zee." Must change the subject! "Want me to bring home some food from Fridays for dinner?"

"Sure, but I asked Coach Dish yesterday if I could pick up more hours at the check-in desk and she said they needed an evening person all week. So I won't be home until after ten."

"I'm sure I can make enough at Fridays to pay for this room so you don't have to work if you don't want to."

"Art, come on, no you can't. At some point you're going to go back to your house and your real life and I'm going to have to fend for myself."

I face the other way on the bed so she can't see me. Or I can't see her. Or I can't see her seeing me seeing her.

After work, I walk to Target on the way to the hotel and pick up some things for the room. Two scented candles, a red pillow that reads *Love*, Bluetooth mini-speakers, water bottles, kale chips, and laundry detergent. I might have also picked up condoms, but I make myself forget this the moment I finish paying for them.

I spend the rest of the night nibbling at the food I brought home from the restaurant and doing my best to transform this motel room into something divine. At nine, I shower, put on the only pair of silk underwear I have and nothing else.

At ten, I light the candles, turn on the music, turn off the lights, get into bed, and wait. But then I get this:

ZEE

Going to be late

ZEE

After I leave the motel that morning, I'm glad to be away from Art. I spend the next hour trying to figure out how I can tell him we need to stop what we're doing without crushing him flat.

But as the day goes on, I start missing him. A little at first. Then it grows. And grows. By the time I clock out from the CrossFit desk at ten, I want to race home and tell him we should get married so we never have to spend a night apart again. I'm acting and thinking like a bigger girl than I ever have and it's all because of the girly guy I'm maybe, sort of in love with.

Except Cam shows up—surprise! yay!—just as I'm getting into my truck. He's hands and tongue and "Want to go park somewhere?"

"Not tonight . . . I'm tired."

"Man, Zee . . ." Cam starts, but pauses. You want to know why he pauses? Because I crushed him. HE CRUSHES EASIER THAN ART! His eyes are watering as he continues, ". . . I feel like you're not really into me."

I suck. Don't suck. "Cam, dude . . . I'm sorry. I think this is just harder than I thought. Transitioning from friends to whatever."

"Yeah, maybe you're right. It's just Abigail always wanted to see me and text with me and you're barely acknowledging I exist."

"I've never been much of a texter. You know that."

"But that's when we were friends. Now that you're going to be my girlfriend—" *Girlfriend?*

"Cam . . ." I don't say it. But he knows.

"You don't want to be my girlfriend?" Dude is teary-eyed again.

"I do . . ." Sure, maybe, if I don't run off and elope with Art. ". . . but I want to work toward it, not jump into it."

"But love is about jumping in. No safety net!" Holy fuck, he's talking like those Hallmark movies my mom watched all the time. I hate those movies.

"Zee, I know you've never been in a relationship, so let me take the lead, okay?"

I kinda want to let him lead himself into a fucking wall. Then I want to tell him I'm staying with my not-so-platonic husband in a motel tonight. But then—

"Yeah, okay."

This makes him so happy, me letting him lead, he bursts into a smile and kisses me. I kinda like it. Reminds me of something Art might do, which reminds me that I should tell Art I'm going to be late and he's going to know why I'm late. . . .

Knowing Zee is probably making out with Cam at this very moment makes me want to text a beautiful girl and flirt, so I think of Carolina but thinking of her makes me think of Jayden.

So I text him instead:

ME

When are you buying me dinner?

I regret texting him the second I do it but he texts me two seconds later, so it's too late to do anything:

JAYDEN

You said lunch, now it's dinner-

Does this mean you broke up with your boyfriend?

ME

What makes you think I had a boyfriend?

JAYDEN

Was I wrong?

I hesitate.

JAYDEN

Exactly. I forgive you.

You didn't know someone as fabulous

as me existed yet ;)

ME

I'm straight.

JAYDEN

Yes, me too;) Shhhhh.

I don't respond because I suddenly feel like this is cheating on Zee more than if I was texting with a girl. (And even though SHE'S the one cheating! Or not-cheating-but-still-cheating. Ugh.)

A few minutes later, Jayden texts me a picture. It's him. In a long white-blond wig, a gold dress hiked up high on his thigh, lipstick, mascara, done excessively but done well. His eyes eat the camera and his tongue is placed on the edge of his bottom lip with an expert touch of seduction.

JAYDEN

So, straight boy, Tell me since you're an expert.

I'm a very pretty girl, aren't I?

Two roads diverged in a yellow wood . . . it was a yellow wood, right? I think. I can't remember. I hate school. Anyway:

ME

Yes very

JAYDEN

oooh, you like me in a dress, don't you?

Yes.

JAYDEN

Does the Art that lives below the border

like me in a dress?

I had been ignoring the lower half of my body. But now Jayden made that impossible.

The answer was yes. The answer was a picture of a boy in makeup and a dress made my penis hard.

JAYDEN

Does Little Art want another picture of me in a dress?

Yes. Yes. Yes. Yes. Yes. Yes. Yes. Yes.

ME

I have to run-sorry

ZEE

I let Cam talk me into getting in his car and making out more. He's pawing at me and pulling at my arms, trying to make me paw at his crotch, which I do for five seconds until I decide it'd be more fun to touch the gearshift.

"Cam . . ." I start to stop him.

"I want you so bad," he says with this heavy breathing.

I don't want you at all. I don't say this. I say, "I need to take things slower," because I probably am in love with someone else.

"But . . ."

"Please."

Then he fucking says, "I'm falling in love with you."

WHAT?

No. You've either been in love with me since Little League or you're horny and want me to jerk you off. It's an either/or. There is no option of *I'm falling in love with you because I saw you in a miniskirt.*

But I say, "I really need to go."

"You're not going to tell me you're falling in love with me too?"

"I've been in love with you for six years and you never had a clue," I say. And I'm gone.

When I walk into the motel room, it's like walking into a corny romance novel. Candles, soft music, everything's clean and warm. He even bought new pillows! I always hate these scenes in movies because I never believe any dude would take the time to do this sort of stuff . . .

. . . but Art did. My beautiful boy did. And, man, the shit works. I feel safe *and* turned on. I feel like a princess and an animal ready to . . . you know.

Art is asleep, new pajama bottoms on, bare otherwise. I strip down to just my boxer briefs and slide up next to him. His eyes bat open as I pull him into me.

"Do you like it?" he asks, still half-asleep.

"I love it," I say, and I kiss him, hard, and he emits this delicate, ache-filled whimper and, man, that makes me want to swallow him whole.

art

I wake up before Zee does the next morning and walk to the strip mall next to the Home Depot, pick up juice and bagels, and bring them back to the room. She's still sleeping, but she's kicked off the blanket, her body naked but for her boxers.

With her short hair, her small chest, her toned muscles . . . she looks like a boy. She kisses like a boy. She dresses like a boy. She swears like a boy. But I love her like a girl.

You do?

Yes, of course I do!

Sure.

What's that mean, "sure"?

It means I think you're confused.

I am not!

Jayden's picture?

I have no idea to what you're referring.

"Hey," she says, waking up.

"I got some food."

"Come here."

I leave the bagels and juice on the motel table, get into bed with her. "I love you," I say.

"I want you," she says, takes me in her hands, strips me down to my underwear, and makes me cry out like a girl.

Afterward, as she's holding me, I ask, "You're not a virgin, are you?"

She hesitates, but then admits, "No, I'm not." Ugh.

"Thanks for being honest. I am."

"I know."

"I want to have sex with you, Zee."

She turns my chin with her fingers so we are gazing into each other. "I want to have sex with you too, Art."

"But is it okay, the first time we do it, that I take the lead?"

Again, she hesitates, but then she says, "Yeah, yes. Of course." Then she kisses me hard.

I pull back. "But I want to wait until tonight, okay? I know you work late. But when you get back, I want to take you to dinner even though it will be late and then I want to come back here and make love."

She laughs. "Make love."

"Yes, I know I can't take your sex virginity. But I want to take your 'make love' virginity."

"You're hilarious," she says even though I wasn't trying to be for, maybe, the first time ever.

ZEE

By the time I leave the gym that night, I'm exhausted (Cam's texted me fifty times) and am hoping Art will want to forget going out and just stay in. But when I walk into the motel room, he's dressed in a fancy fucking suit, with this musky cologne on that he's never worn, and sporting big boots that make him taller than me.

Seeing him I know it would crush him if I bailed on dinner, so I say, "You look very handsome," even though he still looks pretty.

"Thank you. You can just go as you are. I won't mind. I just wanted to look special for you."

"No, I want to look special for you too," I say, which might be the cheesiest crap I've ever said in my life. I take a shower, and as I'm drying off, I'm like, "Fuck it," and—

art

—Zee exits the bathroom in the tight designer jeans and tank top I bought her at Macy's. She's even put on mascara.

"You look so beautiful," I say, and I mean this. I do. Because she looks like a girl. I like when she looks like a girl. I do! I really do.

When we get out to her truck, I ask, "Can I drive?"

She laughs and throws me the keys.

I want to go somewhere special, but at this time of night, the only place open *and* romantic enough is in Evanston, so we have an almost hour drive. Zee doesn't complain, but I can tell she's bored and her being bored on a night I wanted so badly to be perfect. . . . Ugh, I don't have the inspiration to come up a with good metaphor. . . . I just wanted everything to be perfect and it's not.

ZEE

Everything Art is doing is awesome. Really fucking awesome. But I can barely breathe in these jeans and I feel like every waiter at this fancy restaurant is looking at my tits in this skimpy-ass tank even though I barely have tits to look at. And I'm tired, and I just want to be home with him in bed watching TV.

He asks, "Are you going to go to Penelope and Benedict's party this Saturday?"

"I wasn't invited."

"You were. They invited you on Facebook."

"I don't look at that much anymore. And I hate high school parties. Teenagers thinking they're acting mature by getting blasted and puking up on lawns."

"Okay, we don't have to go."

"You can go, Art. We're not . . ." I didn't say it. But the kid knows and he's crushed. "Okay, I'll go to the party with you. But people have to think we're just friends, okay?"

He nods.

I lean across the table, whisper, "Maybe we shouldn't have sex tonight."

"You don't want to?"

Not really. But I say, "I do, but maybe it will be too much for us." For him.

"No, I'll be fine, Zee. I understand the rules."

I fall asleep on the way home.

When Zee fell asleep in the truck, I was relieved. This night felt like a total failure, and I didn't want the first time we made love to be when she was barely awake.

But when I come out of the bathroom after washing my face, she says, "Give me five minutes?"

"Of course," I say, not sure what she's up to.

ZEE

I had packed one pair of panties—can we just admit what a stupid fucking word "panties" is and I might not wear them ever just because of the word?—and I wanted to keep playing the role of the girl since Art was playing the role of the boy . . .

I mean, I am, he is . . .

Never mind. I wanted to wear the fucking panties, okay? I put those on, left the tank on, and then I—Jesus—put some lipstick on. My reflection asked who the hell I was, so I gave it the middle finger and—

art

—Zee exits the bathroom wearing girl underwear and lipstick. I know she's trying as hard as me to feel normal—we are normal! I mean, I feel . . . ugh! I don't know what I feel and it's a disaster not knowing what I feel!—*what I mean* is that I love her for understanding me. Yes, this is what I mean.

She gets into bed next to me. I can tell she wants to kiss me but she waits for me to lead, just as I asked, so I lean over her and kiss her and soon our lips flow into our song.

ZEE

Once Art's kissing me, I stop feeling like a girl pretending to be a girl and feel like me again. When he's leading, I feel like he's making our lips dance together. Like he's got music playing in his mind and he's twirling my body just by touching my lips to his. That sounds crazy or stupid but it feels beautiful. Soft. Slow. Sensual. Yes, sensual. When I'm kissing him, it feels like we're these wild sexual animals. I love it. But I love this too. This sensuality. It feels like we are floating above the bed.

art

Only after we're kissing, after Zee has fallen under my magical powers—and I clearly have magical powers!—do I feel like we're normal. Like I'm a normal boy kissing a normal girl. I indulge in our lyrical connection for as long as I can. For as long as I can hear our sweet song.

But the moment I start thinking about sex, that we should start, or talk about it, or *something*, I realize something horrific—

ZEE

He's not getting hard. Must be he's nervous. Totally understandable.

"Do you want to just kiss tonight?" I ask.

"No," he says, and he knows I know. "I don't know what's wrong."

"Let me try something." I can't believe I'm offering to do this, but I guess this means I really love him.

Zee kisses my chest, then my stomach, and, oh-my-god, she's going to kiss my penis, isn't she? And then she pulls down my underwear and she can see my penis for the first time and I feel sick to my stomach. She puts it in her mouth and it feels good, very good (of course it does!), like a massage for my penis, but I'm not getting excited, am I? Why aren't I getting excited? Why do I get an erection when I don't want one (like when Jayden sent me that picture!) and I can't get one on the most important night of my life?!

ZEE

He's not getting hard, but the kid's still pretty huge if you know what I mean and my jaw hurts instantaneously. How do chicks do this longer than thirty seconds? It's boring *and* painful, and if Abigail really loves doing this, Cam should have stayed with her forever because I will never love doing this. I can't fucking believe I'm thinking about Cam now, I should—

art

"Zee?" I say, then pull her up so our faces are next to each other.

"Sorry," she says.

"Don't be sorry. I'm sorry."

"I don't want *you* to be sorry. It happens."

"I'm nervous, I think."

"Me too," she says, except she isn't nervous at all. She's just trying to be nice. Then she smiles, and runs her thumb along my lips. "My lipstick got on you."

"How does it look on me?" I say, because I don't know why.

"Probably better than it looks on me," she says, and tries to laugh.

"I can't believe you put lipstick on for me." I try to laugh too.

"And I tried giving you a blow job and I hate giving blow jobs."

Oh-my-god. "You must really love me."

"I guess so."

"Zee?"

"Yeah?"

"I really love you," I say.

ZEE

I know the kid loves me, so I say, "I know."

But then he gazes deep into my eyes. More intense then he's ever done it and he's always super fucking intense. When he knows he's got me rapt under that gaze, he says, "Zee, I love *you* you."

I say, "I know," again but this time I feel it.

He says, "Let's not pretend with each other again."

"Okay."

"Zee . . ."

"Yeah?"

"I think I'll get excited if you lead. In fact, I'm getting excited just *thinking* about you leading."

"Really?" I reach down and, yep, he's getting there.

"Really."

"You like when I kiss you like this," I say, and kiss him hard.

"Yes," he says, nodding, shrinking and blossoming at the same time.

"You like when I grab you like this?" I wrap my arm around his back, pull him fast against me.

"Yes," he says, and moans.

"You like when I'm on top of you like this?" I push him onto his back and straddle him.

He nods. I slip off the stupid panties and, listen—"We don't have condoms."

"Yes, we do." He smiles a nervous smile, reaches under the pillow, and pulls out a condom he had hidden there. I take it, unwrap it, and put it on him.

"Are you sure this is okay?" I ask, because no boy ever asked me and the boy should always ask. I'm *not* the boy. But I'm not *not* the boy either.

"Very much," he says.

"I love you, my beautiful boy."

"I love you, my handsome girl."

Part Eight
THE MYSTERIOUS
X
OF SEX

art

I call in sick to the restaurant the next morning. Zee and I don't spend the whole day in bed together, but we spend *almost* the whole day in bed together. It isn't like this soft-core cable movie of nonstop sex. It's us talking and cuddling and kissing and doing things I've never seen on cable.

I put on her lipstick and panties.

She puts on my underwear and suit.

We talk in each other's voices, walk like the other person, call each other the opposite gender. Touch each other in, um, unusual ways. We laugh, like we're being silly, like it isn't real, but it also turns us both on and that is very real and it is very terrifying. It *feels* amazing. At least our bodies feel amazing. But besides how it feels, it's terrifying. I don't know who I am supposed to be anymore, and I've always known who I am supposed to be.

After she leaves for her job at the gym, I spend the next four hours googling everything we said and did. This eventually leads me to clicking on sites of people doing and saying those things to each other in videos. I quickly back click and try to forget what I just saw or might see in these videos.

These videos are also known as pornography.

I know this is very prudish of me, but I've never really looked at porn. My brother, Alex, very inappropriately would try to show it to me when he was in high school and I was, like, eleven. He wasn't evil, just a stupid teenager being a stupid big brother, and we had parents that were clueless. But it was absolutely horrifying and gave me nightmares and I vowed never to look at it again. I've never reconsidered this vow. I always knew I wanted love, then sex, not the other way around. Yes, I knew this made me different from most boys, but I didn't care! I just didn't think it made me *that* different.

But now, sitting alone in this seedy motel room, waiting for my masculine girlfriend to come home so that she can make me orgasm and moan with high-pitched cries, I start to wonder if I've avoided porn because I didn't want to know the truth.

No.

No what?

We can't think about this today.

You're right.

But maybe we can look at videos of what we can't think about today.

So look but don't think?

Yes.

This is very unlike you.

Do we really have any idea who "you" are anymore?

Good point.

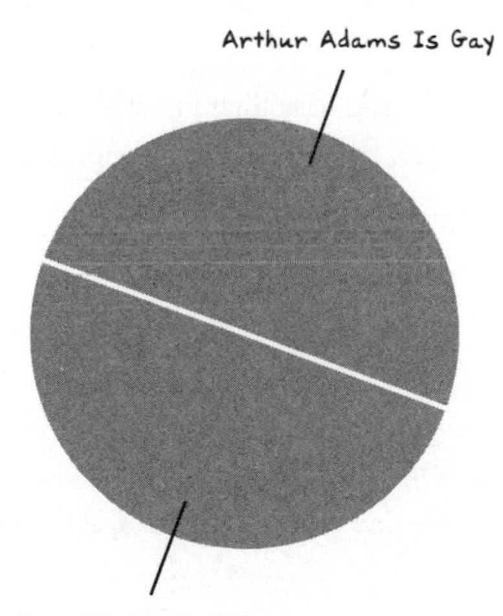

ZEE

On the drive to CrossFit, nothing feels that weird. Yeah, I'm seventeen, I live in a motel room, and I have sex with a boy who looks hot in my lipstick. Yeah. Okay. I'm not going to tell anyone, ever, about it, but whatever.

Yet as soon as I walk into the gym, as soon as I see Glen, Bill, Taylor, even Bryan, I get this queasy feeling that everything Art and I have done with each other is illegal. Or worse, inhuman. That we should be arrested for crimes against biology.

I want to be that girl who Glen booty-calls. Be that girl who has sex with Bill where we never speak before or during or after. Where it never even crosses my mind that I could have an orgasm with a guy. I want to be that girl who silently pines for Cam to twirl me. For me to squeal at the sight of him instead of getting wet when a boy squeals for me.

While I'm working the desk, I feel like I'm still sweating from the workout even though I'm not. It feels like I'm sweating *inside* my skin. Like I have to change my flesh or I'm going to be this sickly, weird, uncomfortable *thing* forever.

Not even halfway through my shift, I start getting excited at the thought of seeing Art. Like *sexually* excited. I'm fucking throbbing. I suddenly feel like I'm a drug addict. Like Art is my drug again. But this time it feels like I need to stop seeing him or I'll overdose and die.

So I text Arshad. My dad. The recovered addict. And ask if he can talk.

art

When Zee texts me she's meeting her dad after work, I text her that I'd like to go. She says she should go alone, which makes me think she's seeing Cam even after we had sex.

It isn't even seven. If I have to stay in this motel room, alone, for the next four or five or forever hours while my brain tries not to imagine them together, I will probably self-combust.

I don't know what to do.

My heart tells me this is the price I must pay for the girl of my destiny.

My brain asks what price is Zee paying if I sit here all night waiting for her.

So my hands text Jayden.

ME

I want to see you tonight

Wow, I'm so demanding. He'll probably love it.

JAYDEN

You're so demanding.

I love it

And then I'm running from the motel to my house.

Yes, me, running!

Why am I running?!

Because I'm going to steal my dad's car and drive to Winnetka to see a boy.

After I shower, I have no idea what to wear. I had seven weeks to plan what I'd wear for my first date with Zee, I've had less than an hour for my date with Jayden. Not that this is a date.

It's totally a date.

I'm going on a date with a boy.

With a boy who is a better dresser than me. (Crucial clarification: Has a better wardrobe, not is a better dresser.) But this point is not a small one. I don't want to be in knockoff versions of what he might be wearing. So I decide I'll dress more casually. Jeans, a gray oxford, and my now faithful Bullboxer shoes. I look good. (I always look good. Ha.) But I look like I don't care if I look good.

When I go to grab the keys from the kitchen, my dad is standing in front of the refrigerator.

"You didn't go shopping this week," he says without looking at me.

"I'll go tomorrow."

"There's nothing to eat."

"Do you want me to run out now? I'll have to use the car." Yes, I'll be late, but expertly so.

"Yeah. Taco Bell," he says, and I don't have the time to argue against my father's horrible diet choices. Thirty seconds later, I'm in the car, driving like I do it all the time. I order my dad an obscene amount of tacos and burritos and nachos, drive home, put it on the kitchen counter, and yell, "It's in here, I have to run!"

And I'm back out the door before he can ask where I'm going. I would have told him if he asked. I would have said, "I'm going out on a date with a boy because the girl I love is with the boy she wishes she loved instead of me." The look on his face would have been worth it alone. But who am I kidding? My dad would never have asked.

It takes me almost an hour to get to Winnetka, which is basically the fanciest suburb in all of Chicago. Jayden, of course, lives in a mansion across the street from Lake Michigan. I text him when I'm parked on the street outside. He texts back:

JAYDEN

In one minute, you'll meet your destiny.

But don't fall in love with me . . . for at least an hour ;)

Who texts stuff like that?

Me. I know.

Being on the receiving end is intimidating! I'm never doing it to Zee again. (Yes, I also know Zee will hate me if she finds out where I am so I'm never telling her and I'm not thinking about her again until I'm on my way back to Riverbend. I'm a horrible person. But she was a horrible person first! Ugh.)

Ten minutes after the one minute is up, Jayden exits his front door. After a brief, distant moment under the front porch light, he falls into darkness as he approaches the car. Should I get out and open the door for him? Who's the boy when it's two boys? Me. I think. I don't know. I've only been (maybe) gay for an hour. I get out just because and move around to the curb.

Jayden descends the last stairs from his property onto the sidewalk and into the faint gleam of the streetlamp. He's wearing a long-sleeve coral T-shirt, and designer jeans (in fact, they may be girls' jeans; in fact, they might be the exact *same* design I bought for Zee), and he bought them just big enough so they fall low over both his hips. I'd be shocked if he was wearing underwear. His shoes are gray canvas, white-soled, expensive. His walk is impossible not to watch, and his big eyes pull me into him even as I stand in the same place.

I am definitely the boy.

He holds out his hand. I take it in mine for a handshake, sort of, but I'm ninety-four point two percent sure he gently caresses my palm with one of his fingers as he says, "Hello, Mr. Art. I'm Mr. Jayden." Then he winks. Winks! Who winks at someone the first time they meet? Yes, me, I know. I'm being hilarious because it's distracting me from my impending nervous breakdown.

"Hi," I manage, and smile, or maybe I just stare. And then I say, "Ready?" which is so boring but I've entered a world where I don't understand the language or the rules.

"Yes, darling," Jayden says, but his eyes say, *I want to have sex with you.* Oh my god, who looks at someone on the first date with eyes that say that?! (And you can't say me because even I have never done that!) I open the passenger door for him, and he slides inside. I walk around the back of the car because I have to adjust my, um, penis in my pants because I have an erection. *So* glad I wore jeans. But, oh my god, how does this happen from just watching him walk down the sidewalk! Ugh.

"Where are we going?" I ask as I start the car. I think (no, I know) he's wearing perfume, and I think (no, I know) I like it.

"You pick," he says.

"Oh, okay," I say, and of course I should have had a place picked out but I don't. . . . "There's a diner in Morton Grove called Seven Sisters that my grandmother used to take us to when we stayed at her place."

Jayden levels his eyes at me. "A diner? In Morton Grove? That your grandmother frequented?"

I feel like the least sophisticated person ever born.

"I know a brilliant place downtown. We'll go there and you'll love it. Just take Sheridan to Lake Shore Drive."

"Where's Sheridan?"

"I just moved here, *Arthur*—you're supposed to be giving *me* the tour."

Um . . .

"I'm kidding. Just take a right up at the next street and we'll run into it," he says, and I do exactly that. I'm officially terrified of being less than he wants me to be.

Once we're on the all-important Sheridan Road, Jayden says, "I'll say this once, and then I want you to forget I said it. Deal?"

Deal?

"You're even more attractive in person. Thankfully, I've sworn off sex and love until college or we'd probably do something irresponsible."

I emit some kind of never-heard-before under-my-breath chuckle.

"You're new at this, aren't you?"

"At what?"

"At *this*," he says, and squeezes my leg just above my knee. Oh my god, I'm going to crash and kill us both.

"I'm . . . I was . . . I thought I was straight."

"I'm sure you did." He's being sarcastic. But I must be sweating sincerity, because he follows up with, "Oh, my, you're serious."

Yes.

"So you've *never* been with a boy?" He has that sex look in his eyes again. I can't function properly when he does that!

"No . . ."

"When did you have your precious moment of self-discovery?"

When he sent that picture? When I liked that Zee looked like a boy? When I looked at porn today? I cannot speak, which is totally normal for Gay Art. Very bizarre how Straight Art was much more eloquent.

"You are this gorgeous vision of a boy, untouched, untainted. If I met you in New York, I'd probably insist on corrupting you at once, but I've decided that Chicago Me is going to be a born-again virgin. So we can both be virgins. That way we can suffer together." He squeezes my leg again, but this time much higher.

ZEE

I meet Arshad back at The Forest Café. I know I said I wouldn't go back, but, fuck, whatever, I'm too desperate to be stubborn.

It's even weirder at night. If that's possible. The ceiling has those glowing stars kids put in their rooms except these stars are giant and feel like they're three-dimensional and about to fall on your head. Colorful spotlights swim back and forth from some unseeable corners, which makes it feel like I'm in a nightclub with trees. It's Thursday in the suburbs and this place only serves coffee but people are moving with that weekend party energy, that alcohol-fueled buzz, appearing and disappearing down paths I don't remember seeing when I was here last.

Arshad is waiting for me this time. At one of the booths. He looks at peace with this trippy place despite being so old. Maybe that's because he's a drug dealer. But I don't know if I can afford to care how he makes his money if I can't get Michael to give me what's mine.

"This place is really weird," I say to him as I sit down, and I can't believe I'm judging anything weird after some of the kinky stuff Art and I did in the motel room.

"I like weird," he says, with a smile. "It feels more honest than not weird."

He likes to say fancy crap sometimes. Whatever. A waitress comes over. At least I think she's a waitress because she just put two teacups down. But she's fortysomething, beautiful, wearing a red suit. She's Asian. Or Latina. Or maybe both. She's tall, taller than me, and super feminine. Her lipstick is as bright apple red as her suit.

"Zee, this is Stephanie," Arshad says, and I guess he's friends with her. I sort of say hello but then she lingers. It's odd. I feel like they have some secret. I can't look at either of them.

"Maybe later," Arshad tells her, and then she walks away.

Once I'm sure she's gone, I smell the tea. "What's in it?"

"Just tea." He laughs. "Herbal tea from Vietnam. It doesn't even have caffeine."

I sip it. Burns my tongue. That's why I never order tea—always too hot or not enough. Never drinkable. Why am I wasting my time thinking about this? Because I don't want to bring up Art. Why the hell did I think I could bring up my kinky sex stuff with a dad I don't know when I doubt I could have even mentioned this to my mom?

"Zee . . ." he starts, after my long silence. "The advantage of almost killing yourself with drug addiction is you can never again fool yourself into self-righteous judgment of anyone else."

I have to replay what he said to even understand it. Then, when I finally get it, it actually makes me want to talk about my Art addiction even less. People always judge, Arshad! I'm judging myself right now! But I have shown up and I suppose I need to pretend I have something to talk about, so I say, "Yeah, well, I've been living in a shitty motel for five days because I can't stay with Michael because he's a creep and he won't give me the money my mom left."

"That's a very difficult strain he has put you under."

Fuck. "Quit it with your therapist talk. Just not in the mood." But that overloads his brain. He has to do his eye-closing thing. I feel like an asshole. "Never mind, sorry, talk however you talk."

"No, I see how I speak can be off-putting. . . ."

"It's fine, Arshad! I'm being a bitch."

"You're not. . . ."

"Yes, I am! Let me admit I'm a bitch. I don't know why I told you the Michael thing. Maybe I just wanted to *bitch* to someone." He laughs. It's nice to have my dad laugh at my joke. Fuck him, though.

Then he says, "Would it be okay if I contacted Michael? I imagine I could convince him that he has misread you and the situation and that it's best to quickly give you what is yours."

Man, he spoke well, but, "No, no, I don't want you talking to Michael. He doesn't like you and he'll say racist crap and you don't deserve that."

"Zee, I can handle whatever Michael has to say."

I think for a second. "Maybe but let me first see if I can solve this without getting you involved."

"If that's what you think is best."

"Yeah . . . I do."

"Okay."

I'm starting to feel comfortable with him, which makes me uncomfortable. "I need to go," I say, even though I don't. I was never going to talk to Arshad about Art anyway. *Art.* Jesus. I can't decide what I want more: him to be naked in bed when I get home or him to be gone.

Arshad says, "Hold on," reaches into his pocket, and pulls out another stack of hundreds. "Will you take this money just in case of an emergency?"

"I don't want your money."

"Then consider it a loan you can pay back, in this life or the next." He does a tiny grin. For the first time, I see what my mom might have seen.

I almost ask him if he's a drug dealer, but I can't be *that* much of a bitch. So I eye the cash. Don't be stubborn, Zee. "Yeah, all right." I take the money and stand.

He stands as well, holds out his hand. "Thank you for meeting me, Zee."

"You just gave me a bunch of money. I owe you, Arshad."

"You will never owe me a thing."

"Yeah, when you say stuff like that, these warning lights go off in my head that you're going to turn out to be the asshole I want you to be."

And, fuck, there's this *look* in his eyes. But I can't deal with any revelations by him tonight, so I say, "Later," and I'm gone.

When I get to my car, I expect fifty texts from Art.

There are none.

Instead, there's this:

CAM

I'm waiting for you outside your house.

I'll wait all night for you

art

Jayden takes us to this multifloor more-club-than-restaurant restaurant called Maroon, which has maroon walls, maroon velvet chairs, maroon velvet couches, and maroon floors. The ceilings are more of a fire-engine red, but that just reminds you everything else is maroon, so maybe that's the point.

The host is as pretty as Jayden, wearing skintight black pants, a black shirt, and a black bow tie. He leads us past the main stairs to an electric-candle-lit circular staircase that leads to a small room with backless couches and small tables between them. The host leaves the tiniest menus I've ever seen and then disappears through a door that a second ago was a wall.

"This is amazing," I say, because it is but *also* because my senses are on overload and I can't think clearly enough to say anything else.

"You like when I show you things?" Jayden says, and oh-my-god, he's seducing me again.

"Maybe," I say, and this is the first time I feel like I'm playing back.

"If I was sensitive, I'd be stressing over why you haven't told me how I look tonight. But I'm not sensitive at all, so you don't need to tell me." And when he says that, Jayden means he is probably the most sensitive person in this dimension.

"You look . . ." Does he want me to say handsome? Beautiful? Ugh, this is hard. *I'm hard.* I'm so crass! Embrace it! So I say, ". . . exciting to *every* part of me." Ooh, there's the old me.

"That wasn't bad. I might have even liked it."

"Five points for me." Time for my movie-star smile.

"Yes, five points for you. Now you're only behind by nine hundred and ninety-five."

The waiter arrives. He doesn't have a shirt on. If I had that many muscles, I might not wear a shirt either. Jayden says, "We'll share the cheese plate. And

I'll have a pear cider martini. My man's driving, so he can't drink with me tonight." Jayden flashes a fake ID before the waiter asks. It works. The waiter leaves, and Jayden says, "I assume I assumed correctly that you don't have a fake ID?"

"You did."

"In New York, you barely need it. But here, with these Midwest puritans, I quickly determined it best to show it like you've been showing it for ten years."

God, Jayden is effortlessly exquisite. He's seventeen with a twenty-seven-year-old's soul. He's what I always thought I was only to now realize I have a lot of work to do.

"So, my gorgeous virgin, since you were straight until yesterday. What did you tell yourself when you somehow never liked a girl 'quite like that'?"

Oooh, this feels dangerous. So I say, "I did like a girl . . . once."

"Beyoncé and Lady Gaga don't count."

"Her name is, was, *is* Zee." I immediately regret saying her name.

"Oh, mmmmh, I'm feeling jealous and I *never* feel jealous . . ." This is doubtful. He goes on, ". . . but I also feel oddly turned on. Was she like your *girlfriend*?"

No, she is more. And as soon as I think this, I ache to be with Zee in our motel bed, cuddling and watching a dumb movie, and not in this fancy, fabulous club with beautiful Jayden.

But I say, "No . . . we . . ."

"Oh, please don't tell me you kissed her. PLEASE don't tell me you had sex with her. I'll never be able to erase that from my memory."

I'm with Jayden to forget about Zee, and all he's doing is making me miss her more.

"Now you have to tell me or I won't be able to think about anything else."

I sit up straight, and in the most mature, confident voice I can find within me, I say, "You're the first boy I've been on a date with. . . . I'd rather talk about you." I know as soon as this leaves my mouth that no matter how many points I was behind in our little game before this, I am in the lead now.

"Dammit," he says as the waiter delivers his drink.

I wait.

Jayden takes a sip, does that vixen thing with his eyes as he whispers over the edge of his glass, "I fell in love just now even though I promised myself I wouldn't."

Later, when the bill comes, I grab it because I do.

He says, "But *I'm* supposed to pay. Our bet, remember?"

"You lost on purpose." I wink.

"Yes, of course I did, but you're just hoping paying the bill and acting all manly will get you laid."

The moment I park outside his house, Jayden says, "Oh, my, you *actually* took me home."

"I, uh . . ."

"Let's *go* somewhere." And he accentuates the go by rounding his lips and holding the vowel while *at the same time* grabbing my upper-upper-upper inner thigh. Subtlety is not his strength. Maybe that's the advantage of being gay. It's two boys, and most boys always want sex. So what's the point of playing hard to get if no one would believe it? Except, as we've established, I'm not most boys and I *am* truly hard to get.

So I just sit there and stare at him and, oh-my-god, I'm brooding, aren't I? I totally am.

Then he says, "I want you to kiss me so badly right now I feel sick to my stomach."

I laugh.

"That wasn't meant to be funny!"

"Okay . . . one kiss."

"No, now I don't want to," he lies.

So I say, "Jayden, shhh," and lean across the center console and—

Wait!

Oh-thank-god you stopped. We shouldn't kiss him!

But . . . maybe we should.

What about Zee?!

She's kissing Cam.

Yes, but—

Shhh.

Using both my hands, I cradle his face in my palms, and pull him gently into me. I keep my eyes open because I know he's going to keep his eyes open, at least until I hypnotize him with my magic, which will be three-two-one, yes, there, he closes his eyes and melts under my hold.

No tongue, because this kiss is meant to linger, not excite, and I keep it short because I know this will leave him thinking about me for days. God, I should probably teach a master's class at Harvard on how to kiss someone.

When I pull back, he can't hide his wonderment. "Okay, I'll marry you."

I laugh, because that's what I would have said. Then I say, "Let me walk you to your door."

I get out, help him out of the car, and walk him to the bottom step of his porch. He's alternating between joy at having found me and panic that I'm leaving. "Come inside. . . . We don't have to do anything. Just hold each other . . . naked."

"You're funny . . . but I have to go." I kiss him on the cheek and float away.

When I turn on the car and see the time, I'm sure Zee will beat me back to the motel and instantaneously know where I was and who I was with.

ZEE

Cam's waiting for me outside Michael's house.

Shit.

All I want to do is go back to the motel and get in bed with Art, but if I do that, Cam will know I never went home. This double-life crap sucks. On the way to Michael's, I almost text Art that I'm going to be even later than I thought, but I don't want him to think I'm doing what I am actually doing.

Need to:

Resolve Cam fast.

Be back at motel before Art suspects anything.

art

On my drive back to Riverbend, I don't text Zee—she would know just by my typed words!—but I don't respond to Jayden's eighteen thousand texts either because Cinderella Art must not-so-magically transform from Gay Art to Straight Art by the time I arrive at the motel room.

I drop my dad's car off at the house and then run—twice in one day!—back to the motel, getting into the room just after eleven and Zee's . . .

Not there.

ZEE

He's asleep, looking like the innocent, rosy-cheeked kid I first met years ago. Is that what I fell for? Not the stubbled sports hero he is now?

"Cam . . ." I say as I knock on his car window. He stirs awake and tries to open the door, but I shut it on him. "Roll down the window."

"I wan-ted to see youuu," he says, exhaustion slurring his words.

"I know. But I . . . can't. I need you to go home."

He's too tired to fight. He nods, turns his head. But then . . . he turns back. "Kiss me," he says.

No.

"One kiss and I'll go. If you don't kiss me, I'm staying here all night."

He thinks this is romantic.

"One kiss, Zee."

No.

"Then I'll go."

So I can get back to Art, I kiss Cam for what I promise myself will be the last time.

art

Zee is probably kissing Cam right now, or more—oh-my-god, please not more—but that is maybe, probably, still better than her discovering I was kissing—but not more!—a boy.

After I've showered and gotten into bed, Zee's still not home. AAAH! So I text Jayden that I had a wonderful time and that I'm off to sleep. But *he* texts me new pictures of himself. He looks gorgeous in each. And I get an erection before I can even tell my penis not to. I never masturbate. You're thinking, *Don't lie, every teenage boy masturbates.* You forget that I am Art Adams, one of a kind in all time and space. But I start masturbating to the photos because won't Zee be suspicious if I have a hard-on? Maybe, I don't know! Maybe I just masturbate because it feels really good to touch myself and look at Jayden's photographs. But then he texts me another photo with the message:

JAYDEN

I'll even let you call me Zee

I knew I shouldn't have told him her name! And seeing her name on my phone makes me think of her, which makes me think of her on top of me, so I close my eyes and, ugh, orgasm to the memory of a girl an hour after I kissed my first boy.

Teenage Boys Who Masturbate But Lie to Even Themselves and Say They Don't

Teenage Boys Who Masturbate and Brag About It

Me (Until Right This Second)

Teenage Boys Who See No Point in Masturbating Because They Think Sex Without Love Is Meaningless

Teenage Boys Who Masturbate and Prefer Not to Talk About It

ZEE

I don't get back to the motel room until close to midnight. Art is there, asleep, curled tightly into a ball. Almost at once, I feel Art's one-of-a-kind energy spin off his sleeping body and into mine, awakening my brain, my chest, my groin. I decide, with certain finality, that we should never, ever be apart.

So I lean over him, down close to his ear, ready to whisper something I know will make him excited to see me . . .

. . . but then I notice his phone edging out from under the pillow. Weird. Yeah. I should ignore it. But. I can't. So I reach over him, gently sliding the phone out and lifting it up. I shouldn't look. What could I find? But I shouldn't look anyway. But I can't not look now. I know his password because he's told me everything—so why I am looking? Is it because of what's happened the past twenty-four hours? Do I blame him for the weird stuff we did together?

All this is bullshit, but whatever, it's "too late," as Art would say, the phone is on, open to a text conversation. There are pictures. A boy. Not Art. *Jayden.* I hate that name. He's beautiful. More feminine than I could be after ten thousand makeovers.

"What are you doing?" A voice. Art's. He's awake. I lower the phone. Drop it onto the bed.

"Nothing."

"Were you going through my phone?" He's angry, still half-asleep, but sitting up, searching. Finds his phone.

"Who's Jayden?"

"Oh-my-god, Zee, you were going through my phone. . . ." He's crushed because he crushes easy. But it's different this time.

I'm pissed. I'm jealous. Jealous of how fucking gorgeous Jayden is. "WHO'S Jayden, ART?"

"You were with Cam!" He doesn't even deny it! (Neither do I.) And he's standing, searching for things. He's getting dressed. Packing his bag. Where does he think he's going?

"Was I just your beard or whatever?" I don't even mean that. I don't think. But everything's wrong. He's leaving and I'm not stopping him. "I'm not driving you anywhere."

"I need to go."

"It's midnight. You're not walking out of a shitty motel by yourself at midnight."

"You can't tell me what to do."

He stops at the door. He doesn't want to go. I should be nicer, make him stay, but I have to know, "*Who's* Jayden?"

Art can't look at me. Only down at the floor.

"Are you gay, Art?"

He looks up, tears starting. "I love *you,*" he says, but fuck you, I'm over your tears.

"No, you're gay. I knew it. And if you're gay, you can't love me. Which means you're the biggest fucking fraud I've ever met." That landed as hard as I wanted it to. He wobbles and then he's gone.

Part Nine

ROMANTIC FLUIDITY AT THE BEND

art

Pulling my suitcase behind me, I make the trip from motel to home for the second time tonight. I'm feeling so melancholy! I don't even know what that word really means, but I'm sure I'm feeling the most melancholy anyone has ever felt.

On the walk, my future world-renowned-artist self tries to convince me that I must experience these depths of total and complete self-loathing and misery so that I can have the material I'll need to become a future world-renowned artist. This sounds fair until I ask my future self if I'm gay and he falls annoyingly silent.

When I get home, it's just past one a.m. After getting some water for myself, I peek in to check on my dad. On cue, he farts in his sleep. My dad may be a fiftysomething, wifeless, unemployed insurance salesman who now sleeps on a gas-filled couch, but at least he knows who he is.

I lean into Abigail's room—yes, I am that desperate for human interaction—but she's not there. Since she and Cam are finished, I don't know where she could be at this hour, but wherever it is, I'm sure she's being very mature and responsible. And when I say that, I mean there's a better-than-average chance that all of Riverbend will be engulfed in flames by sunrise.

When I wake up Friday morning (you know, the first morning after the girl I love dumped me for maybe, possibly, being gay), I hear the strangest sound: My dad is upstairs. He has escaped the den! Freed himself from its tentacles of zombification!

After I dress, I step out of my room and find him pulling the suitcases down from the attic. "Morning, Dad. Doing some cleaning? Need any help?"

"I got a job," he says between heavy breaths, descending the attic ladder.

"That's amazing!" My enthusiasm wakes the hungover mess that is Abigail. She emerges, barely human, from her room before bitching:

"Why are you two making so much noise so early in the morning!?" The fumes of last night's alcohol consumption swirl through the hall at ninety-nine miles per hour.

"It's almost eleven a.m., sister," I say. Abigail has largely abstained from the Adams family curse of chemical dependence. But I guess that was when she could indulge in her Cam dependence.

She flips me off as she cries out, "DAD! Can you please do whatever you're doing later?"

"Dad got a job, Abigail. Isn't that amazing?"

"Yes, because I need more clothes before school starts."

I ignore her, say to my father, "Let me buy everyone an early dinner at Fridays to celebrate."

He says, "No time, Art. We got a lot of work to do before we can go next week."

"Go where?" This panicked mini-me starts hyperventilating inside my heart.

"Your brother got me a job at Progressive, so we got to move to Ohio."

My father says this not looking at either Abigail or me. Casually, almost under his breath, as if it is no big deal. As if it is totally normal for us to move across the country. As if we haven't spent our entire lives in Riverbend, Illinois. As if all our friends and loves and everything weren't here. As if he did not just punch us both in the stomachs with his big, fat, hairy, selfish, heartless words.

Despite my soul being mortally wounded, I remain outwardly composed. Numb, silent, but composed.

Abigail?

"IF YOU THINK I'M MOVING TO FUCKING OHIO FOR MY SENIOR YEAR OF HIGH SCHOOL, YOU CAN FUCK YOURSELF, YOU FUCKING ASSHOLE!"

That shoots some life through my dad: He tosses one of the suitcases hard against the wall and outscreams Abigail's best scream ever: "DON'T YOU EVER FUCKING TALK TO ME LIKE THAT!"

Abigail screams incoherently back, then slams her bedroom door in his face. Though I just stand there as witness, quiet, my dad still feels I need yelling at.

"ART, DON'T JUST FUCKING STAND THERE! START PACKING UP THE HOUSE!"

"Okay, Dad." What else can I say? I'm just a tiny, stupid kid in a big, horrible world.

ZEE

For those first few hours trying to sleep alone in the motel room, I wake up every fucking five minutes. I'd keep hearing Art walk back in the door and I'd get excited that I'd get to kiss him. Or yell at him. Either would have done it for me.

When I finally do fall asleep for good, I end up sleeping late, until almost ten. When I wake up, I have maybe five seconds of thinking Art is next to me on the bed. I can feel him. I swear. Then I turn over and he's not there and

fucking

pow

It hits me that he's gone. That whatever we were is over. Then

fucking

pow

I remember my mom's dead. For the first time since she died, the worst thing I think of when I wake up isn't that she's dead. It's that Art's gone. It makes me fucking hate Art for making me care more about him than her, even if it was only for five seconds.

I check my phone for a text from him anyway. Instead I find a group message from Pen that includes Iris. She asks if we're free for lunch or dinner today. Iris has responded with a *Can't do lunch, but dinner! Yes!* The exclamation mark is such a girl thing. I've always hated exclamation marks in texts. But I like that Iris did it. Never mind. I respond *Sure—off work at 7 tonight.* The girls then rocket a bunch of texts back and forth between each other deciding where we should go and I just type that I'm good for whatever they want.

I decide to look Iris up on Facebook, which I haven't signed into in months but what the hell. I know who she is because we've been in school together since junior high but we were never close and I never thought of her . . . never thought of her as what? Am I really serious about this?

Don't overthink this. I don't. I find her pictures. She's blond. I knew this. She's pretty. I knew this too. She dresses preppy, in pinks and oranges and bright whites. You know who she looks like? You know all those movies about the nerdy teenage boy who pines after the beautiful popular cheerleader except the cheerleader doesn't know he exists? (My mom's favorite was *Can't Buy Me Love*, which came out when she was a kid and she'd make me watch it with her every time she got dumped.) But then the nerdy boy proves himself worthy of her by doing her homework or beating up her mean boyfriend or something dumb like that and the movie ends up all happy and bullshitty with them an only-in-Hollywood couple. Well, anyway, that's who she looks like. A beautiful popular cheerleader straight out of a movie.

Except she's not a cheerleader and she doesn't have a mean boyfriend. And if there are nerds pining after her, they are wasting their time because she likes girls. And if you like girls, you don't like boys no matter how much of your homework they do.

Except I'm feeling like that nerdy boy right now. I fucking am. And I'm getting the urge to put my hands down between my legs for the first time since before my mom died. And it's from looking at pictures of a pretty blond girl even though I dumped Art last night for being gay.

art

My dad has scheduled the movers and U-Haul truck for Monday, three days from today. We will pile into his car on Tuesday, leaving Riverbend forever and ever and ever. I attempt a few more questions about it, but he just yells, telling me I'm making things difficult, so I help him start packing in silence. Move whatever he wants to move, throw out whatever he wants to throw out.

Abigail doesn't leave her room for hours, though she occasionally graces us with an "I FUCKING HATE YOU!" from behind her door. When we're taking a break in the kitchen, I hear the front door slam. I run out and watch Abigail slip into a car I don't recognize . . .

. . . but I do recognize the boy—or is he a man now?—behind the wheel. It's Will Safire. Yes, *that* Will Safire, Abigail's freshman-year boyfriend. Everyone remembers Will Safire for being the famous quarterback who took Riverbend within a touchdown thing of the state championship game three years ago. I remember him as the creepy senior dropping my fourteen-year-old sister off at two a.m. in clothes she hadn't left the house in. He dumped my sister the second he got some big scholarship, and did I mention Will Safire got kicked off his college team last season after an assault charge? So he's worse than just a creep. And my sister just ran off with him and three dudes that look exactly like him in his backseat. I sincerely think this might be the last I ever see of her. If she doesn't somehow get herself killed, Abigail will find a way to stay in Riverbend, or with Mom somewhere, and I'll be shipped off to Ohio with Dad and Alex. Two people I have nothing in common with besides our DNA. Yay.

The only person I want to tell I'm leaving is Zee, but then I think how dramatic it will be for her to show up to school and look for me without admitting she's looking for me and then someone will tell her, *Art moved to*

Ohio. And she'll have to excuse herself, go to a bathroom stall, burst into tears, and yearn for me until the end of time. How great of a scene will that be in the movie about our great love story? Except there won't be a movie because our great love story might have been just a few bizarre days in a motel room and then us never seeing each other again.

ZEE

So, yeah, masturbating while thinking about Iris makes me think about Art and what a hypocrite I am but I also start thinking about Iris and Art at the same time and *then* about Art, Iris, *and* that boy on his phone—*Jayden*—and I'm not sure if I'm getting more excited at all the images in my head or more disgusted at how royally fucked-up I am.

So I give up before I orgasm, check out of the motel, and decide I'm never going back. That my week there with Art was this *thing* I needed to get out of me, this phase, this experiment, this I-fucking-don't-know-what, but whatever it was, I'm never doing it again. Not with him, not with anyone.

Once I have my coffee, I have nothing to do except think about how I'm homeless again. So I text Michael because I need to unleash some venom:

ME

Need my money

He doesn't respond right away and so I fire another:

ME

Or I'm telling my dad to get involved

That feels good. Yeah. Feels good to have an adult in my corner for the first time since my mom died. But then I get this:

MICHAEL

Have you met your father's "boyfriend"?

My dad felt like the straightest of straight guys. Either way,

ME

I don't care if he's gay. Only bigots do.

MICHAEL

You should care and you should care
that your dad probably didn't show you this

Attached beneath that is a picture of a document. After pulling over to the side of the road, I zoom in on the image:

It's a birth certificate.

My birth certificate.

My birthday, my birth hospital, my mother's name, Arshad's name . . . and . . .

My birth name: Zhila Gholbani.

Zhila.

My real name.

Not Rebecca Kendrick, daughter of Katie Kendrick.

Zhila Gholbani, daughter of Arshad Gholbani, the man that never wanted me to exist.

I am not me.

art

While working the lunch shift at Fridays on a Friday, I gaze at every girl and boy I find even the slightest bit attractive and try to determine who I would want to be stranded on a deserted island with.

In the end, I decide I'll refuse to be stranded on any island unless it's with Zee.

(And I'll need cell service on the island so Jayden can still send me pictures.)

I know this is not how this game is usually played but it's how I'm playing so shhhhh.

On one of my breaks, I text Zee.

ME

I miss my not-very-platonic wife

I know this is not what you text someone you are super mad at! She went through *my* phone and said the most horrible, hurtful things in the history of horrible, hurtful things, but, ugh, I don't care. I still love her. Even if I'm gay, I know she'll be the only person I love until I die.

But by the time my shift ends, Zee still hasn't texted me back. And suddenly I feel like I've been thrown into this vast dark ocean, and I'll drown in it if I don't find something, someone, to rescue me soon. So I text Carolina.

ME

Jayden

She would know.

CAROLINA

I knew it ;)

ME

WHEN did you know?

CAROLINA

I always thought, but it wasn't until we kissed that I knew for sure.

Ugh. I like being more complex.

ME

What's the latest on "As the Trevor World Turns"?

CAROLINA

He got back with Betsy. I hate him.

ME

Sorry :(I love you

CAROLINA

If only you were straight ;)

I am. Was. Will be again? I'm a disaster. I'll just confess:

ME

I had sex with Zee

CAROLINA

How??!?!

ME

Penis was inserted into vagina

I'm hilarious.

CAROLINA

Did you like it?

ME

I loved it . . .

I love her . . .

Wasn't going to dive into all the kinky, weird stuff over text.

CAROLINA

You're never boring, Art ;)

I should ask Carolina if we could hang out, or go to a movie. Something safe with someone I have zero sexual chemistry with.

Instead,

ugggggggggggggh,

I text Jayden.

ZEE

Go to CrossFit because I need to sweat every memory of everyone I've ever met out of me. When I park, I notice two people making out in the car next to me. Weird but whatever. But then when I get out of my truck, I actually see their faces.

Taylor . . . and Bryan.

Jesus—IS EVERYONE IN MY LIFE GAY?!

They leap out of the car two seconds later, and Bryan runs up alongside me, saying, "Hey, Zee, let me tell Art about Taylor, is that okay?"

Don't tell him I'll probably never talk to Art again because it's none of his fucking business. "Yeah," I say, because I have to say something.

"And thanks for talking to Cam. He actually called me, and we had a long talk. He's a good person. And you inspired me, so I'm going to play football. That's so strange to say! Bryan Colucci, football player. But thank you. Taylor thinks I'll be good, but it doesn't even matter. I just think I need to do it and fuck being afraid of who I am."

"Cool," I say, and he can tell I'm in a bitchy mood and probably will be until the planet blows the fuck up.

After class, I get a text from Art.

That weird, nervous sweat flashes through me the second I see his name. For a moment, I think I'm excited, turned on, yeah, but then I think about the picture of that boy Jayden. That double life Art will lead. Somehow I decide that this means if I go back to Art, and whatever weirdness we did together, that I will have to lead a double life too. I'll have to become Zhila Gholbani.

And sure-fucking-enough, Arshad texts me right then:

ARSHAD

Zee—talk to Michael?

ME

Don't you mean Zhila?

ARSHAD

I didn't know how to address it.

This is my failing.

But can we please talk so that I can explain?

Nope. Done with you.

But I need to text someone and it can't be Arshad or Art or my mom—'cuz she's fucking dead—so I text Cam:

ME

That was cool of you to talk to Bryan. Thanks.

CAM

When can I see you?

ME

I don't know

CAM

Can we go to that Benedict dude's party together?

No, but I say,

ME

Sure.

art

Just like last night, I pick up Jayden at his place in Winnetka. As he descends from his mansion, the moment his eyes find me, he projects this hypersexuality that tells my penis to tell my brain to do whatever Jayden says and whenever he says it forever.

"Good evening," he says as he steps into me, and with a very confident, strong hand takes me by the back of the head and pulls me in for a kiss that destabilizes my footing on the earth below. As he pulls back, just a bit, his eyes still inches from mine, he uses this deep-throated whisper to say, "I need you to be so turned on that you never go more than ten minutes without thinking of me again."

"Okay," because yes, duh, never again.

ZEE

For our dinner, Pen and Iris eventually settle on a restaurant called The Unknown Artist, which is on the north side of Gladys Park, less than a block from The Forest Café.

The Unknown Artist is tiny and all random, tiny nooks with odd-shaped tables in each one. Framed handwritten poems and sketches on every inch of every wall. Pen and Iris are already there, and as I approach their table, I realize this is the first time I've ever gone and hung out with just girls. It's always been me and my mom, or me and Cam, or me and the CrossFit crew. Yeah, I realize this is sort of a not-so-blind date, but that feels less new than me having actual friends who are girls.

"Hey," I say as I sit down next to Pen. Had to choose one side and it would have been weird to presume I should sit next to Iris. Pen looks like she always looks—black clothes and black boots and black makeup and even a black nose ring today—but seeing her somewhere besides the pizzeria or school makes her feel like a three-dimensional person for the first time. Iris is wearing white pants—aren't they called capris or something?—and I think the same frilly tank top that Art bought me. But hers is this light pink color and it looks good on her, natural, not like she's playing dress-up. I'm wearing my cargos and hoodie because if I'm going to be into girls, she's got to like me for who I am. That sounds stupid. Never mind. Iris is nervous, fidgety, and can't look me in the eyes, so I try to be extra nice and say to her, "Thanks for asking me to hang out." This type of thing usually feels super false coming out of my mouth but I don't mind it today. Maybe, if I'm really a lesbian, I'll be a better person.

"I've been telling Iris," Pen starts, "that I want to hang out with more interesting people more often, and we both decided that you're interesting." Both of them giggle a bit, not fake but nothing I would ever do, and I feel like such a guy. Not just a guy, but a guy who has no idea how to speak girl. Art would know how to speak girl. I miss him. I hate him.

"Well . . . thanks, I think," I say, because I want to talk instead of hate Art.

I can see Iris work up the nerve to speak, and then she says, "How have you been?" She says it in that way that you know she's asking about my mom and, listen, I know she lost her mom and suddenly my heart is ten times the size, which means it hurts ten times as much. Am I gonna fucking cry in front of these girls ten seconds after I sit down? I am.

"Sorry," I say as I try to wipe the tears from my eyes. Penelope loops her arms through my left arm, and Iris leans over and takes hold of that same hand. This is what girlfriends do. They hug. They console. They're good at it. "Thanks . . . yeah, wow, just when you think you're over crying about it, boom."

"It's been eight years since my mom died," Iris says, "and I still cry about it. At least one good sob a month."

"So you're saying it's gonna suck forever?" I say, smiling through my tears.

"Yep, that's exactly what I'm saying." Iris squeezes my hand and smiles with me. It's nice. She's like a girl Art.

art

Jayden directs me downtown again, this time using the Kennedy Expressway. We park on a not-so-clean and not-so-safe street west of the Kennedy and then we go down an even less clean and less safe alley, where a woman as tall as Cam but with bigger biceps sits on a stool in front of a stairway that, probably, leads directly to the afterlife.

Jayden smiles, says, "Hiya, Sam," only Sam doesn't flinch, she might not even be breathing, and we walk on by her and down the steps until I'm sure I've seen the last of the living.

Though my imagination wasn't that wrong, the stairs lead to a small crowded dance club with a big bar. The lighting is cheap and sparse, purposely so, the floor mysteriously sticky, and I cling to Jayden's hand out of fear of getting lost. I feel like a small child at a grown-up party. Besides slowing every few steps to rub his butt into my crotch—which shouldn't be so enjoyable!—he leads us directly to the bar, where he orders the same martini he did on Friday.

"You're not going to drink with me, are you?"

"No," I say as I pay for his drink.

"I think you're afraid of exploring new things." He takes a sip and again flawlessly performs his seduction-over-the-edge-of-the-glass routine.

Mmmmh. Since I understand all subtleties of human behavior, I understand that Jayden is trying to shame me into drinking with him so that *he* won't feel shame for drinking to numb *his* fears. Straight Art was obsessed with being a one-of-a-kind force in the universe and would point this out, but Gay Art is just another typical teenage boy who doesn't want to screw up his chance at getting his penis some action, so I'm going to just nod and shrug.

No.

No?

No, Gay Art has had twenty-four hours of being boring. That's enough.

"Jayden . . ." I lock eyes with him.

"Oooh, you're being so intense."

"I'm never, ever going to drink with you. My family more or less are almost all drunks or stoners, so I have no desire to be like them. And I don't know what your family life is like but I know no sixteen-year-old searches out places like this so they can have pear cider martinis unless their family is more or less horrible too."

Still got it. Ha.

Jayden's sexual smirk fades as his eyes fill with tears. He can't find words to respond, probably because he's torn about whether he wants to insult me or ask me to marry him again.

So I say, because Straight Art and Gay Art have united to form Super Art!, "You should know that you and *only* you could have made me confront and explore my attraction to boys so fast and furiously."

He still can't or won't speak, but he does form this tiny, wounded, lovely smile on his lips. And then he manages, "Hug me?" in this delicate, young voice. And so I hug him, and despite the crowded, dark bar, it feels like we are all alone.

"Want to get out of here?" I say, and, oh, my gosh, I sound like such a dude I don't even recognize my own voice. Jayden nods as I take him by the hand and lead us back to the world above.

ZEE

Dinner with Iris and Pen is nice. I never quite feel comfortable. Part of me is trying to be their friend, part of me is trying to figure out if I want to kiss Iris or not.

Toward the end, Pen asks, "So . . . you and Cam Callahan . . . are you dating now?" She looks at Iris as she asks this. Because she's asking for Iris? Probably, right?

"I don't know," I say. Because that's true. I don't really want to see him or kiss him. But I also feel like you can't spend every day from the time you're eleven until seventeen wanting a boy to love you and then as soon as he shows interest run the other way. I owe him and us more time, don't I? They don't say anything to my "I don't know," which feels like they're waiting for me to explain but fuck that, so I ask Pen, "You and Benedict seem like you're going to get married."

"Yeah, we will. But we're freaks."

Iris adds, "Freaks in a super-awesome way." Damn, Iris just radiates kindness. Like my mother. Am I thinking about kissing a girl because she reminds me of my mother?! I'm more messed up than I thought. I try to shake my brain free of judgmental crap and ask Iris, "You seeing someone?"

"Me?" she says as if I wasn't looking right at her. And, for the first time, she looks *right at me.* Holds my eyes in hers. Blue eyes, long lashes, tiny freckles beneath them. Man, it's peaceful looking at her so directly.

"Yeah . . ." I say.

"No, I'm not seeing anyone." And, yeah.

The bill comes. Pen pays. Then she says, "Have you guys ever been to The Forest Café? It's just down the street, and it's fascinating. Want to get a coffee and talk some more?"

"Yes, that sounds great," Iris says.

And fuck me, I don't want to go there, but I don't want to ditch the only girls that I've ever been remotely interested in being friends with, so I say, "Yeah, sure."

We don't even move our cars since it's so close, but on the walk, Pen gets a call. It's the pizzeria. She needs to go in and work. So she says to Iris and me, "But you two should go. I'll text you later. Zee, can you drive Iris back to Riverbend?" And then she leaves.

Was this part of their plan? To leave me and Iris alone?

Iris says, probably reading my brooding face, "We don't have to go. I totally understand if you want to come back when Pen can stay with us."

"No . . . let's go."

art

I take Jayden to Seven Sisters, the diner in Morton Grove that my grandmother would take us to when I was a kid. When he sees where we've gone, he says, "If two obviously gay teenagers go into this obviously straight white Republican stronghold, everyone's going to stare."

I think before I speak. (It happens from time to time!) Then I say, "Let them stare."

Jayden shakes his head. "God, I hate when you act all confident and manly."

"You mean you love it."

"Yes, darling, obviously." He leans over and kisses me on the cheek and—AND!—grabs my penis through my jeans. "And you love that."

We order french fries (aka the vegetarian's secret weapon) and tell each other our life stories. The short version of his is that his parents got divorced when he was young, after his mother got sick of his father's affairs. His mother had a fancy Wall Street job, so she didn't need his money or his drama. His dad married another rich woman, moved to Miami, and is rarely heard from. His mother moved them here in May, when she became CEO of some big Chicago-based bank. Since she's off making millions, he and his twin sister, Allie, have been raised by a rotating army of nannies. Allie's the jock (who plays travel soccer with Carolina), and Jayden knew he was gay before he could tie his own shoes.

Afterward, halfway through the drive to his place, I reach over and take his hand in mine.

"You're good," he says.

"What do you mean?"

"You'll see." At the next stoplight, he turns my head toward his and kisses me and, oh my god, he's devouring me like Zee does. Sucking my lips between his teeth, tongue deep into my mouth, penetrating me with—just let me say it!—his passion.

I only can break from his control after getting honked at by the car behind me when the light turns green. But at the next stoplight, he does it again. And I let him. And I love it again. There are probably five hundred lights between Morton Grove and Winnetka (I never exaggerate, ha), and so we rotate every few minutes between me driving him home and him driving me crazy. When we get near his house, he steers me down another street.

I say, "But your house is that—"

"Shhh," he says, and slides his hand over my thigh and over my groin. Jayden directs us to a park on the edge of Lake Michigan. We're the only car. It's very private. Oh my god, he wants to have sex. I'm *so* not ready. . . .

"Jayden . . ."

"Shhhh," he says again, and squeezes me down there again. "Let me give the pretty speech for a change." He takes a deep breath. "You are unlike anyone I've ever met, Art, and the way you see through me is terrifying and addicting. I know this is new. This being with a boy. So if you need to pretend I'm a girl to feel normal . . ."

"I don't want to pretend you're a girl . . ."

"You always say the right things—"

". . . but I'm not ready to have sex, Jayden."

"Are you ready for this?" he says and then kisses me, but only for a moment, before he lowers his head downward and oh. Oh. Oh. Ohhhhhhhh—

ZEE

Iris and I walk into The Forest Café, and even as she's in awe of all its trippiness, I'm alert with paranoia, convinced my dad is here even though that makes no sense. I don't want to sit in the main area, where we would be easily spotted, so I steer Iris to a small table tucked between a hill and a silver-bottomed goldfish pond.

"I'll go get us drinks. What do you want?"

"You don't have to—"

"I'd like to," I say. Jesus, I'm polite to girls.

"Then a mint tea, thank you."

"Be back in a minute." I maneuver to the center coffee bar, put in our orders. While I'm waiting, because I'm still flipping out that I'm going to see Arshad, I'm scanning every booth and table for his face. Nothing.

When I turn back to get the drinks, however, I see that beautiful waitress. Stephanie. The one who served Arshad and me last night. Even from across the width of the circular coffee bar, I can see her long nails. Not wanting her to see me, I grab our drinks and disappear down one of the paths.

"Thank you so much," Iris says as I hand her the tea and sit down next to her. I'm trying to be relaxed, to be present with her. But my anxiety is spiking, wrestling with Stephanie's presence, my dad's absence, and whether Iris is looking at me like she wants to kiss me.

I sip my latte and we both avoid eye contact. I should say something.

But Iris says, before I can think of anything, "Has anyone ever told you that you look like Ruby Rose?"

I shake my head. "I don't know who that is."

"She's an actress. Forget it. I'm being dumb."

"No, you're not. Is she at least pretty?" I smile.

"Yes, but more like handsome. That sounds wrong. Handsome in a pretty way." Which is basically how I would describe Art. Though maybe I'd say he was pretty in a handsome way. She adds, "I didn't mean to say you weren't pretty. The actress is pretty. But pretty in a very special way." She blushes.

"That works, thank you," I say, and we're flirting, right? It's such gentle, subtle flirting. Boys are usually so obvious about it, but thinking they're being subtle. Except Art. He's obvious and proud of being obvious.

"Zee?" Iris asks.

"Yeah?"

"Are you . . ." she starts. But pauses. Can't look at me again. Just beyond me. She wants to ask if I'm gay, doesn't she? Just get to it. No more subtle games, I guess. Iris continues, ". . . expecting someone?"

Huh? She lifts her finger, pointing behind me. *My fucking dad.* But I turn and it's Stephanie, the-too-gorgeous waitress. She's looking at me. At us. The *way* she's looking at me . . .

Stephanie says, "Zee?"

I stand fast. Iris stands behind me, slipping her arm through mine, knowing I need someone there even if I don't know why.

The woman approaches. "I'm Stephanie. . . ."

"The waitress from last night," I say.

"Yes . . . and . . ." She pauses. I brace myself. I don't know what for, but something. Then she starts again, unsure, ". . . your father's girlfriend."

Girlfriend? Didn't Michael say my dad had a boyfriend?

I ask, "Is he here?"

"No. But I called him. He really, *really* wants to talk to you. Can you please just stay until he gets here?"

Iris slips her hand through mine, entwining our fingers. It's a lightning bolt of strength, strength enough to say, "No, I can't. We can't. We're leaving."

Iris and I are outside moments later, walking fast, our hands still clasped. We move well together, our legs have a natural rhythm, our pace effortlessly even. Once we're at my truck, I stop. I have to know who I am. And what I want. I pull her into me with my free hand, lean her against the truck door, and—

art

—ohhhhhhhhhh. Oh. Oh—

"No," I say even though my penis is like, *No?!* But I say it again, "No," and I raise Jayden's head up to mine before he manages to unzip me.

"No?"

"It's . . . I don't . . . I'm not . . ."

"So you're saying," Jayden starts, then gives me that look, "we should just skip oral and go straight to sex?"

The. Look. On. My. Face.

"I'm kidding, Art. It's okay. Truly."

"Do you want to know how not ready I am? I wouldn't even know how it works. Do we take turns? Both wear condoms?"

"What about anything we have done would suggest anything but I'm the bottom and you're the top?"

"I was the bottom . . . with Zee."

He laughs. Laughs!

"Maybe I'd find this funny too if it wasn't my own identity crisis." I'm the manic one for once as Jayden lets his laugh settle. He then takes my hand in his. But not as we did it before. No, this is not seduction. This is . . . sympathy? Yes, sympathy. And as if seeing that in him for the first time opened my eyes to the rest of him, Jayden's layers begin to blossom all at once:

"Art, darling, I grew up in New York. As in Manhattan. As in the greatest place on the planet. By fifth grade, I knew boys that liked boys—me, in case you didn't know"—he winked, still better at that than me—"girls that liked girls, boys and girls that liked both, boys born in girl bodies, girls born in boy bodies, and kids that knew they were both or neither or everything. We were gender and sexually fluid before it was cool because we didn't do it to be cool—we did it to be who we truly are."

I'm definitely moving to New York. Ha.

"If you want to be a bottom with her and a top with me or trade off or both at the same time or forget our silly labels altogether, then, my handsome-gorgeous boy, you can. You can do whatever the heck you want to do. You can love whoever you want to love. You can be whoever you want to be. Anyone who says you can't, no matter what religion or bullshit they are hiding behind, are only telling you that you can't be you because they're terrified of the freedom to be who they want to be."

I want to kiss him. A lot. He knows and squeezes my hand to remind me I'm actually a disaster right now.

"You're going to be shocked to hear this, but I've learned I have major abandonment issues"—now he laughs at himself—"and so of course it's inevitable that I fall *almost every single time* for boys that also love girls and their stupid amazing girl parts I can never compete with. I only feign drama with you because—well, mostly because I'm great at feigning drama—but also because I want to trick you into liking only boys so that I can solve all my father issues through our relationship."

We both smile as I now squeeze his hand in that same new, layered way.

Jayden leans in, as if he really needs us both to listen, and asks, "You're still in love with her?"

I was motionless! I swear! But he knows. Of course he knows.

"You are. I hate her. I hate you. But I also love you and I'd probably love her too."

"So . . ."

"What now?" Jayden asks.

Yes.

"You go home, find the girl you love, and know that there's a boy in Winnetka who loves you . . . and is probably stalking you."

I laugh.

"Yes, I'm very funny. But, seriously, Art, I'm totally going to stalk you." Before I can decide if I'm scared at the idea of him stalking me or turned on, Jayden kisses me on the cheek, floats out the door, and disappears into the shadows.

For, like, a second.

Then he's back under the streetlamp's glow, dancing for me, for him, for anyone lucky enough to witness the magical creature that he is.

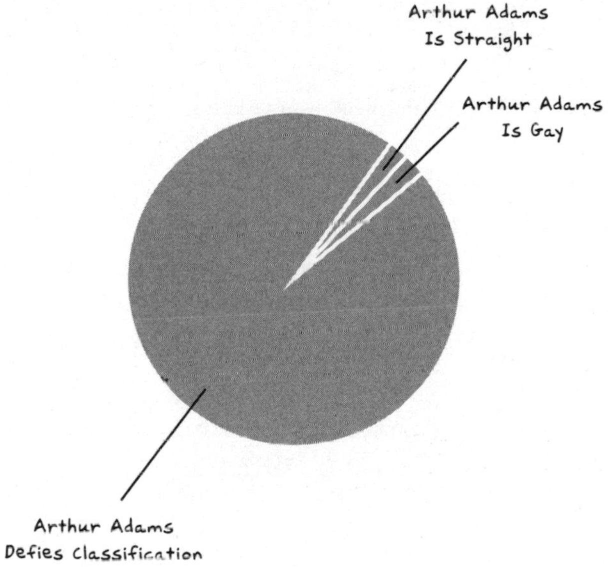

Arthur Adams
Is Straight

Arthur Adams
Is Gay

Arthur Adams
Defies Classification

ZEE

—I kiss Iris
    and she lets me
    and she's a girl
    and she's beautiful,
    and
    I suck her soft essence in through my mouth,
    and I think of Art,
    but I don't want to think of Art, so
    I kiss deeper, tongue, hungry lips.

"Zee . . ." Iris says, her free hand against my chest, pushing me gently away. Away?

"Sorry," I say, and I see me in her eyes. Like when Cam wants more than I can give.

"No . . . it's okay . . . I'm not . . ." She searches my eyes for the words. I love her finding things inside me. But I'm impatient.

I say, "Ready? You're not ready."

"Probably . . ."

I wait.

"I'm not ready . . . for someone who isn't ready."

Me. I'm not. Of course I'm not. I'm a fucking fireball destroying everything in my not-ready path.

Art. Cam. Iris.

I start nodding, needing her to be the strong one as I feel my identity dissipating with every breath. She knows at once, takes me into her arms, hugs me. A friend hug. The one I needed.

On the way back to Riverbend, she asks me about how things are at home living with my mom's boyfriend.

"How do you know?" I ask.

"I don't know any particular thing, but I can sense things. Lesbians are all witches, you know." And then she giggles, and maybe because that giggle of hers does it for me, I tell her I haven't been home in a week.

"Then you'll stay with me tonight."

"That wouldn't be weird?"

"Sure, maybe a little . . . but lovely ideas are always a little weird, right?"

At her house, we say hello to her dad, who had fallen asleep reading a book waiting for Iris to come home. Then we go up to her room. There's one bed. Of course. She hands me a pair of pink flannel pajamas.

"Not your style, I know, but it's all I have." She giggles again, and then I put on something pink for the first time since I could dress myself.

Once she's in pajamas that are, impossibly, pinker than mine, she climbs into her bed. It's a queen, but all the pillows make me feel like we'll be spooning the second I lie down. I just have to say, "I can sleep on the floor."

Iris sits up, reaches out her hand, and pulls me into bed beside her. Both of us on our sides, faces less than a foot apart, I try to avoid looking directly at her. I know she doesn't want to kiss me, and I know I don't know what I want, but my body is vibrating. Not like it does with Art. No. More like my skin is molting off. And then,

I say, "Iris . . ."

"Yes, Zee . . ."

"I want . . ."

Iris turns my head until my eyes can't escape hers.

". . . to tell you everything."

So I do. I tell her. Everything. My mom. My dad. Michael. Cam. And, fucking of course, Art. I even tell her about all my weird sexual stuff.

And because I'm feeling like an idiot for doing that, and telling her I did that, I say in a whisper, "Bet you're even happier you stopped our kiss now."

"Zee . . . more likely, years from now, I'll look back and regret not letting myself be consumed by you even if it killed me." Jesus, I love how gentle she is with me. Art was often gentle, but in this larger-than-life way.

Iris's gentleness shrinks life's madness down until it all seems delicate and harmless.

I ask, "I'm going to ask you a weird question, okay?"

"Okay."

"I fucking don't know the answer, but maybe you do . . ." I cannot believe I am about to ask this. But what the hell, ". . . do you think I'm straight or gay?" I laugh. Just to release my nerves.

Iris smiles, kindly, then says, "Mmmh," pauses, then, "Instead of guessing what you are, I'll tell you one of my secrets that I've told no one. Not even Pen." She pauses again, giggles. Yeah. "Oh my god, I'm so nervous."

"I just told you stuff that's got to be stranger than anything you could possibly tell me."

"I find what you said very normal compared to my secret, but we're probably just all terrified of our own secret stuff."

"Good point."

"Okay, here I go." Iris takes a deep breath, "When Stacy and I . . . when she would be, doing . . . down there . . ." She lowered her eyes toward her lap.

"I got it."

"She was great at it, she broke my heart, but she was great at that . . . *but* I couldn't finish, you know . . ."

"I got it."

". . . I couldn't finish unless I imagined a boy was . . ." Iris did this tiny thrust, with her tiny giggle. ". . . you know . . ."

"I know." I even giggle. *Me giggling.* Jesus.

". . . and, god, I have never once wanted to kiss a boy. Seriously, not once. Well, maybe Justin Bieber when I was eleven, but he looks like more of a girl than most girls." We both laugh. Then Iris's laugh fades, and this serene yet baffled aura falls over her face. "So I have no idea if I'm one hundred percent gay, or you're one hundred percent anything, or anyone is, really, because if I never think of kissing a boy but fantasize about a boy"—she did her funny mini-thrust, overbite thing—"then who knows, right?"

Right. God, I like what she said. It makes me feel better. I'm not even sure exactly why. But it does. All the tension of lying in bed next to her evaporates. I know what we are supposed to be, and so I just have to say, "I'm more nervous saying this than I was trying to kiss you, but Iris, I really, really would like if we could be friends. Good friends."

"I'd really like that too." And her freckle-bordered blue eyes say *I promise.*

Part Ten

TIME TO BLOW UP THE FUCKING PLANET

art

Saturday morning, I don't get a text from Zee (heart breaks) or Jayden (penis stays broken, ha).

But I do get a text from:

BRYAN

I need to tell you something.

Meet me at Uncle Josh's for an early lunch?

When my dad takes a break from packing to drink his liquid lunch, I slip out the door. I feel bad but not that bad. I get to the sandwich shop early. As I'm waiting for Bryan to arrive, a lightning bolt of Art brilliance strikes me. If at least half of me likes boys, then I should be *with* Bryan! He's my best friend and I already love him and I know he loves me. I've never thought of him "in that way" but I didn't know I liked boys until two days ago, so maybe I'll think of him "in that way" now. In fact! Aren't I already? Yes! So it's settled, then. (I know I'll be in Ohio in three days, but being a couple will just give us more reasons to visit each other.)

And then he walks into Uncle Josh's and as he approaches me, I realize that Bryan dresses like Zee. Sweaters instead of hoodies, cargo shorts instead of cargo pants, but *remarkably* similar. Maybe this is a sign that my attraction to Zee has been a subconscious attraction to Bryan all along! And they are both super athletic! And super moody! They're like the same person except different genders!

Well, that's not entirely true. Bryan *is* loud and dramatic where Zee is internal and cool. (But maybe that's better because *I'm* loud and dramatic?) Another big difference is Bryan's gruff and burly and manly where Zee is this androgynous creature from another dimension. . . . Ugh, I don't know, everything's so confusing when you're gay *and* in love with a girl.

He asks, "What do you want? I'll order." I tell him and then he goes to the cash register. Bryan always buys our meals together. Mostly because he's got a no-limit credit card his parents pay for. But it's also just who he is.

When he returns, I say, "I love you," to see if I say it differently now in my post-Jayden existence.

"I love you too," he says, fast, not paying attention.

"No, Bryan, I *love* you."

"Oh-my-god, Zee told you!"

"Told me what?" Suddenly my heart turns into ice and demands we move to the North Pole.

"She told you about Taylor."

"Zee went out with Taylor last night?" Frozen heart now bursts into flames and promises to never rise again until we stop torturing it with all this romantic turmoil.

"Never mind. She didn't tell you."

"TELL ME WHAT? YOU'RE GIVING ME A PANIC ATTACK!"

"I . . ." Bryan starts as the counter guy delivers our order. Except it isn't two sandwiches, it's *three* sandwiches. Before I can ask why, Taylor walks through the door.

Yes, Taylor and his muscles and multi-ethnic universal sex appeal, and I know at once.

Pause time? Thanks.

I let out a wail that travels the circumference of the globe to release all my agony and shame and loneliness.

Okay. Time to be a better person.

"Taylor!" I say, standing, smiling—and a real smile too because I'm that good!—and hugging him. "Bryan was just telling me. I'm so excited. If you hurt him, I'll have to castrate you, but as long as you treat him like a king—"

"Or a queen," Bryan adds as he pulls Taylor into a kiss. They're kissing. And that makes it real. Amazing. It is. Also debilitatingly painful. But amazing too! Taylor excuses himself to use the restroom.

"I'm happy for you," I say as I start wiping the tears from my eyes.

"Why are *you* crying?" he asks.

"These are tears of joy that my best friend has found love." Oh my god, I should win ten Oscars.

"You're such a bitch," he says, smiling, and then delivers one of his Bryan "affectionate" punches to my shoulder, which today just hurts.

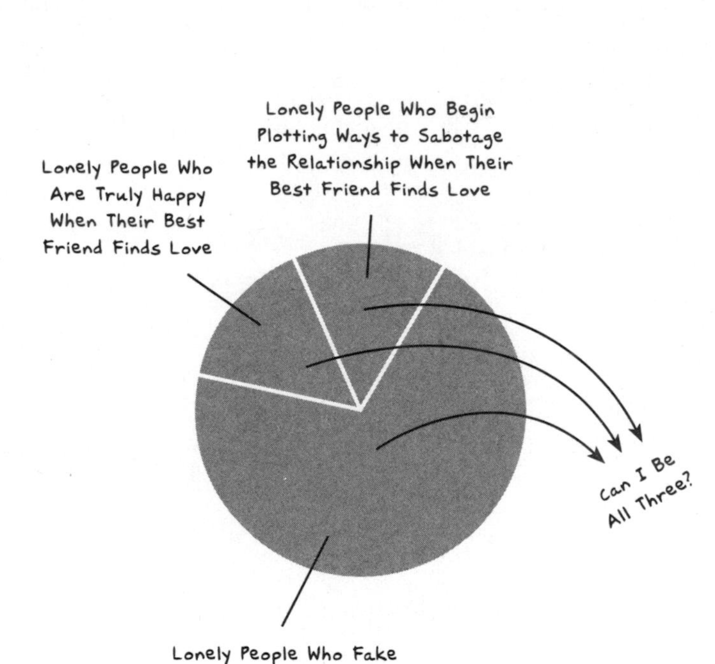

ZEE

Iris and I spend all Saturday eating bagels in bed, watching *Friends* on Netflix, and taking silly photographs of me trying not to squirm as she paints my toenails. I feel like I'm part of some chick-lit bonding scene. Even weirder? I kinda like it.

When we're getting ready for Pen and Benedict's party, Iris's dad yells from downstairs, "There's someone here for Zee."

Iris tilts her head, guesses, "Art?"

"I wish," I say, because I know who it is.

I go downstairs to find Cam waiting by Iris's front door in a sports jacket and the only pair of dress shoes he owns. He also has flowers. Jesus. Before I even reach the bottom stair, he says, "I know you've avoided me this week because I screwed up. I don't know how I screwed up but I know I did. So I wanted to come early and take you shopping as an apology."

"Cam . . . it's fine . . . you don't need to take me shopping."

"You don't even look happy to see me."

"How'd you even know I was here?"

"Iris tagged you on Instagram. See? You're not happy."

"I'm happy to see you."

"Show me, don't just tell me."

Fucker. This is annoying. But what the hell, I make sure Iris's dad can't see us, then push Cam against the wall and kiss him. But he stops me. Mr. Horny All the Time *stops* me.

"No, Zee . . . man, I don't . . . I do . . . I guess I was hoping when I showed up early, all dressed up with flowers, that you'd be super excited, scream my name, and then jump in my arms. That sounds dumb."

"It's not dumb . . ." I say, but I think, *That's so fucking dumb*, because that's what Abigail always did and Abigail's fucking dumb.

*

But maybe I should do it anyway.

He wants a girl for a girlfriend. And I am a girl! But he wants the kind of girl that boys think girls are supposed to be. A girl who jumps into her boy's arms when they haven't seen each other for four days or even four hours.

So, listen, what do you want, Zee? And how will you know if you never even try?

"Cam . . . let's try again." I'm stealing this trick from Art.

"What do you mean?"

"Go outside and ring the doorbell again," I say as I lead him out the door and close it and wait. He rings the doorbell. I scream inside my head, *BE A DELIRIOUSLY HAPPY CHICK!* I open the door, scream, "CAM!" and jump into his arms and he twirls me.

Yep.

Got my twirl.

He's so happy, kissing me, and it makes me happy to make him happy.

But I'm even happier when he puts me down on my own two fucking feet. And then, even though I know it will annoy him—and maybe *because* I know it will annoy him—I say, "Is it cool that Iris is coming with us to the party?"

art

Lunch with Bryan and Taylor is great. And when I say it's great, I mean it's like having a tiny chipmunk trapped inside your lungs trying to gnaw its way free while you have to pretend nothing is wrong, pretend you're even happy that there's a chipmunk trapped inside your lungs. Anyway, nothing *is* wrong! Everything's great. Just great. Yay.

After Taylor leaves to go do whatever hot soon-to-be college boys do, I decide it's time to tell Bryan my secret-only-to-me secret:

"Bryan . . ."

"Yeah?" he says as he stuffs a handful of chips into his face.

"I'm gay."

"Ha, ha." But he fast senses this isn't me being hilarious.

So I add, "I kissed a boy."

He spits out his food and punches me. Like the hardest punch ever.

While I'm trying not to cry, he says, "WHY DIDN'T YOU TELL ME?"

"It only started two nights ago."

"Oh-my-god, you bitch, you need to tell me everything." So I tell him everything about Jayden but only the G-rated storyline of Zee.

Then, at the end, I say, "And my dad got a job . . . in Ohio."

He twists his head. Like a dog trying to understand human.

"We leave Tuesday."

"School starts Wednesday," he says, still in denial.

"For you. I'll be starting school in Ohio next . . ." I don't even know. I'm gonna cry. Bryan jumps out of his chair, taking hold of me. I say, "So will you please break up with Taylor and be my long-distance boyfriend?"

He laughs.

"I'm kidding, but will you take me seriously and do that for me?"

He lets me go from his hug, slurps his orange Fanta, and avoids eye contact.

"You don't love me anymore, do you?" I ask.

"Art . . ." Bryan starts, and I'm pretty sure my heart is going to get broken *yet again*. "I love you. . . ."

"I love you." I really mean this with Bryan!

"And maybe before Taylor, I wanted you to be gay *and* in love with me so I didn't have to feel alone all the time. But we would be a terrible couple."

"No, we wouldn't!"

He says, "I bet you'd try to get me to stop eating fast food and make me dress like you."

"No, I wouldn't," I say, but yes, of course, I would.

"You're too pretty. Though my mom immediately asked why you aren't my boyfriend."

I prefer "flawlessly handsome" to pretty, but now is a bad time to point this out. "Wait . . . you told your parents?"

"Taylor and I got in a fight a couple days ago because he doesn't want to be exclusive when he goes off to UCLA in two weeks. BITCH! I love him. So after I spent all night crying in my room, I had to tell them something and I actually almost called you and asked you what I should say and I heard your voice and your voice said, 'The truth, Bryan!' and so I just told them."

"And?"

"My dad couldn't look me in the eyes. He left the room and started drinking his whiskey by the liter. But my mom told me they loved me for exactly who I was and then my dad, when he was drunk enough, said the same thing. Well, first he asked me again when football practice starts. Then he told me how much he loved me. But, yeah, you were right, asshole, they were pretty great about it."

"That's amazing . . ." but, "and *I'm* clearly amazing . . . how can I not be your type?"

"Does the boy you kissed look anything like me?"

No. But.

"See? I bet he's gorgeous and dresses better than you."

Annoying he knows all that! "But you look like Zee."

"We don't look anything alike. You just think because we both wear cargo pants we look alike."

"No . . ." But maybe. God, I miss her. I possibly start crying again. And when I say "possibly," I mean I cry *a lot*.

"You totally made this lunch all about you, didn't you?"

I nod and sniffle.

"It's okay. If you were my boyfriend and pulled this shit, I'd fucking murder you. But since you're just my best friend, I can do this." He punches me again, and it hurts so much that I stop crying over my drama and cry over the pain in my shoulder instead. He's the best.

I ask, "Want to go to Penelope and Benedict's party tonight?"

"Will Zee be there and will the two of you make a big scene?"

"Probably."

"Then yeah, of course I want to go."

ZEE

I insist Iris sit in the front next to Cam on the drive to the party. With him in his sport jacket, her in a single-strap white dress and white heels, they look like more of a couple together than I would with either. But the more I study them from the backseat, like some invisible alien voyeur, the more I think that they're only a perfect couple in some straight white America fantasy archetype that doesn't exist here or anywhere anymore.

Benedict's house is this huge estate out in the unincorporated part of Riverbend. His driveway is long enough to be its own street. His dad is some rich author but I think he ran off to Asia or somewhere and now it's just Benedict, his mom, and his sister, who's gonna be a freshman at The Bend next year.

We're the first people there because we offered to help Pen set up. Iris leads us around a twisting stone path to the backyard, where there's this big pool with a waterfall. There's also a gazebo, a bunch of lounge chairs and tables, and this epic food spread ready to feed everyone in Chicago.

His mom and sister are moving in and out of the house, carrying food and other crap, and seeing adults and young kids makes me think this might not be a drinking party. Which is cool. No one else might show up. But it's cool they're trying.

Pen waves when she sees me, then moves fast to give me a hug. Then Benedict steps up, holding his hand out, and he says, "Hello, Zee and Cam, I'm Benedict. We're in the same class but you might not know me because I have social problems."

Um.

But then he laughs, and so do Iris and Pen, and Pen says, "That's just what he tells everyone. It sort of made me fall in love with him, so he thinks it will make everyone love him." Man, they are an odd couple. But it works, I guess.

Iris then pulls this other boy who is eating the shrimp two at a time away from the spread. "Zee, you know Gator Green, don't you?"

"Yeah," I say, and I know he lost his dad a few years ago. So when we shake hands, we lock eyes and our hands too. It's like we have this two-second transfusion of our broken fucking hearts and I really don't want to get emotional, so it's nice when Gator says, "Sorry life sucks, but they have shrimp cocktail, so it sucks less sometimes." And everyone laughs, including me.

Cam says, "I didn't bring my swimsuit."

"Go in your underwear," Pen says.

"Are girls gonna go in their underwear?" Cam asks.

"Sure, why not," Pen says. Then Cam looks at me.

"Not a fucking chance," I say. And everyone laughs, which is better than them thinking I'm a bitch. Which I am.

After Benedict drags Cam and Gator off to help him move some coolers, Iris asks me, "How are you?"

"Because you look miserable," Pen adds.

"Well, you two know . . ." And I can't believe I have girlfriends that *know* things. It's nice. Scary. But nice. ". . . I'm a fucking disaster."

They hug me because they're girls but I like it so it's fine. And then, as if Pen knows Art says "disaster" all the time, she says, "Do you know if Art is coming tonight? We invited a bunch of juniors along with the entire senior class."

"That's a *lot* of people," I say.

Iris adds, "On the Facebook invite it says there won't be alcohol, so a lot of the party kids won't show up."

"Or," I say, "they'll show up with their own alcohol."

Pen's eyes widen. "I really hadn't thought about that, but it's something I would have done pre-Benedict. I should warn his mom." She jets off into the house.

Iris touches my shoulder. "I'm sure if Art shows up, nothing dramatic will happen."

I laugh. "Yeah, right."

art

Because I can see the future, I put clothes in a backpack for my lunch with Bryan. That way we could shower and get ready at his house, which is much better because (A) his bathroom is twice as nice and twice as big as mine, and (B) I wouldn't have to go home and get yelled at by my dad for not helping him pack.

Moving on before I move Tuesday!

Since I was pretty sure I'd see Zee at the party, I needed to look amazing. White-on-white Nikes (pristine white!), no socks, white pants, white button-down, black bow tie (yes, bow tie!), and a white jacket with gray and black stripes. I modeled this outfit after a Korean teenage television star who no one will know except me but if they knew of him, they'd know he was preppy perfection.

When I come out of the bathroom, Bryan sees me and says, "You look fabulous!" Ha, he didn't say that at all. He said, "You look like a fucking tool."

"Bryan, you look amazing in your cargo shorts and blue *Star Wars* T-shirt. It's such a bold choice by you."

He ignores my witty comment, heads out of his room and downstairs. "There better be good food at this party so I have something to eat while watching Cam beat you up."

"Why would Cam beat *me* up? He tried to steal Zee from me! I should beat *him* up!"

"Okay, I can't wait to see you beat Cam up." Then he laughs really loud.

"If he does try to beat me up, you better stop him."

"I'll think about it." He screams good-bye to his parents, who tell us to have a good time.

His mom even yells, "Flirt with a cute boy to help you forget about Taylor going to college!"

So as we get in his car, I have to say, "You have the best parents ever."

"Fuck you."

"Why are you saying that to me! I just said you had the best parents ever!"

"Because you're saying that so you can gloat about knowing they'd be cool about it."

"Well, yes, but that's because you have the best best friend ever too." I get a text. It's Carolina. She wants to go with us to the party. So I ask Bryan, "Can we pick up Carolina on the way?"

"Will Trevor be there with his new girlfriend and will they cause as much drama as you and Zee?"

"Probably."

"Then yeah, of course we can pick her up."

So we swing by Carolina's house. She's always ready early and walking out the door before we even come to a complete stop. Carolina's one of those girls that doesn't really know she's beautiful, so she usually dresses like she's in fifth grade. But tonight she's wearing (and almost pulling off) a small, tight purple dress because her ex is a walking erection who will probably need to have sex with every girl in Illinois before he realizes he's still in love with her.

"Bryan, thank you sooo much for picking me up," Carolina says as she gets into the backseat.

"As long as you entertain me by getting in a big fight with Trevor, I won't make you pay me gas money."

"He's kidding," I say. "I'm sure Trevor won't be there."

"Oh, he'll be there . . . with Betsy. I hate him." She loves him.

Bryan says, "My first boyfriend is going to be having sex with college boys in two weeks, so we can eat our feelings together."

"Thanks, Bryan." Then she turns my way. "Art . . . will Zee be there?" Hearing Zee's name suddenly makes me fidgety, and I start breathing like I forgot how to breathe.

Bryan notices. "What's wrong with you?"

"I think I've been in denial about seeing Zee."

"You're being overdramatic like always. It's not like you had sex with her."

Carolina utters this tiny "Oh," but it's plenty.

Bryan yells, "ARTHUR ADAMS! You had sex with a girl?"

"I loved her!"

"And *then* you kissed a boy?"

Now Carolina yells, "You kissed Jayden?!"

"Yes."

Bryan: "You're such a slut!"

Carolina: "He's discovering things, right, Art?" She's so nice.

But she's set up Bryan: "He's discovering he's a slut!"

That may actually be true. But I say, "I was emotionally vulnerable because Zee dumped me for being gay!"

"But you ARE gay!"

"Or maybe he's sexually fluid."

"Thank you, Carolina."

"A fluid slut. Get it? Get it?" Bryan says with a laugh.

Ha, ha, um, I think I might vomit. Like really. I can feel that gross, smelly, acidy stuff rising in my throat. It tastes like Bryan's jalapeño kettle chips and I didn't even have one.

Carolina reaches into the front seat and caresses my arm. "Maybe Art is so special that normal biology doesn't apply to him."

Bryan can't come up with a clever retort to that, so he punches me in the same spot Carolina was just caressing as he turns down Benedict's long driveway.

And yes, I'm definitely going to puke.

ZEE

The party arrivals start slow, but by seven—an hour after the official start time—Benedict's three-hundred-yard driveway is a parking lot and the food table is being assaulted. There are at least a hundred people here, which is a ton, but more than twice that number were invited, so if everyone shows up, things could get nuts.

Since I brought it up, Pen asks me to keep a lookout for kids bringing alcohol. Kind of a sucky job, but Pen's panicking that the cops are going to get called and Benedict's mom's going to get in trouble and then blame her. Since Pen's been so awesome to me, I owe her, and I say, "Sure, I'll be your narc."

I perch myself up in the gazebo, which is raised on a miniature hill on the opposite side of the pool from the house. I can see pretty much everything and everyone from here. One eye is looking for booze and the other eye is looking for Art. Cam sits with me because he thinks he has to, but I tell him to go have fun and so he does. I watch him a bit as he talks to people. How everyone loves him. They should. He's handsome, a great athlete, and nice to popular kids and outcasts alike. I sort of hate him, but maybe I'll love him again if I watch everyone else loving him. And while I'm watching for alcohol and Art, and keeping an eye on Cam, I also might be catching glimpses of Iris and trying to decide if I'm really a lesbian or maybe I just really like Iris or maybe I just really hate Cam and he's making me a lesbian.

So I guess I'm watching for booze and Art to arrive *and* I'm watching Cam and Iris socialize as people jump in the pool with their clothes on. Now people are being thrown in the pool. And now some people are in only their underwear in the pool. And the music just got turned up and people are screaming for the hell of it. Fuck, the cops are going to get called even if no one's drinking.

"Hey," I hear this barely audible voice say. I look at the path leading up to the gazebo, and it's some junior whose name I can't remember. A track guy. Intense guy. Always walking the halls like he's fucking pissed. Maybe that's what people say about me.

"Hey," I say.

"We've never met, officially, but I'm Trevor Santos."

"I'm Zee." And *Zhila* is like this sharp thing in my throat.

"Yeah, just wanted to say I really dug your mom."

"How'd, uh . . . ?"

"My mom was a client of your mom's. And they became friends and my mom's not the easiest person to be friends with, so that just shows your mom was fucking awesome."

"That's cool . . . thanks," I say, but he doesn't leave. He sits down next to me. So now I feel like I have to say something. "Didn't you win the sixteen-hundred-meter race at state?"

"Fifth place. But thanks for thinking I won." He smiles. It's effortless. He's dark like me, inside and out, and wiry, and tall, and fuck, am I thinking he's hot? Am I just one big hormone who wants to make out with anyone that I have even the slightest chemistry with?

But I fake like I'm not thinking anything dumb and say, "You were only a sophomore, so I'm sure you'll win next year."

"I heard you're into CrossFit," he says.

"Yeah, how'd you hear that?"

"I asked around." Is he flirting with me?

"Yeah. You should try it. You'd be good. I'd kick your ass, but you'd be good for a guy."

"I think I'd like that. Getting my ass kicked by you." He's *definitely* flirting with me.

"THERE you are," this girl says as she comes up the path. It's Betsy Kwon. A senior. We always have a bunch of honors classes together. She's on the track team too. She drapes herself over Trevor, then kisses him on the neck.

"Heya, Zee," she says, and gives me that "bitch, stay away from my man" smile.

"Heya, Betsy." I give her the "I want to move to another planet and not think about guys—or girls—for a decade" smile.

"I'm hungry," Trevor says to neither of us, "let's grab something. Nice to meet you, Zee." And he, before walking away, gives me the "maybe in our next life" smile. So I give him the same smile back and then they're gone.

And then I see the one person I don't want to see.

Or the *only* person I want to see.

Art.

art

Since I didn't throw up inside Bryan's car, I decide this means I'm ready to get out and see Zee. She'll probably be in the pool, kissing Cam, and I'll wave and pretend I'm so happy to see her and—

I puke onto the roots of a tree on the edge of the driveway.

"Are you okay?" Carolina asks. Bryan hands me gum.

"Yes, I'm amazing."

Carolina says, "'Amazing' is my and Art's favorite word."

"You two are dorks. Come on, let's go already."

I make sure there's nothing gross on my lips, give myself a pep talk inside my head, and then step out in front of Bryan and Carolina as we round the house toward the backyard, where the party is already at a ten out of ten on the crazy scale.

ZEE

Art.

The kid.

The beautiful boy who was once, briefly, *my* beautiful boy.

From my shadowy, distant perch in the gazebo, I watch him. He'll never notice me, so I just study his movements. The way he greets other kids, the way he listens, how he holds himself. Maybe seeing him exist when he doesn't know I'm there will help me understand why he penetrated my life so deeply and so quickly.

He looks happy. Really happy. Maybe he's over whatever it is we were. Maybe he's forgotten all about us. He's dressed like this is a wedding. Like it's *his* wedding. Like he should be the center of everyone's attention. And you know, he probably should. He just looks different from everyone else. What did I call him when we were in the shower together? An angel. Yeah. He looks like a supernatural being floating an inch off the ground among the rest of Riverbend's mere mortal teenagers.

art

It takes me four point two seconds to find Zee hiding off by herself in the gazebo on the other side of the pool. And she's watching me! She thinks I don't notice her but, *Zee, you forget that you are my mythical creature and I'll know where you are even if you take a rocket ship seven galaxies away.*

But I pretend I don't see her. I love this plan.

Yes, my heart is thumping so hard I can hear it in my head even though there's a million teenagers here all talking far louder than necessary. And I still have the taste of vomit in my mouth even though I'm on my third piece of Bryan's gum. But I'm such a good actor, she won't notice. She'll only see how much I'm enjoying talking to other kids, how I haven't thought about her at all, how—

Oooh, there's Cam. I'm going to talk to Cam. This is a terrible, brilliant idea—

ZEE

He's going to talk to Cam, isn't he?

I stand.

No.

I sit back down. What could the kid even say? Tell him about the motel? You can't just say something like that. He would never.

He fucking might.

I stand up again—

art

"Hello, Cam!" I hug him. That was awkwardly enthusiastic, even for me.

"Hey, Art."

"How are you and Zee?"

He can't answer fast enough for me because I-will-hate-anything-that-leaves-his-mouth.

"I hope you're great, you two are so perfect for each other. I've always thought, 'Why's he dating Abigail? He should date Zee! She's so great. She's the best.' " I'm reasonably confident I am no longer attached to my body.

"You okay, Art?"

"I'm great. I'm so great. I'm the greatest I've ever been, in fact."

"Hey." He leans in, whispers, "Abigail hasn't returned any of my texts. She doing okay?"

Why's he texting Abigail? Now I'm feeling like he's betraying Zee even though I should want him to so she can be mine again.

"Never mind. Don't tell Zee I asked about Abigail."

I'm wondering why he changed the subject so fast right up until I hear *her* voice. "Hey, Art . . ."

ZEE

He turns away from Cam when he hears my voice. And suddenly there we are. Less than a foot apart. We're so close. And so far. That's dumb. Dumb but true.

"Hi, Zee, so great to see you," he says, and, listen, up close, he's not . . . *he's so fucking beautiful I want to press him into me until we're the same fucking person* . . . but he's not happy like I thought from a distance. The way he's looking at me . . .

art

She doesn't say anything. I say it's great to see her because I'm a great performer and I'm not going to make this dramatic. I'm going to be happy she's happy with Cam and she won't know how unhappy I am because I don't want anything but for her to be happy—

—oh-my-god, I'm going to cry—

ZEE

He's going to cry. In front of Cam.

"Are you crying, Art?" Cam says.

"No," Art says as tears are falling down his fucking cheeks.

I take him by the arm. "Cam, give me a minute with Art." I start pulling him away. We'll go to the gazebo. Yeah. Or maybe another country and be what we were in the motel but we won't judge ourselves because no one we know will be around to judge us.

"Why do you need to talk to *him*?" Cam says, clueless. I want to say because Art would never be clueless but that's Bitch Zee and I don't want to be Bitch Zee. I just want to take care of Art right now.

But then I hear the scream.

More like a squeal of some giant dying beast.

Abigail—

art

—Abigail:

"AAAHAAAHHAHAHHAHAHA!"

It's pretty amazing how loud she screams. There are ***hundreds*** of people here, dancing and screaming and swimming and Abigail makes a noise *so* loud that all of them stop what they are doing and look toward her.

Someone even turns down the music so everyone else can hear what happens next.

ZEE

I'm holding Art by the arm, standing on the patio near the diving board. Cam's a few feet away from us toward the middle of the pool. Every other kid at the party has gone still, whether they were in the pool or at the buffet or in the grass making out. They're watching. Ready for a show.

Abigail's standing at the shallow end, next to the pool steps. She's shoeless, in a short leather skirt and the same orange top I was in a week ago. Her makeup is sliding off her face from the sweat pouring down her head. Abigail is drunk. Beyond drunk. So drunk she looks possessed. And worse? She's not alone.

Behind my sister is her uber-creepy ex Will Safire and at least a dozen other former Riverbend preppy high school jocks. Except no one looks preppy anymore, or even athletic, just mean and old—so old! One of them must be almost thirty! Above anything, they're all drunk. Abigail can barely stand. Will Safire and his cronies have those droopy, enflamed red eyes. They're all drunker than I've ever seen my parents. (And I've seen my parents pretty darn drunk.) Drunker than you see on TV, because it's not a funny drunk or even a pathetic drunk, it's—

ZEE

—the kind of drunk when they're two seconds from passing out or two seconds from killing someone.

Cam takes a step toward Abigail. "Abigail, you haven't been hanging out with Will again, have you, babe?"

Babe? I don't love hearing him call her "babe," but she likes it even less.

Abigail runs full-raging-bull at Cam, throws two fists into his chest, and yells, "DON'T CALL ME 'BABE' WHEN YOU'VE BEEN HAVING SEX WITH ZEE!"

I flinch because I know my whole careless summer is about to land on my head. I can't even look back at—

Zee can't look at me. It's okay. It's not okay at all because I can't believe she had sex with someone else and, yes, I know I kissed Jayden but it was just kissing, sort of, and my brain can't do anything right now but—

ZEE

Cam says, "We didn't have sex!"

Which is true, but it feels weird that Cam's saying it. Abigail keeps hitting him, hard, a few to the side of the head, and Cam's just taking it. And I don't know what's supposed to happen between all of us but no one should be hitting anyone. So I step forward and try to pull Cam away and Abigail grabs back at him with one hand, slapping at me with the other, spit flying from her blitzed face as she screams, "Let him go! He was mine for two years! I get to have him for three more days and then you can have him forever because I'm moving! YEAH, I'M MOVING AWAY FROM ALL YOU FUCKING LOSERS! GOING TO OHIO, WHERE I DON'T HAVE TO SEE ANY OF YOU LOSERS AGAIN!"

Cam says, soft to her hard, "You really moving?"

And I turn back to Art, who can't look—

art

I can't look at Zee, but when I turn away from her, I see Bryan and I can't look at him either and so I look away from both of them and I see:

Jayden.

OH-MY-GOD.

And he's standing in the grass, far behind Abigail, but he's wearing a *hoodie and cargo pants*. He even did his hair like Zee! Oh-my-god, he really is stalking me and Abigail's still yelling and Zee and Bryan *and* Jayden know I'm moving to Ohio and Zee has let go of Cam, is grabbing me, looking at me and saying—

"You're moving?" I ask, and as I'm waiting for Art to respond, I feel like I'm waiting for him to tear me in half.

art

"Surprise," I say, because I always try to be funny even when the world is ending.

Abigail has officially won the award for "craziest-meanest-drunk Adams" and that's impressive because there have been a lot of crazy-mean-drunk Adamses. She shoves Cam toward Zee and me, slapping at his face so he'll look at us. She yells, "And see those two? You want to know why she cares more about Art than you? Because they had sex! Yeah, so you got my gay brother's sloppy seconds! How's that make you feel?"

Guess who forgot to throw Abigail off the Zee-Art secret-love scent?

ZEE

Now Cam shrinks to half his size as he looks at Art and me. He can barely say, "Is that true?"

And no more bullshit. "Yeah."

"How could you have sex with Art?" Cam's fighting tears, and he's about as good at fighting them as Art.

I look back at the kid, and I don't even need to think twice about saying what I want to say.

art

"Because I fell in love with him," Zee says. And oh-my-god, my girl just declared to the whole school and Cam and the whole world that she loves me.

"HE'S GAY!" Cam yells.

"I DON'T CARE WHAT HE IS!" Zee yells back. And her words, plus Abigail's fists to his head, are too much for him, so he just collapses to the ground. On his hands and knees.

"GET UP!" Abigail's now crying too. Her punches dissolve into the exhausted slaps of a toddler. "Be a man, Cam . . . be a man, yell at me . . ."

Zee looks back at me, and I know before she says it. "You pull Abigail away and I'll get Cam." I nod and—

ZEE

As I'm trying to lift Cam up off the ground, Art moves around to try and contain Abigail, but that Will Safire dude and his equally gross friends—tired of just watching the spectacle—are suddenly beside us. They start kicking and punching Art. He's fine, managing . . . until Will swings a vodka bottle down onto his head. Boom, my beautiful boy falls fast and limp to the ground.

Abigail's rage ricochets into horror. "Art! That's my brother! Get away from my brother!" And now she's attacking Will, who starts hitting *her* back.

I let Cam go so he can save Abigail from the blitzed older kids and I can rescue Art. Someone's pawing at me, and I'm preparing for a bottle across my head as I try to pick up Art when I see—out of the corner of my eye—Bryan barrel out of the crowd, arms wide, and he tackles Will Safire and two of his lackeys into the pool along with himself.

The rest of the drunk punks leap in after Bryan, and Bryan's fucking strong but I don't know if he's twelve-on-one strong. Abigail pulls away from Cam toward Art, crying hysterically, repeating, "I'm sorry, I'm sorry," until she starts puking uncontrollably. With Art and Abigail by me, I yell, "CAM! HELP BRYAN!" and he leaps into the pool like the hero I kind of always knew he was. He and Bryan are fighting side by side. It's twelve on two, but they're holding their own as I lift Art up off the patio floor. He's bleeding. It's over my hands, on my pants, on his forehead, seeping into his eyes.

"Let me help," another kid says. A boy. He's dressed in a hoodie. I don't recognize him and I'm not leaving Art with someone I don't know. Then this soccer girl Carolina steps in, says,

"We got him."

"Can you sit with him?"

"Yes. Go help your friends."

And I turn and leap into the pool, picking off one of Bryan's attackers.

Trevor, Benedict, Gator, and a couple of the other football players are in the pool now, each trying to pull away the party crashers, but these dudes are drunk and they're fucking insane, kicking and yelling and punching like rabid animals.

Bryan yells, "Get them in headlocks and yank them out one by one," which Cam does, and more football players have jumped in, some of Trevor's track buddies, and even Benedict's friend Robert. And suddenly we outnumber them three to one. Will Safire and the drunk dudes, once they're in headlocks, go limp and let us pull them to the shallow end, where almost every other kid at Riverbend is waiting to help pin these idiots down.

When Bryan drags the last drunk stranger out of the pool, every kid from Riverbend—and there must be almost two hundred of us now—does this huge cheer for Bryan and Cam. Not just for them, but also for all of us who jumped in, and maybe for all of us period. For like one second, it feels like I go to the greatest high school in the fucking country.

Then I remember Art and, sopping wet, I sprint over to where Carolina and the boy in the hoodie are sitting with Art. Hoodie boy is crying, which is weird, and hyperventilating, which is weirder.

"He's not breathing," the boy says. "Art's not breathing."

art

Oh-my-god, I died!

This is even worse than Zee having sex with Cam. Mmmh. I don't know. I think I'd rather be dead than for Zee to have sex with Cam again. I'm hilarious when I'm dead.

Did you know when you're dead you can see and hear the living? You can. Because I can see and hear Zee and Jayden right now. Oh-my-god, Jayden's going to tell Zee that we kissed and I won't be able to be mad at Zee for having sex with Cam if she knows about Jayden. *This* is definitely worse than me being dead.

Zee's holding my hand, and leaning next to my face, then away, then back. She should kiss me! Yes! Jayden might kill her, but then we would be dead together, which is better than just one of us being dead. That's so selfish of me. Okay, she can stay living, but I get to haunt her.

"He's breathing," Zee says.

"He is?" Jayden's barely functioning. Wait—did they say I'm breathing? Does that mean I'm not dead? Well, I guess that's good news. I mean, it would have been rather memorable if I died young. But, clearly, I'll be even more memorable if I live forever.

"Art? You okay?" she asks.

I tell her yes, I'll be okay as long as she never leaves me again.

But Jayden says, "He's not answering."

ZEE

The ambulance arrives pretty fast after the cops get there. Me and the hoodie kid stay with the stretcher as the paramedics roll it from the backyard to the driveway. Bryan and a few others are just behind.

One of the paramedics says to us, "Only one of you can get in the ambulance with him. The rest of you will have to meet us at the hospital."

I look at the new kid and Bryan, and they know before I even employ my evil eye. I give them a nod of thanks, then climb into the ambulance with Art.

The kid's breathing okay. But his eyes are closed, and I always thought I kept my mom alive by making her look at me. Except I *didn't* keep my mom alive. She died. And Art's going to die, isn't he? He's going to leave me like my mom left me.

Kid, if you die, I'll hunt you down in the ghost world and kick your ass.

And then, I swear, I can hear him say—yeah, I'm nuts! I know!—but I hear him say, *And my queen, if I don't die, do you promise to love me until the end of the universe?*

"I promise," I say, and yeah, I fucking say it out loud because I want to make sure Art hears me.

When we get to the hospital, they wheel him off into an examination room—just like they did my mom—and I have to wait. Wait in the waiting room. By myself. My phone's busted from the dive in the pool, so I can't call anyone and I don't know who the hell I'd call anyway.

Except two minutes later, Bryan and the new kid arrive and we're all hugging even though I hate hugging people. Then I have to say, "Who are you?" to the kid who's dressed like me.

"I'm Jayden."

"He's—" Bryan starts.

"I know who he is." The pictures. *Jayden.* And yeah, he's prettier than Art and a hundred times prettier than me and I'm sure they did stuff and I want to punch him but I hug him again just because who the fuck cares about that now.

Not too long after that, Pen, Iris, Benedict, and Gator Green show up. They all hug me and I'm a hugger now, so I hug them back. Me and the girls do this chick group cry and it feels good even though I want it to feel wrong. I guess this means I have friends. It feels so fucking good that it hurts.

Then that soccer girl Carolina arrives holding hands with Trevor Santos, which I don't understand but also don't judge because who knows what their story is. I pull them both into our giant embrace because right now I'd hug everyone on planet Earth if it helped Art be okay.

Pen and Iris tell me the cops put Will Safire and the rest of the drunk kids in cuffs and into the police cars. Since they weren't invited, and they were the only ones drinking (at least the only ones caught), Benedict's mom didn't get in trouble.

Cops arrested Abigail along with them. And before I even have to ask, Pen says, "Cam followed the cops to the station."

Iris adds, "But he did tell us to tell you that everything's cool."

"Everything's cool?" I don't even know what he means by that. In fact, I don't know if I should be mad at him or he should be mad at me. But you know, "Fuck it. If he's cool with me, I'm cool with him."

Pen has pizzas delivered to the waiting room (not just for us, for everyone there), but I can't eat food right now and neither can Jayden. *Jayden.* So he sits next to me while everyone else dives into the pizza.

"I can see it," he says. The boy has this flair. Like he's an actress from the nineteen-fifties.

"See what?"

"How you could turn a gay boy straight." He laughs. It *is* funny.

"Yeah, well . . . I might say, seeing how fucking pretty you are, how you could turn a straight boy gay."

"Oh, you're smart and interesting too. I never had a chance."

"I have to ask," I start, "do you always dress like that?"

"No, this was a one-time event and I'll demand any photographic evidence be destroyed."

"I think you look good." I smile at him. Just because.

Jayden says, "I promised I'd stalk him, and I always keep my promises. Okay, and maybe I also dreamed he'd see you and me in the same place and choose me. But after witnessing the two of you together, well, maybe I'm meant to be your guest star. A very important, very famous guest star, of course. And yes, I mean that in every way possible." He tries to smile, but he starts crying instead. So I pull Jayden down against my chest. He closes his eyes. I close mine. And since I know we're both thinking of Art, it feels like we are on the same side.

At midnight, a doctor comes out and the first thing she asks is,

"Are Art's parents here?"

The admitting nurse behind the doctor says, "I left voice mails on multiple numbers we had on file, but there's been no response."

"Is anyone family?"

I raise my hand before I think not to. *I'm his not-so-platonic wife.*

But Bryan rescues us again, says, "She's his sister."

I'll be whatever I need to be so that I can be with Art.

"Where are your mom and dad?" the doctor asks.

"They're shitty parents," I say, and the doctor nods, like she knows there are parents out there that just suck, so she directs me back through the doors, tells everyone else, "The rest of you will have to wait out here."

Once we're into the guts of the hospital, the doctor says, "He's stable. The CAT scan of his head didn't reveal anything. We'll keep him under tight observation. It's probably just a concussion . . ."

I feel a big fucking *"but"* coming.

". . . but he has yet to regain consciousness. This does happen. It's not ideal, but it does happen. Will you be able to sit with him? Talk to him? It might help."

"Anything."

And that's when I realize the doctor is leading me into *the same fucking room my mom died in* and I almost say *I can't* but I don't because I can't not be there for him. The tears start before I even see him. The doctor says, "A nurse will be back here in a few minutes. And we will update you as more test results come in. Please try to get ahold of your mom or dad."

"Okay," I say, and she leaves me alone with Art.

He looks terrible. His hair is a mess, dried blood caked in deep. Drool running down his chin. Eyes look lopsided. But . . . Jesus . . . he still looks gorgeous. Even this way. Even when he's a disaster, he's beautiful.

I sit down on the chair, same chair I slept in that last night with my mom, and pull it up alongside him. "Hey, kid . . ." I say, and I feel like an idiot. I stare down at the floor and wish I could just talk like he talks, with that joy and freedom. Talk like my mom used to talk.

A voice. "I love him . . ."

I look up.

Mom.

She's there. Lying next to Art on the bed. Alive. Glowing. She's crying, but the tears only make her more radiant.

She keeps talking. "I love him. . . . I've been watching you, Zee, watching the two of you, and I know you two are different and it doesn't make sense like the world wants things to make sense, but you were never going to settle for something less than extraordinary. The ordinary makes sense because making sense is what makes it ordinary. But the extraordinary is exceptional because it's the exception. You and Art, you're the exceptions. You're the extraordinary."

"Your mom's brilliant," Art says—ART SAYS?

"Thank you, Art," my mom says *back to him*.

"I really wish I got to meet you when you were alive," he says.

"Yes, well, I *was* pretty great."

"Wait . . ." Art looks around. "Is this a dream or an out-of-body experience or all part of Zee's imagination?"

"Let's not put labels on things," my mom says, then laughs at her own joke. So Art laughs and I think I'm laughing too but not sure exactly. Then my mom kisses Art on the cheek, says, "I love you," and then she leans over him and I lean into her. Our faces are so close, everything is so real, or beyond real, like it feels more true than what everyone else says is real.

"I love you, Mom."

"I love you, Zhila," she says, and kisses my cheek. I close my eyes to feel it, and when I open them, she's gone and Art's still unconscious.

But.

Then.

He's not.

Art's eyes flutter open with such grace it's almost as if he thinks he's in a movie. "We're in a hospital," he says, his voice raspy.

"We are," I say, smiling and crying as I ring for the nurse.

"I had a dream . . ."

If he says he had a dream about my mom, I'm going to check myself into a mental institution.

". . . that I was pregnant."

"That makes sense," I say.

"That doesn't make *any* sense," he says.

"Or it makes perfect sense. Either way, it's all okay."

Part Eleven

art

The doctor says I died, but because I'm so vital to the universe's plans, I came back from the afterlife. And when I say the doctor says this, I mean she says that with her mind but has to use actual words to say boring stuff like I had a minor concussion and some blood loss, which caused temporary loss of consciousness. But that explanation is so boring! So I'm only retelling this story how I want to tell it from now on.

I'm allowed to go out into the waiting room, where Bryan, Carolina, Penelope, Iris, Benedict, Trevor, and this Gator person that I didn't know existed are all waiting.

Oh, yeah, and Jayden is there too. Dressed like Zee. He's so crazy! But also so attractive. Seeing him and Zee in the same room . . . I'm going to say something dramatic (yes, even for me!) . . . but seeing them in the same room makes me feel like a whole person. I don't even know what that means! But that's okay.

The nurses keep asking where my parents are and I say, *My mom is a slut and my dad is a drunk* but I don't actually say that, I just say, "I don't know," because I'm still (sort of) a kid and you can't just tell other adults that your parents are terrible or else they think you're the one that's terrible.

They make me stay the night at the hospital. Zee stays with me. She curls up into the bed with me. We don't kiss. Neither of us talks about it. Just before we fall asleep, she says, "I love you, Art."

"I love you, Zee." And then I think of a funny joke to say, but I fall asleep before I can say it.

In the morning, Bryan picks us up from the hospital and the three of us go to Bagels at the Bend. After we're sitting down with our egg sandwiches, Bryan says to Zee, "Have you beaten him up for moving to Ohio?"

She shakes her head. "I'm trying not to think about it."

"That's fine, I'll do it for both of us." Then he hits me—twice!

Then Zee, trying not to get emotional, says, "Is this for real?"

"My dad got a new job. He told me Friday. He says we leave on Tuesday."

She whispers and yells at the same time, "That's *two* days from now."

I can't even say anything. I always can say something! But just the idea of moving makes me stop breathing and my heart stop beating and then I die but I'm immortal now so I come back to life but just because I'm immortal doesn't mean I want to think about it.

After bagels, Bryan takes us back to Benedict's to get Zee's truck. Penelope and the rest of them are still there, cleaning up. Since I missed the big fight in the pool, they tell it to me again. Bryan was basically Superman, they say, and so I say, "I always knew Superman was gay." And everyone laughs because I'm hilarious. Except Bryan. He punches me. Which means he loves me. Even if I'm too pretty for him to kiss, I'm not too pretty for him to love.

Zee and I then get in her truck and we start driving and I have no idea where we're driving, so I ask where we're going and she says,

"To see my dad."

ZEE

I don't really want to talk about why I want to go see my dad.

I might not even know.

Okay, fuck, but maybe seeing my mom in the hospital room had something to do with it.

art

Zee drives us to The Forest Café, which I've always wanted to visit this time of year. And when I say "visit this time of year," I'm being hilarious because it's only twenty minutes away.

We enter through a revolving door at the same time this strangely luminous boy (with green eyes and the best hair on this planet or any planet) is leaving. He waves at me. Or maybe at Zee. Or maybe both of us. So I wave back and he smiles, and then when I turn, he's gone.

"Did you know that boy?" Zee asks.

"No . . . you?"

"No, but, never mind." And then as soon as we are inside the café, I decide I want to live here. Trees and coffee and paintings hang by wires as if they're floating in the sky.

This beautiful older woman in a gray suit meets us near the entrance. "Art, I'm Stephanie. Arshad told me all about you."

"Arshad didn't tell us all about you. I feel cheated."

"She's his girlfriend," Zee says, then leans into me. "And stop trying to be funny. None of this is funny."

I'm feeling more me than ever, so I just let this nugget fly: "But that's exactly when we need to laugh the most."

"Oh," Stephanie says, "I like that, Art. Where did you hear that?"

"Just now, as it left my mouth."

"You're special," she says, and now I love her.

Zee says, "He knows. No need to tell him."

Stephanie then leads us past the center coffee bar and sitting area, back down a winding path, up in an elevator, and into a private office that overlooks Laedi College and all of south Gladys Park. No Arshad, but there's a wide wooden desk, a big soft couch, a shiny huge TV, and a refrigerator with glass doors.

"Oooh," I say, because I've always loved refrigerators with glass doors.

But Zee's all business. "Where's Arshad?"

"He'll be here in a moment. Make yourself comfortable and take whatever you want from the fridge." So I do, taking a Fiji water.

After Stephanie leaves to get Arshad, Zee asks, "Why do you think Michael would have said my dad had a boyfriend?"

"Because Michael's an idiot."

"It's just weird for him to say that—"

"Zee, Stephanie is beautiful and feminine—"

"Yeah, duh."

"And part of what makes her so beautiful is she earned that femininity."

Zee thinks for a second longer.

I say, "She's trans."

"Oh! I literally would have had no idea. You're right, Michael is an idiot. Which reminds me, I have no house and no money and no anything."

"You have me."

"You're moving to Ohio in two days."

God, I don't like hearing that. Before I can say anything to make either of us feel better, Arshad walks in.

ZEE

My dad—Arshad—doesn't try to hug me, doesn't even approach me. He knows better. Stephanie enters as well, closing the door and situating herself behind the desk. Arshad says, "How are you?"

I say nothing.

Art, of course, says everything. "I'm being forced to move out of state by my tyrant father and Zee is homeless and broke because of her idiot step-father figure."

"Okay," Arshad says, then looks toward Stephanie. "Then let's start there." Stephanie opens a drawer on the desk, takes out a several sheets of paper. She hands them to Arshad, who then hands them to me. I take them, and pull away so I'm halfway across the room.

"What is this?" I ask. It's bank stuff. An ATM card is attached with a paper clip.

"I opened a bank account several years ago for you. There's not much, but it will help."

"I don't get it."

Art tries to explain: "It's money he gave you. It's in the bank."

"How could you open an account with my name?"

Arshad says, "My name is also on the account."

"So you can take it back. You control it."

"I would never do that," he says.

"I don't believe you."

"Then tomorrow, because today is Sunday and the bank is closed, go to the bank, open your own account. Transfer all of it from our joint account into an account that only you have access to."

Fuck, I'm so overwhelmed. "Why are you doing this? What's the catch?"

"There's no catch. It's your money. You owe me nothing."

"WHY ARE YOU DOING THIS?"

He answers with this calmness that makes everything still: "Because you're my daughter." And as soon as it makes everything still, I start crying. Just bawling. And then I can see him crying but I don't want to cry and I don't want to cry with him.

So I ask, "Are you rich?"

"No, not rich."

"But you own this place, don't you? The Forest Café?"

"Yes, I bought it from the original owner several years ago."

"Why?"

He pauses, then, "Because your mother and I had our first date here."

I *knew* he'd say that and yet the mention of my mother trips my warning light. "I have to go."

"Whatever you wish," my dad says.

"*Where* are you going to go?" Stephanie asks, then gives my dad a look.

Arshad says, "Stephanie and I would love for you to live with us."

I say, "No," before I can think about it.

Art again takes my hand. "I think Zee just needs some time to think about everything."

"Of course," my dad says.

Fuck, I hate how nice he is. "Bye," I say, and I move toward the door, pulling Art behind me.

art

Once back in the truck, Zee turns to me but doesn't look at me. "Do you need to go home?" And I want to die, again,

But I manage to say, "Do you *want* me to go home?"

And she starts crying again, and between her sobs, Zee says, "I never want you out of my sight again." And oh-my-god, I lunge over the center console and hold her and it's our best hug ever and all our hugs were the best ever too, so this hug should probably be studied by aliens as the embodiment of perfect human love.

When our hug is over, she says, "Where do you want to go?"

Back to the motel. But I can't say it.

"Want to . . ." she says.

And I know she can't say it either, so I just say, "Yes." And she knows.

We first go to a bank, stop at the drive-up ATM.

"If this doesn't work . . ." Zee starts, holding the card her dad gave her.

"It will work," I say, and, duh, it does.

She shows me the receipt as she wipes the tears from her eyes.

"He's a good person," I say.

"Yeah, maybe, but I still want to hate him."

We pick up Thai food because I think even Zee has reached her limit on pizza, and go back to The Last Riverbender motel. Zee pays for the room, and we walk up the stairs and inside. It's been just over two days since we were here but also ten lifetimes.

Sitting in front of the bed, we eat and watch Comedy Central. We don't talk much. After we're done with dinner, we curl up on the floor without a word spoken. Spooning. I'm the outer spoon. This is important or not at all.

She says, after we lie there for three episodes of *Tosh.0*, "I don't want you to go to Ohio."

"Maybe I can stay if you marry me." I laugh.

"You're not an illegal immigrant, Art. You don't need me to marry you so you can stay in Riverbend."

"Are you saying you wouldn't marry me if it would allow me to stay?"

"I'm not . . ." She stops. Thinks. "Yeah, fuck it, I would marry you."

Later, she says, "Let's get in bed."

"Okay," I say. She stands, strips down to her underwear, and gets under the covers. So I do the same. Then we're both lying on our sides, our eyes pouring into each other.

She says, "I didn't have sex with Cam."

"I don't care." I do, but I don't.

"We kissed and groped each other a little."

Ugh. "I don't want to know."

"I want you to know," Zee says. "And I want to know everything about you and Jayden."

"Why?" Please, please, please don't make me tell you.

"Because . . . I want to understand . . ." She reaches out and caresses my face. ". . . us."

After something so profound and perfect, I clearly have to tell her everything. And so I do! Which is terrifying, but also extraordinary, like she was there with me when I was experiencing all these new things with Jayden.

Then, after I finish telling her everything, we just lie there in silence until she says, "I kissed Iris."

"Really?" And I'm excited, not jealous, which is crazy, but okay.

"Yes."

"Did you like it?"

"I didn't not like it. But she stopped it. Which was good."

"Do you want to kiss her again?" I ask, and now my excitement turns jealous. Or maybe into panic and I can't breathe for a second.

But she doesn't answer me. Instead she asks, "Do you want to kiss Jayden again?"

*

And he's nuts and needy and, ugh, I have an erection just thinking about him.

"Yes." I can't lie to her. Ever again.

"It's okay."

"I would never cheat on you, Zee."

"I know. . . ."

"Would you cheat on me?"

"No . . ."

"But?"

"Tonight, can we not kiss or do other stuff? . . . Can we just hold each other?" she asks.

"And keep our underwear on?" I say, because I'm hilarious, always.

"Yes." She smiles.

"Yes . . . I would love that." I really would. Is that bizarre? Does this mean I'm one hundred percent gay? No other straight or even bisexual teenage boy in the world would be just as happy holding a girl all night as he would be getting naked.

Oh, who cares what other teenage boys would do?

Because they're not me.

And they wouldn't be holding Zee.

ZEE

I fall asleep on Art's chest super early, like before eight p.m. But then I wake with a jerk, as if from a nightmare but I don't remember dreaming. I know it isn't morning yet. I reach toward the floor to grab my iPhone from my pants, but then Art says, "It's one twenty-two."

"Have you slept at all?" I ask.

"I told you I gave sleeping up."

I smile, sit up, pull his head down onto my chest.

"Zee . . . ?"

"Yeah?"

"When all that stuff happened at the party, when you said you loved me . . ."

"I do."

"But you couldn't . . . or shouldn't. What if I'm meant to only like boys . . . ?"

"Kiss me," I say.

He sits up, faces me. "But you said . . ."

"If you don't want to kiss me, then don't kiss me. If you want to kiss me—"

He kisses me before I finish. His lips against mine, his smell seeping into me. It is at once a jolt of electricity to my flesh and a warmth that calms my bones.

I say, "Still great? Even after you've kissed a boy?"

"Still the greatest ever," he says.

"Iris said some things that made me think. Maybe connections between people are mystical and mysterious. Who knows why you like me *and* Jayden. Or I like you *and* Iris *and* Trevor—"

"Trevor?!"

"Yeah, sort of, for like two seconds. And that green-eyed boy—"

"Yes, me too." He shrugs and grins because there's no one ever born who wouldn't find that guy attractive. "Do you still like Cam?"

I didn't have to think long. "No. I'm officially over Cam. Whatever combination of stuff you and Iris and whoever else has, he doesn't have it."

Art started wiggling, excited, ready to leap. Then he says, "Let's figure it out."

"Figure what out?"

"Figure out the 'combination of stuff.' Maybe we'll come up with a more eloquent title, but let's me and you figure out why we like each other and then other people even when those people seem like they have nothing in common, not even gender, and maybe we'll figure out the secret to all the mystical and mysterious connections people have with each other."

I laugh even though I know he's serious.

"I'm serious!"

"I know you are. What makes you think a girl like me and a boy like you can figure out what nobody else in history has ever really figured out?"

"Because *only* a boy like me and a girl like you could ever figure this out." And then he takes my face in his hands. His eyes bloom. Inside them is both this little child that believes magic is real and this old soul that knows it is.

"Okay."

"Great, let's get started."

"Now? It's one thirty in the morning."

"Could you possibly go back to sleep right now?"

Fuck. "No."

"Then, my queen, let's get to work."

"All right, kid."

So we do. We stay up the whole night, talking about everything. Everything we feel. Everything we've seen, heard, read. We look stuff up online, stuff like the Kinsey Scale, which we stole from, and we stole a lot of other people's stuff too. But we truly thought, by the time the sun was long up and we were overtired and overhungry, we created something original and brilliant and important. Maybe we're just two teenagers in a motel room. But maybe we're more than that.

Our final title? The Zert Scale: The Combination of Stuff Love Is Made Of.

Maybe we'll put it online someday. Or publish it in some book or something. Art even made these great charts. Who knows what we'll do with it, if anything, but I'm glad we did it together.

And then Art gets this:

ART'S DAD

Need you home. A lot of work to do before we leave tomorrow.

art

When Zee and I get to my house, there's a huge moving truck parked on the street outside. Professional movers are loading the den's couch—my father's summer bed—into the back.

"That makes it real, huh?" I say, trying to make it light. But that's impossible, even for me.

Once we're inside, the house—the only home I've ever known—looks like a gutted animal carcass. Most of the furniture is already in the truck, drawers and cupboards are open, emptied or close. Boring brown boxes are stacked in every room as if that's all this house ever had in it.

I hear voices upstairs. At first I assume it's my dad—who else? But then I take Zee by the hand, start climbing the steps. When I realize it's not my dad, I say, "We can go."

"No, it's okay," she says. And upstairs, side by side on the bed, looking at an old photo album, are Abigail and Cam. We stop in the doorway but don't say anything. They look up at us.

"Hey," Abigail says, only she starts to tear up at the sight of me and has to look down. This is—*literally*—the first time my sister has ever been sentimental about me. Cam nudges her until she leaps to her feet, facing us.

"Hey . . . so I know I was fucking horrible on Saturday night. Like unforgivably horrible. I wish I could say I was so drunk that I couldn't remember what I did but I remember, even if I was so fucking drunk I should probably be dead. I'm going to have to see a counselor in Ohio and go to AA meetings and all this shit that I deserve but, I don't know, I still hate myself, and I know you don't have to forgive me. . . ."

"I forgive you," I say without hesitation.

"Me too," Zee adds.

She hugs Zee, then me, and—because the world is spinning in the opposite direction today—Abigail says, "I love you, Art."

My sister Abigail, the bitchiest bitch in all of Riverbend, just told me she loves me. So I say it back.

ZEE

Cam then stands up and engulfs me in his arms in a way he never has before. Not when we were friends, not when we were the weirdest of weird couples this past week.

"Zee . . ."

"Yeah?" I'm nervous. No idea why.

"The pitching staff is terrible."

And that's when I know, for the first time since we were eleven, that Cam has always loved me. It's just that neither of us ever understood it wasn't a boy-girl kind of love. It was a Chicago Cubs kind of love. And nobody can understand that except Chicago Cubs kind of people.

art

After we say our good-byes, and are in my room alone, I ask Zee, "Is it hard to see Cam and Abigail back together?"

"Yeah, no," she says. "I mean . . . I always thought Abigail was terrible for Cam, but now I think she's perfect for him."

"A perfect match on the Zert Scale," I say, because I'm brilliant.

Then Zee says, "How can I help you pack?"

Oh. I guess that has to happen now. I look around my room, at Alex's stuff, at mine, at my clothes, at magazine covers, at my poster of my white kitten in his pink tie. "Will you take this to remember me by?" I say as I take the poster out of the broken frame.

"I'd remember you even if I was lobotomized," she says, "but I'll take your kitten poster anyway."

"Thank you." And then I look at all my stuff again and I say, "Okay, let's go."

"Art, you need to pack. Your dad will flip."

"Maybe I'll pack tonight when you're sleeping, maybe I'll travel back in time and pack last Friday when we were sort of fighting. But I'm not packing today, on my last day with you."

She nods because she knows I'm right, and then we leave.

Outside, my dad is pulling into the driveway, bags of Taco Bell piled in the passenger's seat. He rolls down the window. "Where have you been?"

"I was in the hospital. Thanks for coming by."

"Your sister got arrested, and I had to deal with her. I knew your friend here would take care of you."

"Her name's Zee."

He ignores me, says, "Art, you need to get back inside and help pack the house."

"Dad, I took care of you all summer. . . . Today I need to take care of me," I say as I grab Zee's hand and move fast toward her truck, hoping to outrun his inevitable yell.

But that yell never comes.

Once at the truck, I turn back and find my father staring at me. Our months together, without Mom, replay in my head. It's possible they do in his as well. In silence, he raises his hand. Because I love dramatic interpretations, I decide my dad is not saying good-bye but rather hello. As if he sees me—the real me—perhaps for the first time.

I wave back and then, as Zee might say, we are gone.

ZEE

Sometime not long after driving away from Art's dad, a plan starts forming in my head. I don't share it with Art right away because I don't know if my plan is possible and I don't want Art making me believe in another thing that is impossible today.

I text Arshad, tell him I want to talk. Tell him we could come to The Forest Café.

When we get there, my dad is waiting for us in one of the booths in the center of the café. Art gives him a hug. I don't. We sit on one side; he sits on the other. Art and I hold hands under the table.

"Okay . . ." I say.

"She's very serious suddenly," Art says.

"Here's my proposal. I'll live with you—"

Art shouts, "I love this proposal!"

I ignore him, continue: "—if Art can live with you too."

"Zee," Arshad starts. "Art has his own family."

I raise our clasped hands from under the table and lay them on top. "Art's family is gone, just like mine. I'm Art's family. And he's mine. And he loves you, he loves Stephanie, and the only way you and I have a chance is if he's there. So use your money, hire lawyers, get him emancipated like me. But we come together or I don't come at all."

Arshad closes his eyes. Does his mini-meditation thing. When he opens them, he says, "Okay. If Art wants this . . ."

I look to Art, whose eyes are filled with tears, whose chin is quivering, and I say, "He wants it so much he's been rendered speechless for the first time maybe ever." He does manage a furious and enthusiastic nod.

"Okay, then I will make it so," Arshad says, and smiles this beautiful smile and I see myself in him, or maybe even the self I wanted to be when I was my best, kindest self. But then his smile dies, and he says, serious and sharp, "Stay here."

Since I don't take orders well, I'm up from the booth and next to Arshad a second later.

It's Michael. Standing across from us in a wrinkled suit, unshaven, shaking, sweaty, hollow. Looks like he escaped his own funeral casket.

"Rebecca . . ." he says when he sees me. He tries to approach, but Arshad is blocking his path toward me.

Arshad says, "Michael, this is not a good time—"

Michael spits out, "You won, Arshad, okay? You won . . . just let me give Rebecca something . . ."

I try to move around my dad, who's sweating almost as much as Michael. Both of them twice as terrified as me. I say, "Arshad, it's okay."

"No . . ." Arshad and Art, who's behind me, say at the same time.

But I give them both that look that says I'm in charge, not them. I step past my dad and face Michael straight on.

"The money your mom left . . . it's gone . . . I'm sorry . . . but I have this . . ." he says, then he reaches inside his suit jacket.

It's the letter.

My mom's letter.

Michael holds it out. He can't look at me. Like he's the kid and I'm the disappointed parent. "I loved your mom so much for so long and I really just wanted to be the man that took care of you and her and I can't do that now." His broad face and broad shoulders are just melting toward the floor, his whole big manly-man life turning into a puddle at his feet.

"It's . . ." I had all this venom for this guy five seconds ago, but now I got nothing. So I just say, ". . . all good. We're all good."

"You forgive me?"

Sure. "Yeah," I say, but that's all he gets from me, so I add, "Good luck." And he knows I mean good-bye. So he nods, still never looking at me, and walks away.

art

After Michael leaves the café, Stephanie races over to Arshad, Zee, and me.

She says, "So, all four of us?"

And Arshad says, "Yes."

Then Stephanie starts tearing up, which makes me start crying, so we hug, and Zee looks at us like we're nuts until I drag her into our embrace and then I can tell Arshad feels left out, so I shuffle us over to him and we all pull as tight as we can.

ZEE

Art and I move into Stephanie and Arshad's house, which is a couple blocks from the café on the edge of Laedi College campus. It's a hundred-year-old house, once owned by the founder of Triple S Motors. It's huge with hallways that go nowhere and rooms that don't make sense. Art insists it is a "work of art" and Stephanie makes it feel comfortable and warm, despite the size. She does insist on playing this classical music by some long-dead composer named Dvořák through the entire house's speaker system. She says it's the music my dad and her fell in love to. I tell her it makes this old house feel haunted. To which she says, with an Art-like wink, "But only by ghosts with exquisite taste in music and people."

Art's father doesn't fight the emancipation or Art staying with us. Art likes to joke that he and his dad have never been closer now that they're a thousand miles apart.

We technically live in Gladys Park now, but my dad worked it out with the school districts so we can both finish high school at Riverbend. Which is cool, because Pen and Iris are the best girlfriends I've ever had—they are the *only* girlfriends I've ever had—and senior year means a lot more being able to share it with them. God, I sound lame. Whatever.

My dad and I get along. We do. But it's a lot different living with someone every day from just having coffee with them for an hour. He's still super nice and interesting, even wise, but he's also super moody. (And despite what Art says, he's even moodier than me.) But when he gets in a funk, Stephanie tells him to go have a time-out in their room, and when he comes out, sometimes not until the next day, he apologizes for indulging in his "existential despair." Art and Stephanie make fun of him, we all laugh, but yeah, I get it. I get "existential despair." So I get him. And, yeah, I guess I love him too.

*

I can't bring myself to read my mom's letter until Art holds my hand and reads it out loud while I try to contain my sobbing. This is how the letter ends:

All right. Okay. I guess I have to tell you about your dad . . . Wow, your dad . . . SO! I've been talking with him. For years actually. This makes me feel like such a terrible person saying this now! I loved him deeply, but he said and did some horrible things after I got pregnant with you. And for almost ten years, I did a pretty good job of forgetting he existed. But then he wrote me and apologized in this very profound way and I didn't tell him to go away. He wanted to meet you. But I had just gotten sick again and I didn't want him to get you when I was losing you. That probably doesn't make sense. But it's why I never could talk to you about him. I knew he would have you, if you wanted him, for the rest of your life. I wanted you for myself the rest of my life. . . .

You have me for the rest of my life too.

When you feel you might be ready, I've included his number at the end of the letter. Just remember that no matter what you think of him, I'm glad I met him because he gave me YOU.

And he gave me you.

Last thing? Once more! I LOVE YOU, ZEE! I'm crying when I'm writing this because you make life so meaningful and gorgeous for me and I'd die from this fucking disease infinity times as long as it meant I got to share this world with you again and again. Hugs and kisses and hugs and kisses forever and ever and ever, Mom

This exhale pours from me a moment after Art finishes reading the letter. My body calms. My eyes clear, not totally, but enough that I can open them again. The room returns to the present reality, and I turn to see Art, who has cried as much as me. Maybe more.

"I love your mom so much," he says.

Without hesitation, I say, "I love *you*."

Art and I get our own rooms at my dad's house (we could have gotten two each), but we spend every night those first couple months together. Sometimes his bed, sometimes mine.

We kiss. Great kisses. They really are. But we never do more than that. He never asks to do more, and I never really want to. He gets excited once in a while, but not that often, and I never hunger for more. So we kiss and cuddle. Stephanie asks me once about it, and she says, "You two sound like ninety percent of married couples." She thinks she's (almost) as funny as Art.

art

On November 1 (of course I remember the day), Zee falls asleep in her bed while I'm still doing my homework. And then, I don't know, I just don't feel like waking her up or maybe I don't want to cross the cold hallway floors, so I sleep alone in my room.

And this happens more often, sometimes her, sometimes me. Then, over Christmas break, Jayden asks if he can give me a Christmas present and I know what he means. I don't go see him, but I decide if Zee and I are going to be honest, we have to stay honest, so I ask, "Are we still a couple?"

"I don't know," she says.

And I say, because I'm brilliant, "Couples can break up. Since we will never break up, maybe we were never a couple."

"Okay . . ." She doesn't know where I'm going.

"So, maybe we're more than a couple."

"We're family," she says.

"Yes, but families can break up too. The Adams clan is example A. So . . ." I get down on my knees. "I didn't buy a ring. . . ."

She laughs.

"Zee . . ."

"If you're asking what I think you're asking, call me Zhila."

"Zhila . . . will you, from now, until the end of time, be my platonic-but-not-neccesarily-always-platonic wife?"

"Yes, I will . . . but only if you stand up." So I stand up. Then *she* gets down on her knee, holds my hand, and asks, "Art . . . will you, from now until the end of time, be my platonic-but-not-necessarily-always-platonic husband?"

"A thousand yeses," I say.

"A thousand yeses?"

"Would you prefer just one yes?"

"No, in fact, for you and me, I don't think a thousand is nearly enough."

Odds of Zee and Art Being in Love (in Ways that Defy Classification) Until the End of Time and Space

Infinite %

author's note

(This was originally supposed to be at the beginning of the book, but then Art made it beautifully his own and it made more sense to put it here.)

With a novel entitled *The Handsome Girl and Her Beautiful Boy*, it might be obvious that the book will be exploring issues of gender and sexuality but I—

"No," Art said, midthought.

"Art, you and Zee are really just here to help out with the dedication and the acknowledgments."

"b.t., please, you've been silently begging for my help ever since you sat down to write this."

"But don't you think something called the 'Author's Note' should actually be written by the author?"

"So you should be beholden to labels in a book trying to deconstruct them?"

I, um, had no retort to that. So I shut up and listened as Art said:

"Dear people about to read this book: Zee and I are not archetypes. We don't speak for all teenagers. Nor do we speak for all people who share any of our unique traits. We're one-of-a-kinds just like you. So let my journey be mine, Zee's be hers, and yours be yours. Because that's where we want this whole amazing evolution revolution to go, right? To get to the point where everyone knows they get to be whoever they want to be and get there however they want to get there and everyone else loves us not in spite of those things but because of them."

He said a lot. I tried to replay it in my head. I had to do it fast because I also knew Art was about to say:

"Tell me you love what I said or I'll die."

I love it.

acknowledgments

When I write the acknowledgments, I invite my narrators to join me because they prove even more in tune than I am to who was important in writing this book and why. With *Forever for a Year*, I arranged a meeting between Trevor and Carolina, painfully awkward at first because they had broken up but in the end cathartic for us all. With *The Nerdy and the Dirty*, Benedict and Penelope insisted I meet them for pizza in Riverbend, which began a new understanding of who I am to my characters and who they are to me.

Art and Zee?

They showed up at my door, months before I planned to write this.

"Surprise! We're early!" Art said as I opened the door, leaping to hug me.

"Or not surprising at all," Zee said, offering me only a handshake. "He insisted if we waited until you invited us that it would be boring."

"My exact words were 'The most boring thing in the history of the universe.' "

"Well," I finally spoke, "I usually wait to write the acknowledgments when I have a theme I can weave through the thank-yous—and I don't have a theme yet."

"Perfect," Art said, "because we do."

"You do?"

Zee said, "I told him you'd figure it out after we thanked the first few people."

Since my two small sons had left my brain zombie mush, the idea of Zee and Art doing some of the heavy lifting was very appealing. So I took a small leap of faith and let them do their thing.

"First," Art said, "Kate Farrell, your editor. Kate, when you read this, just know I love you too, you beautiful soul you."

"Art," Zee said, "we should also thank her for cutting out all the lame stuff Brad thought our story needed."

"Zee, we decided we're calling him b.t. because we are honoring that identity. And it makes us special compared to Carolina and all them. And we don't want to call that lame stuff lame, you know what I mean, it's just that was stuff b.t. had to experience in order to write the story that was meant to be."

"What Art said, sure," she said. "I'll just add: Kate, you rock for knowing our story didn't need any fancy bells and whistles to be special."

"God, I love her," Art said.

"Me too," I said, and then Art hugged me for no reason except he's Art.

"While we're hugging," he said, "you should thank everyone else at Holt/Macmillan who helped make me a literary star. Ha."

Art means, of course, all-star assistant editor Rachel Murray, Starr Baer in production, Kelsey Marrujo in publicity, Kathryn Little in marketing, and Rich Deas and Carol Ly in design.

"Second," Zee began, "your agent, Jill Grinberg—"

"Your agent–soul mate," Art added. "Or would it be soul mate–agent?"

"You're not the easiest of clients—"

"He's super nice!"

"I meant b.t. is not the easiest of people to sell. And your career and ambitions are all over the place—"

"It makes you special like us," Art said, and hugged me *again*.

"Sure, yeah, it makes him special. But special doesn't always put food on her kids' plates."

"But special puts food into their souls!"

"Thank you, Art," I said, and we high-fived.

"Am I going to be the only mature one today?" Zee asked.

"That does fit in with our theme," Art said, and winked. *Winked*.

"I guess the answer to my question is yes. So I'll add a second shout-out to Jill and the subtle powerhouse of a human being that she is and also thank her whole team, including Denise St. Pierre, Cheryl Pientka, and Katelyn Detweiler."

*

"Third," Art said, and hugged me before he even said who number three was. "Your mom."

"My mom? I usually thank my family together."

"We know, but . . ." Art stopped, looked toward Zee.

She took a moment, before saying, "I know you started writing our story—my mom's story—not too long after your mom was diagnosed with stage four breast cancer. And you thought she'd be gone by the time this book came out but she's still here. . . ." Zee had to stop.

Both Art and I leaned over and hugged Zee.

"Your mom was the one who taught you the joy of reading, the importance of language, not just for communication with others, but also even more important for communicating with your own inner self."

I laughed. They didn't find it funny.

"She reads anything you write, even the bad stuff, and she always finds something nice to say. She's a great mom."

You are, Mom.

"Plus," Art said, "once I discover interdimensional time travel, it will be probably be proven that I'm her father." Zee and I both gave Art a look. "You both know what I mean and you know it."

"Can we also thank my dad here?" I asked. "Structurally it doesn't make sense to thank him later."

"No," Zee said, "because you haven't guessed our theme yet."

"I think I know," I said.

"Oooh," Art said, "what is it? What is it? I want to see if he gets it."

"Well," I started, "ever since the election that shall not be named right now, I've been thinking about how the future is female and the first three people you listed are three of the strongest, smartest, and most intuitive women I know."

"Yeaaaaaa . . ." Zee said. "But no."

"No?"

Zee went on, "No. The future being feminine is a part of it—and you better fucking believe that part is true—but you're missing the whole picture. To prove it, I'll thank your dad now: He's the type of man who's strong enough to have a strong wife and at once sensitive enough to have a sensitive son. That combination—especially of men from his era—is far more rare than it should be."

Thanks for being you, Dad, so I could be me.

"Fourth, the Wolfpack, your writing crew," Art said, "and even though that name isn't nearly as brilliant as Zert, it's still pretty great."

Zee added, "Jennifer Wolfe, Gretchen McNeil, James Matlack Raney, Julia Collard, and Nadine Nettmann. They've become some of your best and most trusted friends while being indispensable at responding to your work."

"Oh, please, Zee's just trying to sound like an intellectual," Art said. "You and your writer friends mostly tell sex jokes and eat Gretchen's homemade desserts."

I said, "Those jokes aren't really appropriate for teenagers to overhear, Art."

"b.t.," Art said, "teenagers today have this thing called the internet. We know more and have seen more than your teenage self could have possibly imagined."

"Fifth," Zee began, "your CrossFit family. Which strangely feels like bizarro world of my CrossFit family." She winked at me. "Not only did they inspire a lot of things you wanted to explore with our story, but they also took the time to read it."

Art said, "First, let's thank your CrossFit sisters and brothers, Glen Clarkson, Taylor Montana Catlin, Malinda Guerra, and Bryan's big brother in another dimension, the one and only Michael Colucci."

"And everyone's CrossFit mother—who's younger and in far better shape than you—Meridith Harris. And finally—"

"Zee!" Art screamed. "You better let me be the one that brings up Bill!"

"I just wanted to see how you'd react."

Art ignored her, stood up. "And MOST IMPORTANT, we want to thank your CrossFit husband, Bill Sindelar, who is—of course—my BFF even though we've never met."

I asked, "Should we explain what we mean when we say he's my CrossFit husband?"

"No! Absolutely not," Art said. "Anyone who would judge what you two have is not worth explaining it to. And everyone who has an open heart to all forms of love wouldn't need an explanation anyway."

Zee said, "Sixth will be four important fellow writers. All vital to this book and your life. We'll start with Katherine Carlson, who taught you about sexual and gender complexities before the wider world was talking about them."

"And of course we have to thank the beautiful Jen Richards. She was instrumental in giving insights into all themes, big and small, and particularly important in helping Stephanie be the Stephanie she was meant to be."

Art continued, "Your high school literature teacher, Mr. Ruter—there are rumors his first name might be Allan—who challenged you back then because you deserved it and has supported you since because you needed it."

Zee said, "Last of our special three is Christine Lavaf. She's ten years younger than you but, in many ways, ten times as wise as you. Her ability to offer sage advice both literary and personally is a gift from the universe."

"All right, guys," I said. "This might be the longest acknowledgments in history and you haven't even told me the true theme yet."

Art said, "b.t., before we tell you that we have to thank your amazing—and yes, she deserves my favorite word!—AMAZING wife, Danica."

Zee nodded with approval. "She's a badass. More degrees from more Ivy League schools than I thought possible. Emergency room doctor who dedicates her life to helping children. Wakes up at five a.m. to run. Doesn't take crap from anyone. Like, literally stares people down to let them know she doesn't have time for their bullshit."

"Your wife is one of Zee's heroes, if you couldn't tell. She is also the greatest partner to you, in running your lives together and in raising your kids together."

"Your boys are both these weird combinations of Art and me."

"And by weird, Zee means Axel and Leif are special enough to love playing *Star Wars* and singing princess songs."

"The reason we saved your wife for last is because she best captures a key element of our theme. She's the doctor, the bigger breadwinner, the payer of bills, and, not that I want you to feel bad about yourself, the better athlete."

"What Zee's trying to say is that she's a beautiful strong woman and you're a beautiful sensitive man. Your partnership works because you don't judge—at least judge too much, ha—each other for not fitting the outdated traditional gender roles."

"On your best days, you are especially grateful that she is who she is so you can be who you are."

"That's great," I said, "but that doesn't feel like you stated a theme. . . ."

"So," Zee began.

"Yes, so," Art began himself, and winked.

I said, "You two are acting funny." They had fused in a way none of my other characters had. There was no tension between them. Not like with all other couples I knew, no matter what side of the page they were on. Just a united energy, free-flowing back and forth.

"The answer to your question, b.t.," Art started, "is yes, Zee and I have reached a higher plane of existence." He laughed.

Zee said, "He's being silly. But we do have a question for you."

"Okay."

"Why do you think you write all your books in alternating between the boy and girl characters?"

I knew the answer to that. At least I thought I did. It's what I always said in interviews. That I did it, "because I write love stories above anything else. And not to know both sides of the love story would make the story feel one-dimensional. It would make the love itself feel one-dimensional."

"And that may be true," Zee said, "but Art and I have discussed this a lot recently—"

"It feels very close to our own lives." Art stood and hugged me again as Zee continued, "And I think just like you found a balance of masculine and feminine in your marriage, you are still searching for that right balance of masculine and feminine inside yourself."

Mmmmh. As she said that, my brain started vibrating. Didn't know what that meant.

"We think," Art said, "you have been trying to understand your feminine side through Zee, Carolina, and Penelope. And your masculine side through Trevor, Benedict, and me."

"Only," Zee said, "when you were telling our story, who was masculine or who was feminine and when or why became impossible to predict."

"True," I said.

"So now," Art said, "you wonder if you'll ever be able to balance the masculine and feminine inside yourself."

Maybe.

"But here's the thing—that's what all aware people are trying to do, consciously or unconsciously. We're all searching for that balance. But this moment in history is not just any moment in history."

Art leaped up and screamed, "IT'S THE MOST IMPORTANT MOMENT EVER!"

"It's," Zee said, looking me straight in the eyes, "when the Age of Masculinity is ending and the Age of Femininity is beginning. A thousand years from now—"

"Or even, like, five years from now!"

"Doubt it will happen that fast, but that's not the point. The point is that up until this Age of Transition, to succeed in life—publicly or professionally—you had to stress your masculine traits. Didn't matter what gender you were born, you had to be those clichés of masculinity—tough, independent, assertive—in order to gain and keep power of any kind."

"BUT NOT FIVE YEARS FROM NOW!" Art yelled.

"Thank you, Art." Zee laughed. "But in the very near future, it will be the feminine qualities that will be looked to in our leaders. Sensitivity, empathy, intuition, patience."

"And it doesn't mean just because you're born with a penis, you have to sit out the rest of history!" Art said.

"But it does mean that *just* being born with a penis will no longer be enough. Men will have to do what women have done for thousands of years—find that balance of masculine and feminine inside of them."

"And then ignore all natural male instincts."

"Art's kidding. They don't have to ignore those instincts. They just have to learn to prioritize their feminine side if they want to be one of the leaders going forward."

I said, "It's funny you guys are saying all this now when the election of 2016 was supposedly a sign that the patriarchal society was taking control back."

Zee said, "I read somewhere that that election will be remembered as the last hard kick of a dying mule. I think every day since that election proves we are right. There were more people at the Women's March than the inauguration—"

"Let's not dwell on what's-his-name; by the time this book comes out hopefully the Age of Femininity has put him where he belongs. And if it hasn't, it will soon."

"Well said, Art."

"So keep doing what you're doing," Zee said. "Keep searching and finding that balance. I think you'll find the more you talk about it, the more you will find other people are doing it too."

Art then added, "And the more other people do it, the faster the Age of Femininity and all its amazingness can truly begin!"

Zee turned to me with that gaze, at once intense and peaceful, and said, "Because you're right, the future is female . . . and for it to truly work, that means the feminine in all of us."

addendum

Before the Addendum, an Addendum to the Addendum from the Author, b.t. gottfred:

On the following page is the Zert Scale, something Art and Zee wrote entirely on their own. I know they would want me to include it—and I want to include it—but I would also suggest to read it separately from the novel itself.

So put the book down. Come back in two weeks or two months, when you miss Art and Zee and *also* find yourself in the mood to read a strange, beautiful, and academic (and yet not at all academic) theory on what love (and maybe the universe) is made of.

the zert scale:
The Combination of Stuff Love Is Made Of

by Dr. Zhila Kendrick & Dr. Arthur Gholbani

"Art, I don't think we can call ourselves doctors."

"No one checks those things."

"People *always* check those things."

"Is this better?"

by Dr. Zhila Kendrick & Dr. Arthur Gholbani of the Zert Institute

"Not really."

"If someone actually publishes this, we'll consider this a high-class problem."

"Fine."

This paper shall explore the balance of the masculine and feminine that exists between two people when they form a physical, emotional, intellectual, chemical, or spiritual partnership.

"Art . . . maybe we should say 'might exist' so we don't sound like we know everything."

"But we do know everything. Ha. Okay, okay, I'll add that later. Do you think we should include attractions between three people, like you, me, and that green-eyed boy?"

"I think we keep it to just two people because this is already way too complicated."

First thing, people should know that we stole a bunch of information from the internet. Like Wikipedia's general definitions of masculinity (courage, independence, and assertiveness) and femininity (gentleness, empathy, and sensitivity). And stuff like the Kinsey Scale we sort of stole from but also are trying to evolve beyond.

"Art, I think we will have to do more than just say we stole from them. Also, we shouldn't use the term 'sort of'—it makes us sound unprofessional."

"Okay, you can do that later because you're better at school than me. You know, I think we need to come up with new terms to replace 'masculine' and 'feminine.' Like, you're sensitive and empathetic but you're ALSO courageous and independent. And I'm assertive, clearly, but I'm also very gentle and empathetic."

"And sensitive."

"Ha, ha . . . I'm serious, Zee!"

"And that's why we are writing this paper. To expand people's definitions of masculine and feminine."

"But wouldn't it be easier to just come up with new words altogether? It will take hundreds of years for people to lose society's stupid assumptions that boys are more independent than girls and girls are more gentle than boys."

"Yeah, okay, maybe. But this is going to get really fucking complicated."

"I love complicated. How about—"

- *All traits that old people (and people that think like old people) associate with "masculine" shall now be known as Xulo and ancient assumptions of "feminine" traits shall be known as Olux.*

"Did you just make up those terms right now?"

"Yes, how did you know?"

"Because they sound like made-up terms."

"But do you see how they are the same letters but in different order? It's to suggest that all of us—no matter if you're a feminine boy like me or a—"

"You just used the word 'feminine.'"

"UGH! See! I've been brainwashed by society too. I'm just going to write this down—"

These words use the same letters to suggest that we are all made up of the same qualities, no matter our gender or genitals, but these qualities prioritize themselves in different people depending on a variety of factors, including environment and the prioritized qualities of the other person. In no way do the authors believe Xulo qualities apply to males predominantly (or Olux qualities to female), only that these terms represent what was assumed to be predominantly male or female qualities. To further clarify, if we were to somehow be able to test every male and female on earth for the Olux (old idea of feminine) and Xulo (old idea masculine) qualities, we believe there is just as good a chance that the planet's female population (on average) would have as much if not more Xulo qualities as the male population.

"Did you see one word begins with 'X' and the other 'O,' so it's like 'xoxo,' hugs and kisses. Tell me you love it or I'll die."

"That's very good. For the sake of this paper, we still should occasionally remind people Xulo equals the old idea of masculinity and Olux means old notions of femininity."

"Okay, okay, maybe, but I also want to suggest that Olux and Xulo qualities number far beyond the generic list of typical masculine and feminine qualities. . . . Are you listening? What are you doing?"

"I'm looking at the Wikipedia entries for 'estrogen' and 'testosterone,' which they call the female and male sex hormones. . . ."

"Yeah, and?"

"Did you know that these hormones are found in all vertebrates and some insects? And *that* means these hormones have an—this is Wikipedia's phrase—'ancient evolutionary history.' "

"Zee . . . you've totally confused me."

"I think what we are looking to understand is the balance of masculine and feminine. . . ."

"Olux and Xulo."

"Yes, that too."

"Ha, ha."

"And the hormones that might help shape these old ideas of masculine and feminine are testosterone and estrogen. But if these hormones aren't limited to humans or even mammals, then that means the balance isn't either. The balance existed *before* penises and vaginas existed. And that means that attraction was never meant to be limited to one's genitals. It has been around since the dawn of time."

"Oooh, like if God were real—"

"Please don't make this religious."

"Okay, let's not call it God. What do you want to call the beginning of time, then?"

"The big bang and we're not coming up with a different term."

"The big bang! I love it. It's *even* sexual, Zee. Like you and I had a 'big bang' in this very motel room last week."

"You're hilarious. I'll write this part—"

For instance, if the known universe was birthed by the big bang, one must assume that this birth was proceeded by "something." And this "something" most likely wasn't something as existentially arbitrary as a penis entering a vagina but rather the combination of forces with a conscious or unconscious desire to unify. . . . To unify, birth the universe, then expand the universe. To unify, birth, then expand.

"Zee . . . you have a really good vocabulary. It's kind of a turn-on."

"Keep your underwear on, kid."

"Ha. But seriously, I love this. Unify, birth, then expand. This is genius. You basically just described our relationship."

"Did I?"

"I think you might have described the objective of all relationships."

"Which . . . mmmh . . . which, if you think about it, would make sense. If the universe was birthed by this combination of forces—"

"The combination of Xulo and Olux."

"Sure. If the universe started with this combination, then wouldn't all of us—not just humans, but all animals, insects, trees, everything—be biologically wired to repeat this. Wired to combine in the same way the big bang did. Unify, birth, and expand. Repeat. Repeat. Repeat. And if you can't repeat it with the same person, nature almost demands you do it with someone else."

"Zee, I think you're the one that might be making this even more complicated than me."

"Yeah, maybe. Let's give examples."

"I'll start."

For instance, Dr. Gholbani could be considered both an Olux (feminine) prioritized Boy emotionally and spiritually attracted to Xulo (masculine) Girls as well as a Xulo prioritized Boy sexually attracted to Olux Boys. The qualities he prioritizes changes depending on the partner he is trying to unify with.

"Art, we're not using ourselves as examples!"

"That's the whole point!"

"And why didn't you say you were sexually attracted to me? Are you just sexually attracted to Jayden?"

"Of course I'm attracted to you. Only you can make me squeal, ha. But for the sake of the paper, maybe we should show that we can take on different Olux and Xulo qualities depending on what the dominant interest in the other person is. So, yes, in this case I guess I am saying my dominant interest in you is emotional and spiritual, while my dominant interest in Jayden was physical."

"Fine, whatever. I still can't believe you insist on calling yourself by my dad's last name."

"I love your dad four point trillion infinities."

"I'll just give us different names later. Let's keep going. It's almost dawn."

Dr. Kendrick prioritized her Xulo (masculine) qualities when her dominant partner was her Olux-prioritized mother or the Olux-prioritized Dr. Gholbani. But when Dr. Gholbani prioritizes his Xulo (masculine) qualities, then Dr. Kendrick naturally, perhaps unconsciously, prioritizes her Olux (feminine) qualities.

"Art, fuck, we're not talking about me being partners with my mom even if it's probably true."

"Zee, since we have moved beyond genitals and gender, we have to move beyond this being limited to sexual partners. The vast, vast majority of connections we make in this world are not sexual but still thrive on a Olux-Xulo balance. Whether it's me with Carolina and Bryan or you with your mom, Pen, or Iris. You said you feel feminine around Pen, who you don't want to kiss, and masculine around Iris, who you do. It was *you* who said the big bang wasn't about genitals or gender or sex. It's about who we partner with, who we combine with. Who we yearn to unify, birth, and expand with. For instance, you and I—right now—are combining to birth and expand an idea. We aren't kissing or naked or even thinking about sex, not really."

"Okay, fine. I want to give an example of why some attempted partnerships fail. . . ."

"Like you and Cam."

"We are definitely changing these names later!"

When the Xulo-prioritized Dr. Kendrick tried to emotionally and sexually partner with a Xulo-prioritized male (Cam Callahan), the partnership failed to take root. It would have required one of them to prioritize their Olux qualities, neither of whom was willing to do so for the sake of the potential unification. This probably suggests that it was not a partnership that would or should organically occur.

"Art, I just thought of something. For a *girl*, I am masculine-prioritized, and for a *boy*, you are feminine-prioritized. But if we remove genitals—which is kind of the point of all this—then I would say we are more of an equal balance of masculine and feminine. That's why we work. Because both of us are pretty much equal weighted between masculine and feminine—"

"Xulo and Olux! You're right. Of course you are because you're brilliant. Genitals and gender are too sex-focused. If you separated our auras from our bodies—"

"'Auras' is a bit too cheesy for me."

"Well, we won't put that word in the paper. But you understand what I mean. So if our auras separated from our bodies, from our genitals, I agree with you. Our auras would look remarkably similar in their Olux-Xulo balance. For instance, let's say you and I never have sex again—"

"You really don't think we will have sex again?"

"Of course I do. I'm just saying let's say we don't. Do you think you and I will ever stop unifying, birthing, and expanding even if we never had sex again?"

"No."

"So, the Zert Scale is not about sex or gender or genitals. It's about who we search to unify with."

"And *why* we search out that particular person to unify with."

"I think we should put a chart here."

"A chart?"

"I make charts on my phone whenever I'm bored or even not bored. Here, look—"

"That's a lot of Art Charts."

"These will be known as Zert Charts."

"Art Charts sounds better."

"Yes, rhymes are the best, but we're *expanding* beyond that. Ha. Okay, let's put the Kinsey Scale in first since the internet talks about that the most when it comes to the subject of fluid sexual attraction."

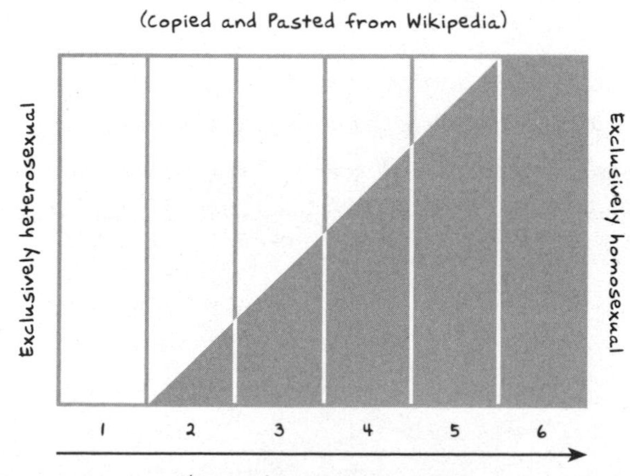

"Should we talk about this or just write it down?"

"Let's just write it."

"Should we mention we're high school students and it's five a.m. and we only know what we know by googling stuff?"

"Let's not worry about that now."

The Kinsey Scale is an attempt to explain, illuminate, and make people comfortable with both their own and other people's attraction to both sexes. And while this was revolutionary back in the seventeenth century . . .

"It was 1948, Art."

"Wow, it really was that recently? No wonder no one was ready for the Zert Scale until now."

"Let's just keep writing."

While this was an important step back in the mid-twentieth century, it was limited in both scope and ambitions. The result being that a male, if he had never physically acted on his emotional or chemical attraction to another male, assumed that he was in category 0. This allows too many people to assume there is a "normal" and that gives unspoken permission to bigotry and homophobia. It assumes that sexual activity is the goal of all partnerships versus one of the many by-products of a certain type of partnership.

With the Zert Scale, we are hoping to begin a dialogue about why and how we form relationships of all kinds. Sexually physical ones, yes, but also just as important (if not more so) emotional, spiritual, intellectual, and chemical.

THE ZERT SCALE

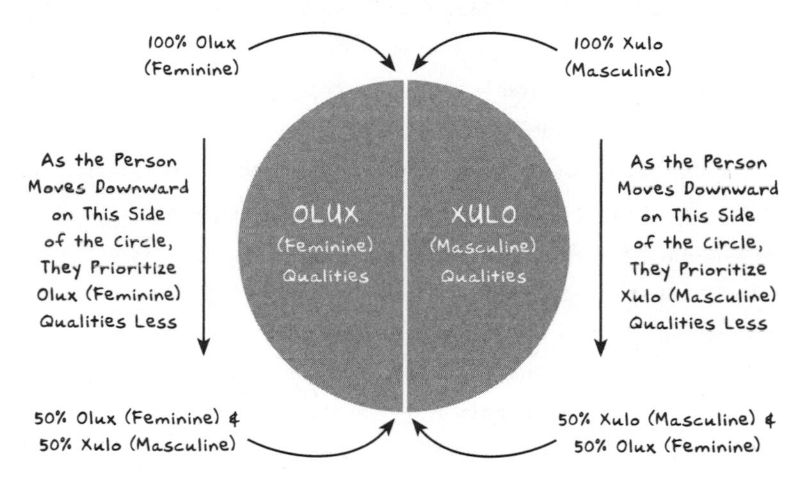

The assumption of the Zert Scale is that all beings are searching for partners that they can "Unify, Birth, and Expand" (UBE) with. In order to achieve the state of UBE, they must find someone who balances the Olux-Xulo (Feminine-Masculine) qualities.

EXAMPLE: If Dr. Gholbani is approximately 50% Olux and 50% Xulo, he will consciously or subconsciously search out a partner who is 50% of each as well (AKA Dr. Kendrick).

Thus the Zert Formula is: UBE = 100% Olux + 100% Xulo

"How's that look?"

"Complicated."

"Complicated is good and inevitable. Confusing is bad."

"It's a lot, Art. Should we explain why we made it a circle?"

The circle serves many purposes. First is the obvious: it's an infinite loop that has no points of disconnection. We are all part of the same circle. The second reason for the circle is to show how the point of 50–50 balance of Olux-Xulo (Masculine-Feminine) Qualities (at six o'clock) is at the opposite point of the 100% Olux–100% Xulo meeting point (at twelve o'clock).

We are suggesting that someone that prioritizes an equal 50–50 balance will search out someone at 50–50 as well just as someone who prioritizes a 100–0 balance will search out a 0–100.

"Zee, no one who has ever lived is one hundred percent masculine or one hundred percent feminine."

"Yes, I know, but we're trying to be scientific about it. Would you rather I write someone that is a balance of 32.4% Olux (feminine)–67.6% Xulo (masculine) will search out a 67.6% L–32.4 % X?"

"For math-challenged people like myself, I think we stick with the easy-on-the-eyes fifty–fifty or one hundred–zero."

"And it's not like we have an exact equation to determine everyone's masculine-feminine balance anyway."

"Unless we come up with a list that's a lot longer and more specific than masculine equals independence and courage and feminine equals sensitive and gentle. We could say, 'If you like watching sports more than shopping, you get two Xulo points. If you like being the bottom in bed, you get five Olux points. . . .' "

"Okay, Art, okay. That's enough. The list would be infinite and impossible and—"

"Limiting too. Even dangerous. We don't want to suggest that people can change their masculine-feminine balance by shaving their legs less or paying for the dinner bill more. We want them to prioritize whatever they feel best prioritizing, and that will attract the partner that balances them out organically."

"Agreed. I think we should also add . . ."

Everyone's balance is fluid, both in purpose and time. For instance, your Olux-Xulo balance for a sexual partner may be different from what masculine-feminine balance you are seeking when it comes to an intellectual or spiritual partner. Even if the same person serves as your partner sexually, intellectually, and spiritually, almost assuredly the balance you each bring to the UBE will be different prioritized qualities for each of the three connections.

Temporally, we are fluid as well. Meaning, you may prioritize a dominant Xulo (masculine) balance today but prioritize a 50–50 balance or even a dominant Olux (feminine) balance in the future, whether that future is five days or five years from now.

"I just thought of something my mom used to tell me when I'd complain about someone saying I was androgynous."

"I love your mom."

"She would tell me, 'Zee, all babies are androgynous-looking and as humans reach extreme old age, they start looking androgynous as well. So androgyny is both where we came from and where we are going.'"

"Oooh. Like the big bang. The universe was androgynous at birth and is moving back toward androgyny."

"If you think about it, as far as humans go, it makes sense. With modern technology and science, we have less and less need for the traditional places that our physical stature put men and women in."

"Let's just say it—"

To conclude, it is our belief that the universe is evolving toward a fifty–fifty balance of the Olux (feminine) and Xulo (masculine), and that each individual is striving for the same balance internally.

"But it's okay if we don't balance out."

"What do you mean?"

"Cam and Abigail. I've been thinking about them. He prioritizes masculine qualities; she prioritizes feminine ones."

"Abigail *definitely* has masculine qualities. Like starting the war at the party."

"Yes, and Cam has feminine ones. But they both are *prioritizing* their traditional gender-based qualities. And they work as a couple because they still are fulfilling the UBE formula. And it's okay if they stay that way. We can't try to make everyone the same as us or then we are judging them for not being like us when we are making this Zert Scale to encourage less judgment."

"You're right. I love you."

"It's daylight, Art."

"I'm hungry."

"Me too."

"Pancakes!"

"We should proofread everything."

"My brain is mush. Let's do that later."

"You mean, I'll have to do that later."

"Let's just come up with a big finish."

"What do you mean?"

"Zee, we need something that sums up what we are attempting to communicate but does it in a fun, grand way."

"Okay . . ."

"But *also* makes people feel good about themselves even if they disagree or don't understand what we were trying to do with the Zert Scale."

"Give me your phone."

"What are you doing?"

"How about this?"

"Perfect."

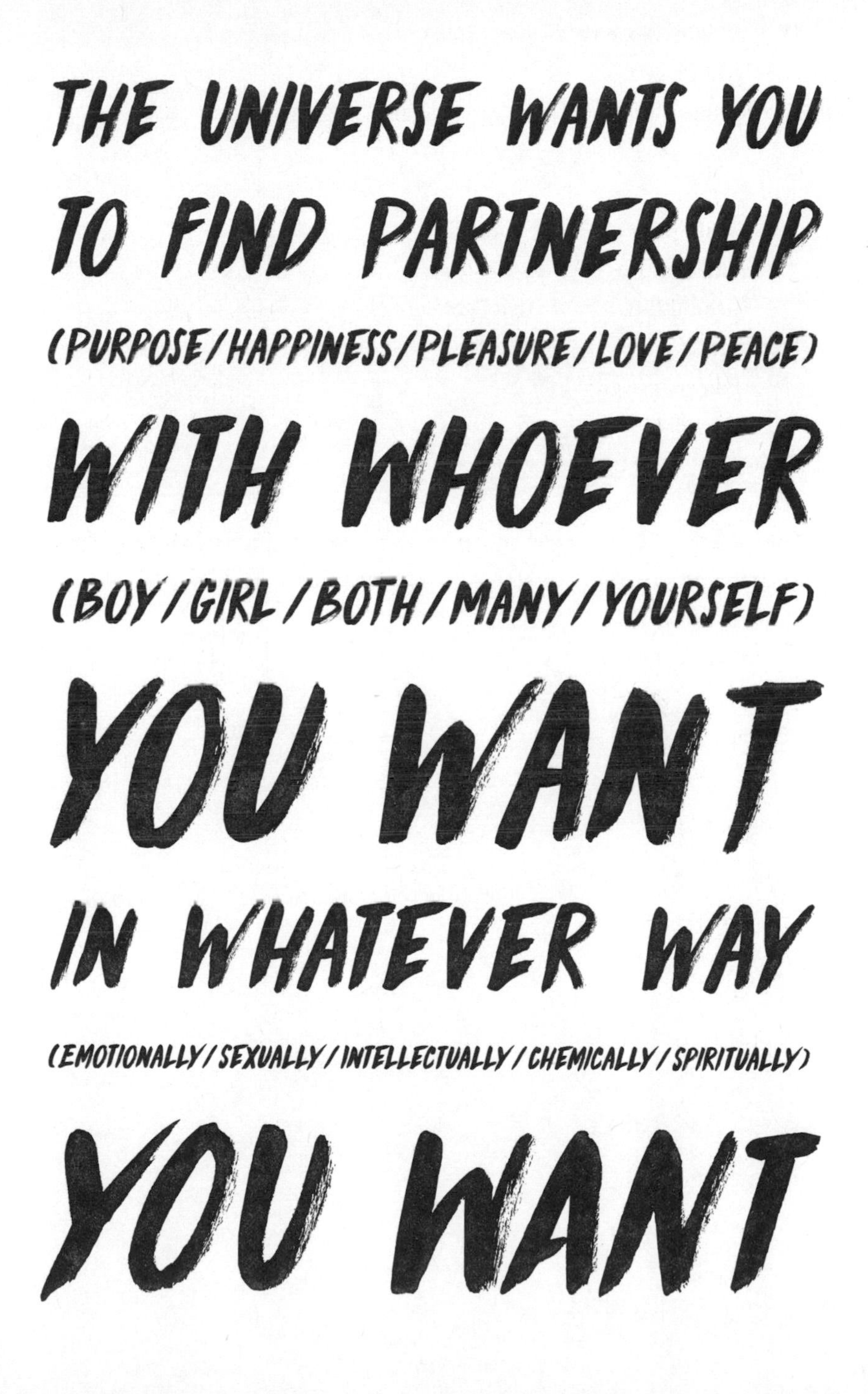
THE UNIVERSE WANTS YOU
TO FIND PARTNERSHIP
(PURPOSE/HAPPINESS/PLEASURE/LOVE/PEACE)
WITH WHOEVER
(BOY/GIRL/BOTH/MANY/YOURSELF)
YOU WANT
IN WHATEVER WAY
(EMOTIONALLY/SEXUALLY/INTELLECTUALLY/CHEMICALLY/SPIRITUALLY)
YOU WANT